Tree-House Comix Proudly Presents

DOG MAN AND CAT KID

WRITTEN AND ILLUSTRATED BY **DAV PILKEY**

AS GEORGE BEARD AND HAROLD HUTCHINS

WITH COLOR BY JOSE GARIBALDI

graphix

AN IMPRINT OF

SCHOLASTIC

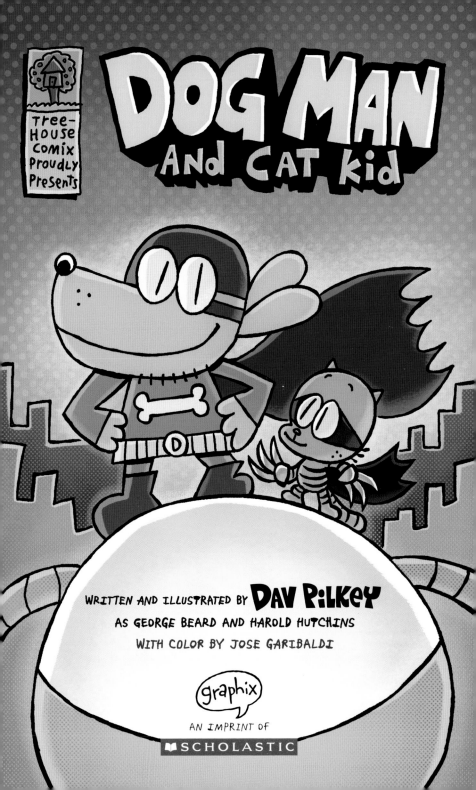

FOR A REAL HERO,
BILLY DIMICHELE

With thanks to John Steinbeck, whose novels, particularly
<u>East of Eden</u>, still resonate with readers today.

Library of Congress Control Number 2017939754

978-0-545-93518-0 (POB)
978-1-338-23037-6 (Library)

10 9 8 7 6 5 4 3 2 1   18 19 20 21 22

Printed in China   62
First edition, January 2018

Edited by Anamika Bhatnagar
Book design by Dav Pilkey and Phil Falco
Color by Jose Garibaldi
Creative Director: David Saylor

CHAPTERS

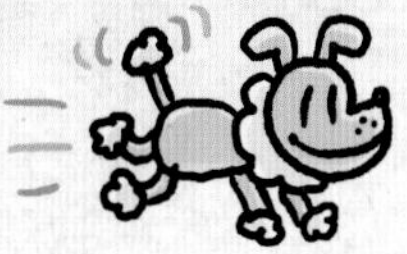

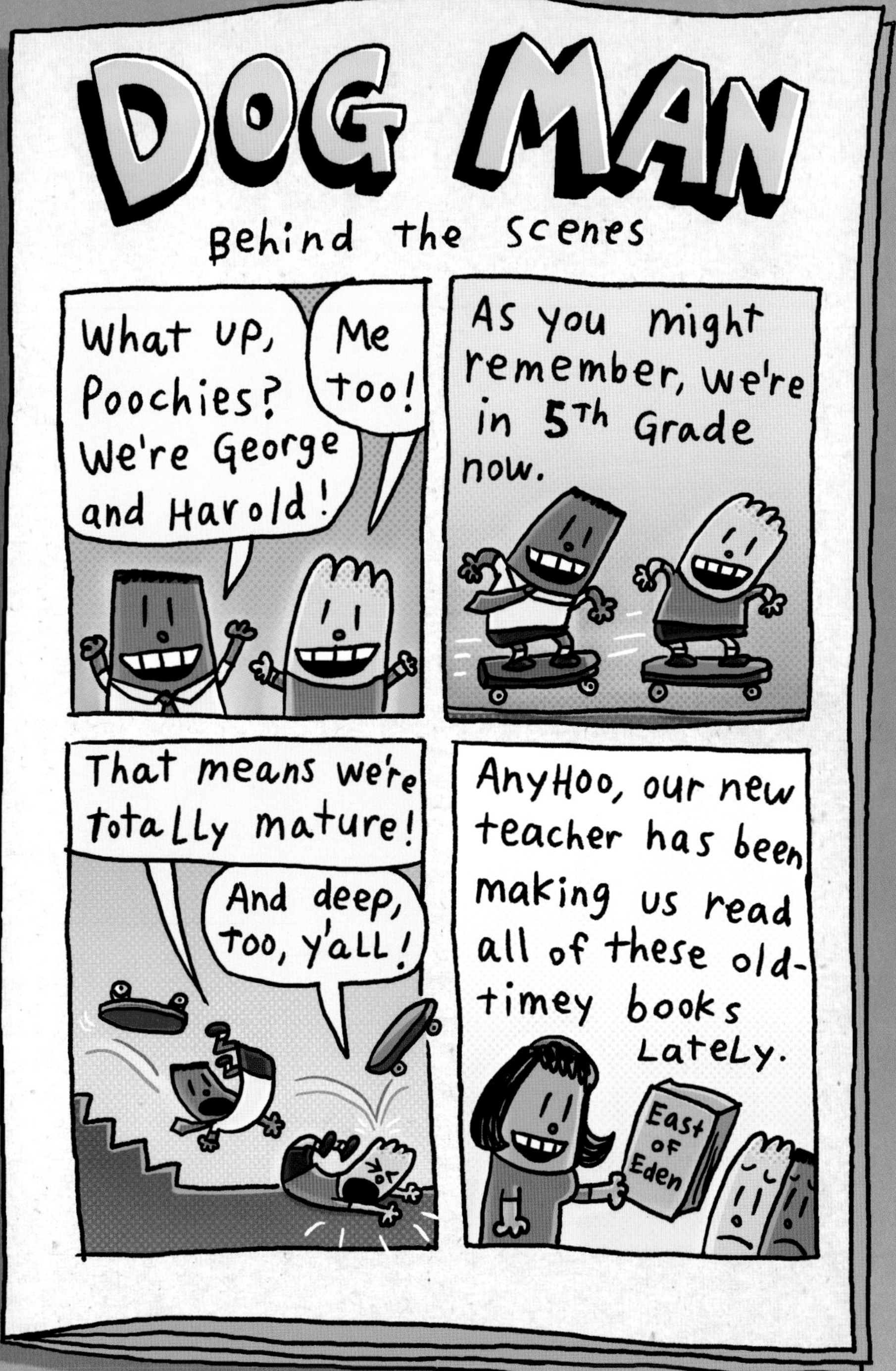

DOG MAN
Behind the Scenes
What up, Poochies? We're George and Harold!
Me too!
As you might remember, we're in 5th Grade now.
That means we're totally mature!
And deep, too, y'all!
AnyHoo, our new teacher has been making us read all of these old-timey books lately.
East of Eden

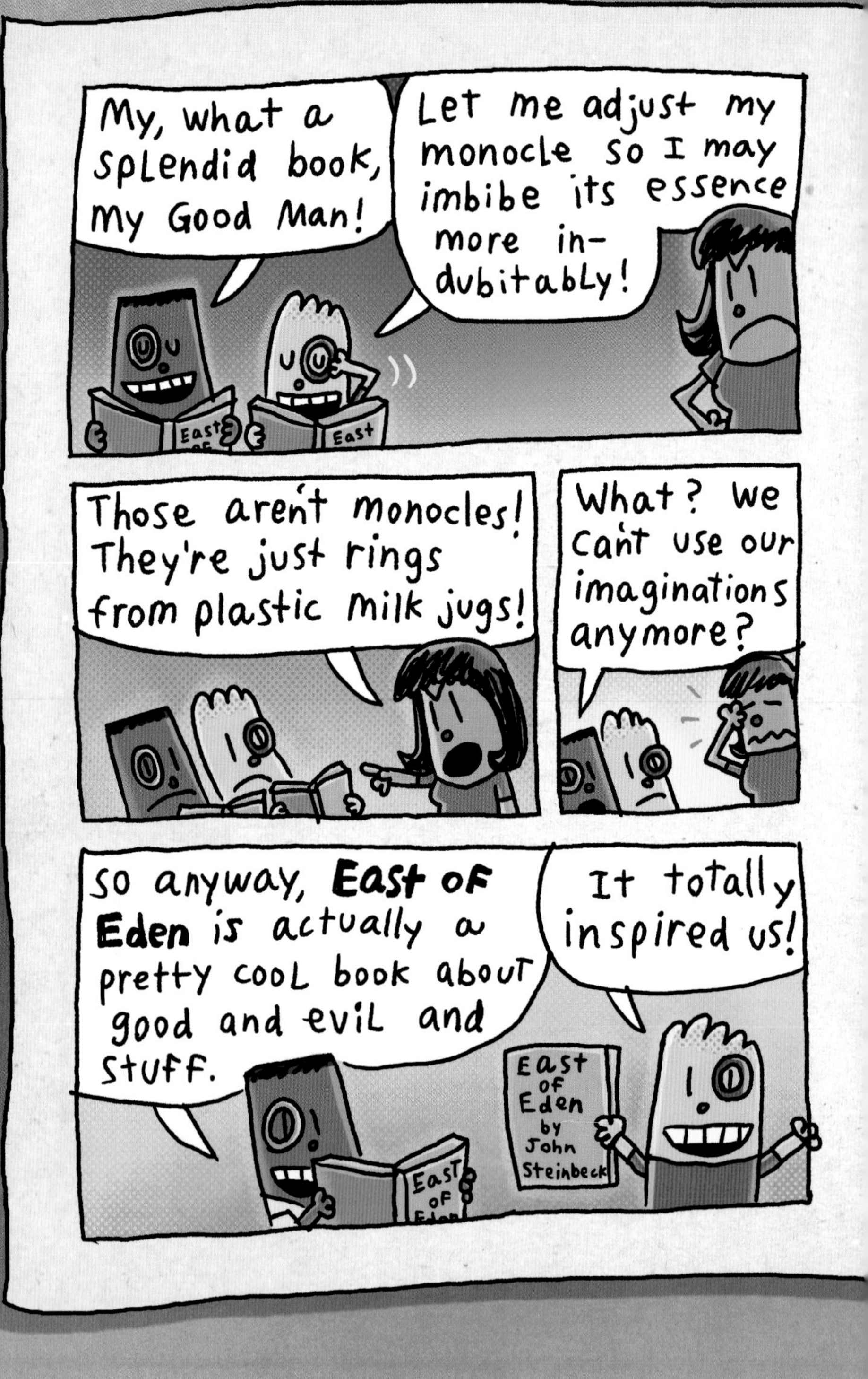
My, what a splendid book, My Good Man!
Let me adjust my monocle so I may imbibe its essence more in-dubitably!
East
East
Those aren't monocles! They're just rings from plastic milk jugs!
What? We can't use our imaginations anymore?
So anyway, **East of Eden** is actually a pretty cool book about good and evil and stuff.
It totally inspired us!
East of Eden by John Steinbeck
East of

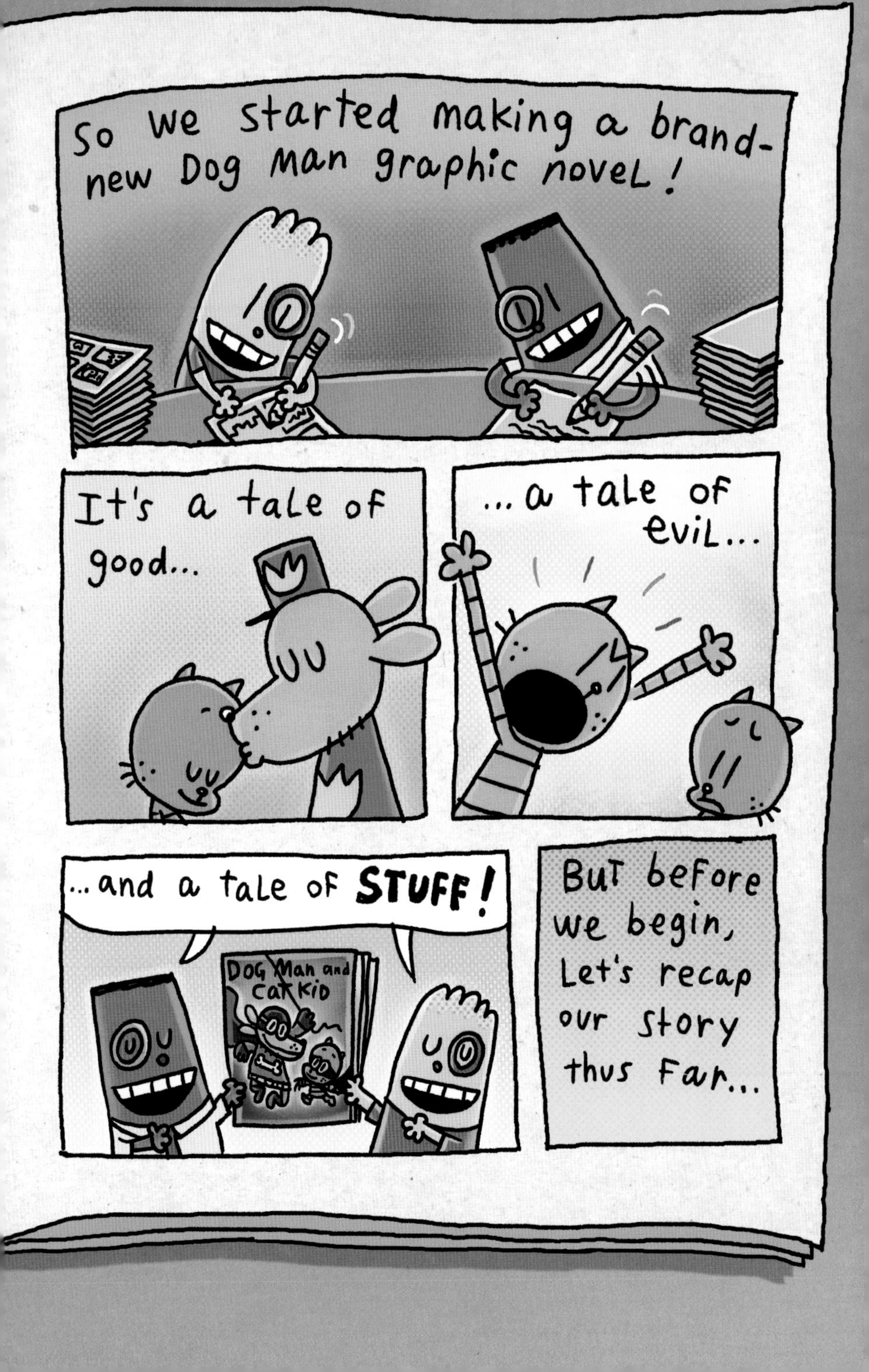
So we started making a brand-new Dog Man graphic novel!
It's a tale of good...
...a tale of evil...
...and a tale of STUFF!
DOG MAN AND CAT KID
But before we begin, Let's recap our story thus far...

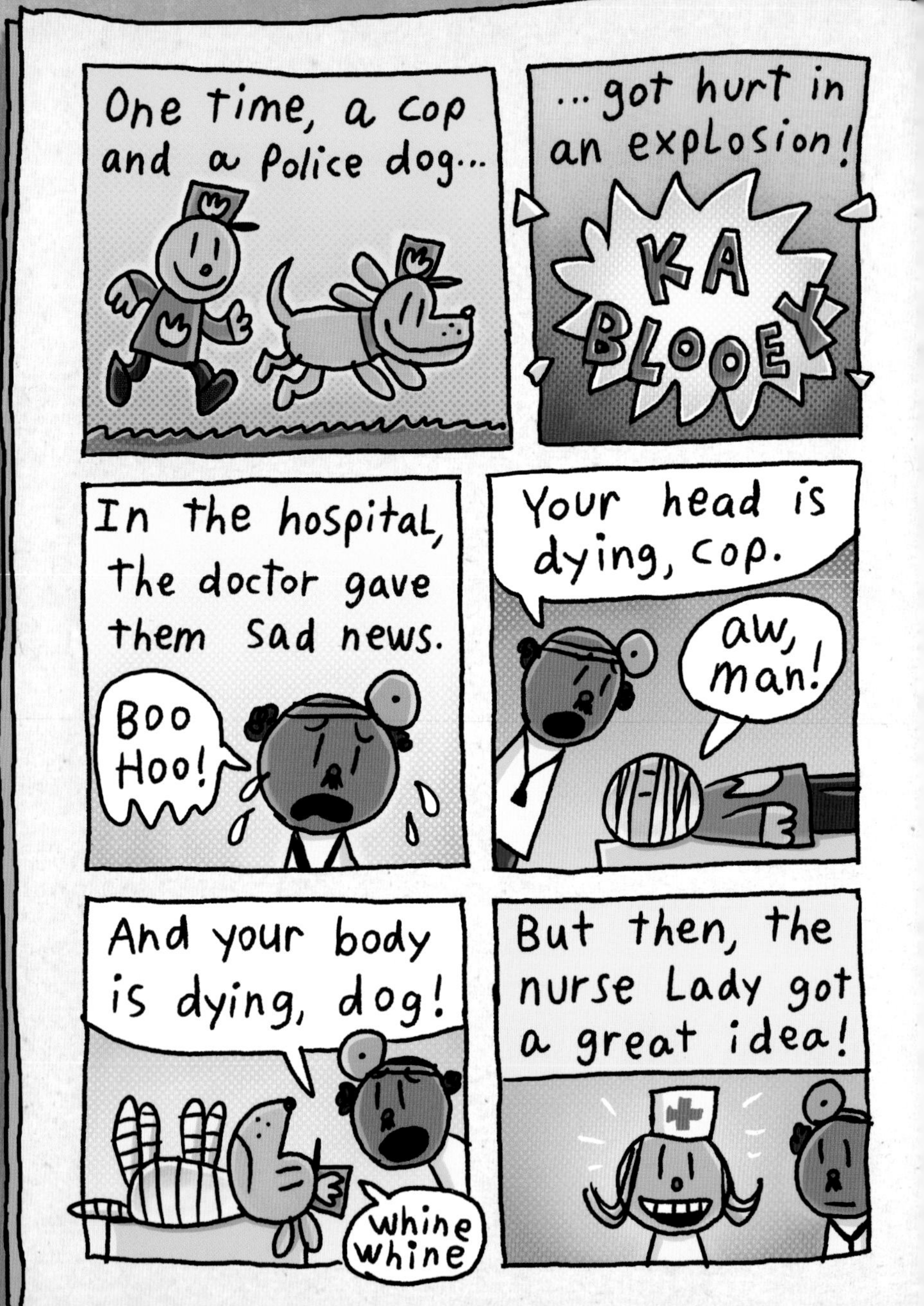
One time, a cop and a police dog...
...got hurt in an explosion!
KA BLOOEY
In the hospital, the doctor gave them sad news.
BOO HOO!
Your head is dying, cop.
aw, man!
And your body is dying, dog!
whine whine
But then, the nurse lady got a great idea!

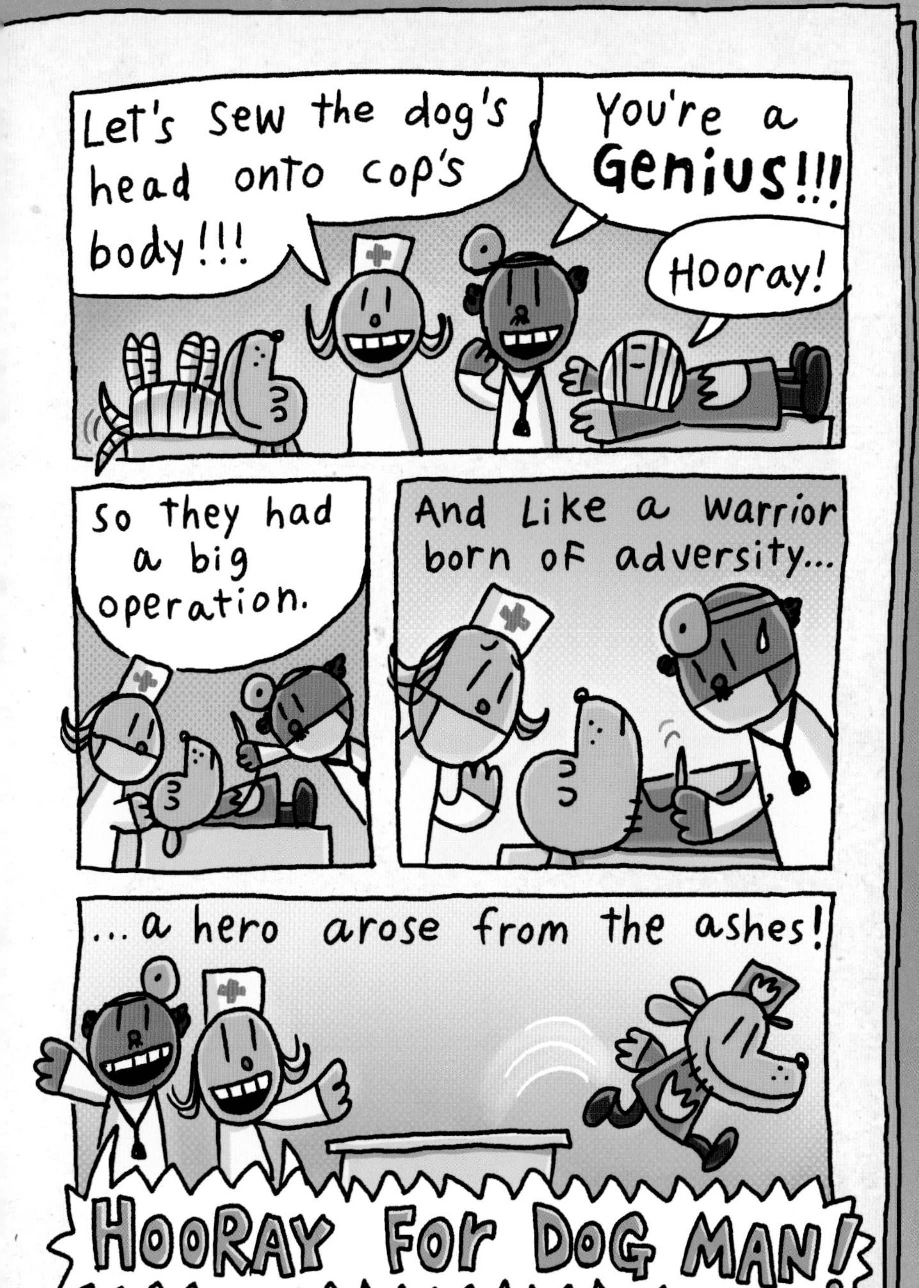
Let's sew the dog's head onto cop's body!!!
You're a Genius!!!
Hooray!
So they had a big operation.
And Like a warrior born oF adversity...
...a hero arose from the ashes!
HOORAY FOR DOG MAN!

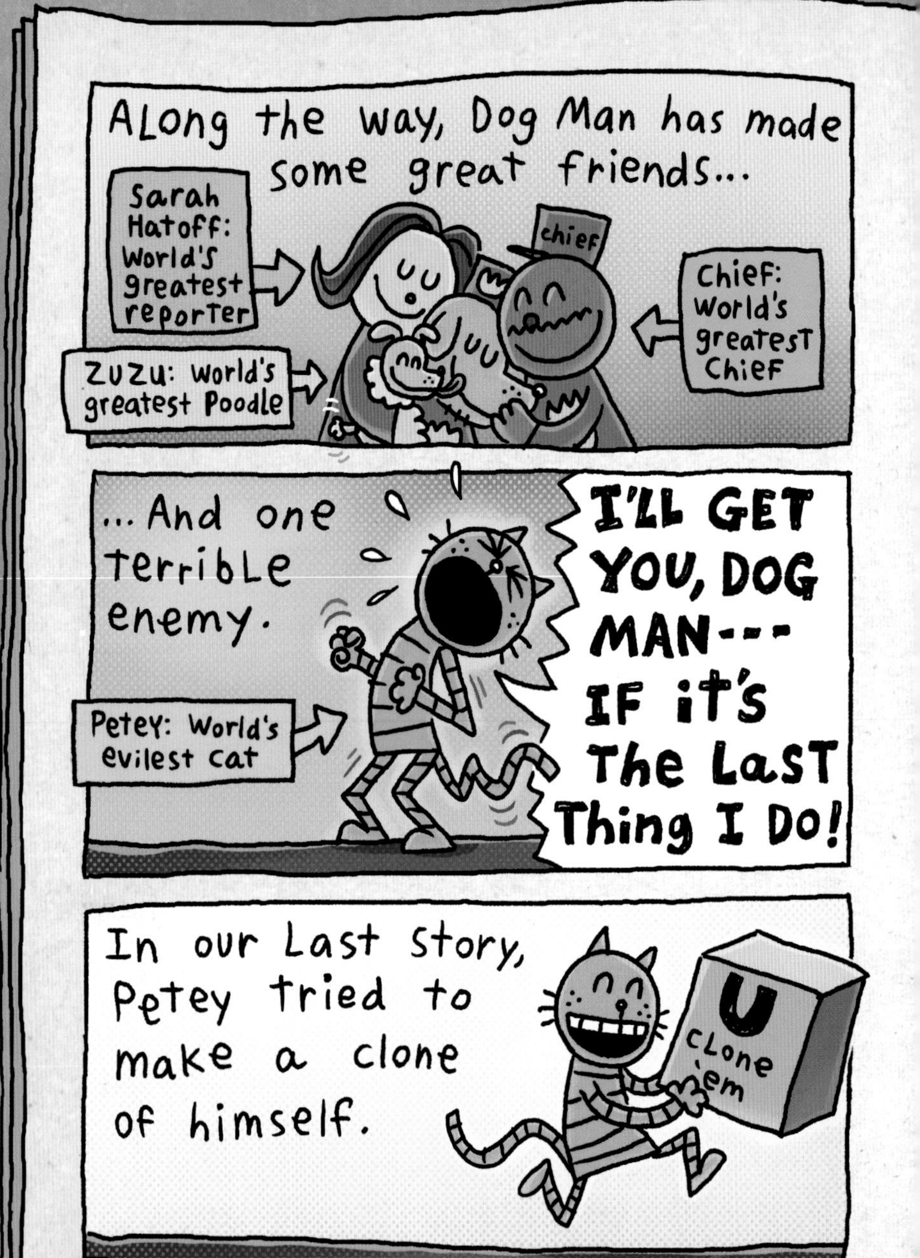

ALong the way, Dog Man has made some great friends...
Sarah Hatoff: World's greatest reporter
chief
Chief: World's greatest Chief
ZUZU: World's greatest Poodle
... And one terrible enemy.
I'LL GET YOU, DOG MAN--- IF it's The LaST Thing I DO!
Petey: World's evilest cat
In our Last story, Petey tried to make a clone of himself.
U
CLone 'em

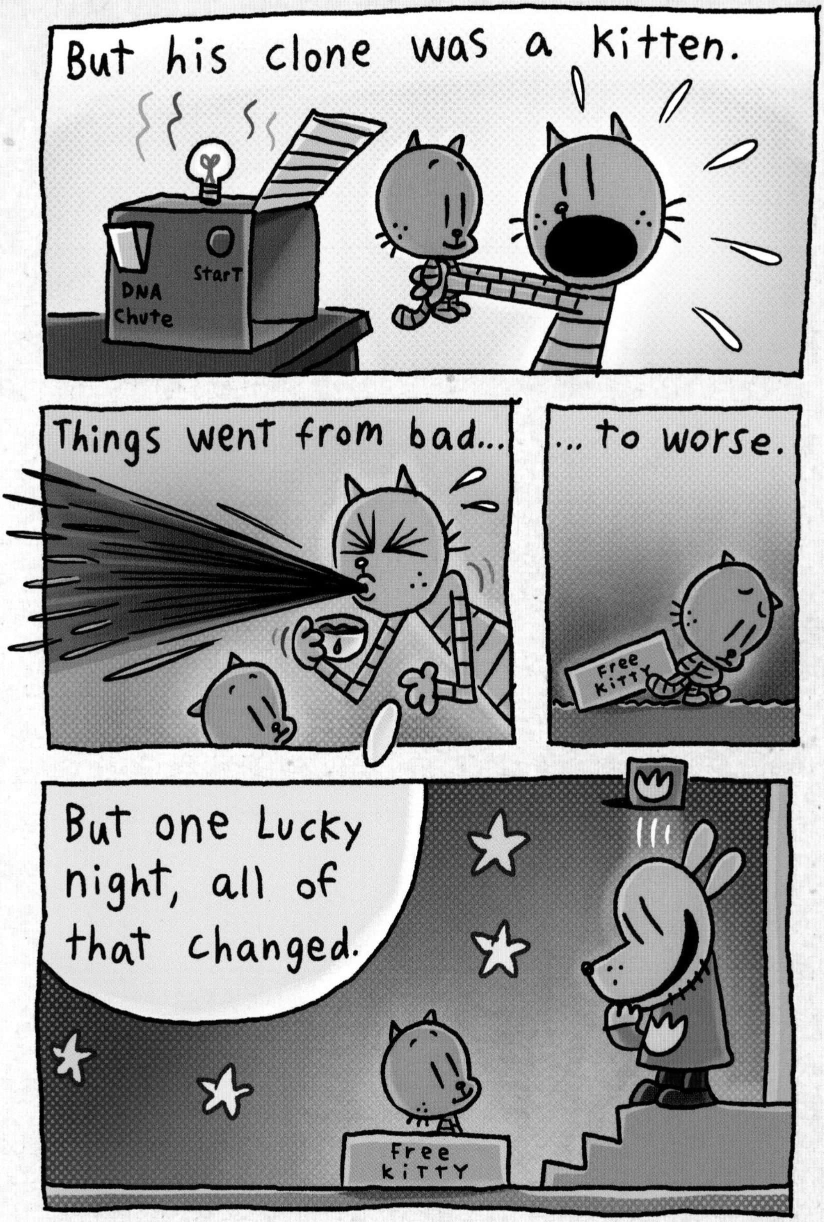
But his clone was a kitten.
DNA Chute
StarT
Things went from bad...
... to worse.
Free Kitty
But one Lucky night, all of that changed.
Free KiTTY

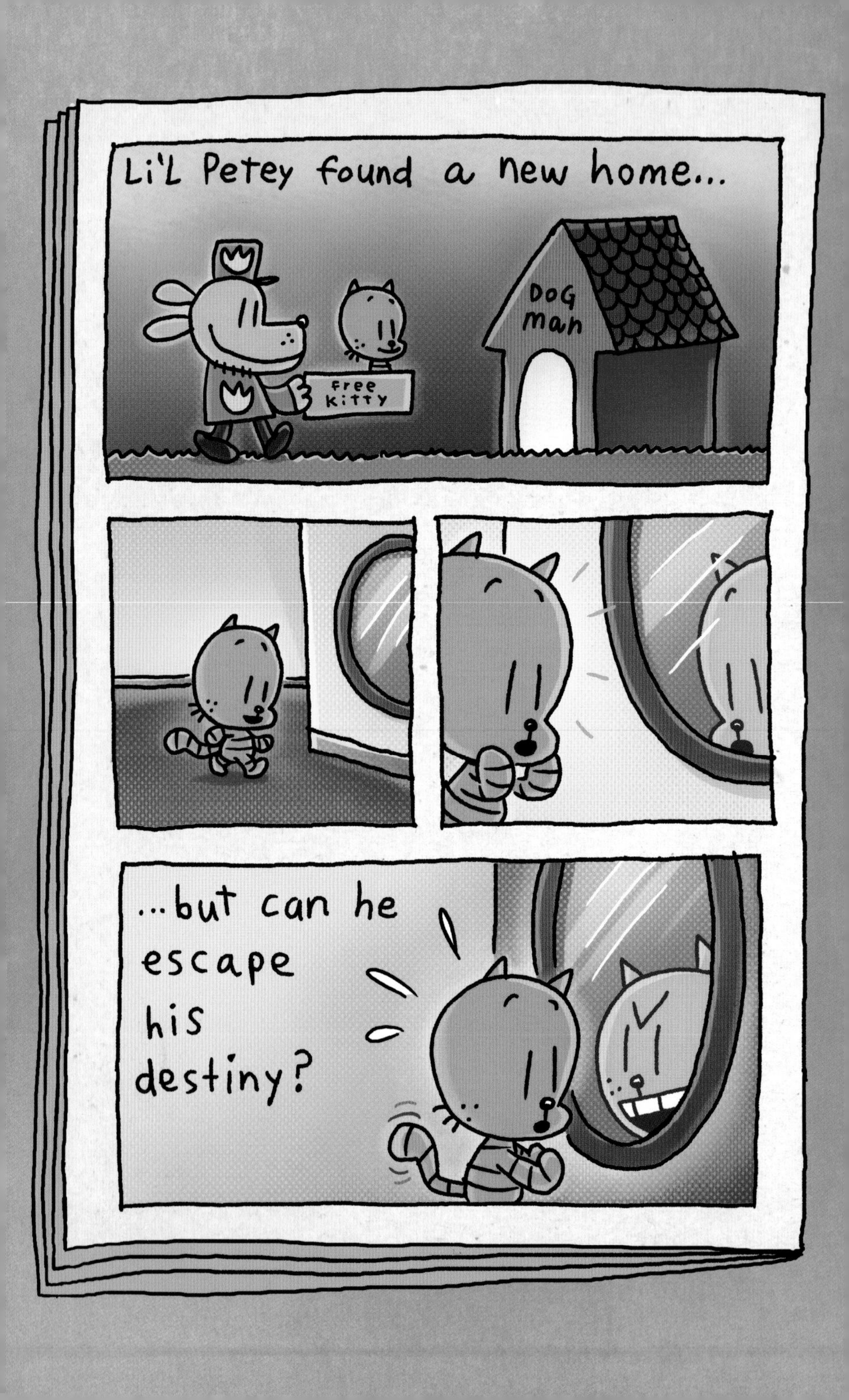
Li'L Petey found a new home...
DOG man
Free Kitty
...but can he escape his destiny?

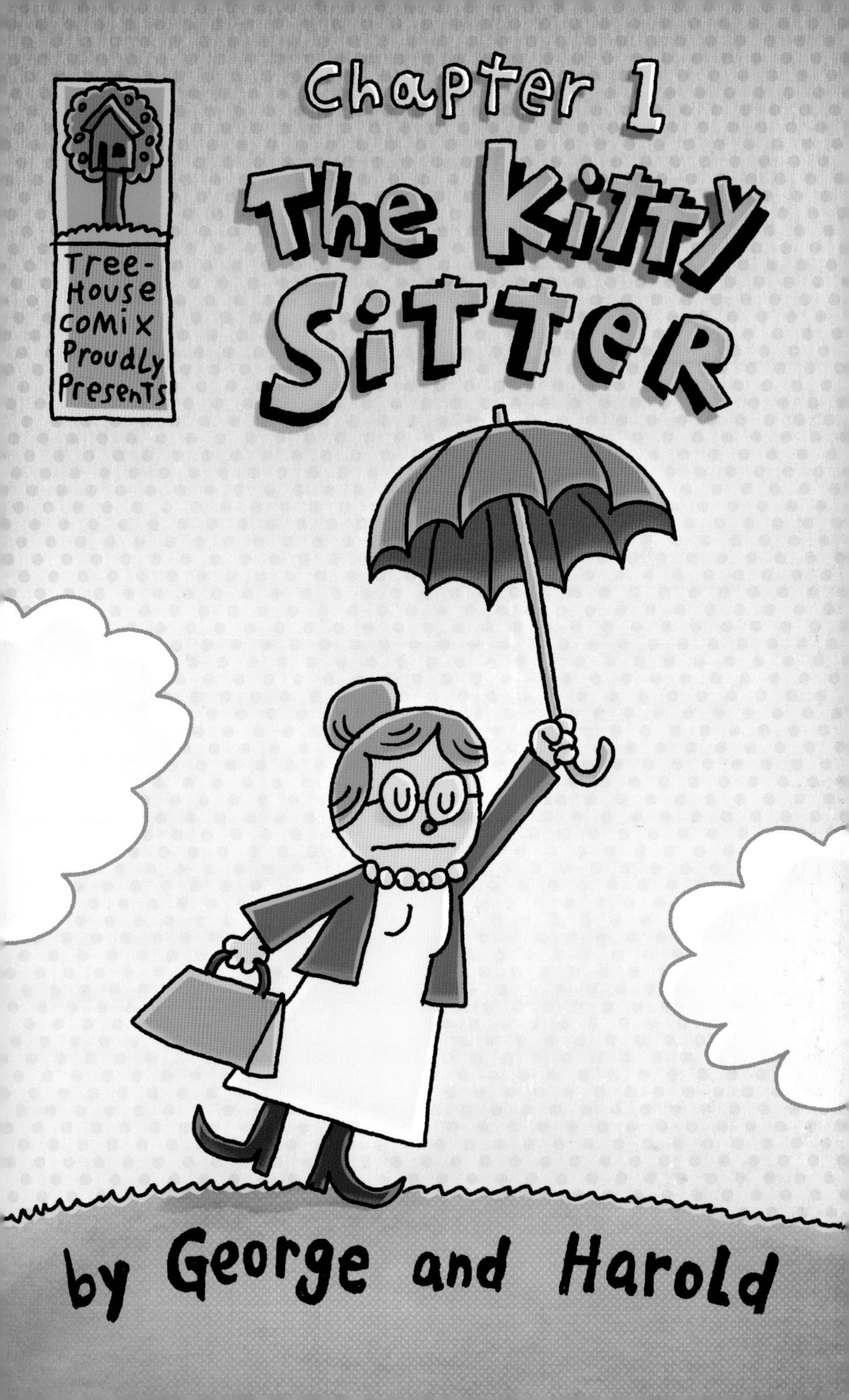
Tree-House Comix Proudly Presents
Chapter 1
The Kitty Sitter
by George and Harold

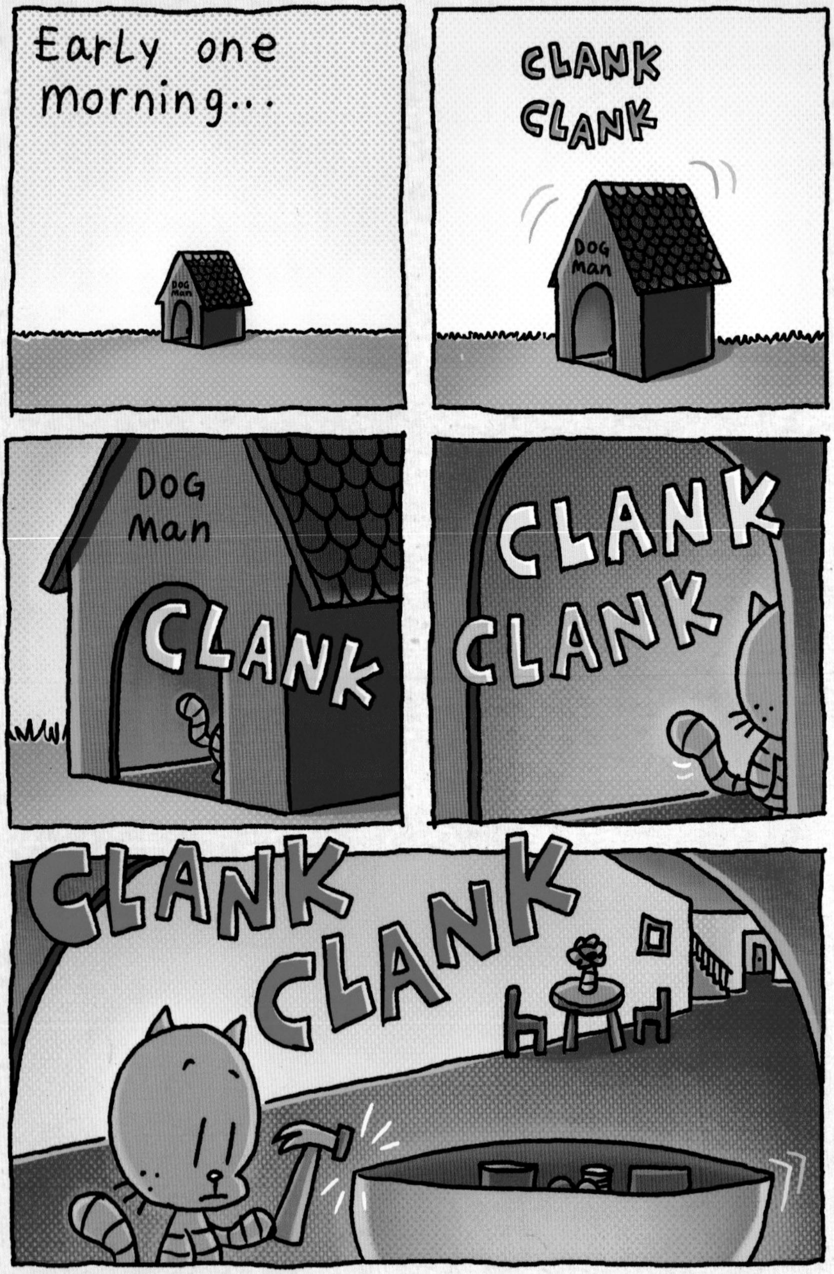
Early one morning...
CLANK
CLANK
DOG Man
DOG Man
DOG Man
CLANK
CLANK
CLANK
CLANK
CLANK

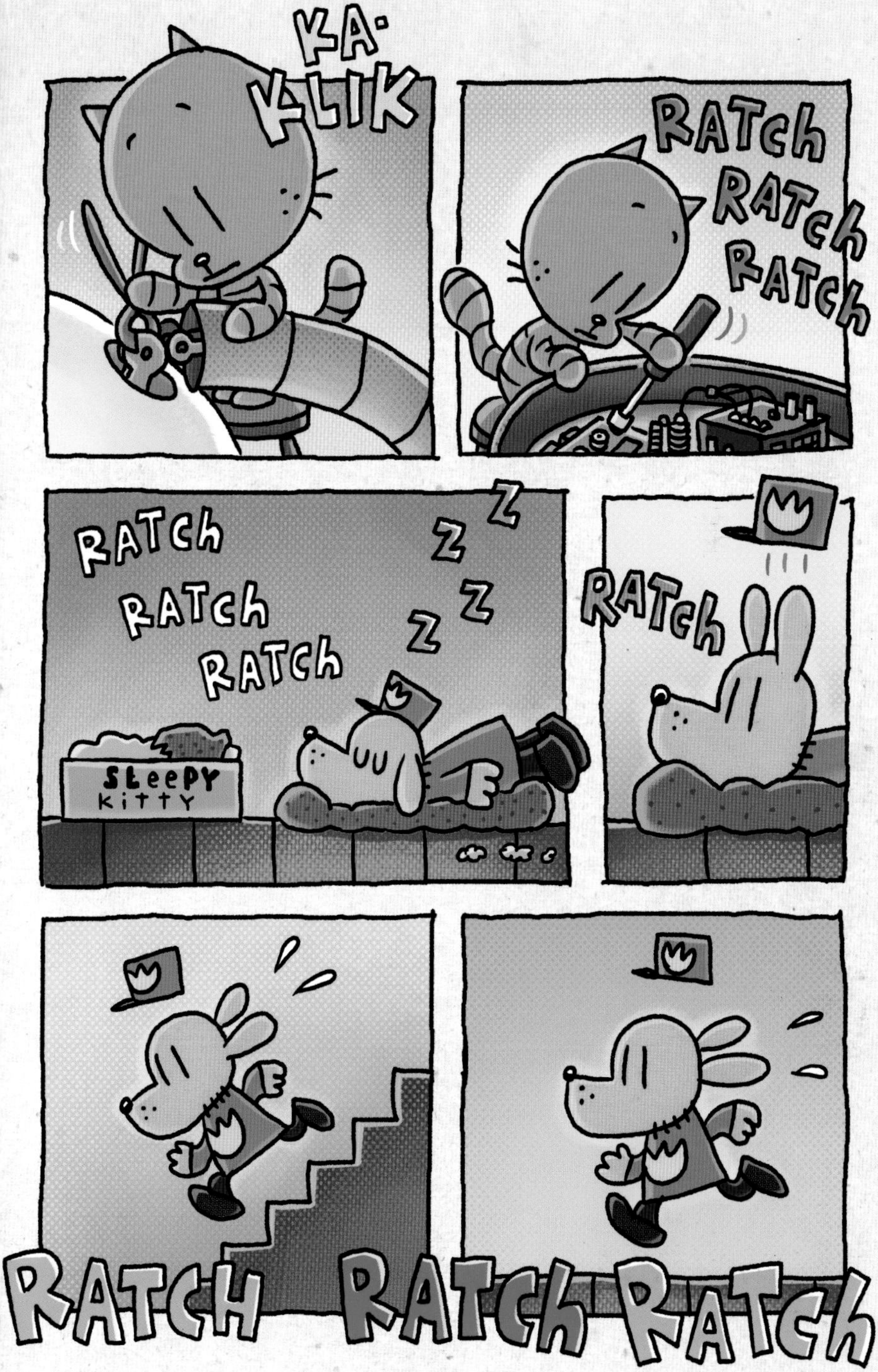
KA-KLIK
RATCH RATCH RATCH
RATCH RATCH RATCH
Z Z Z Z
SLEEPY KITTY
RATCH
RATCH RATCH RATCH

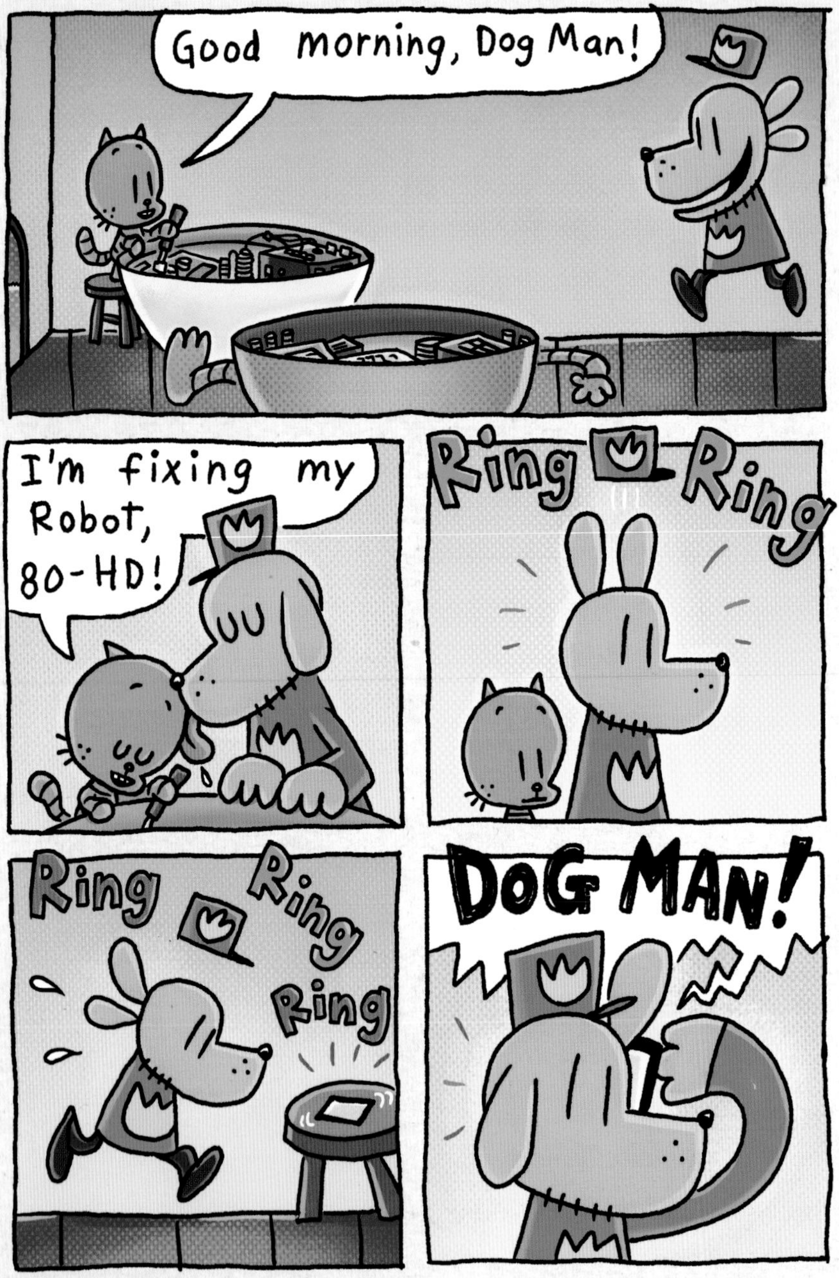
Good morning, Dog Man!
I'm fixing my Robot, 80-HD!
Ring Ring
Ring Ring Ring
DOG MAN!

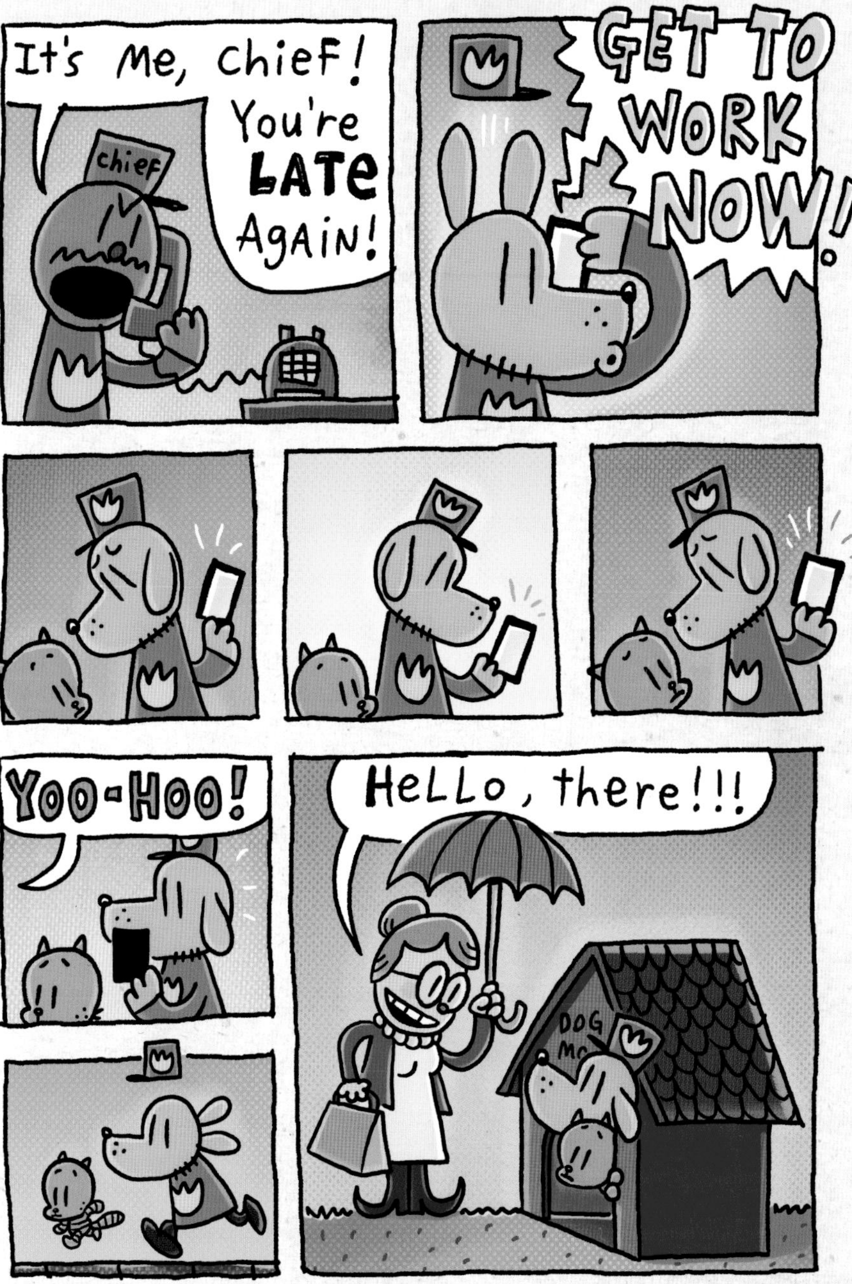
It's Me, chieF!
You're LATE Again!
chief
GET TO WORK NOW!
YOO-HOO!
HeLLo, there!!!
DOG
MC

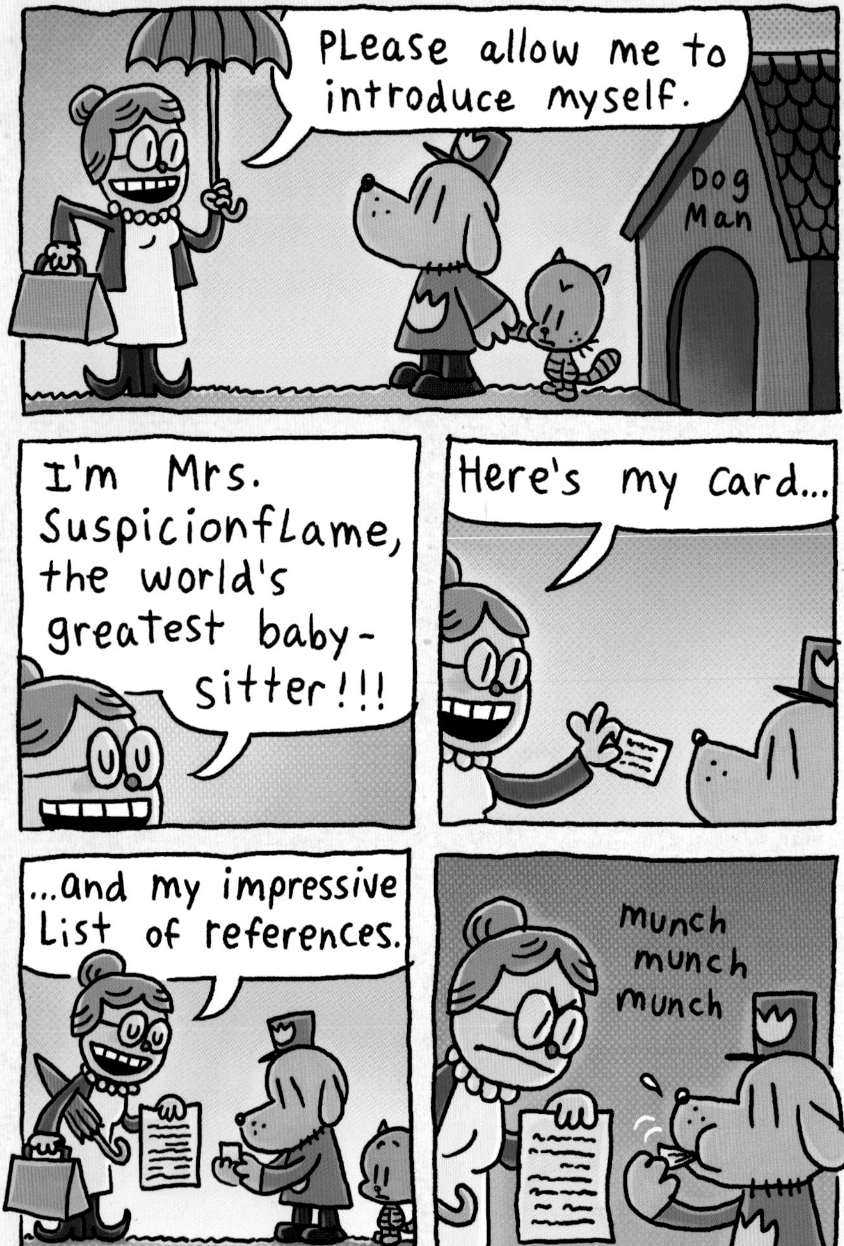

Please allow me to introduce myself.
Dog Man
I'm Mrs. Suspicionflame, the world's greatest baby-sitter!!!
Here's my card...
...and my impressive List of references.
munch munch munch

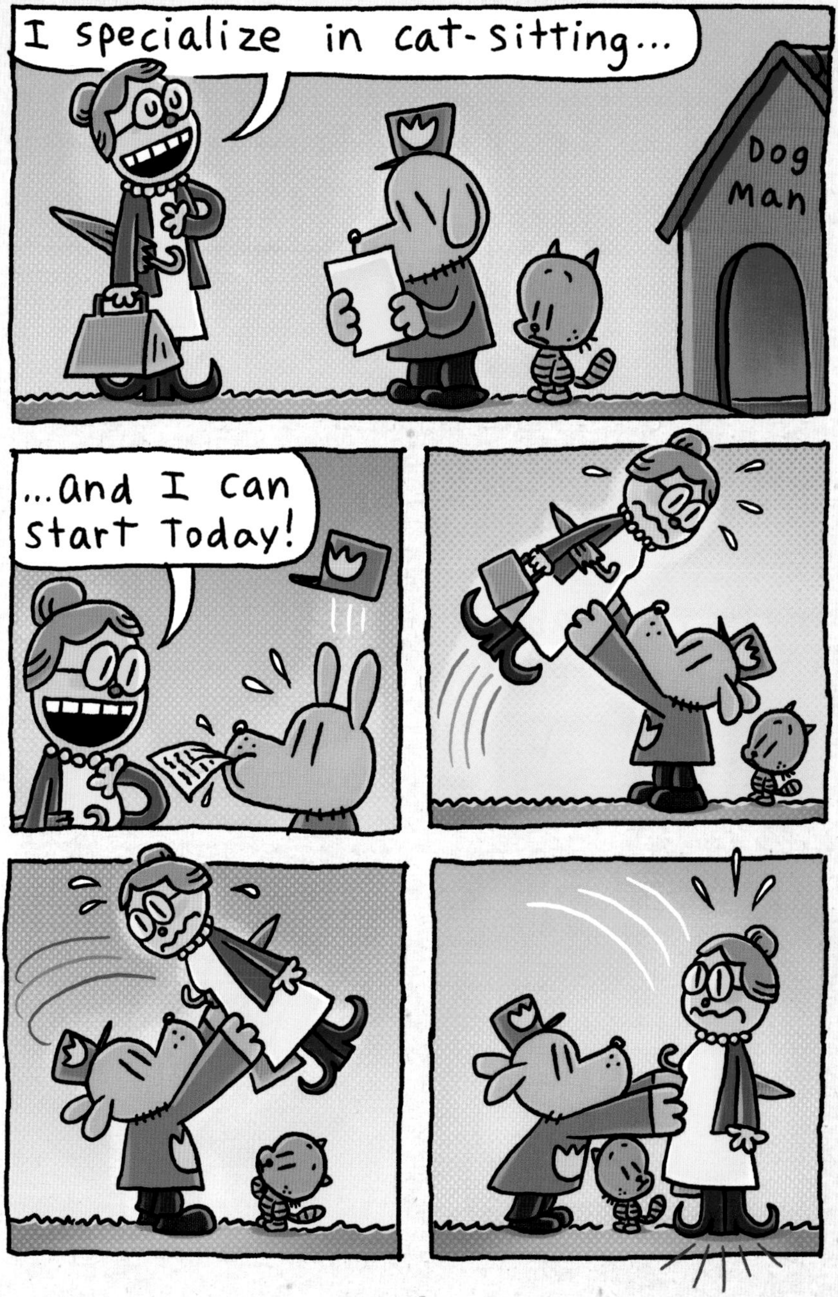
I specialize in cat-sitting...
Dog Man
...and I can start Today!

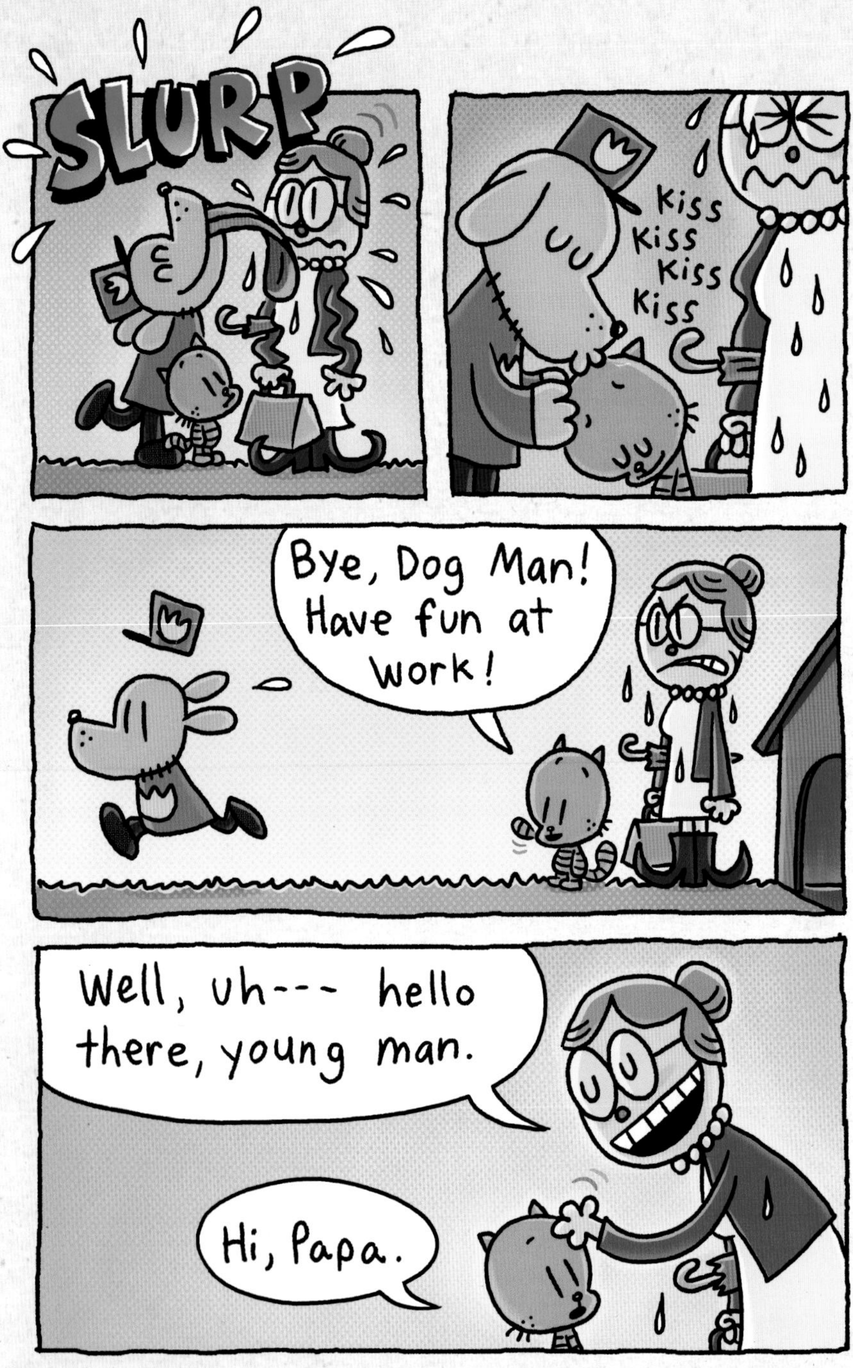
SLURP
Kiss
Kiss
Kiss
Kiss
Bye, Dog Man! Have fun at work!
Well, uh--- hello there, young man.
Hi, Papa.

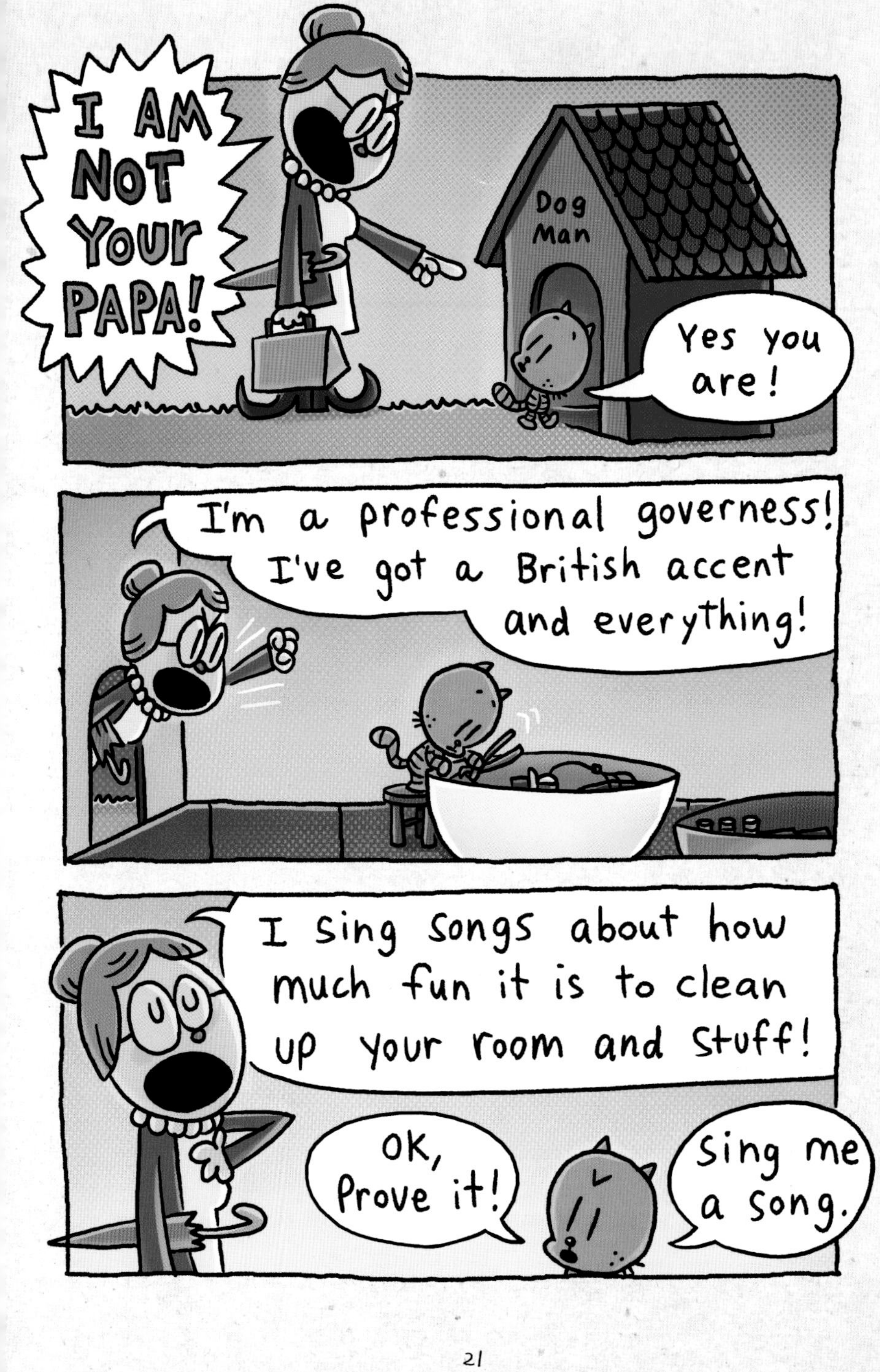
I AM NOT YOUR PAPA!
Dog Man
Yes you are!
I'm a professional governess! I've got a British accent and everything!
I sing songs about how much fun it is to clean up your room and stuff!
OK, Prove it!
Sing me a song.

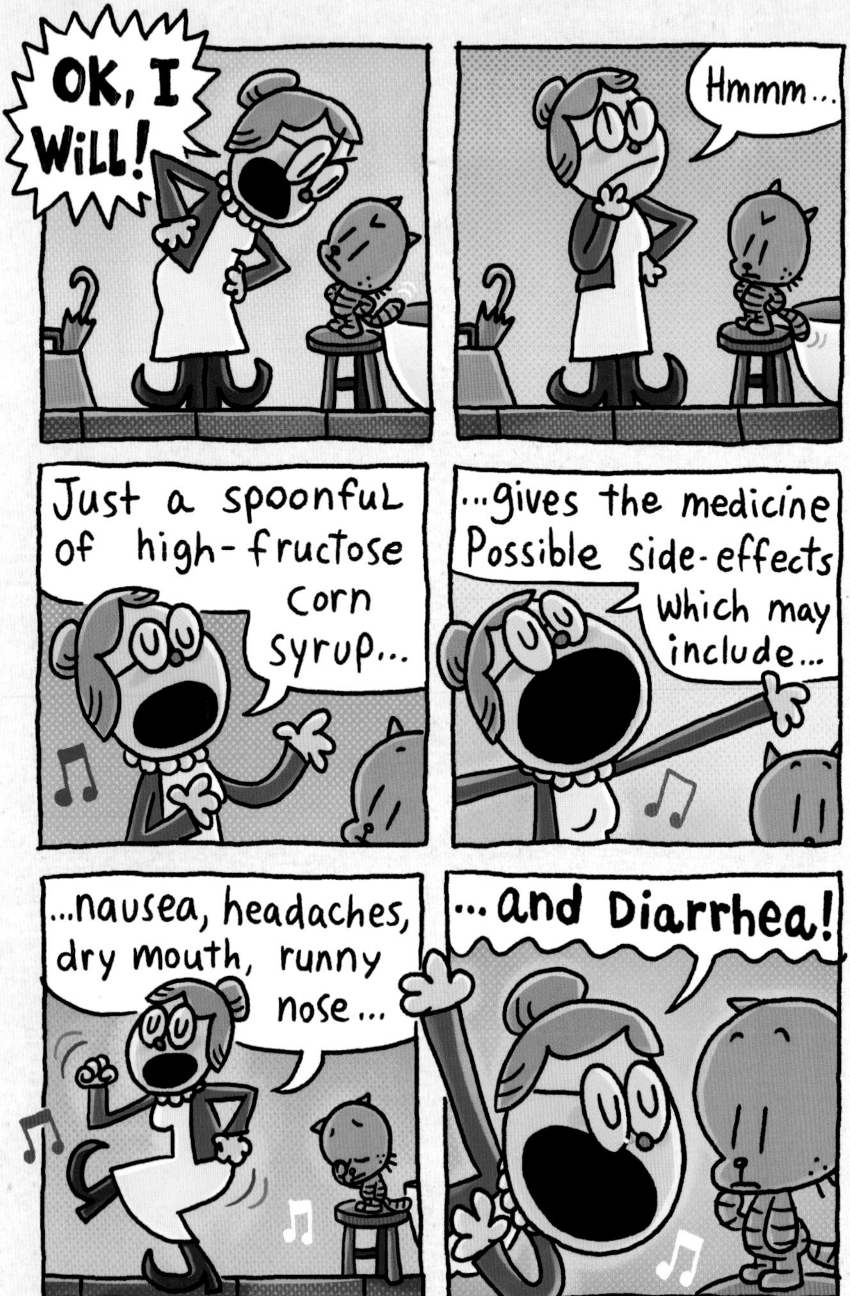
OK, I WiLL!
Hmmm...
Just a spoonful of high-fructose corn syrup...
...gives the medicine Possible side-effects which may include...
...nausea, headaches, dry mouth, runny nose...
...and Diarrhea!

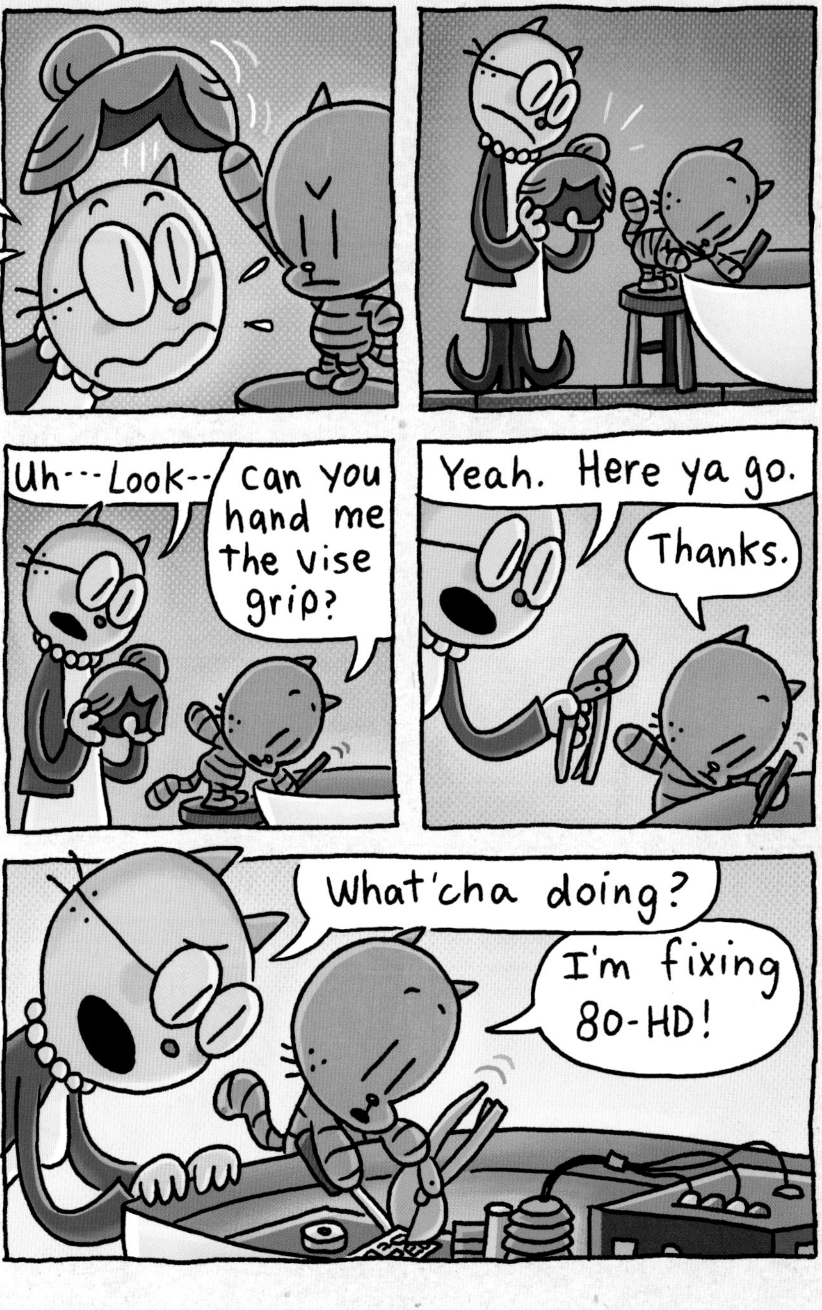
Uh---Look--
can you hand me the vise grip?
Yeah. Here ya go.
Thanks.
What'cha doing?
I'm fixing 80-HD!

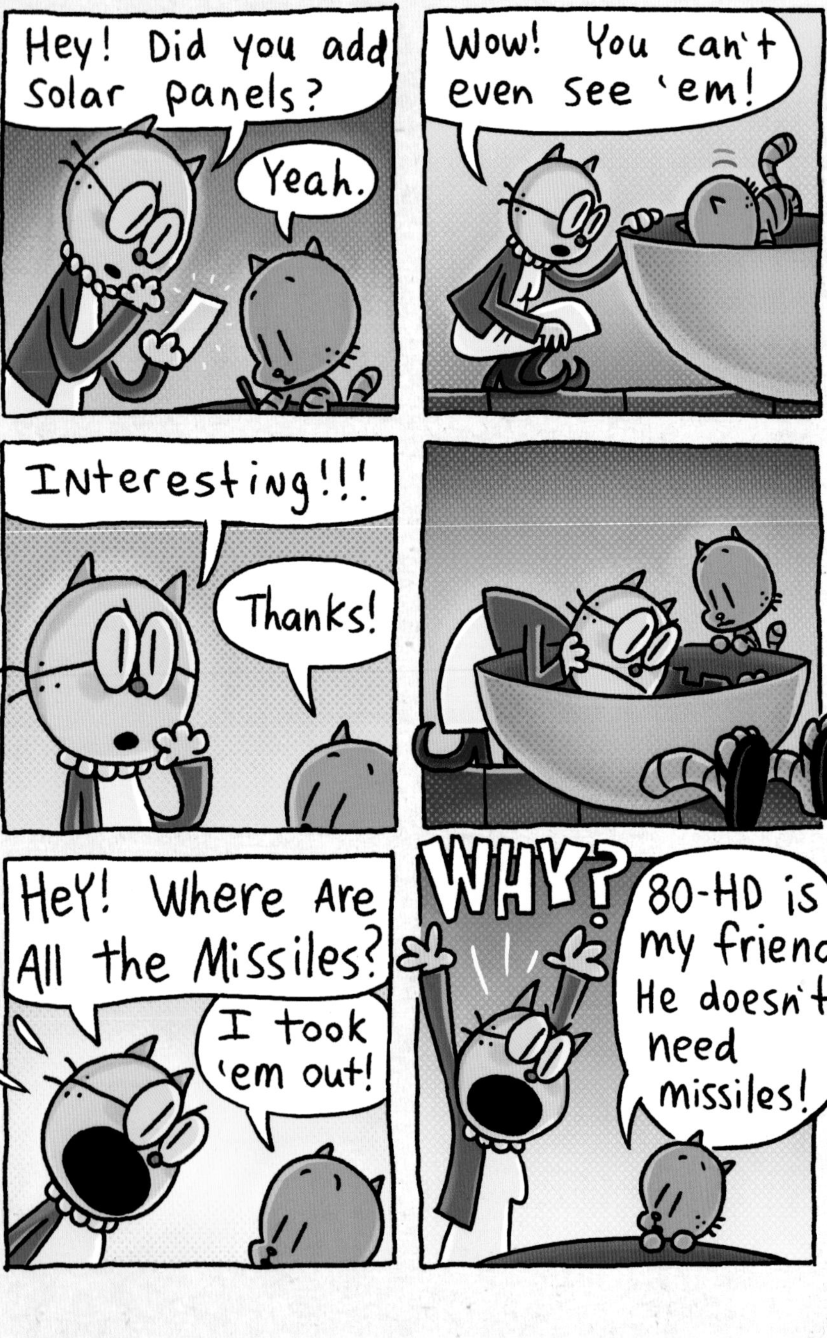
Hey! Did you add Solar panels?
Yeah.
Wow! You can't even see 'em!
INteresting!!!
Thanks!
HeY! Where Are All the Missiles?
I took 'em out!
WHY?
80-HD is my friend. He doesn't need missiles!

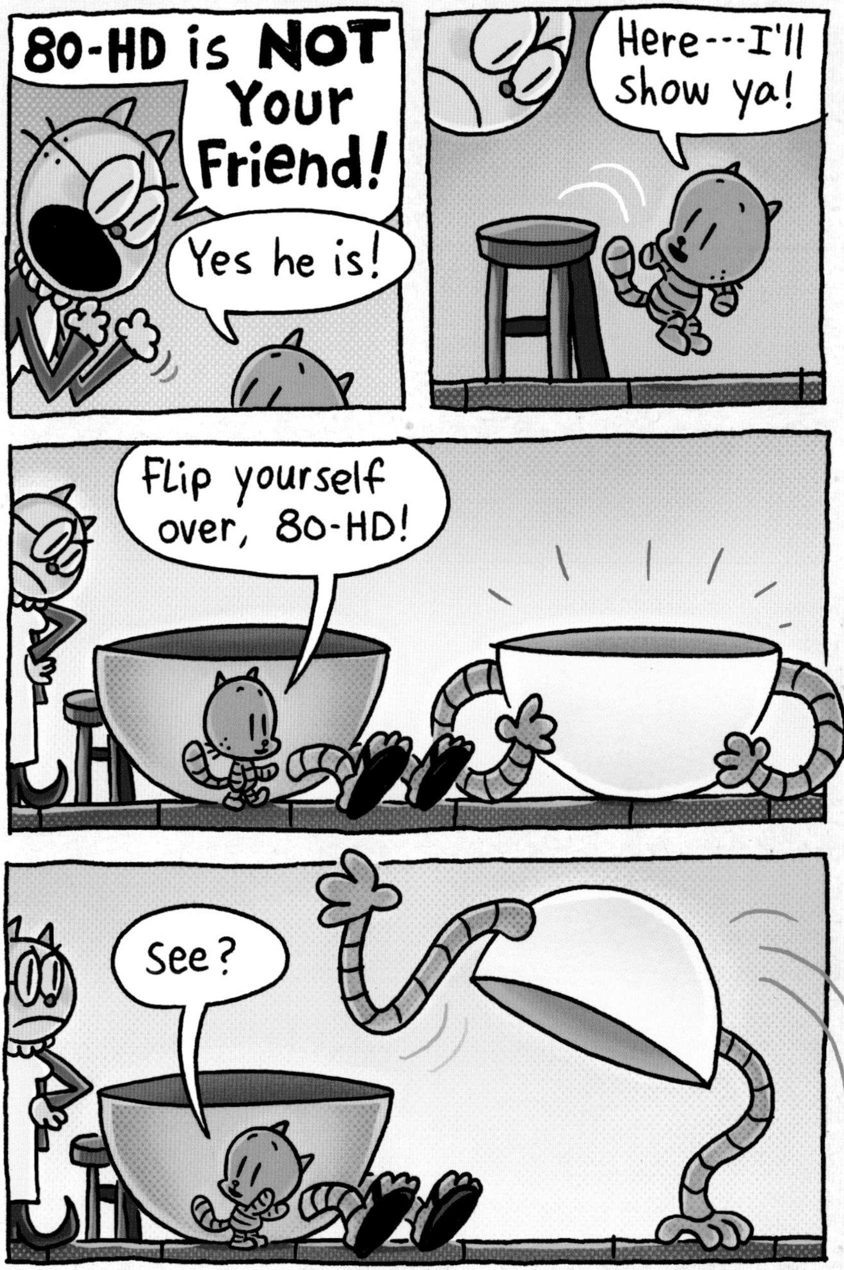
80-HD is NOT Your Friend!
Yes he is!
Here---I'll show ya!
Flip yourself over, 80-HD!
See?

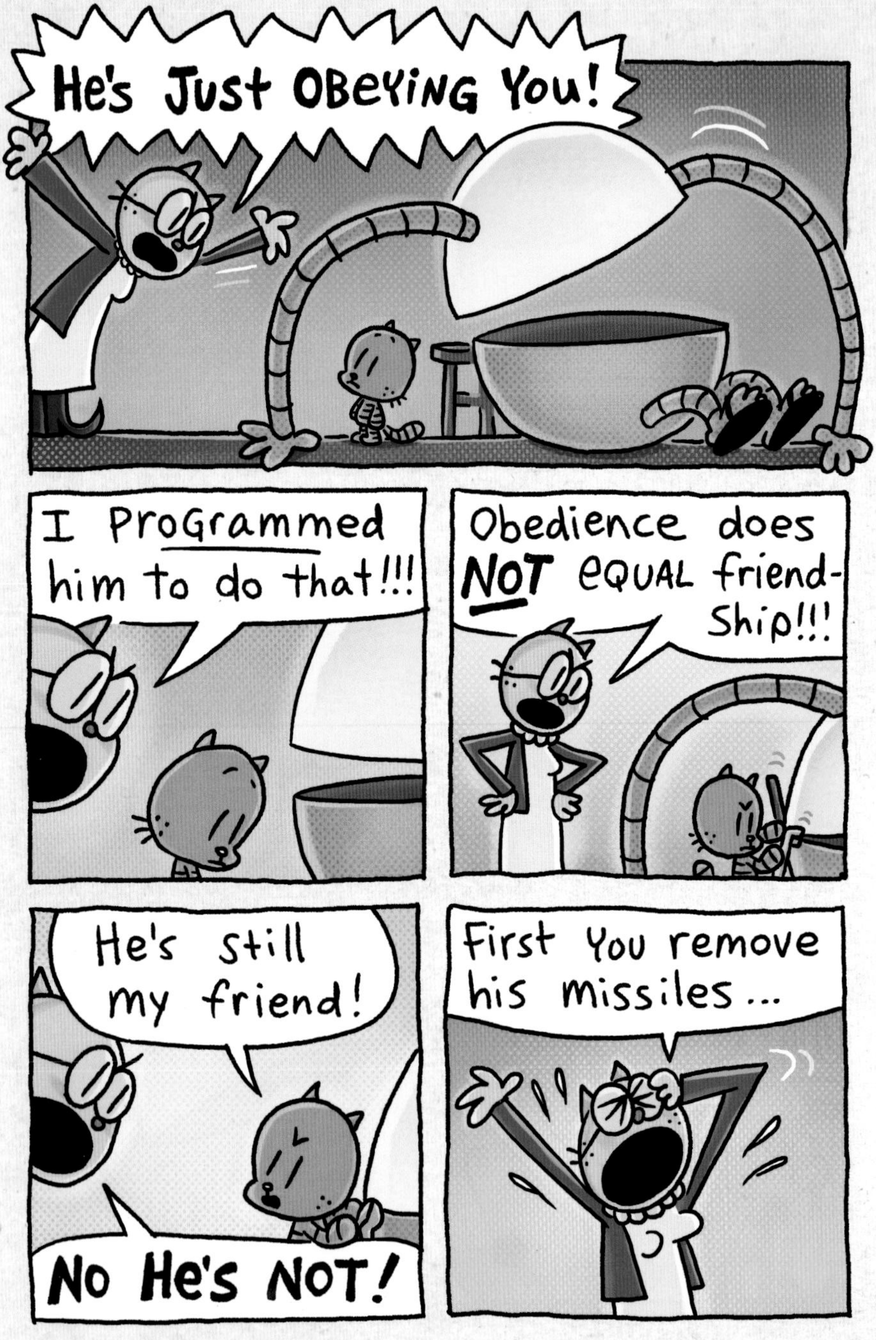
He's Just OBEYING You!
I PROGRAMMED him to do that!!!
Obedience does NOT EQUAL friend-ship!!!
He's still my friend!
No He's NOT!
First You remove his missiles...

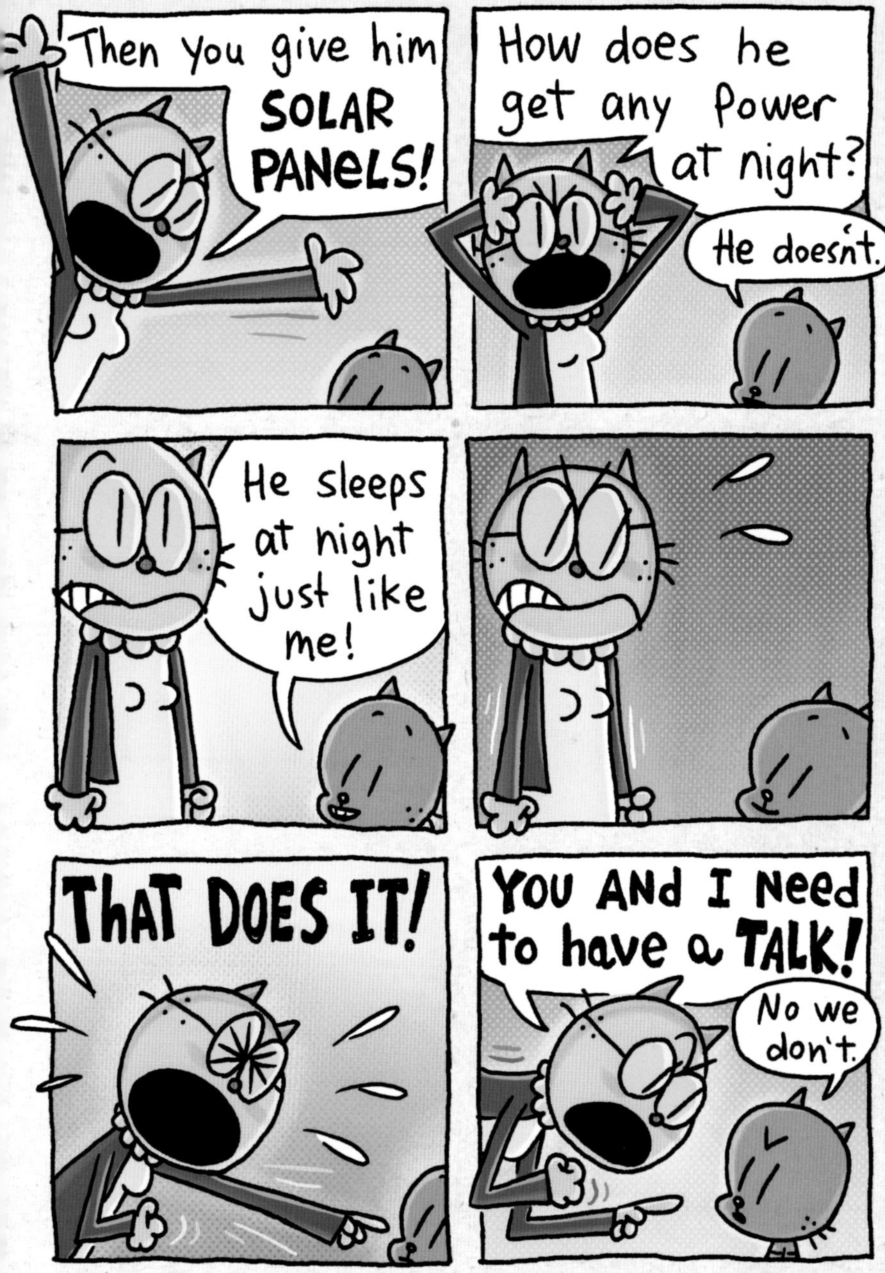
Then you give him SOLAR PANELS!
How does he get any power at night?
He doesn't.
He sleeps at night just like me!
THAT DOES IT!
YOU AND I NEED to have a TALK!
No we don't.

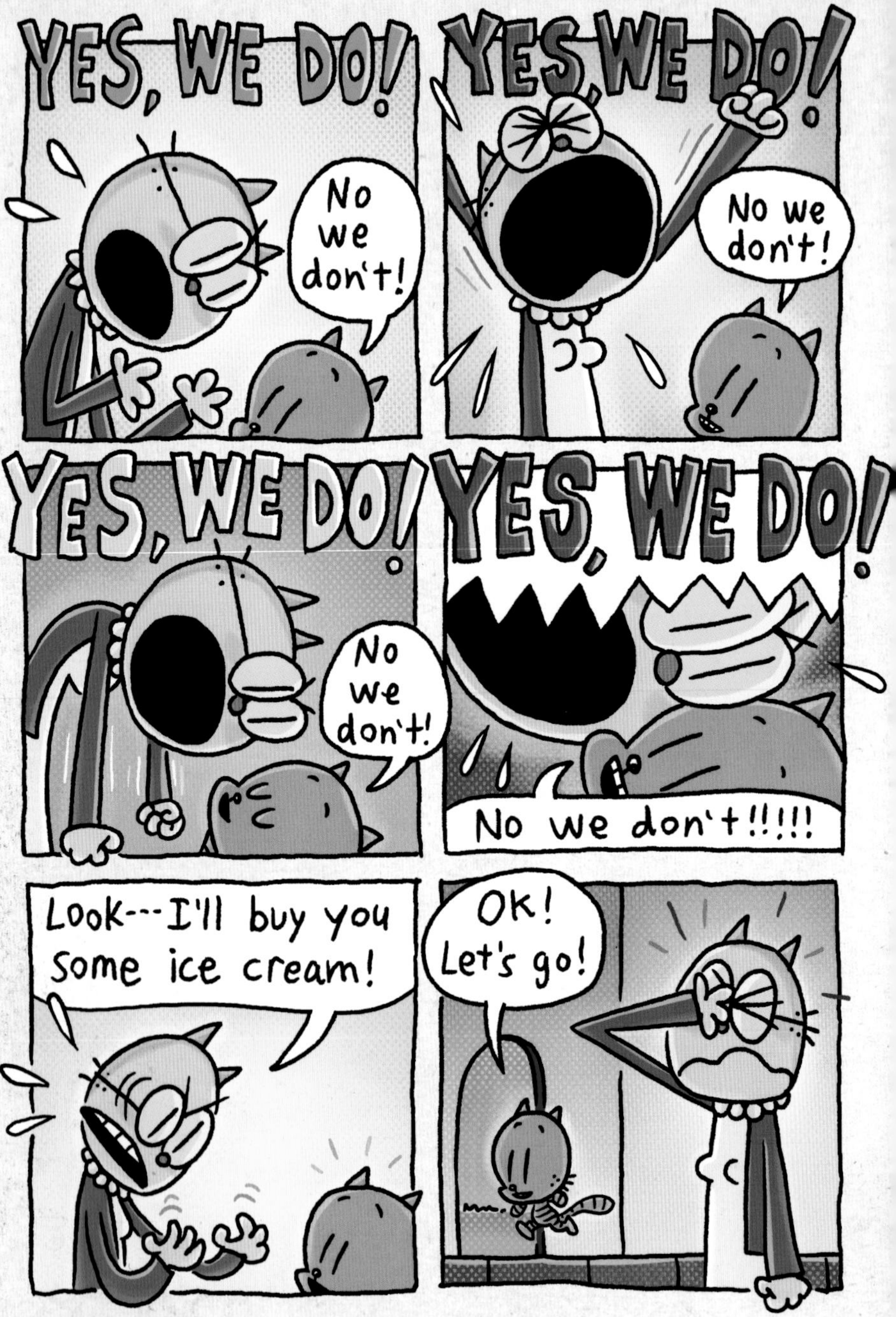
YES, WE DO!
No we don't!
YES, WE DO!
No we don't!
YES, WE DO!
No we don't!
YES, WE DO!
No we don't!!!!!
Look---I'll buy you some ice cream!
OK! Let's go!

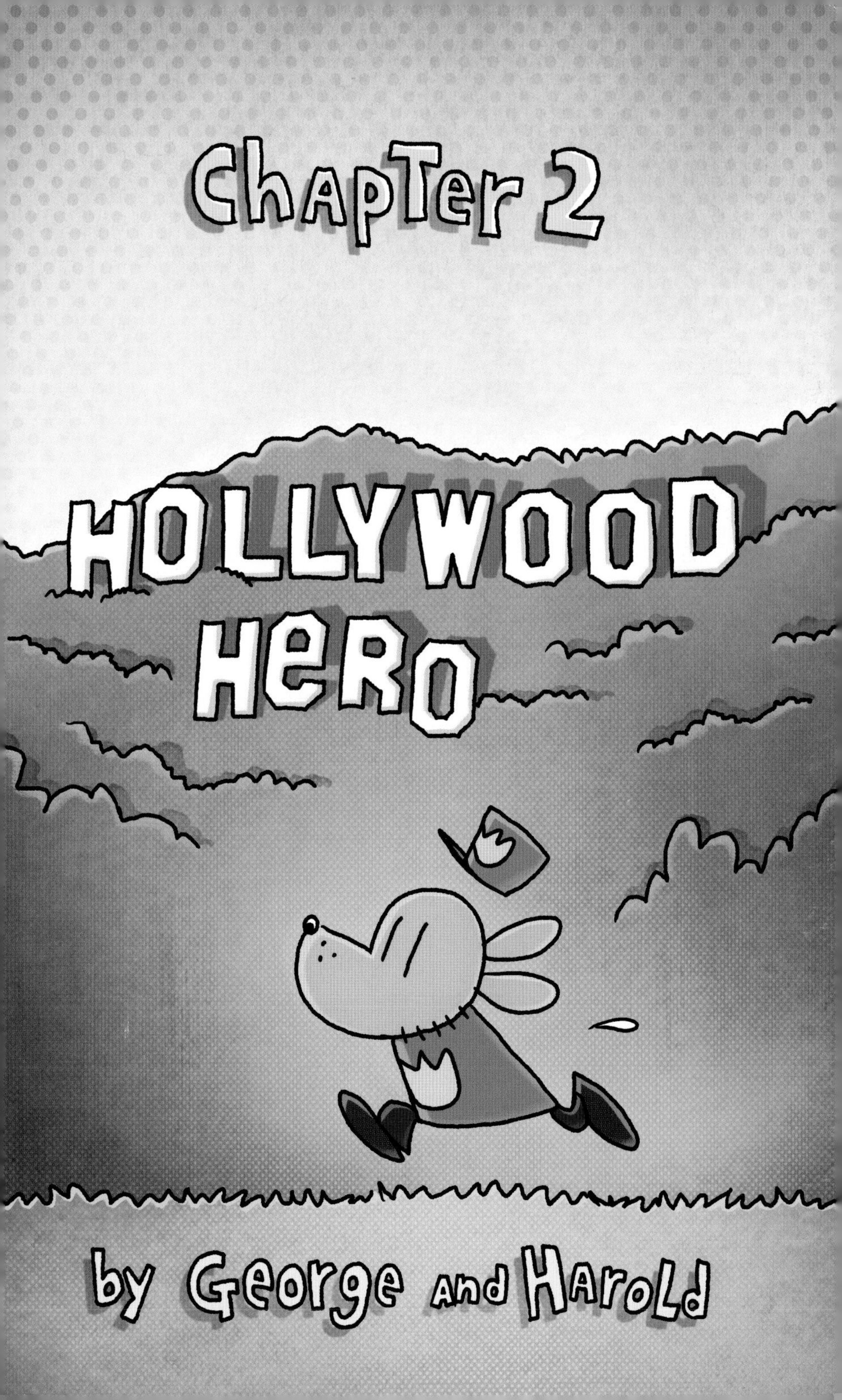
ChapTer 2
HOLLYWOOD
HeRO
by George And HAroLd

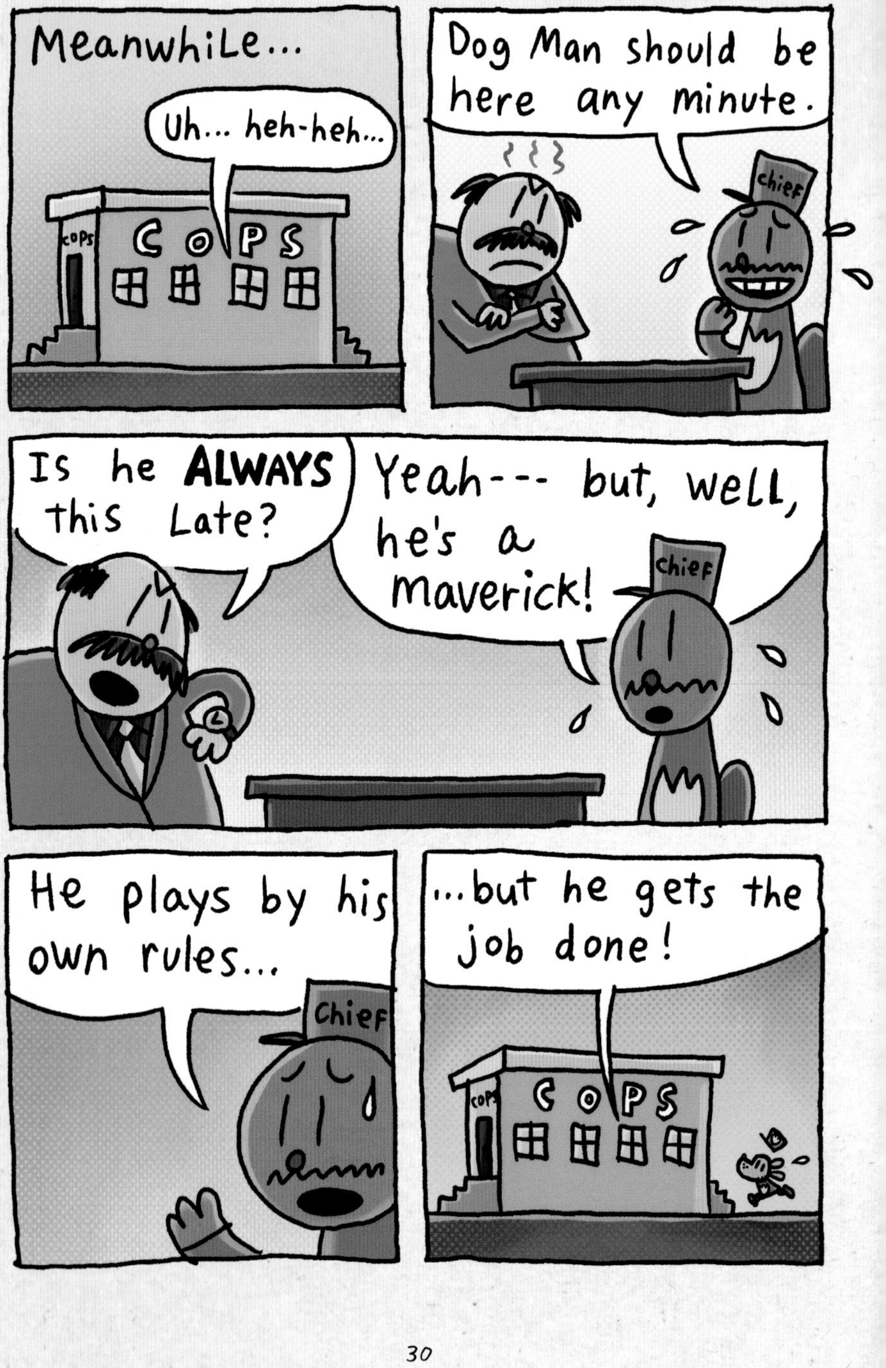
Meanwhile...
Uh... heh-heh...
COPS
COPS
Dog Man should be here any minute.
CHIEF
Is he ALWAYS this Late?
Yeah--- but, well, he's a maverick!
CHIEF
He plays by his own rules...
CHIEF
...but he gets the job done!
COPS
COPS

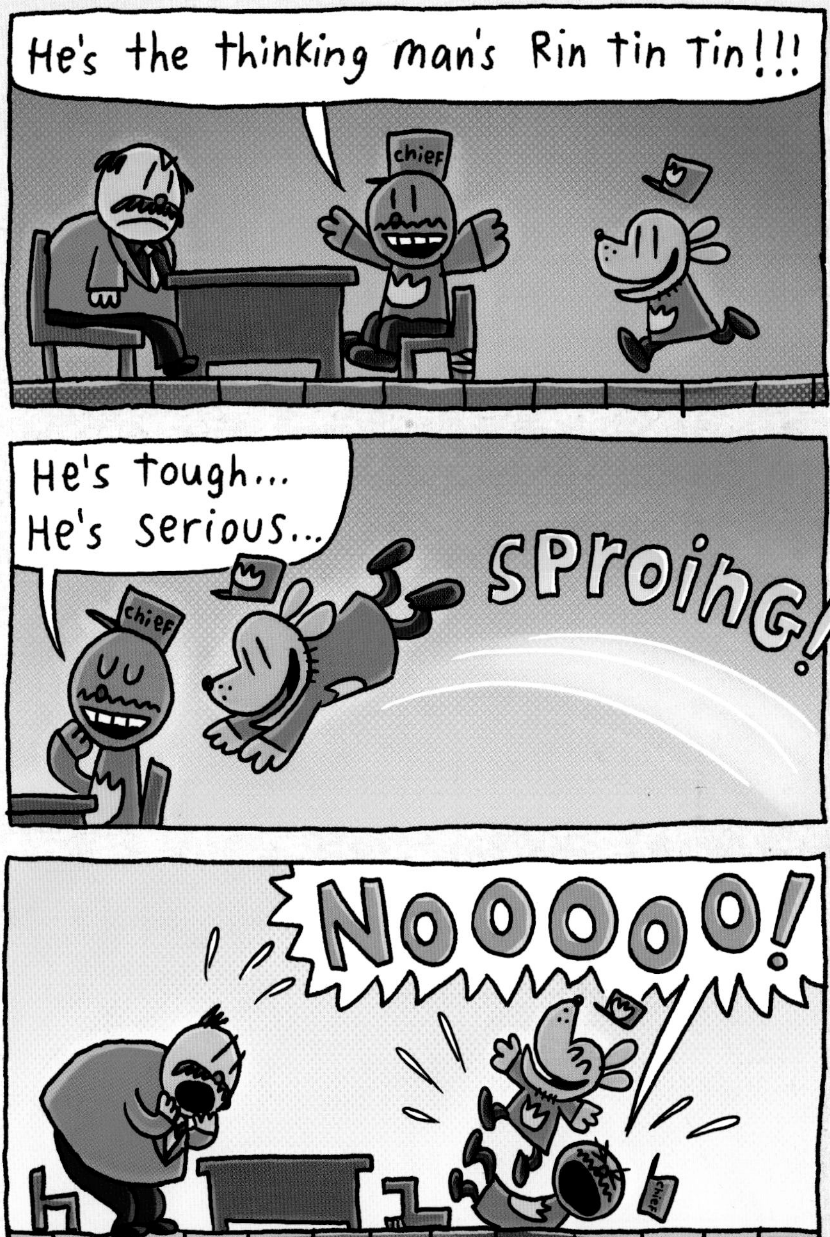
He's the thinking man's Rin tin Tin!!!
chief
He's tough...
He's serious...
chief
SProing!
NoOOOO!
chief

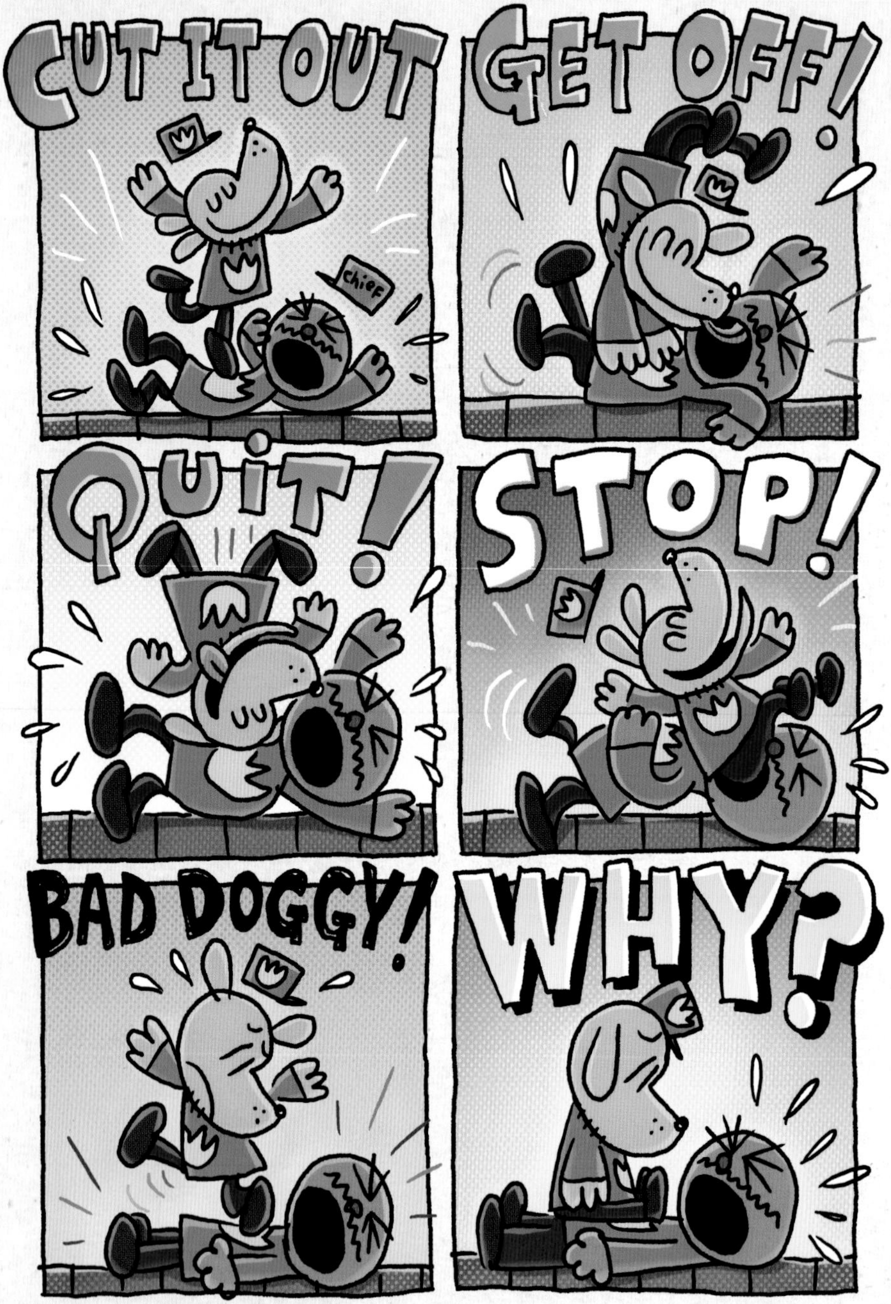
CUT IT OUT
chief
GET OFF!
QUIT!
STOP!
BAD DOGGY!
WHY?

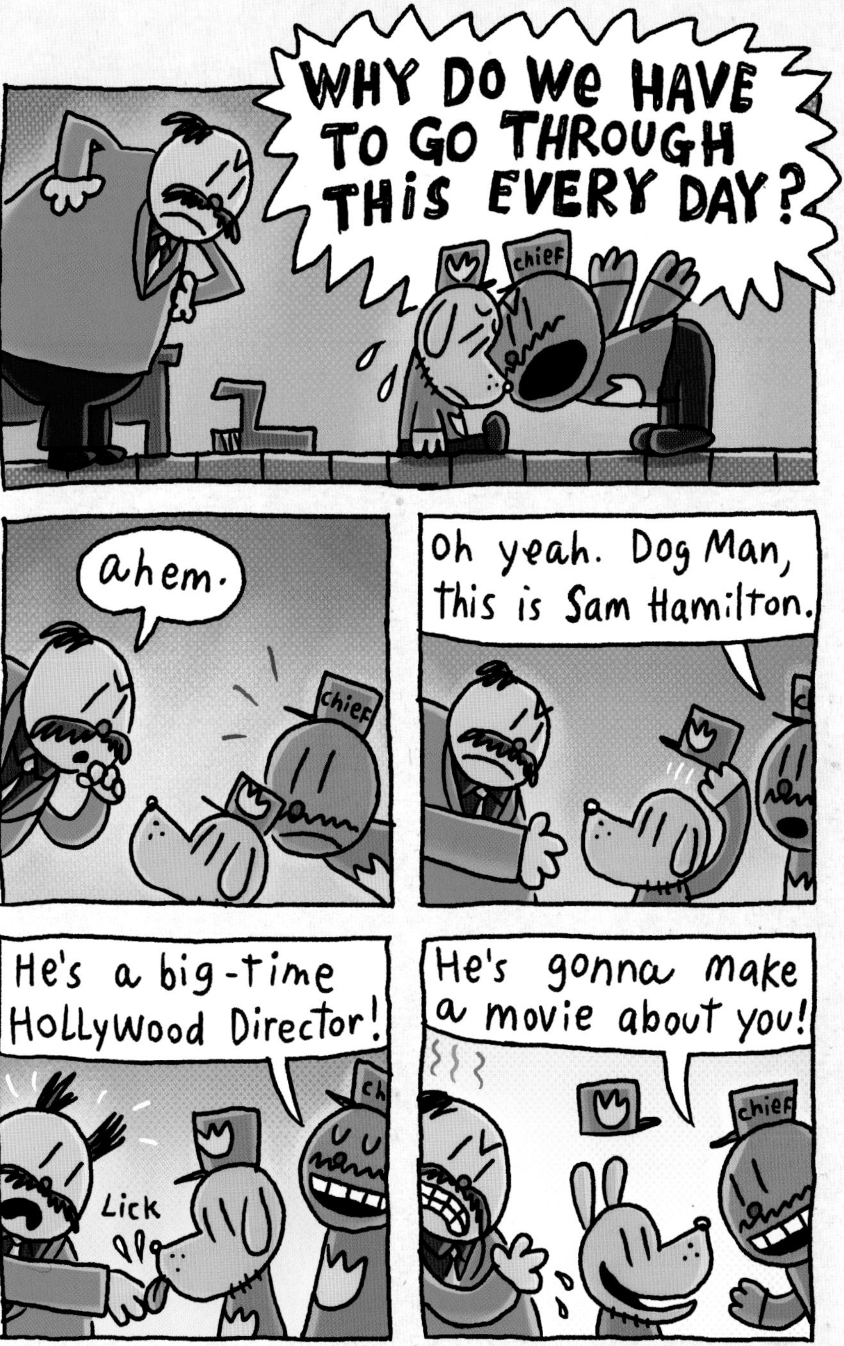
WHY DO WE HAVE TO GO THROUGH THIS EVERY DAY?
chief
ahem.
chief
Oh yeah. Dog Man, this is Sam Hamilton.
He's a big-time HOLLYWOOD Director!
Lick
He's gonna make a movie about you!
chief

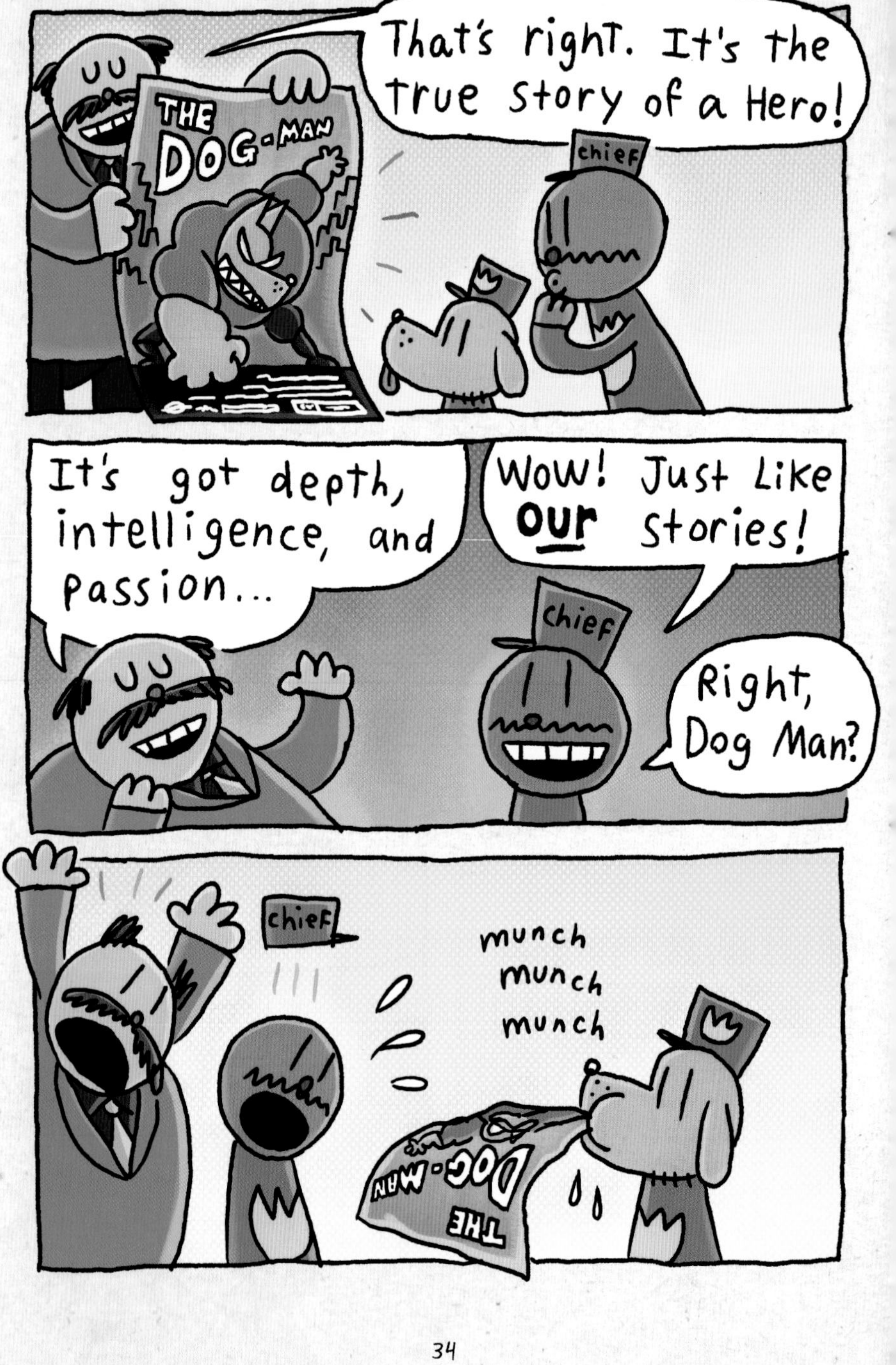
That's right. It's the true story of a Hero!
THE DOG-MAN
chief
It's got depth, intelligence, and passion...
WOW! Just Like **OUR** stories!
chief
Right, Dog Man?
chief
munch munch munch
THE DOG-MAN

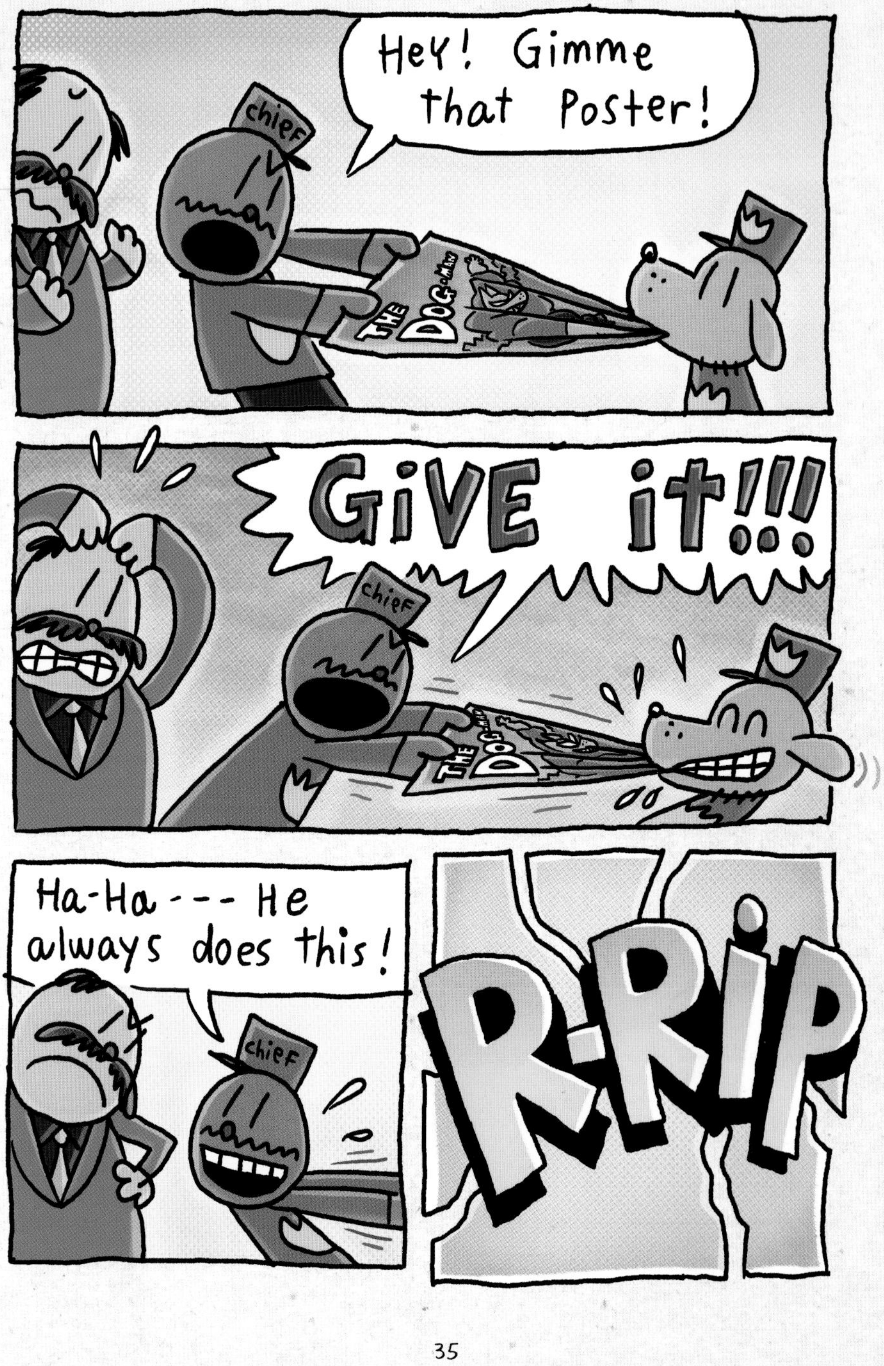
Hey! Gimme that Poster!
chief
GiVE it!!!
chief
Ha-Ha --- He always does this!
chief
R-RiP

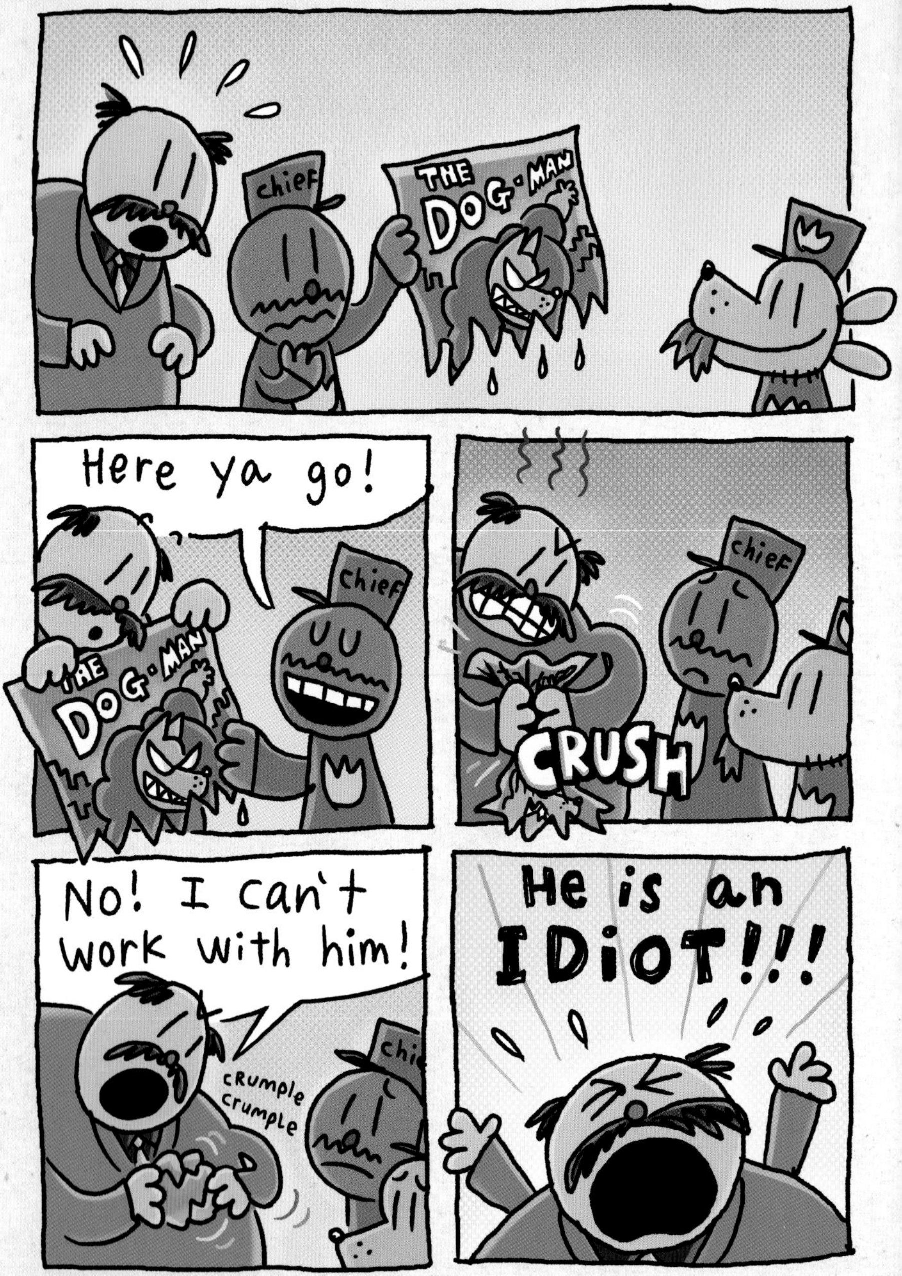
THE DOG-MAN
chief
Here ya go!
chief
THE DOG-MAN
chief
CRUSH
No! I can't work with him!
crumple crumple
He is an IDIOT!!!

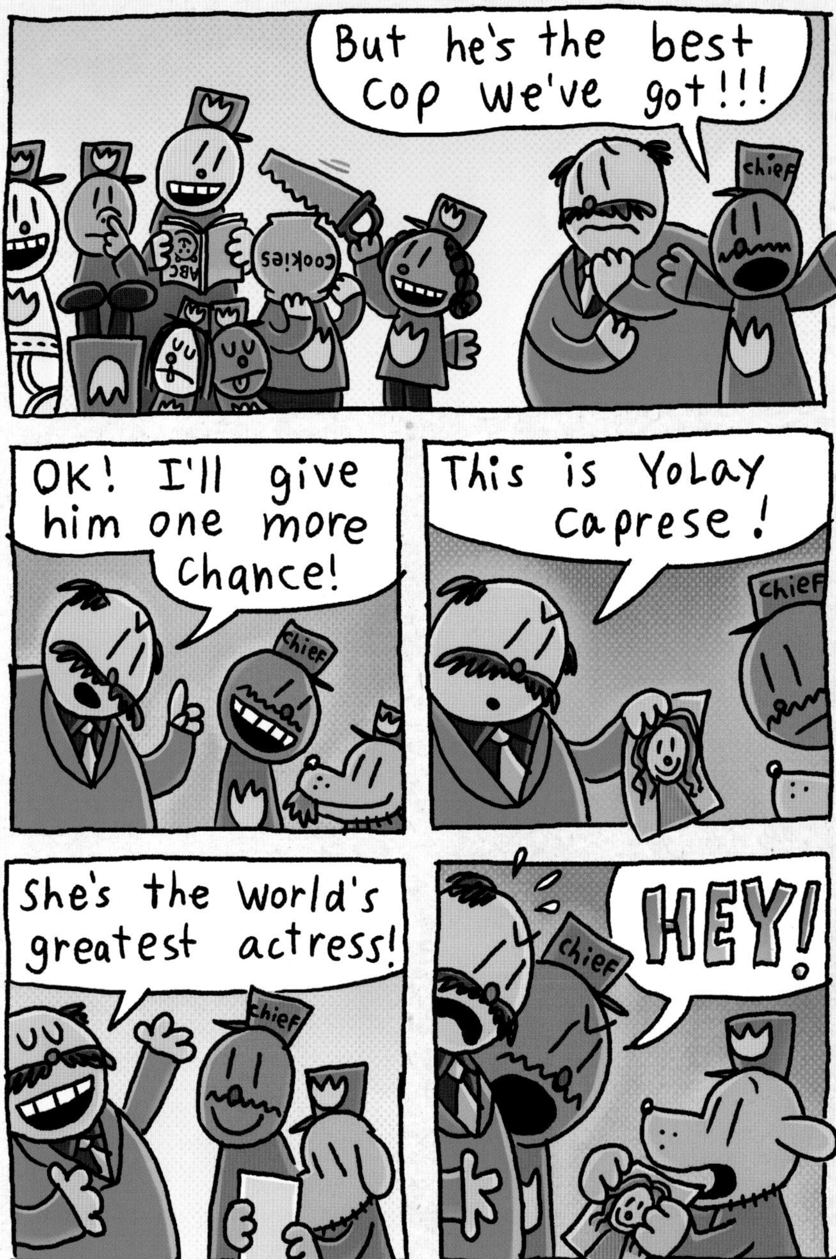
But he's the best cop we've got!!!
chief
Cookies
ABC
OK! I'll give him one more chance!
chief
This is YoLay Caprese!
chief
She's the world's greatest actress!
chief
chief
HEY!

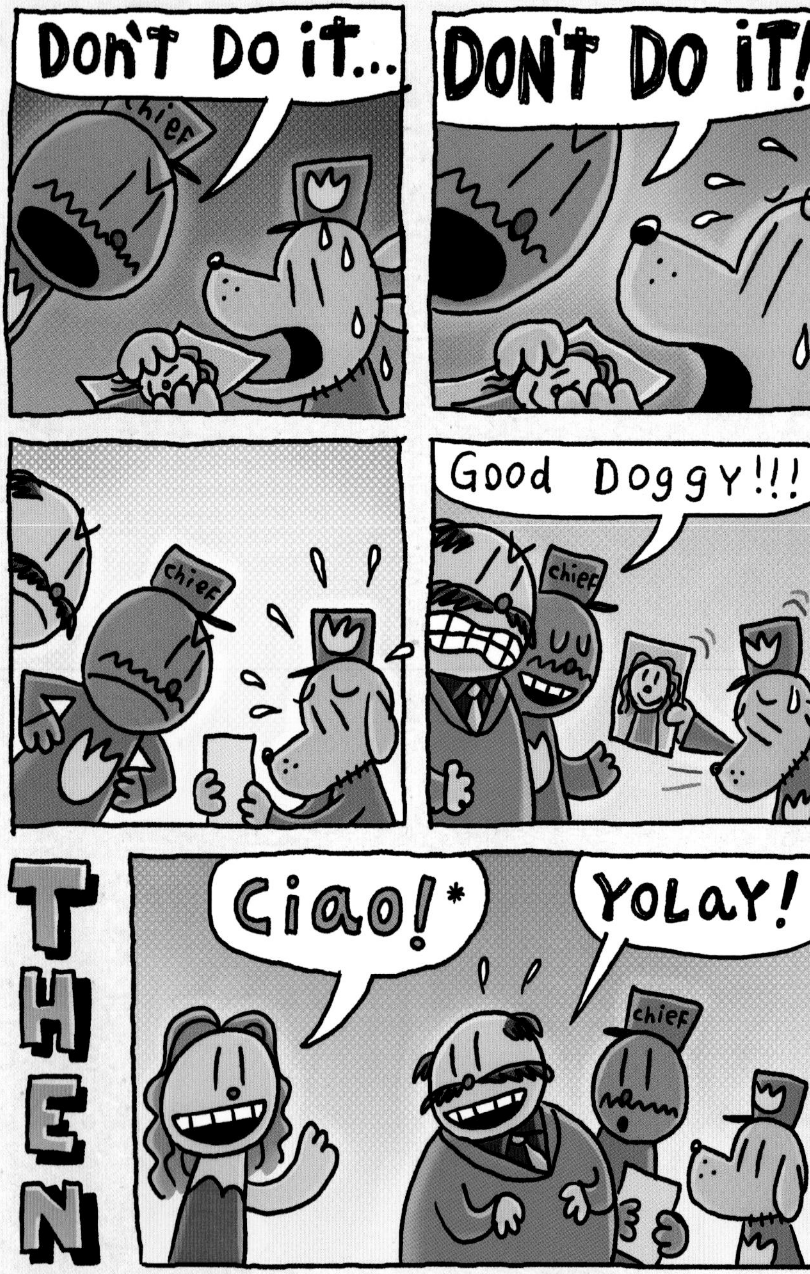
Don't Do it...
DON'T DO iT!
chief
chief
Good Doggy!!!
chief
THEN
Ciao!*
YOLaY!
chief

* Italian for "hello." (Pronounced "chow.")

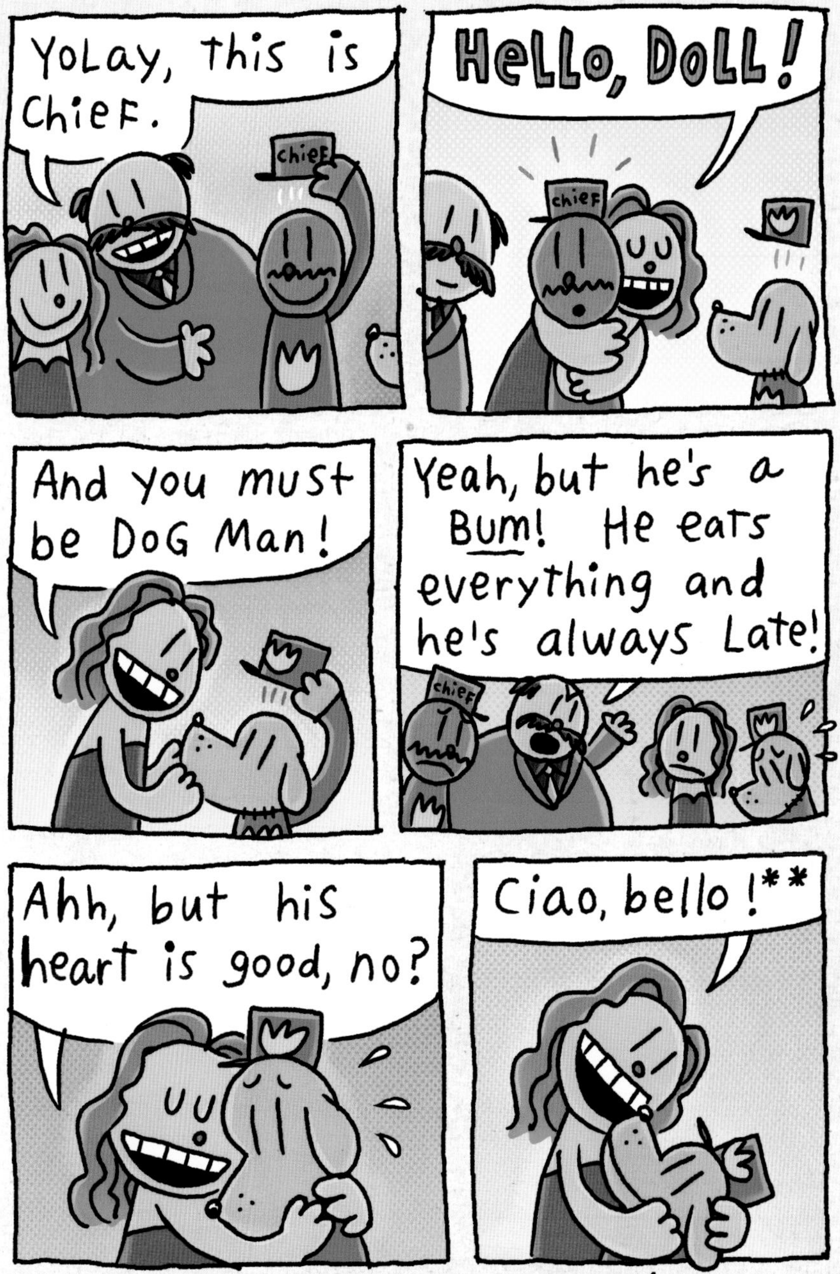

YoLay, this is Chief.
chief
Hello, Doll!
chief
And you must be DoG Man!
Yeah, but he's a Bum! He eats everything and he's always Late!
chief
Ahh, but his heart is good, no?
Ciao, bello!**

** Translation: Hello, handsome!

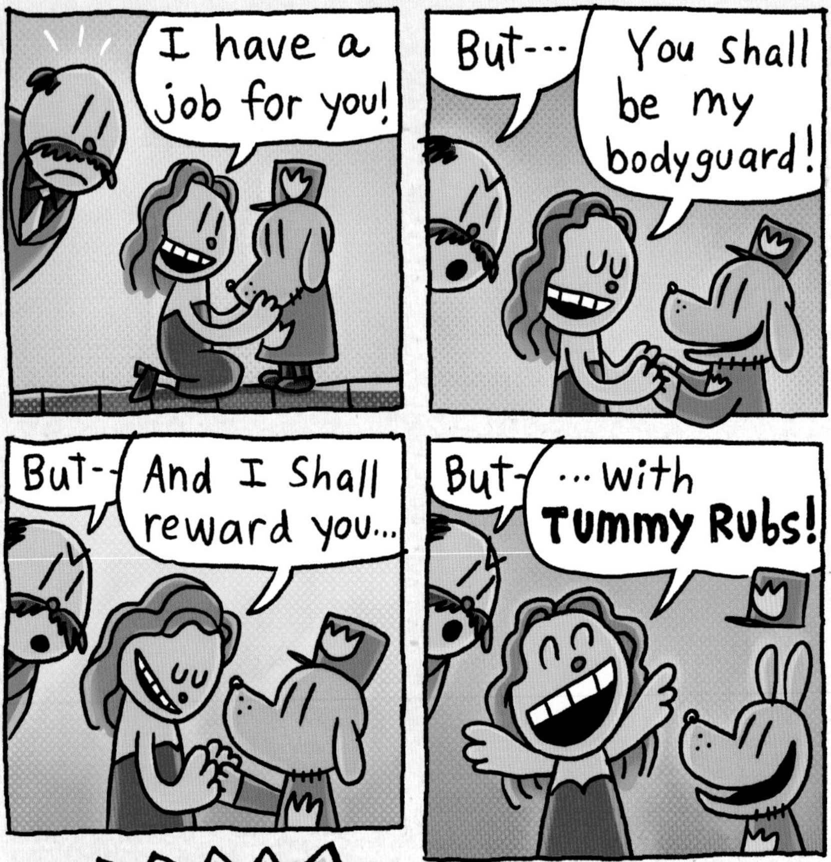

I have a job for you!
But---
You shall be my bodyguard!
But--
And I shall reward you...
But-
...with **Tummy Rubs!**

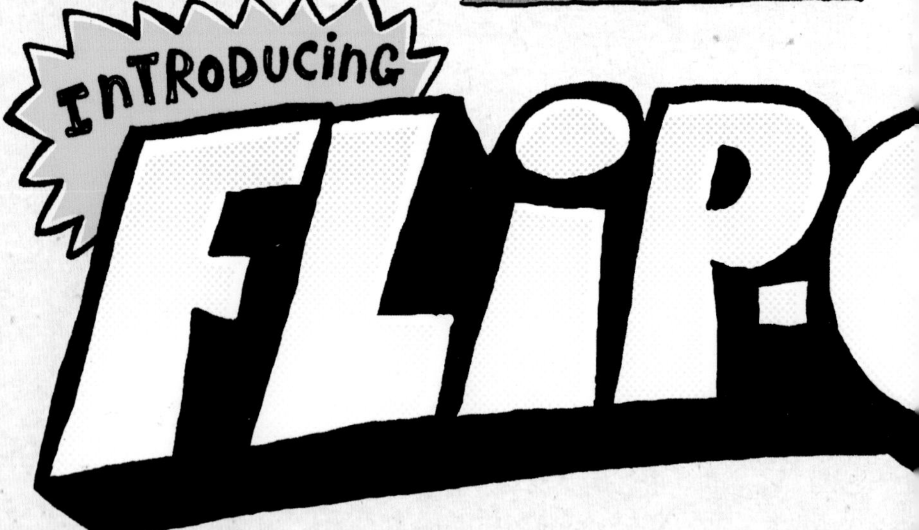

INTRODUCING
FLIP

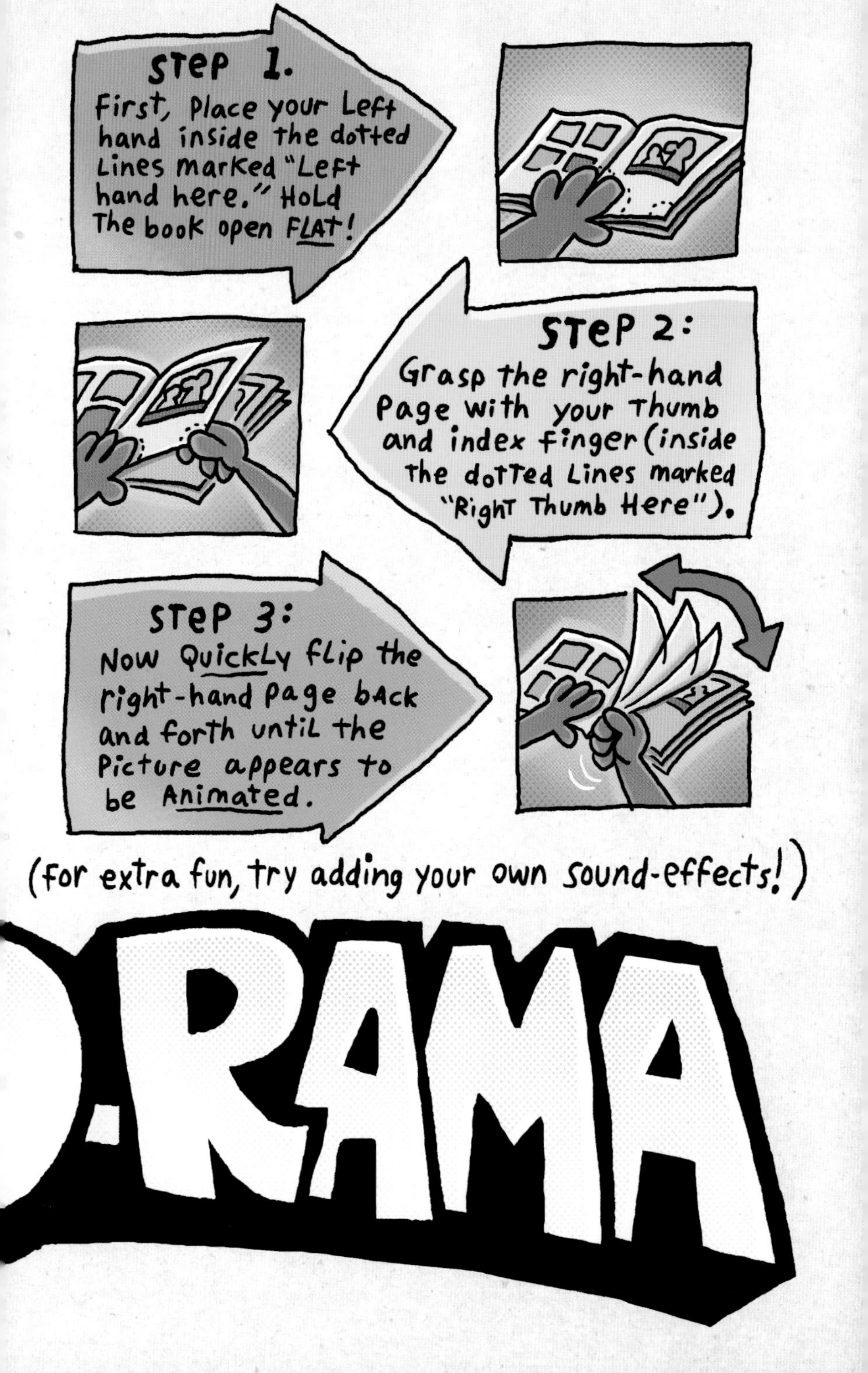
STEP 1.
First, place your left hand inside the dotted lines marked "Left hand here." Hold the book open FLAT!
STEP 2:
Grasp the right-hand page with your thumb and index finger (inside the dotted lines marked "Right Thumb Here").
STEP 3:
Now QUICKLY flip the right-hand page back and forth until the picture appears to be Animated.
(for extra fun, try adding your own sound-effects!)
-RAMA

Remember,

while you are FLipping,
be sure you can see
the image on page 43
AND the image on page 45.

If you FLip QuickLy,
the two pictures will
start to look like
one **ANimated** cartoon!

Don't Forget to
add your own
sound-effects!

Left
hand here.

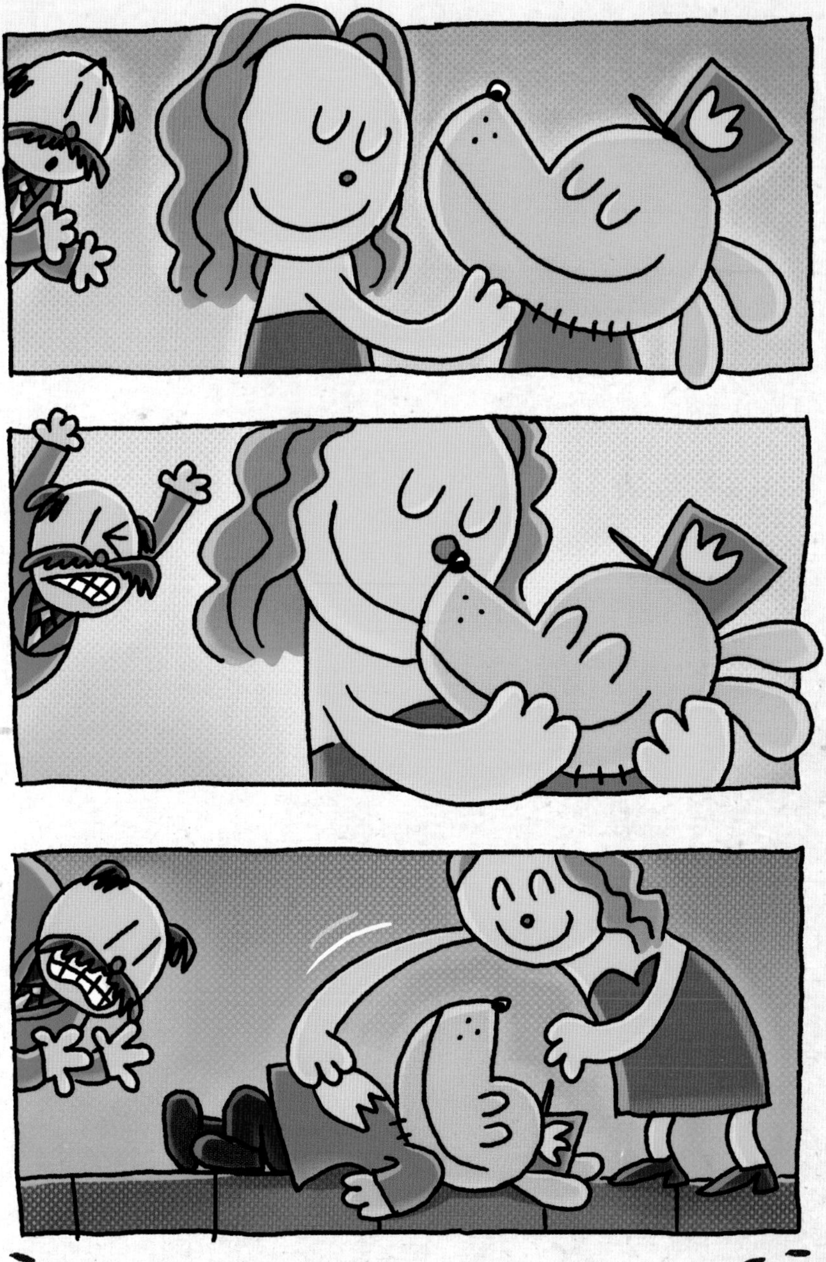

Right Thumb here.

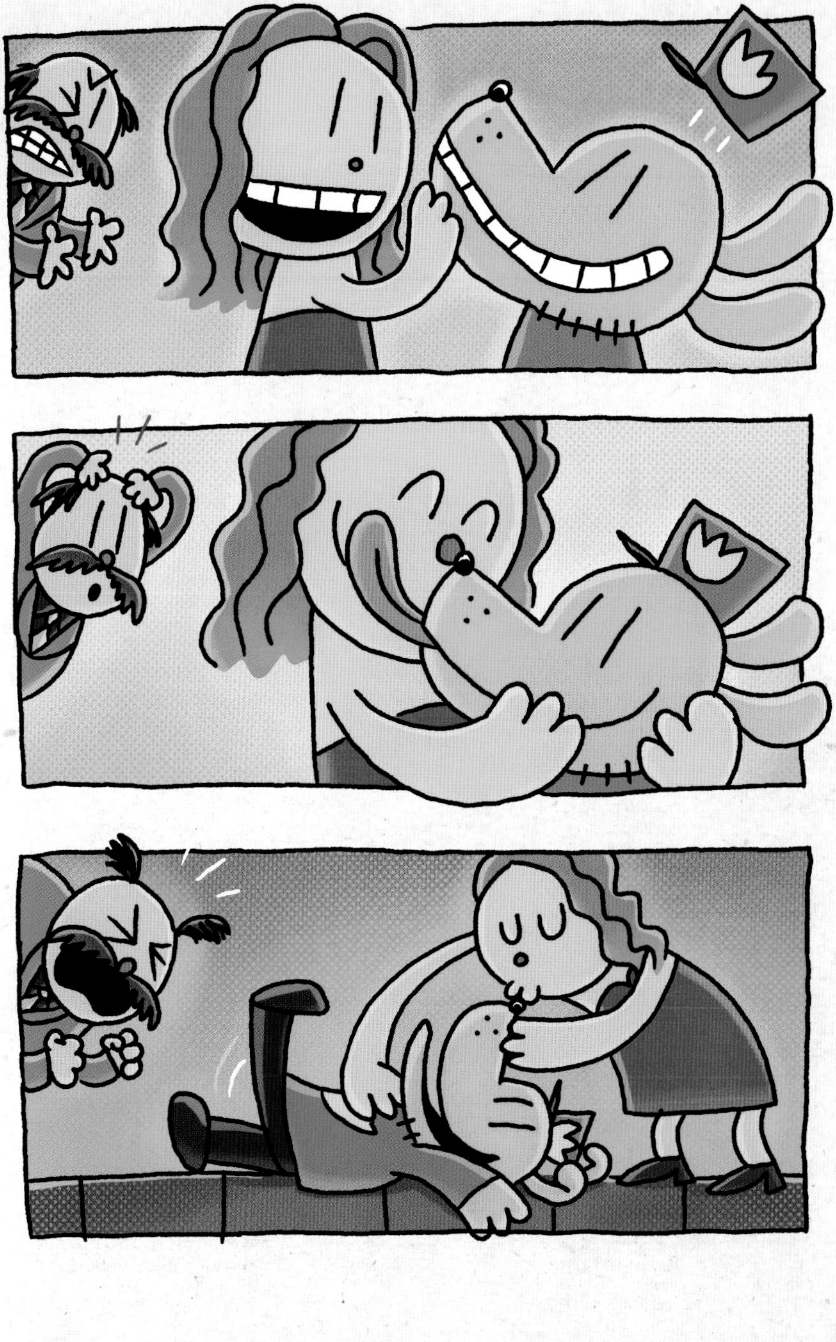

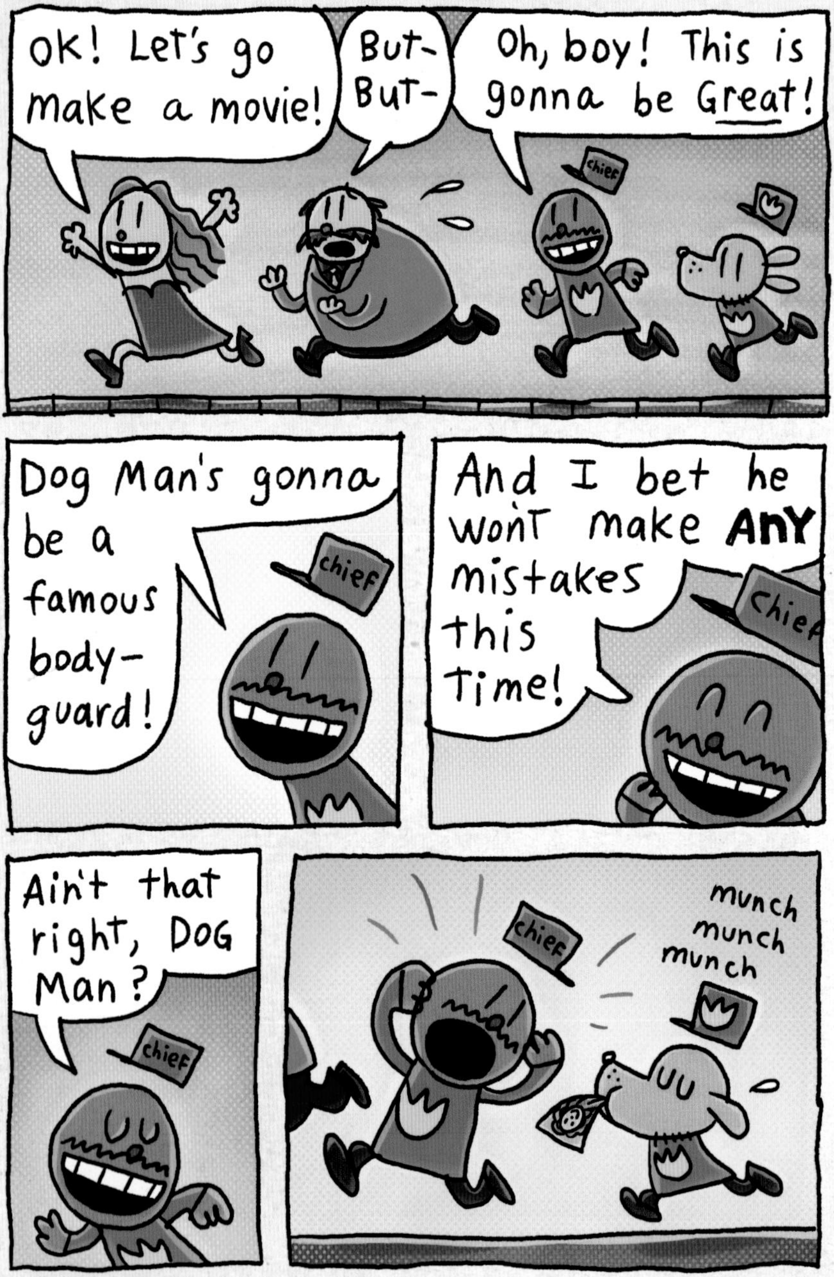
OK! Let's go make a movie!
But- But-
Oh, boy! This is gonna be Great!
chief
Dog Man's gonna be a famous body-guard!
chief
And I bet he won't make ANY mistakes this Time!
Chief
Ain't that right, DOG Man?
chief
chief
munch munch munch

Chapter 3
The Talk

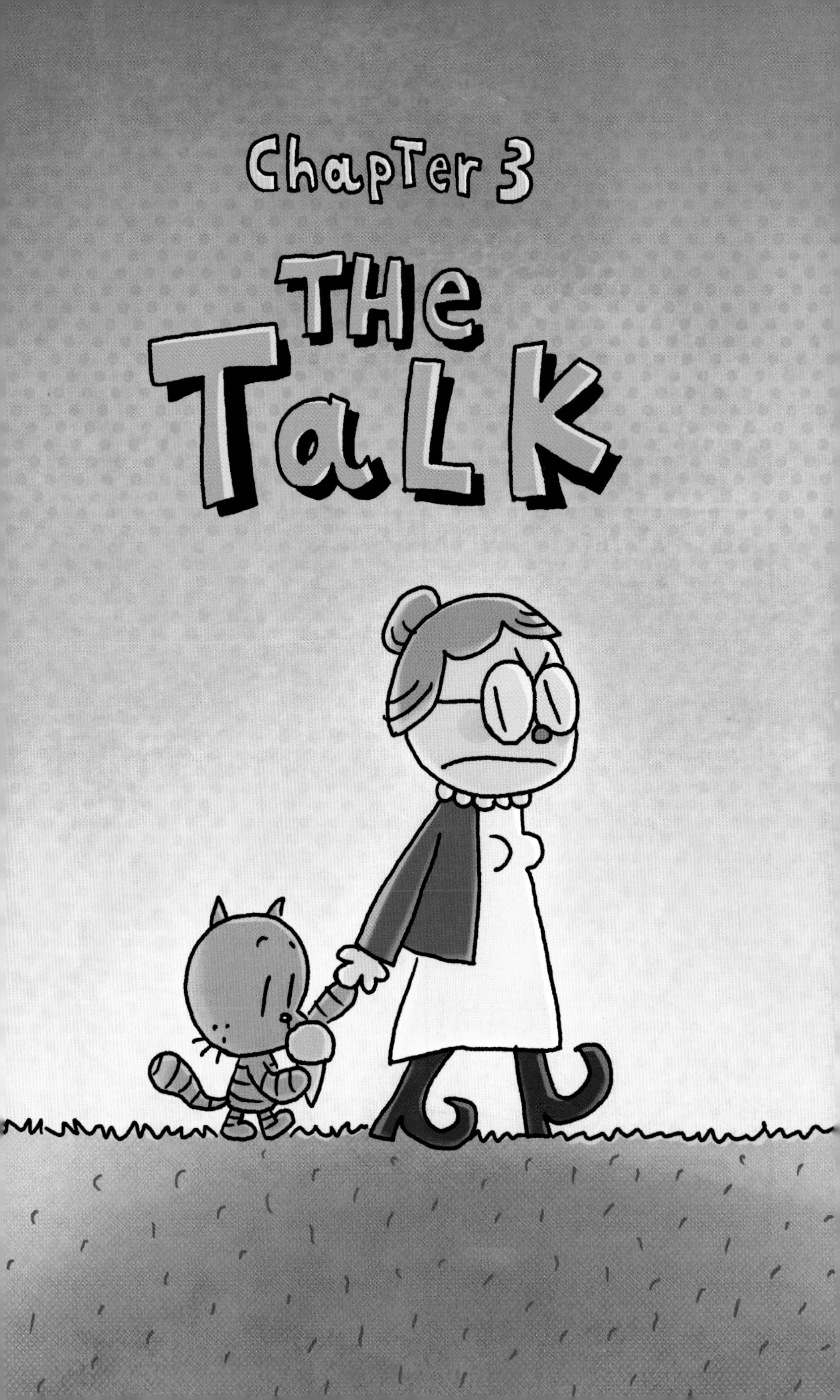

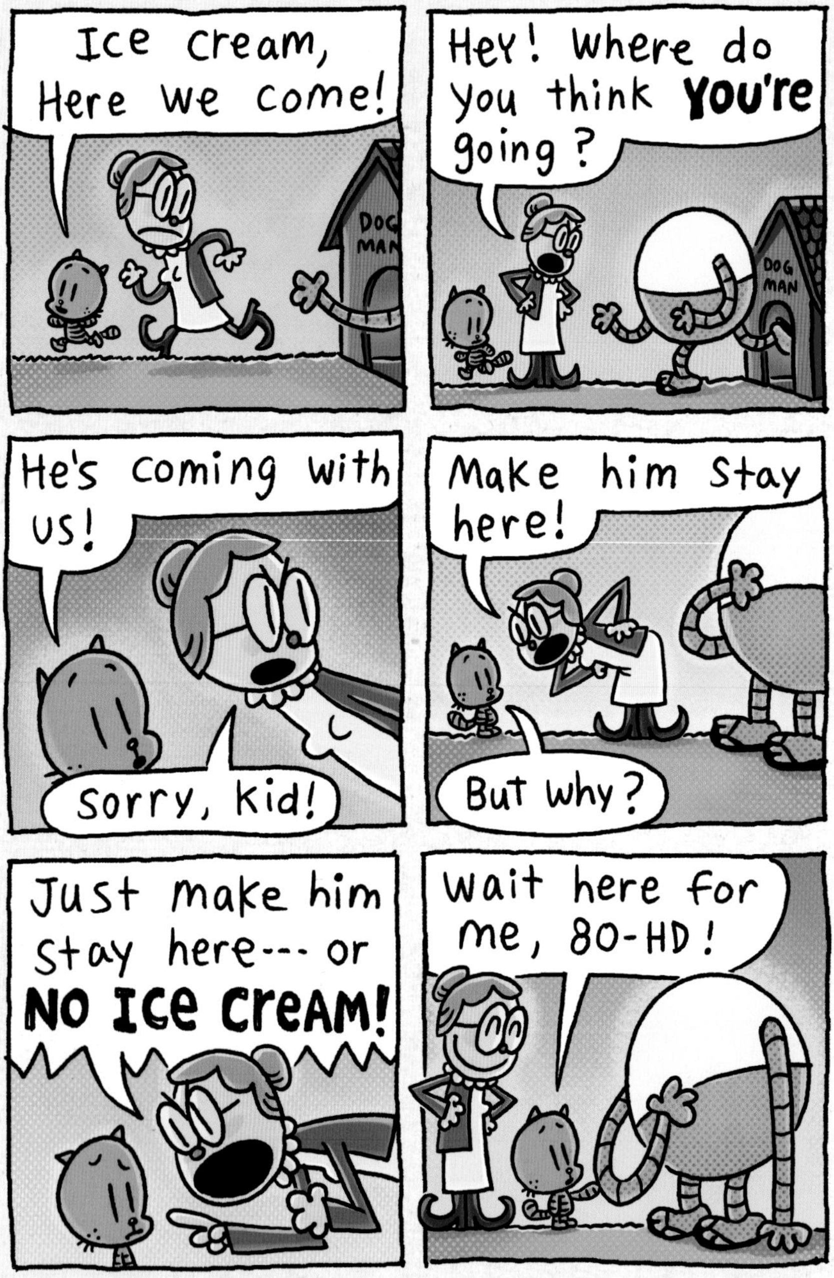
Ice cream, Here we come!
DOG MAN
Hey! Where do you think **YOU'RE** going?
DOG MAN
He's coming with us!
Sorry, kid!
Make him stay here!
But why?
Just make him stay here--- or **NO ICE CREAM!**
Wait here for me, 80-HD!

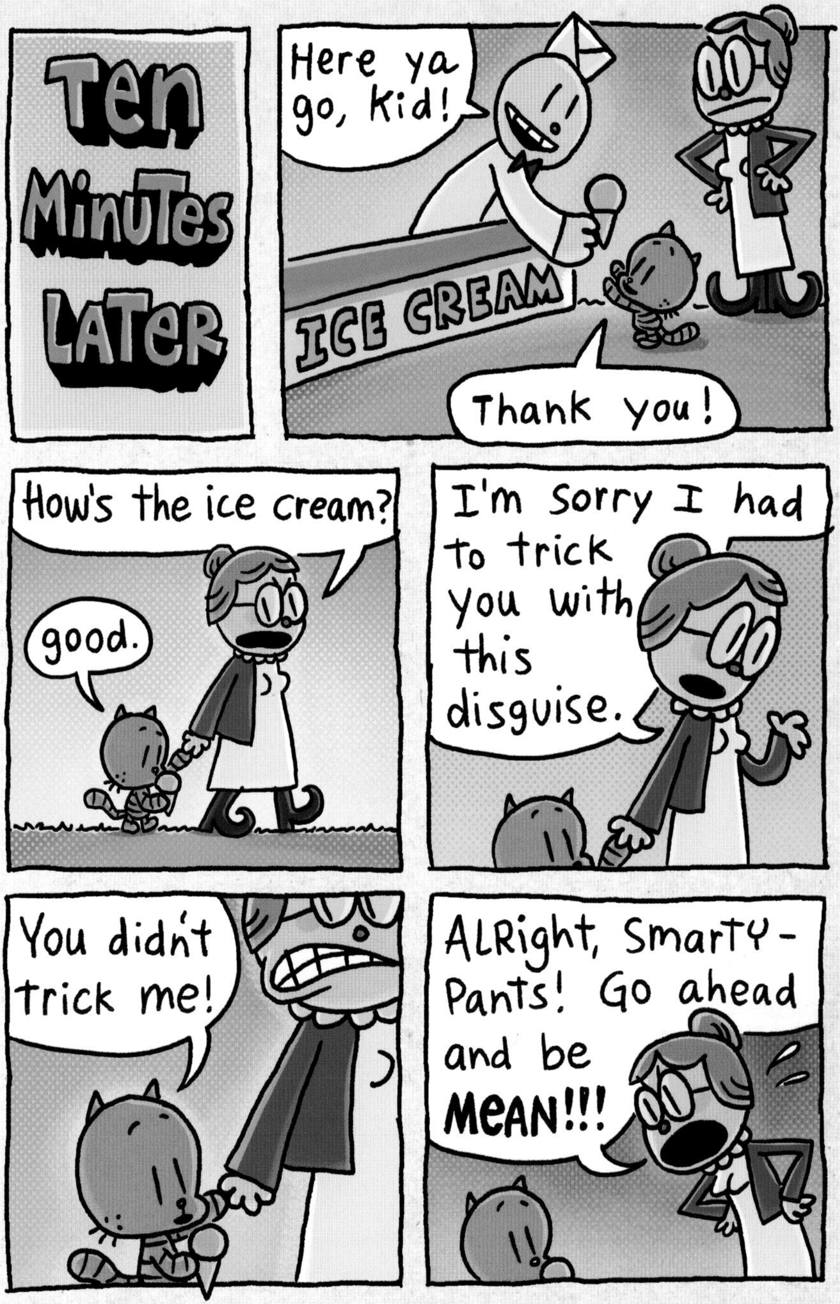
Ten Minutes Later
Here ya go, Kid!
ICE CREAM
Thank you!
How's the ice cream?
good.
I'm sorry I had to trick you with this disguise.
You didn't trick me!
ALRight, SmarTY-Pants! Go ahead and be MEAN!!!

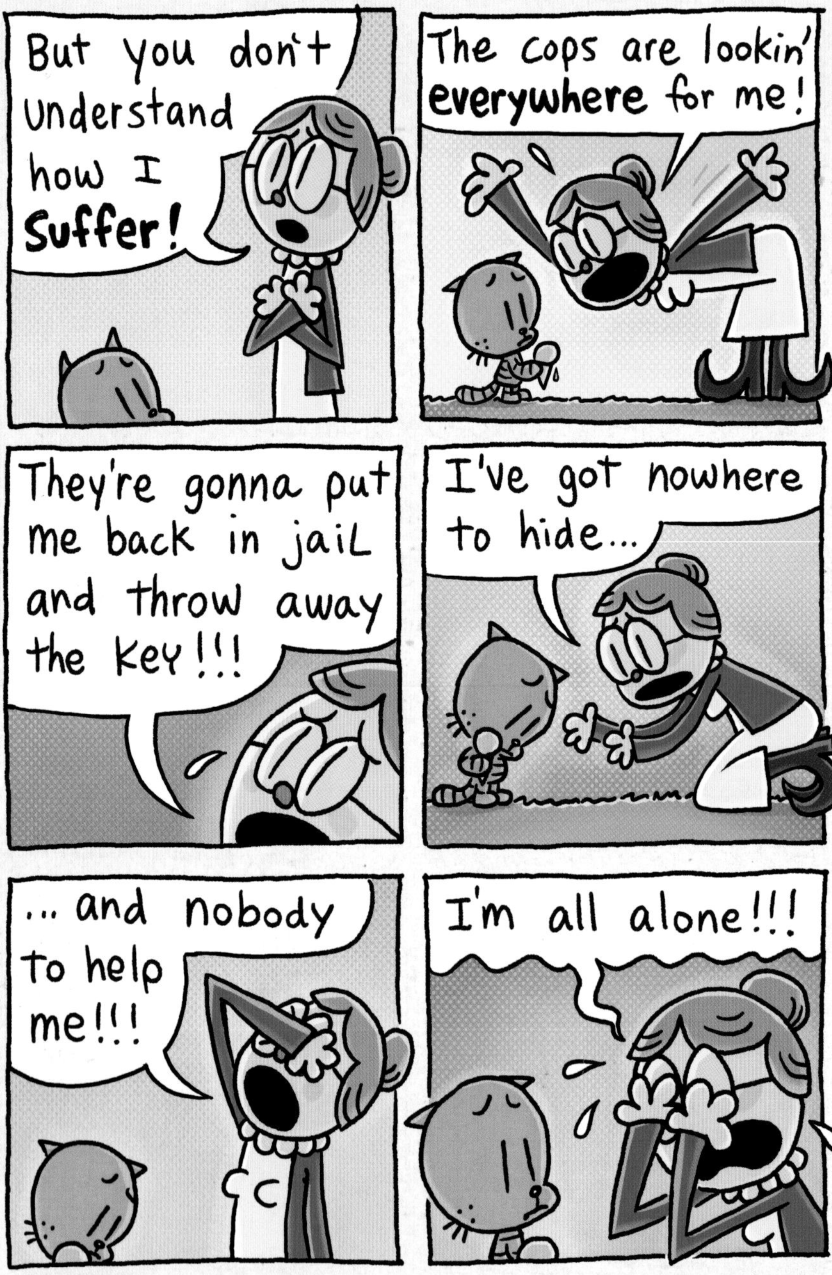
But you don't understand how I **Suffer**!
The cops are lookin' **everywhere** for me!
They're gonna put me back in jail and throw away the key!!!
I've got nowhere to hide...
... and nobody to help me!!!
I'm all alone!!!

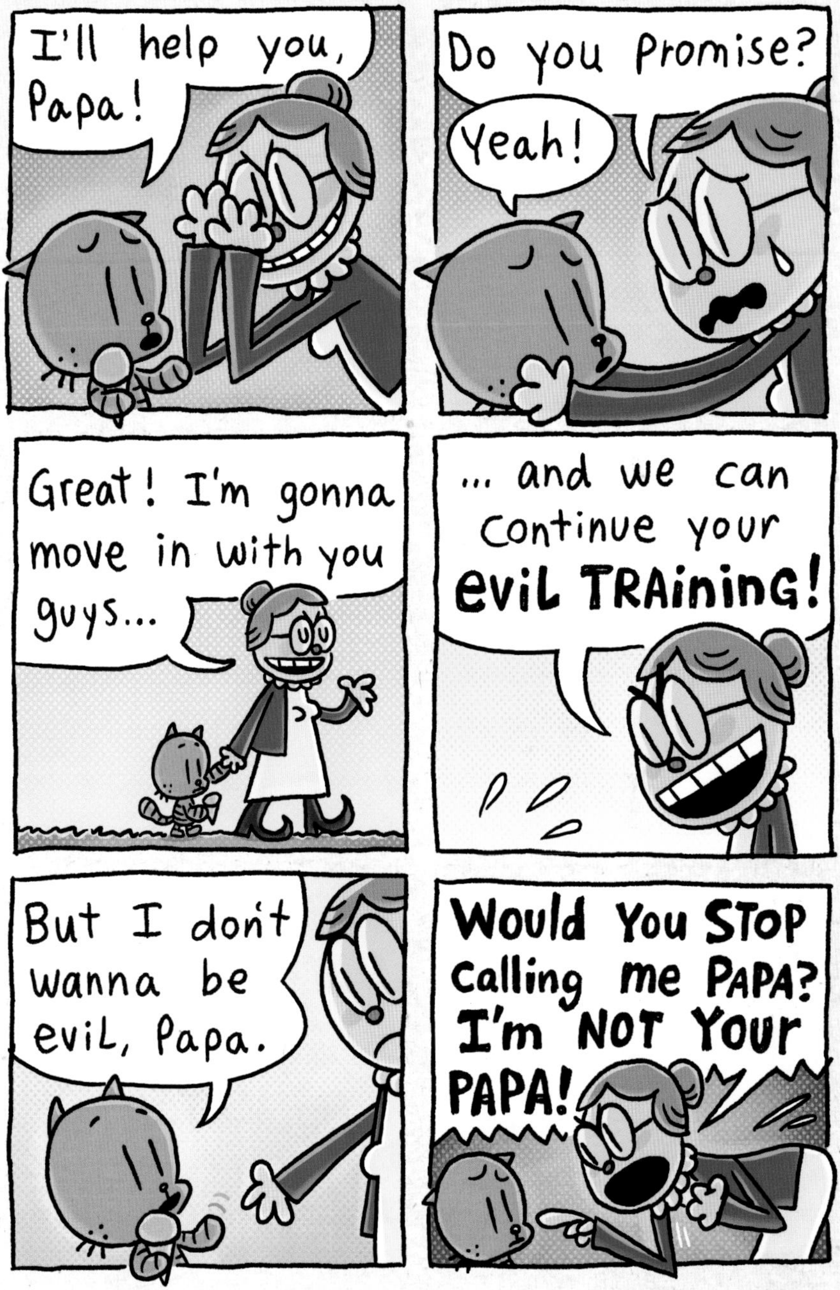
I'll help you, Papa!
Do you promise?
Yeah!
Great! I'm gonna move in with you guys...
... and we can continue your evil TRAINING!
But I don't wanna be evil, Papa.
Would You STOP Calling me PAPA? I'm NOT YOUR PAPA!

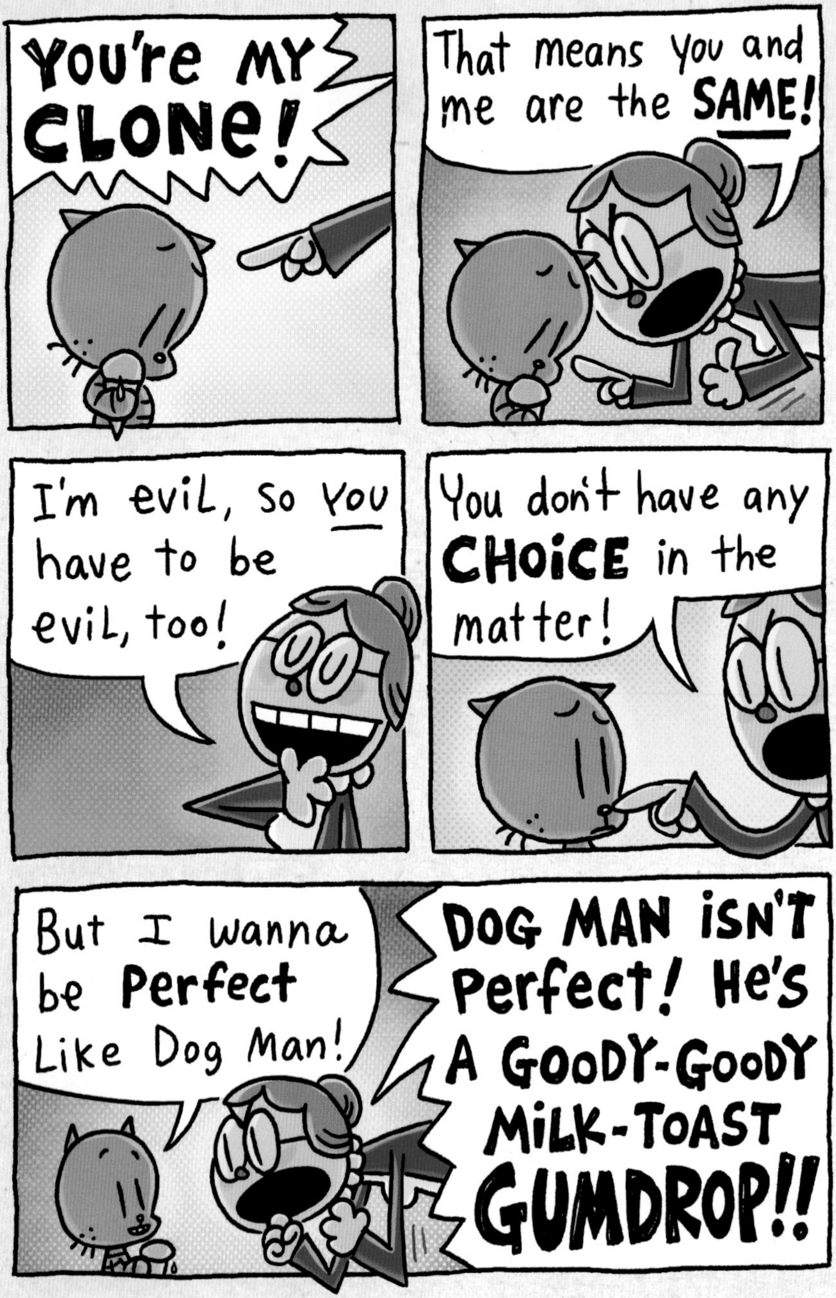

YOU'RE MY CLONE!
That means you and me are the SAME!
I'm evil, so you have to be evil, too!
You don't have any CHOICE in the matter!
But I wanna be Perfect Like Dog Man!
DOG MAN ISN'T Perfect! He's A GOODY-GOODY MILK-TOAST GUMDROP!!

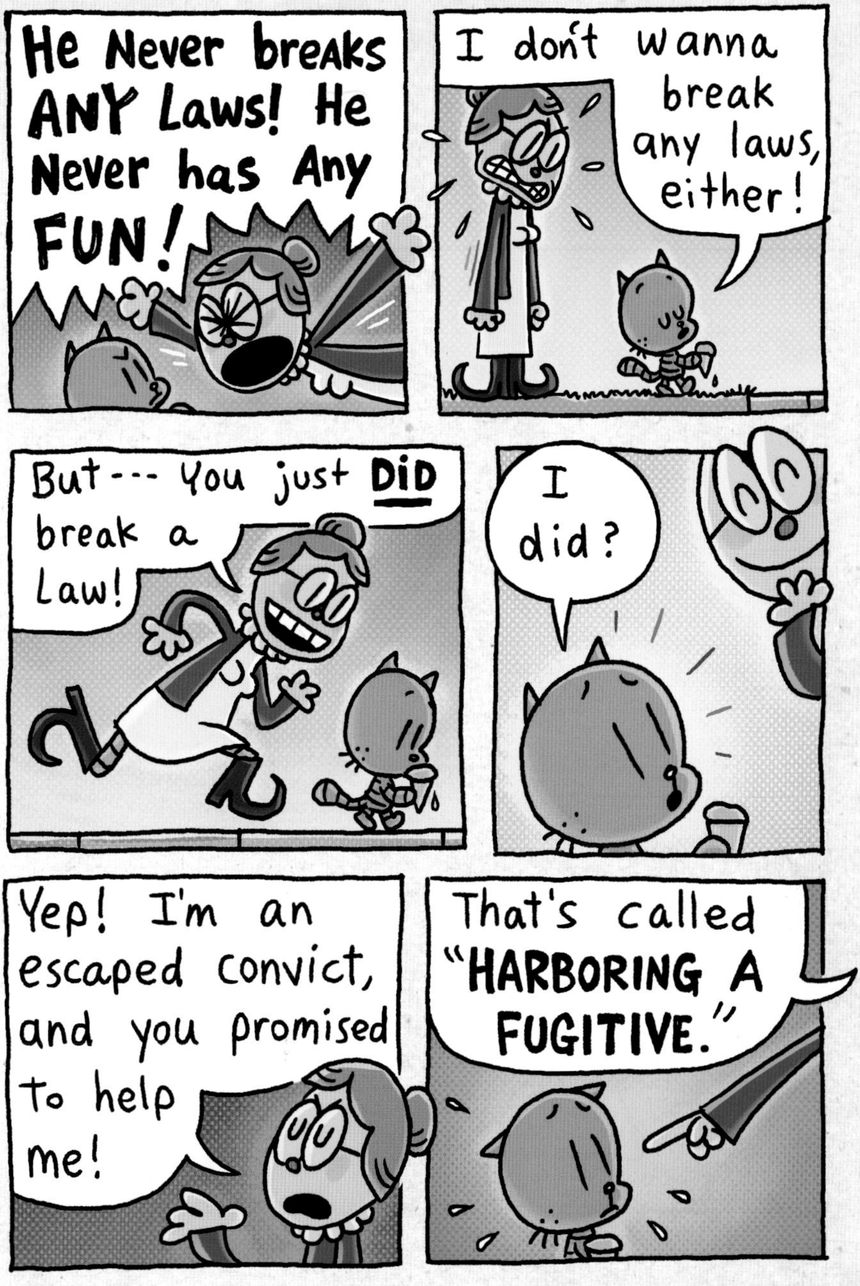
He Never breaks ANY Laws! He Never has Any FUN!
I don't wanna break any laws, either!
But--- You just DID break a Law!
I did?
Yep! I'm an escaped convict, and you promised to help me!
That's called "HARBORING A FUGITIVE."

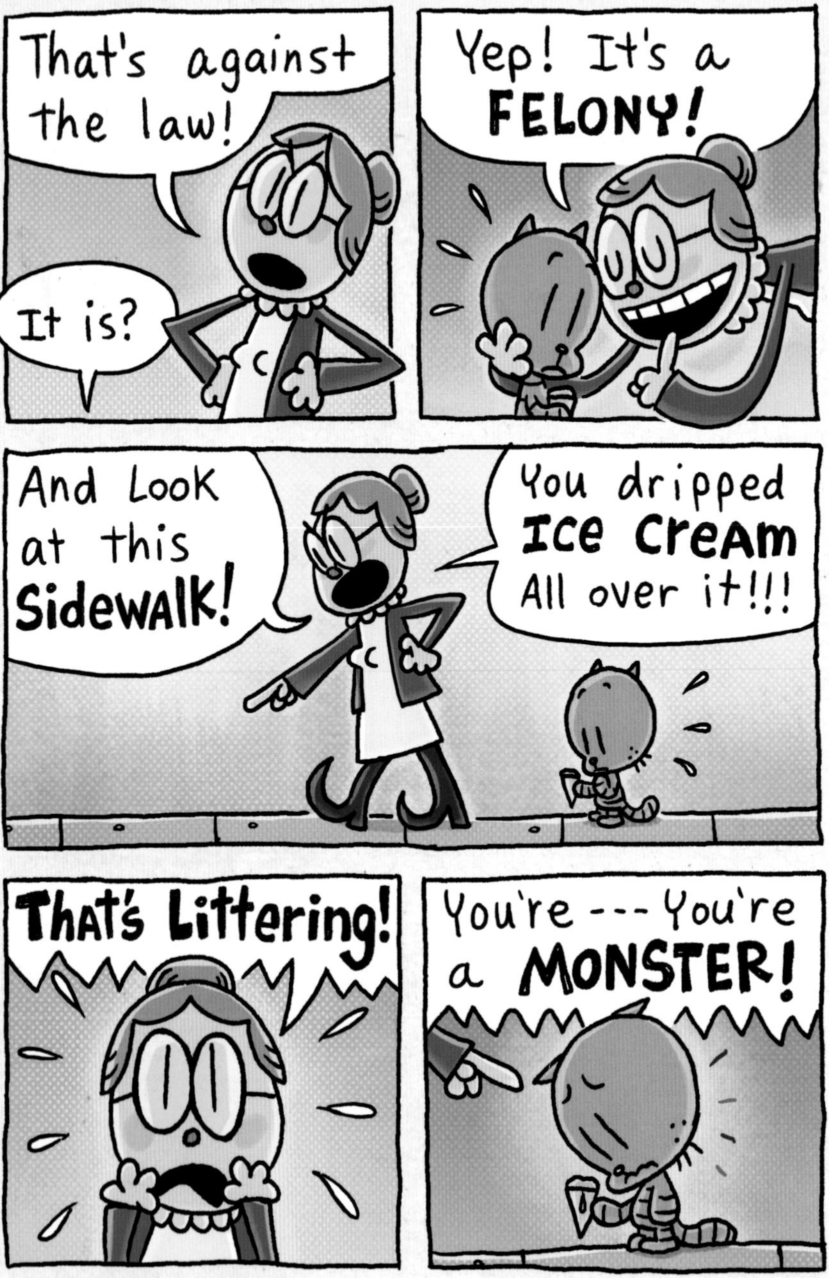
That's against the law!
It is?
Yep! It's a FELONY!
And Look at this Sidewalk!
You dripped Ice Cream All over it!!!
That's Littering!
You're --- You're a MONSTER!

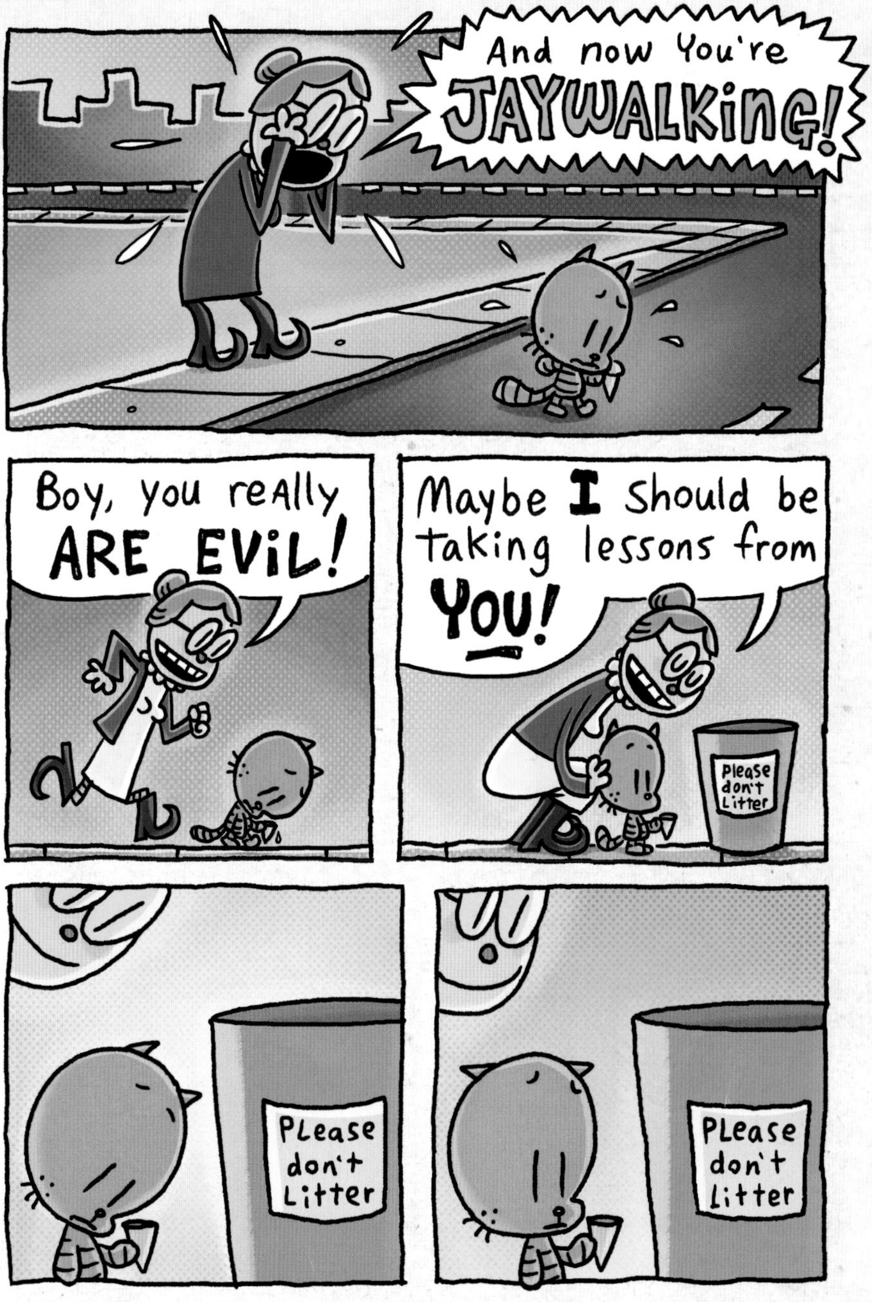
And now You're JAYWALKING!
Boy, you really ARE EViL!
Maybe I should be taking lessons from YOU!
Please don't Litter
Please don't Litter
Please don't Litter

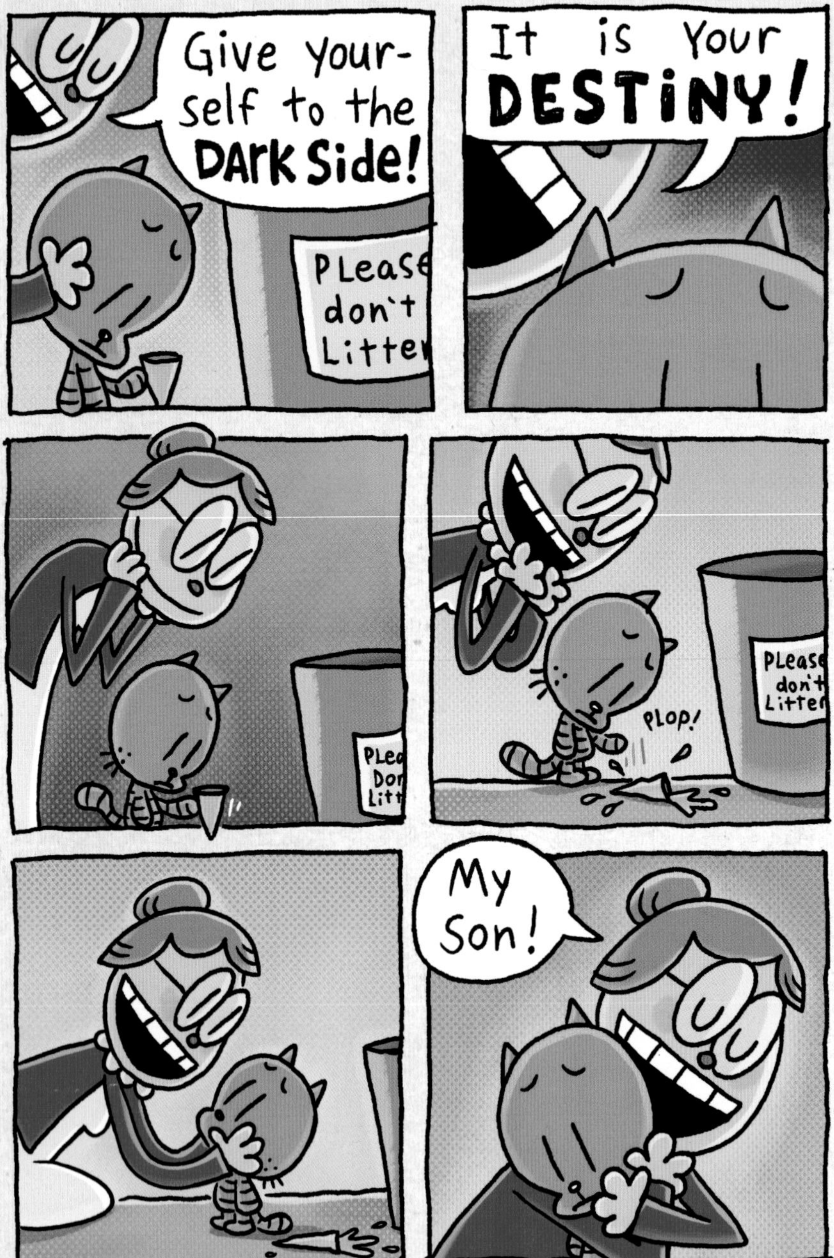
Give yourself to the DARK Side!
PLease don`t Litter
It is Your DESTINY!
PLea Don Litt
PLease don't Litter
PLOP!
My Son!

Chapter 4

An Aching Kind of Growing

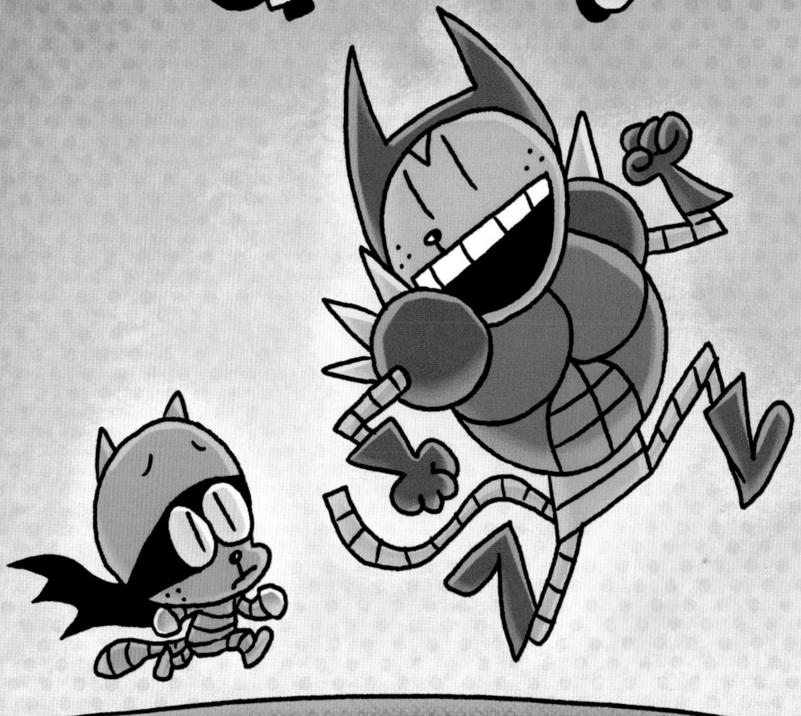

By George and Harold

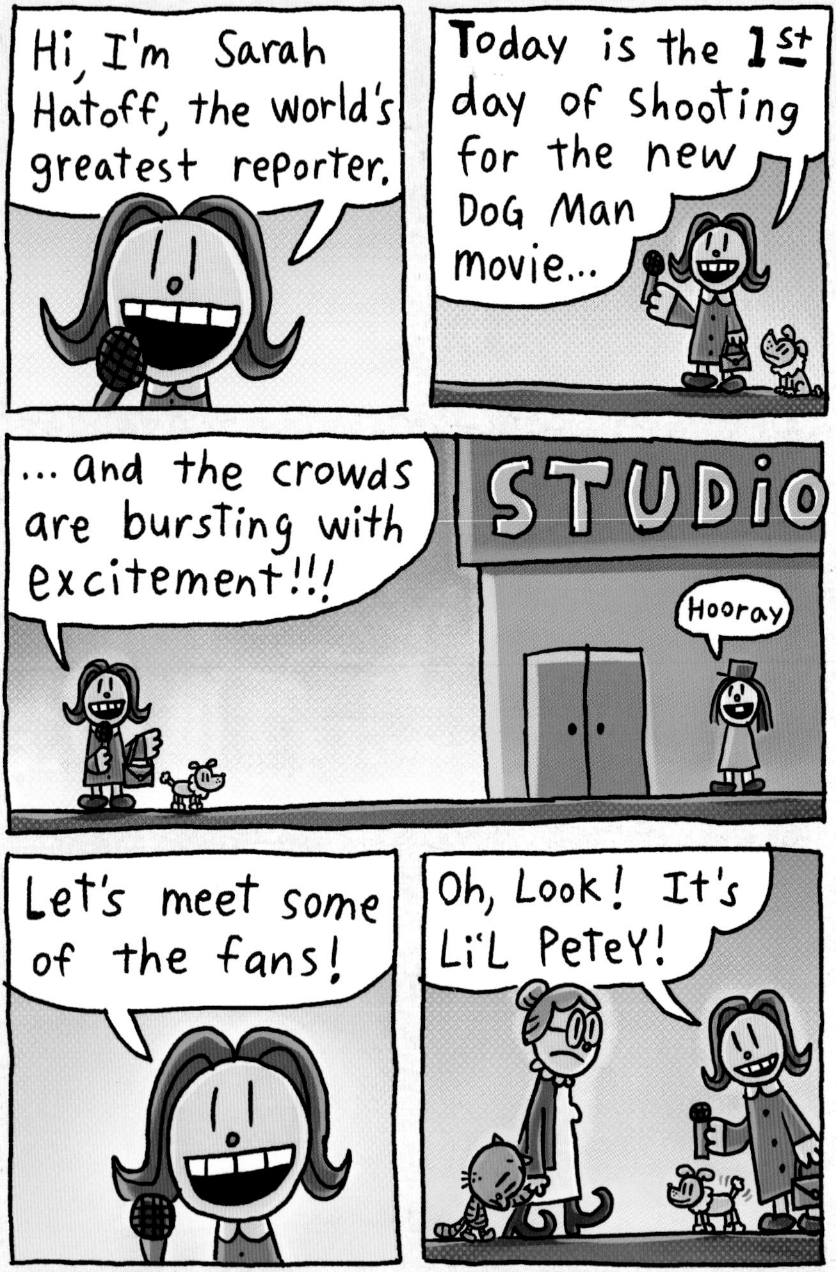
Hi, I'm Sarah Hatoff, the world's greatest reporter.
Today is the 1st day of shooting for the new DOG MAN movie...
...and the crowds are bursting with excitement!!!
STUDIO
Hooray
Let's meet some of the fans!
Oh, Look! It's Li'L Petey!

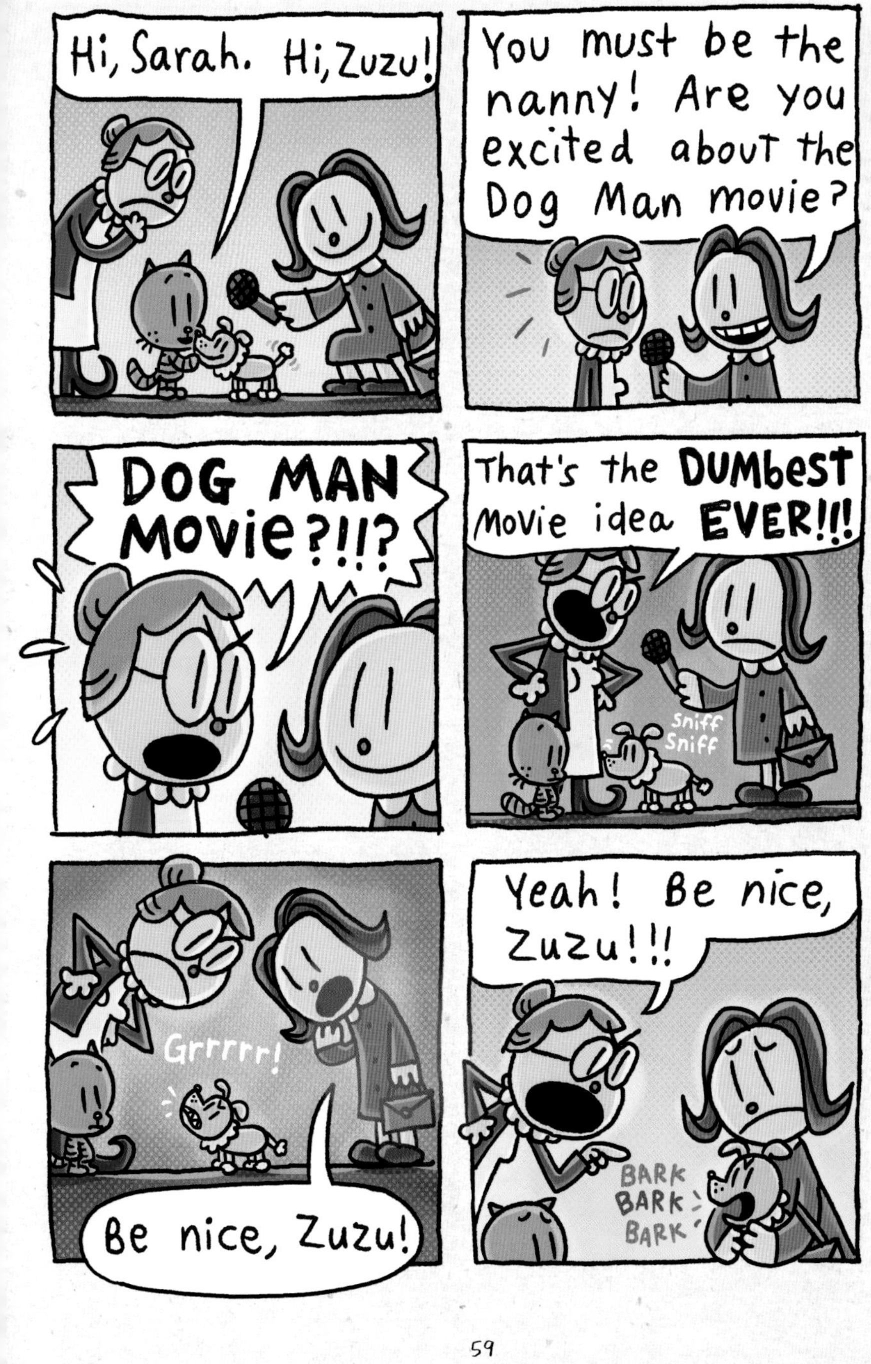

Hi, Sarah. Hi, Zuzu!
You must be the nanny! Are you excited about the Dog Man movie?
DOG MAN MOVIE?!!?
That's the DUMBEST movie idea EVER!!!
sniff sniff
Grrrrr!
Be nice, Zuzu!
Yeah! Be nice, Zuzu!!!
BARK BARK BARK

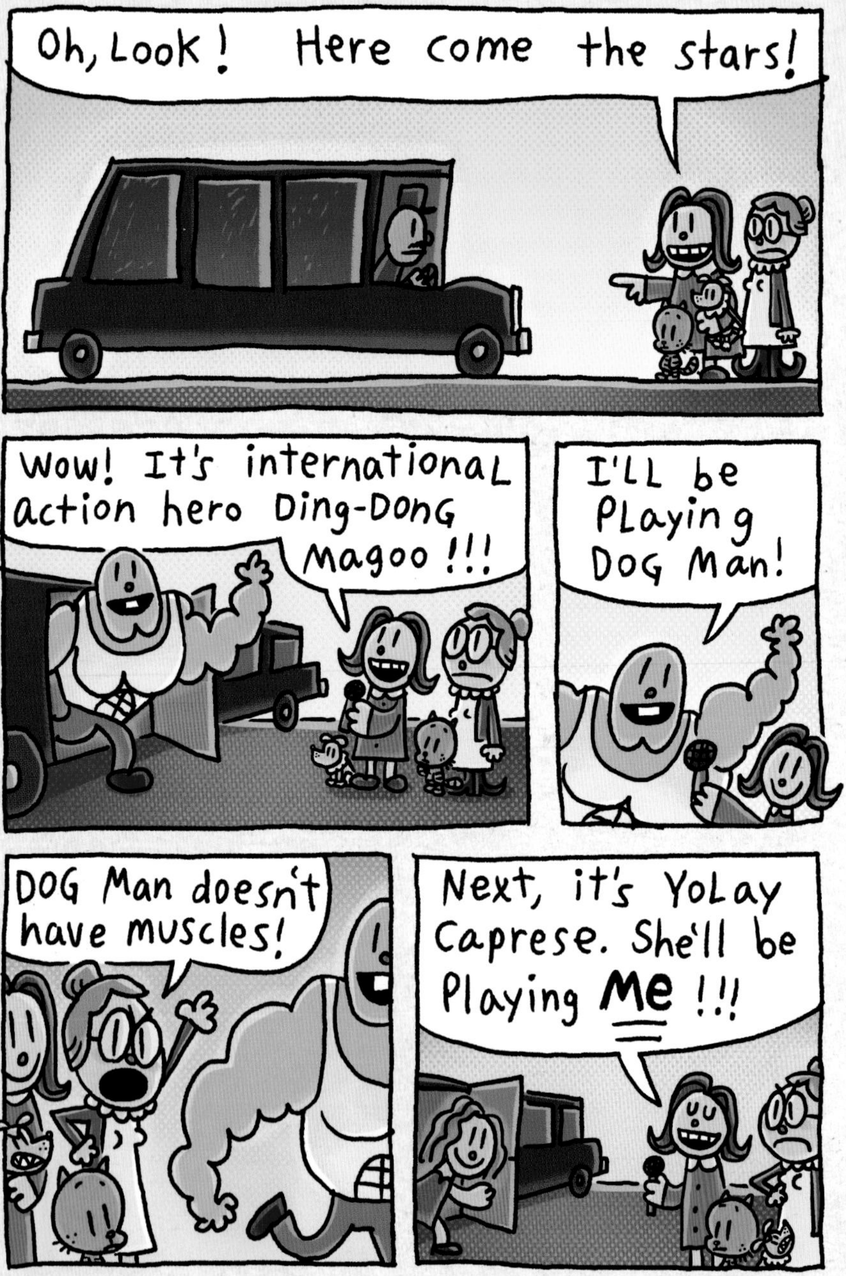
Oh, Look! Here come the stars!
Wow! It's international action hero Ding-Dong Magoo!!!
I'LL be Playing Dog Man!
DOG Man doesn't have muscles!
Next, it's YoLay Caprese. She'll be Playing ME!!!

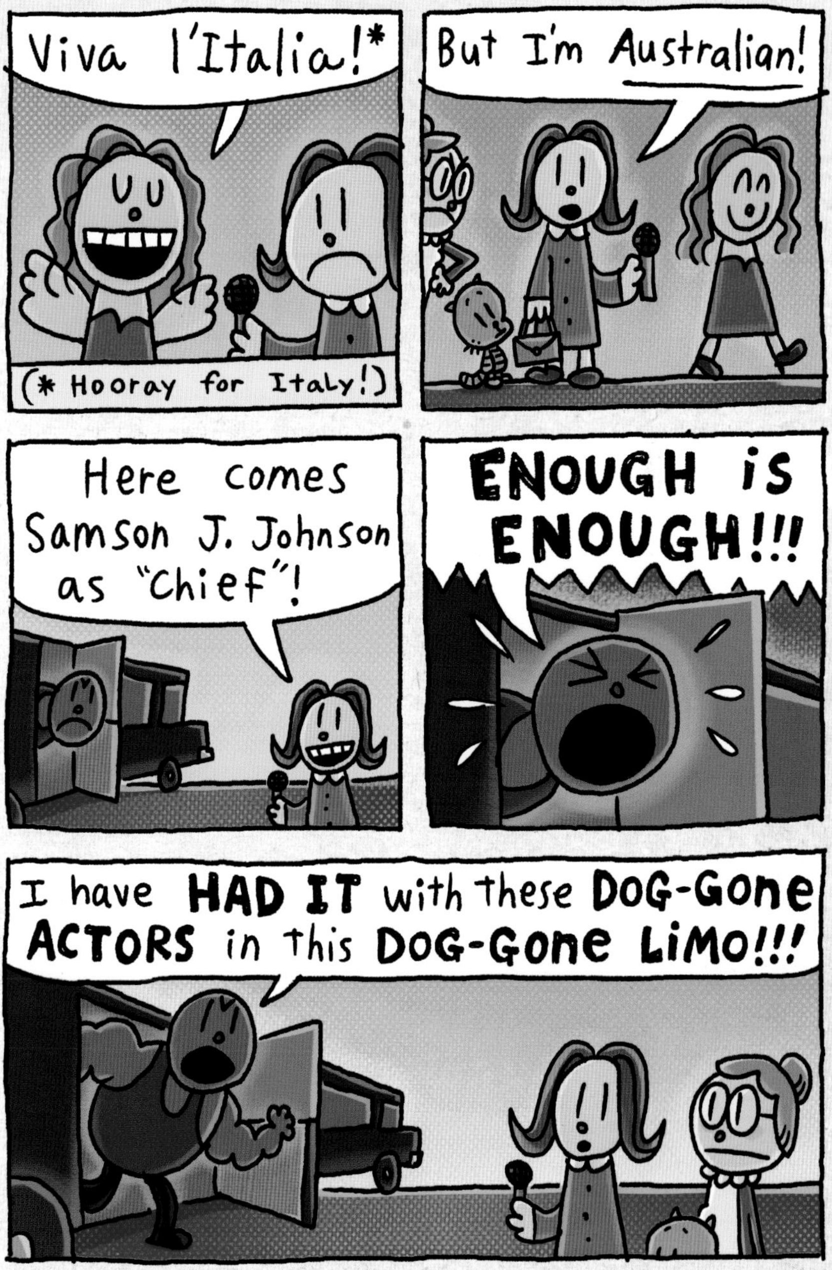

Viva l'Italia!*
(* Hooray for Italy!)
But I'm Australian!
Here comes Samson J. Johnson as "Chief"!
ENOUGH is ENOUGH!!!
I have HAD IT with these DOG-Gone ACTORS in this DOG-Gone LiMO!!!

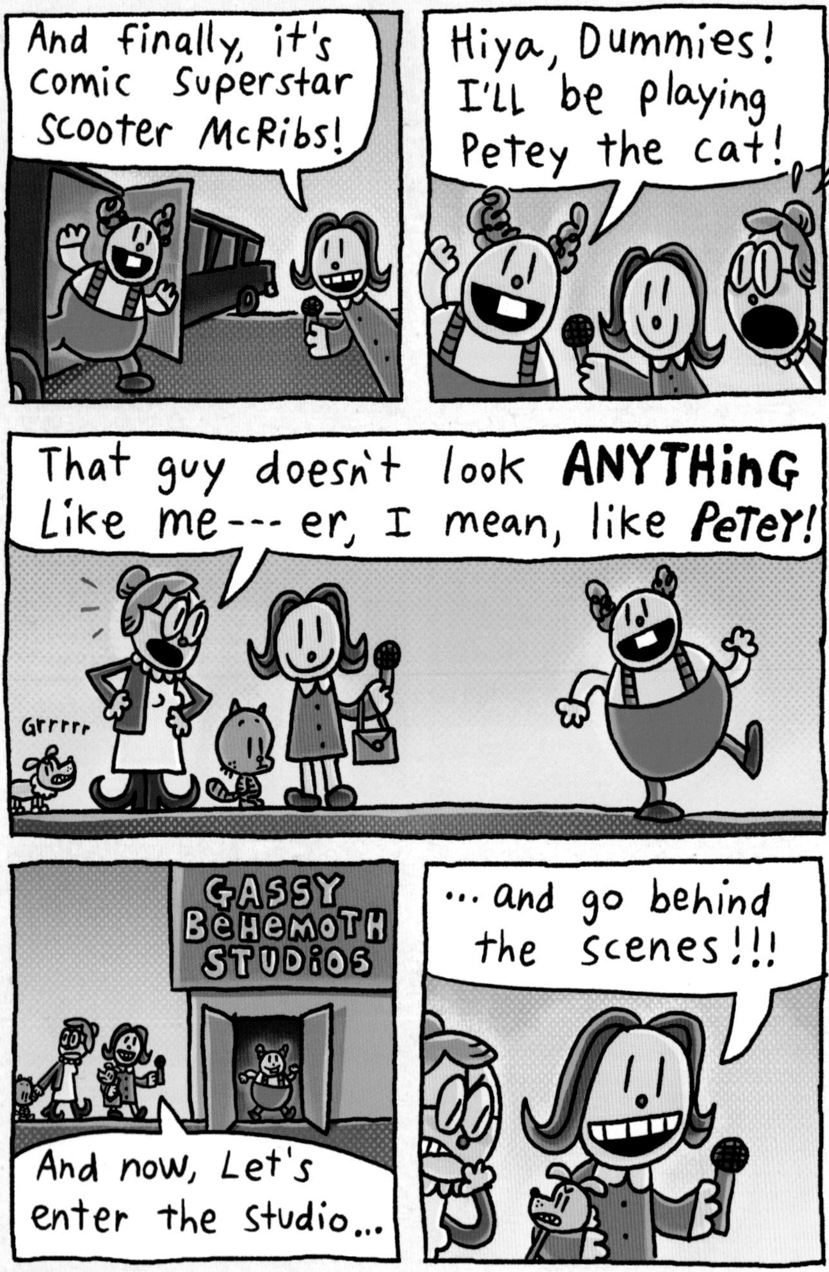
And finally, it's Comic Superstar Scooter McRibs!
Hiya, Dummies! I'll be playing Petey the cat!
That guy doesn't look ANYTHING like me--- er, I mean, like PETEY!
Grrrrr
GASSY BEHEMOTH STUDIOS
And now, Let's enter the studio...
...and go behind the scenes!!!

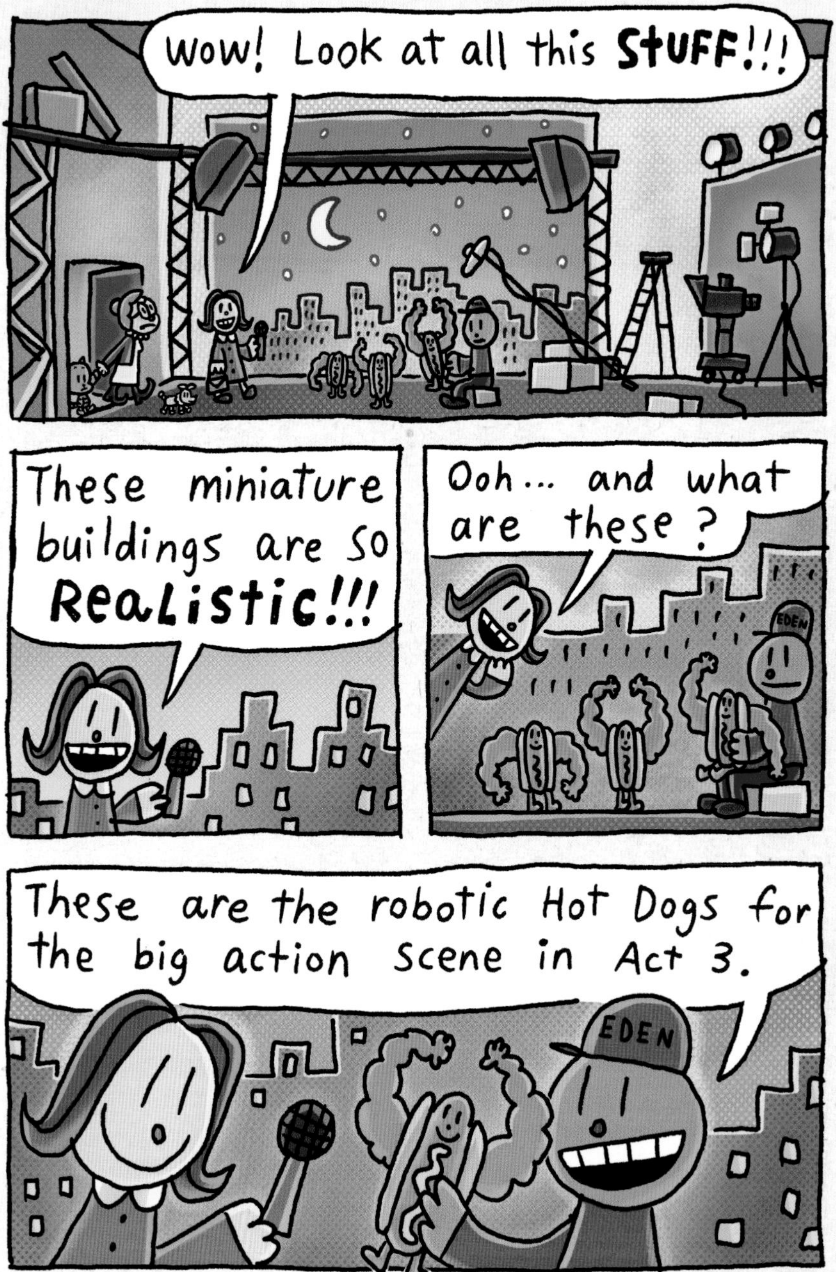

WOW! Look at all this STUFF!!!
These miniature buildings are SO REALISTIC!!!
Ooh... and what are these?
EDEN
These are the robotic Hot Dogs for the big action scene in Act 3.
EDEN

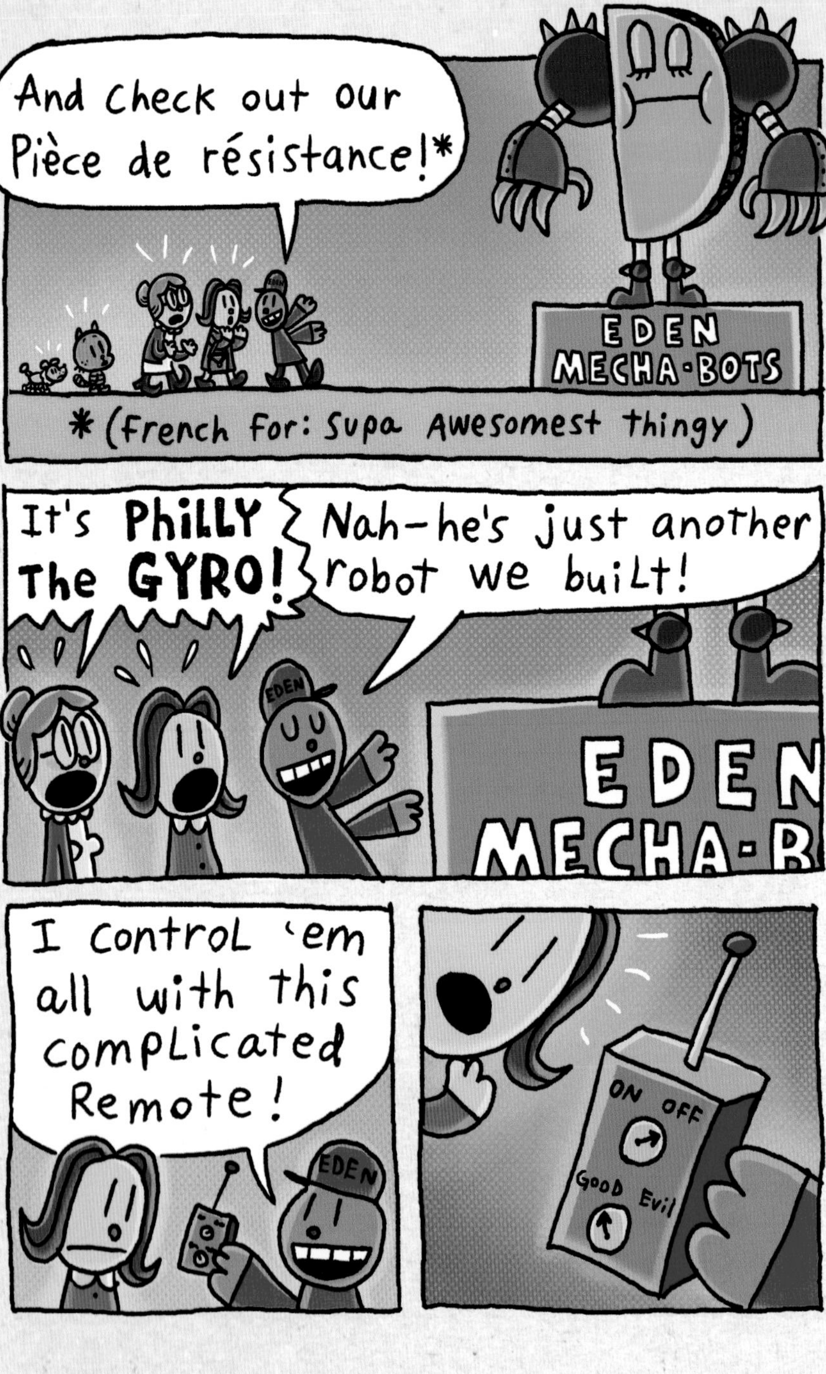
And check out our Pièce de résistance!*
EDEN MECHA-BOTS
*(French for: Supa Awesomest thingy)
It's PHILLY The GYRO!
Nah-he's just another robot we built!
EDEN
EDEN
EDEN MECHA-B
I control 'em all with this complicated Remote!
EDEN
ON OFF
GOOD EVIL

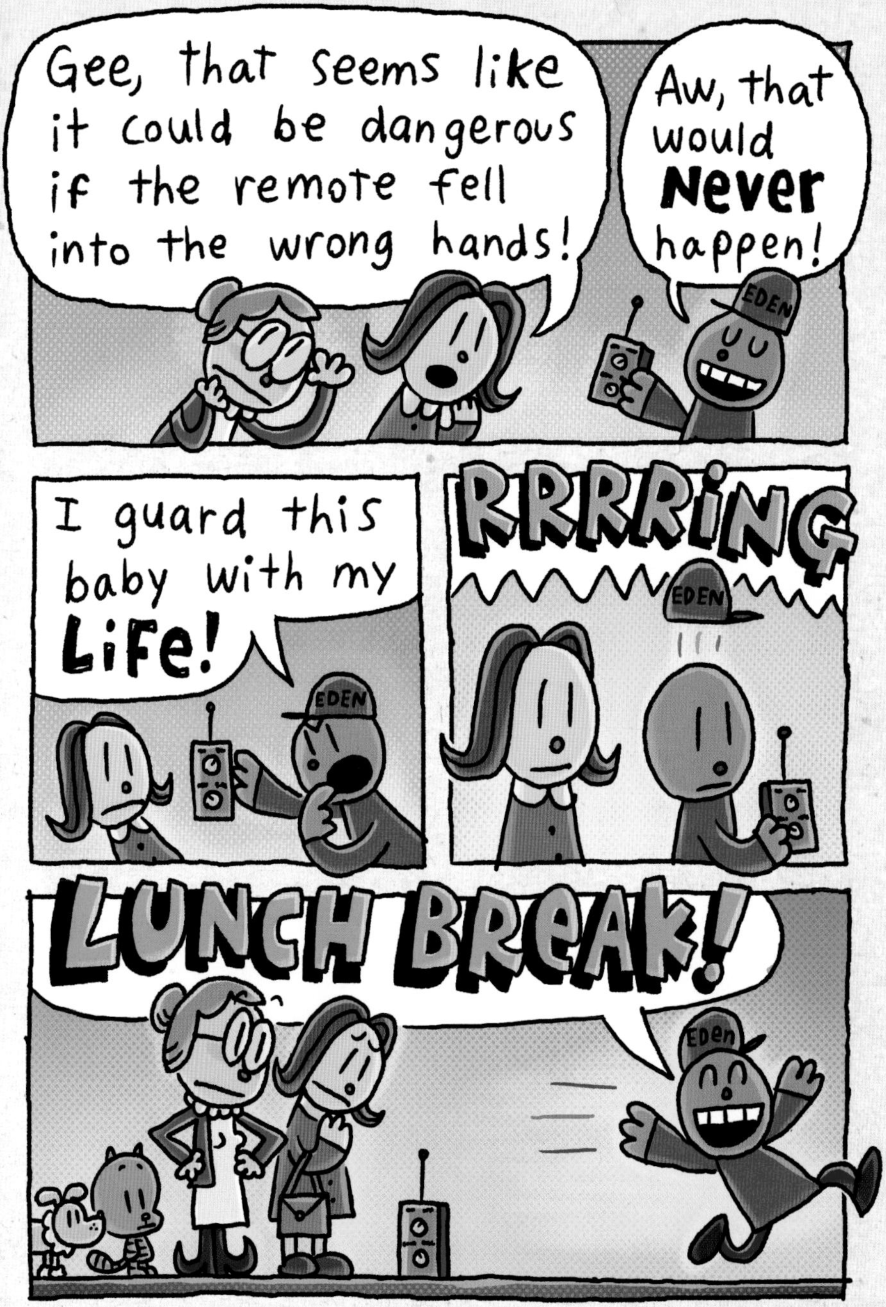
Gee, that seems like it could be dangerous if the remote fell into the wrong hands!
Aw, that would **Never** happen!
EDEN
I guard this baby with my **LiFe!**
EDEN
RRRRiNG
EDEN
LUNCH BREAK!
EDEN

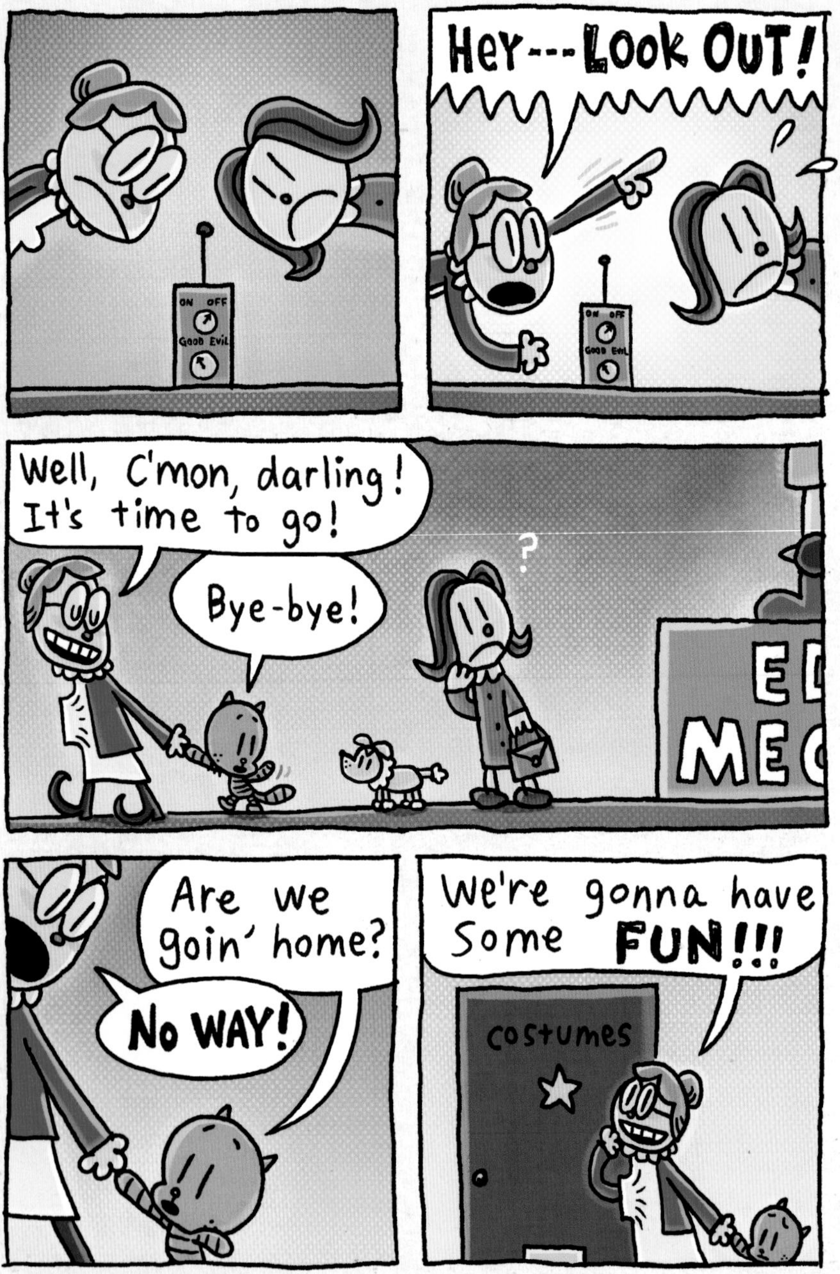
ON OFF
GOOD EVIL
HEY---LOOK OUT!
ON OFF
GOOD EVIL
Well, C'mon, darling! It's time to go!
Bye-bye!
?
ED
MEG
Are we goin' home?
No WAY!
We're gonna have Some FUN!!!
costumes

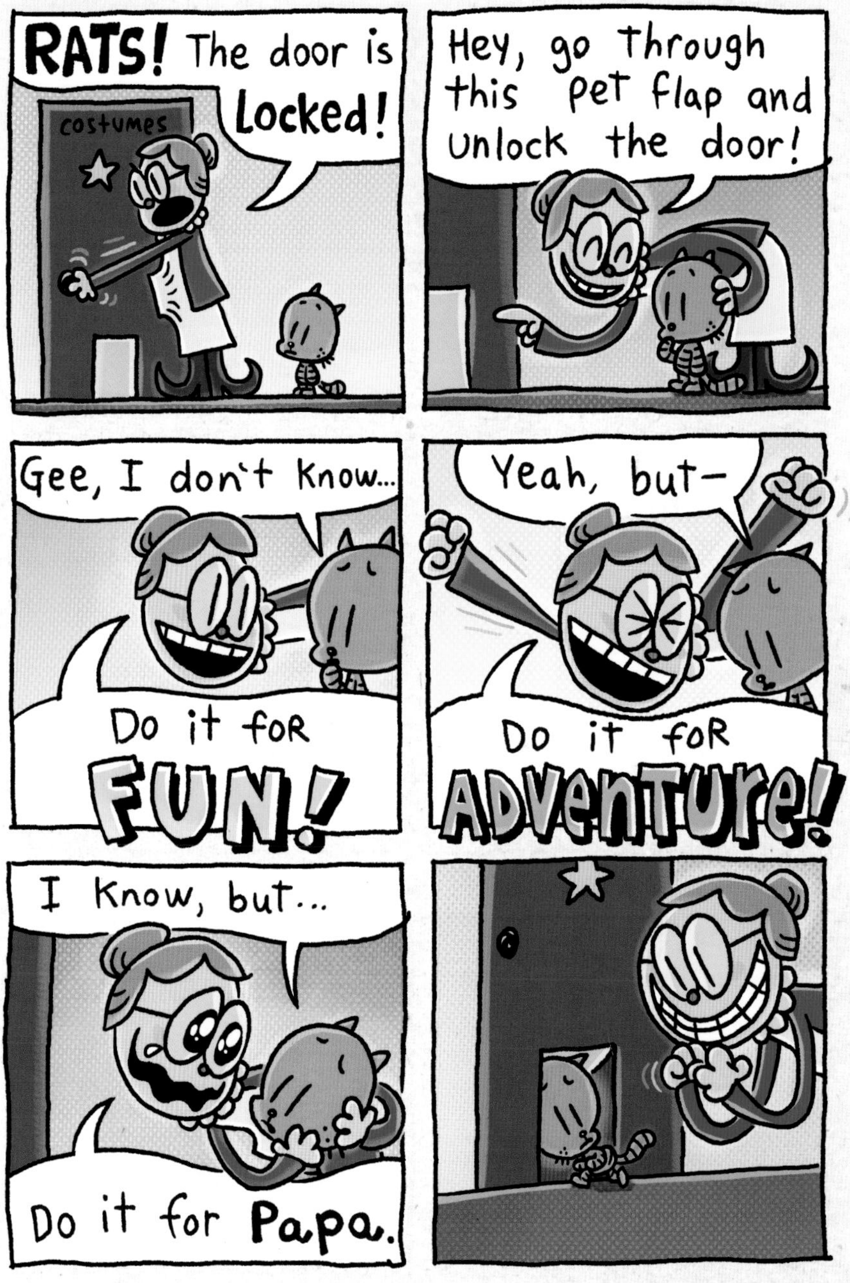
RATS! The door is Locked!
costumes
Hey, go through this pet flap and unlock the door!
Gee, I don't know...
Do it for FUN!
Yeah, but–
Do it for ADVENTURE!
I know, but...
Do it for Papa.

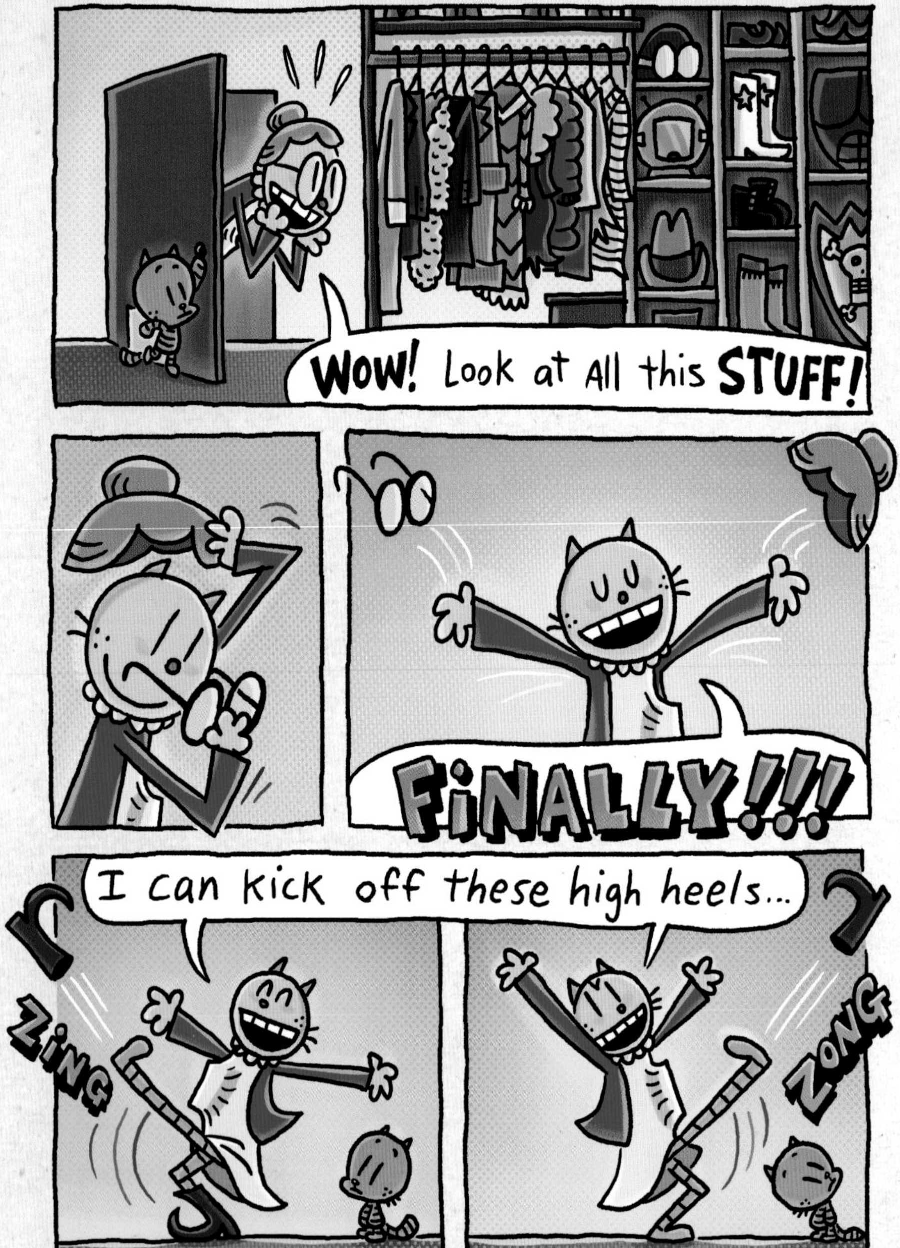
WOW! Look at All this STUFF!
FiNALLY!!!
I can kick off these high heels...
ZiNG
ZONG

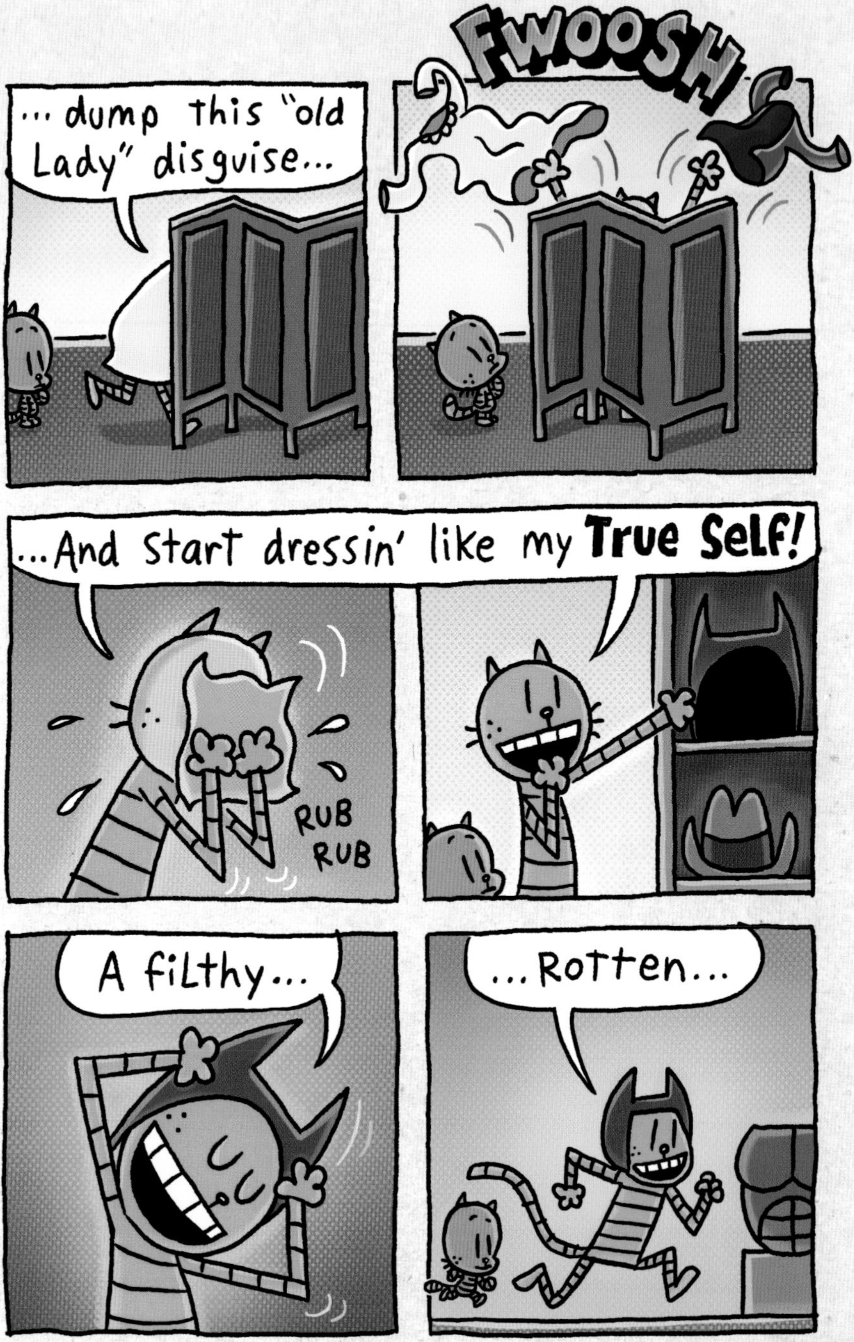

... dump this "old Lady" disguise...
FWOOSH
...And start dressin' like my **True Self!**
RUB RUB
A filthy...
...Rotten...

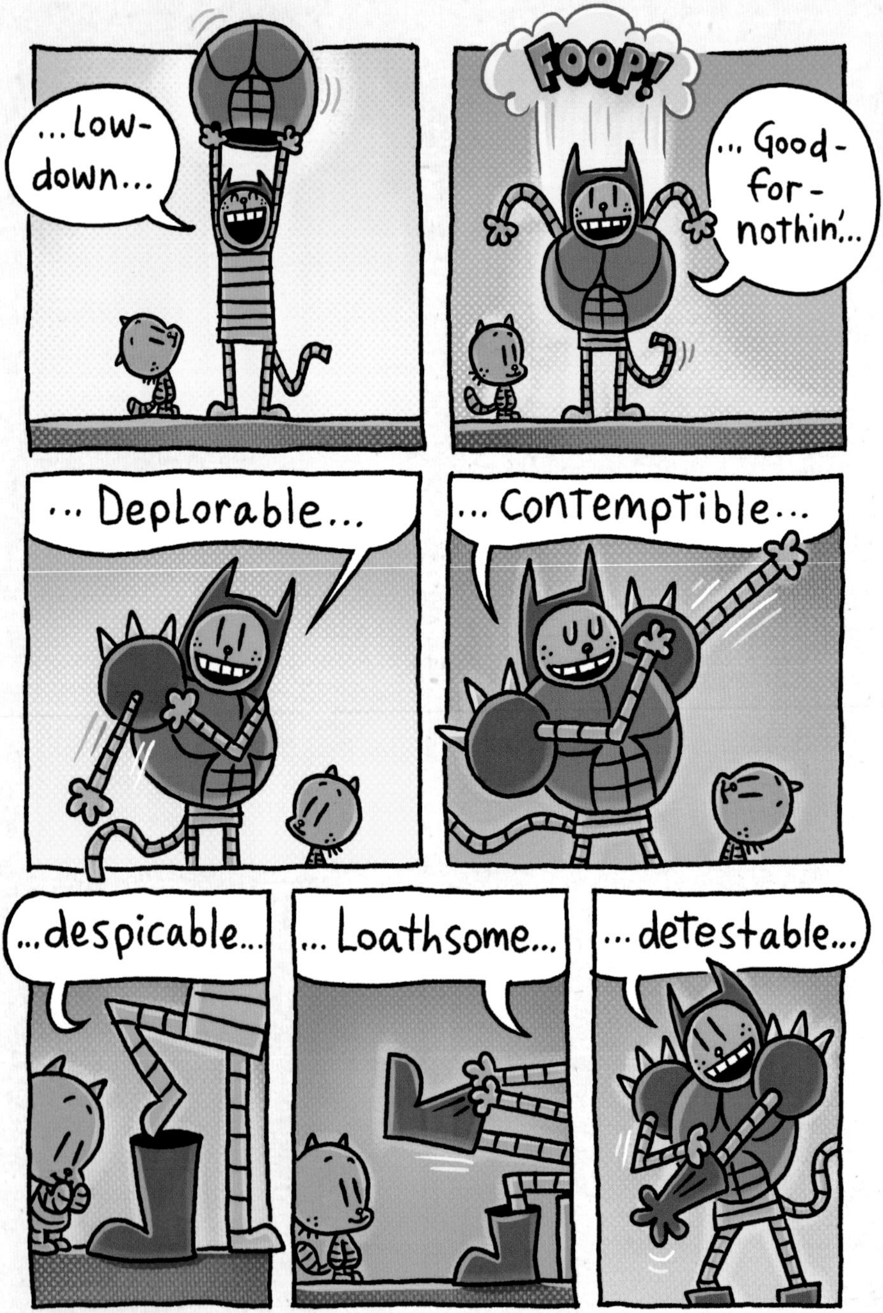
...Low-down...
FOOP!
... Good-for-nothin'...
... Deplorable...
... Contemptible...
...despicable...
... Loathsome...
... detestable...

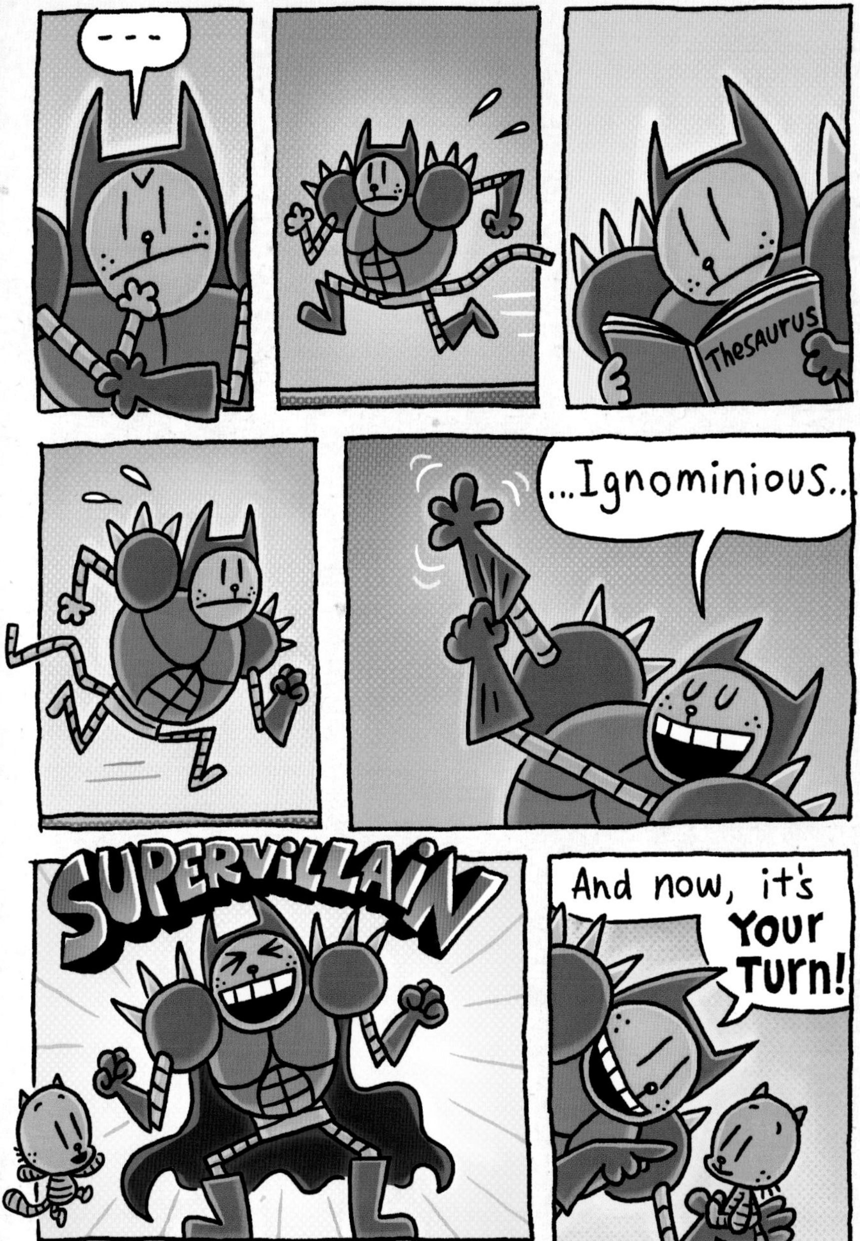

Thesaurus
...Ignominious...
SUPERVILLAIN
And now, it's YOUR TURN!

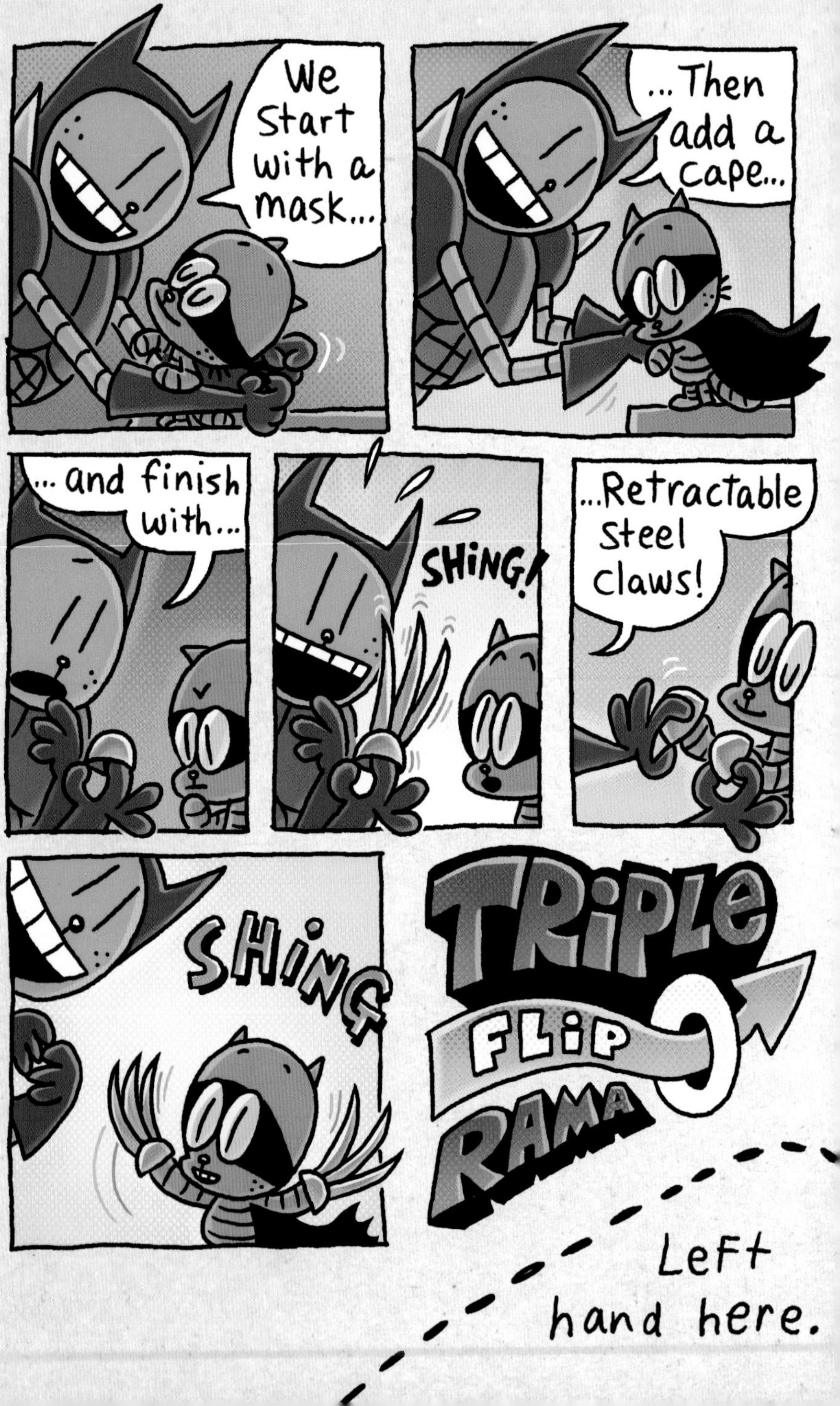

We Start with a mask...
...Then add a cape...
...and finish with...
SHING!
...Retractable Steel Claws!
SHING
TRIPLE FLIP RAMA
Left hand here.

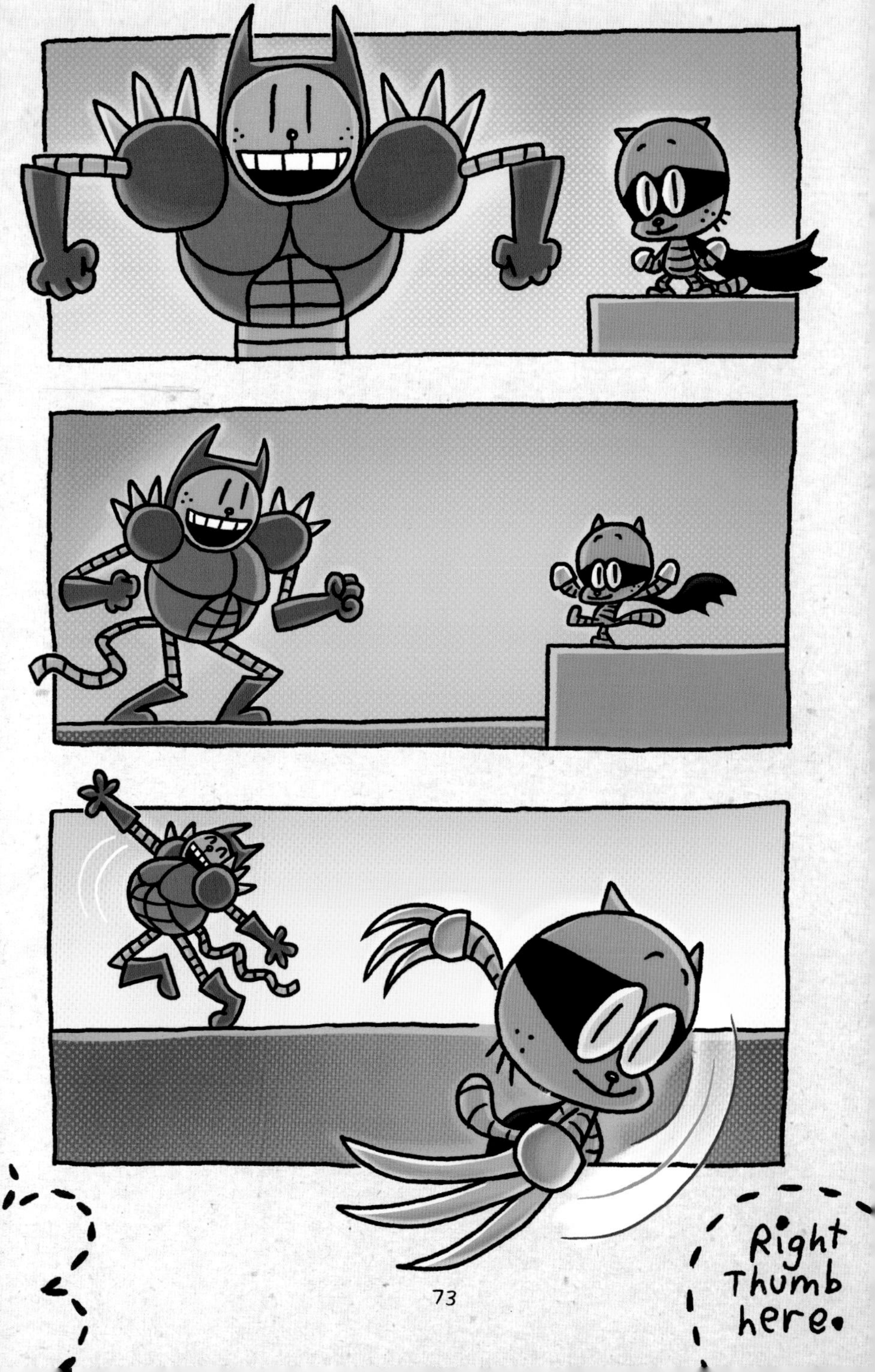
Right Thumb here.

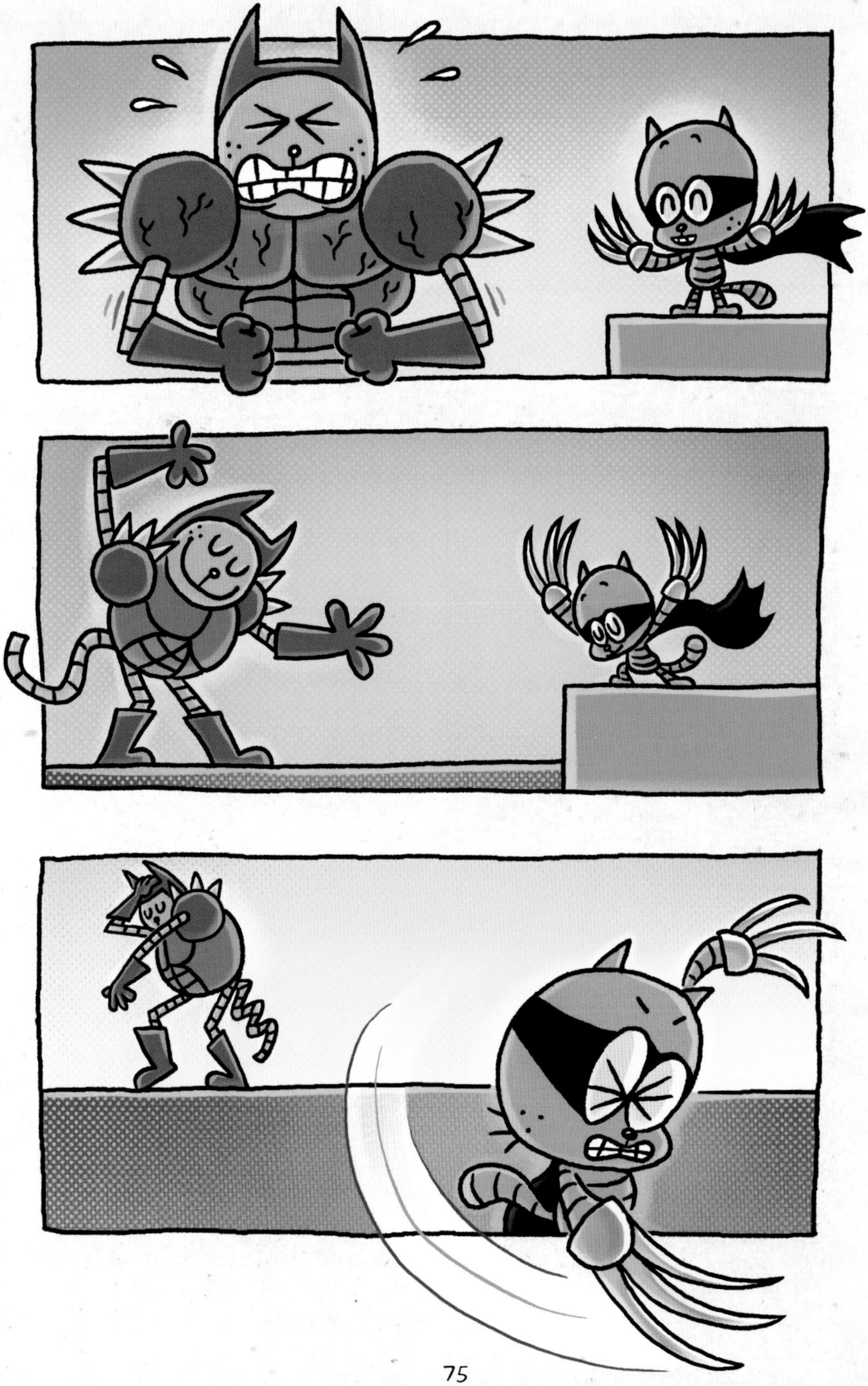

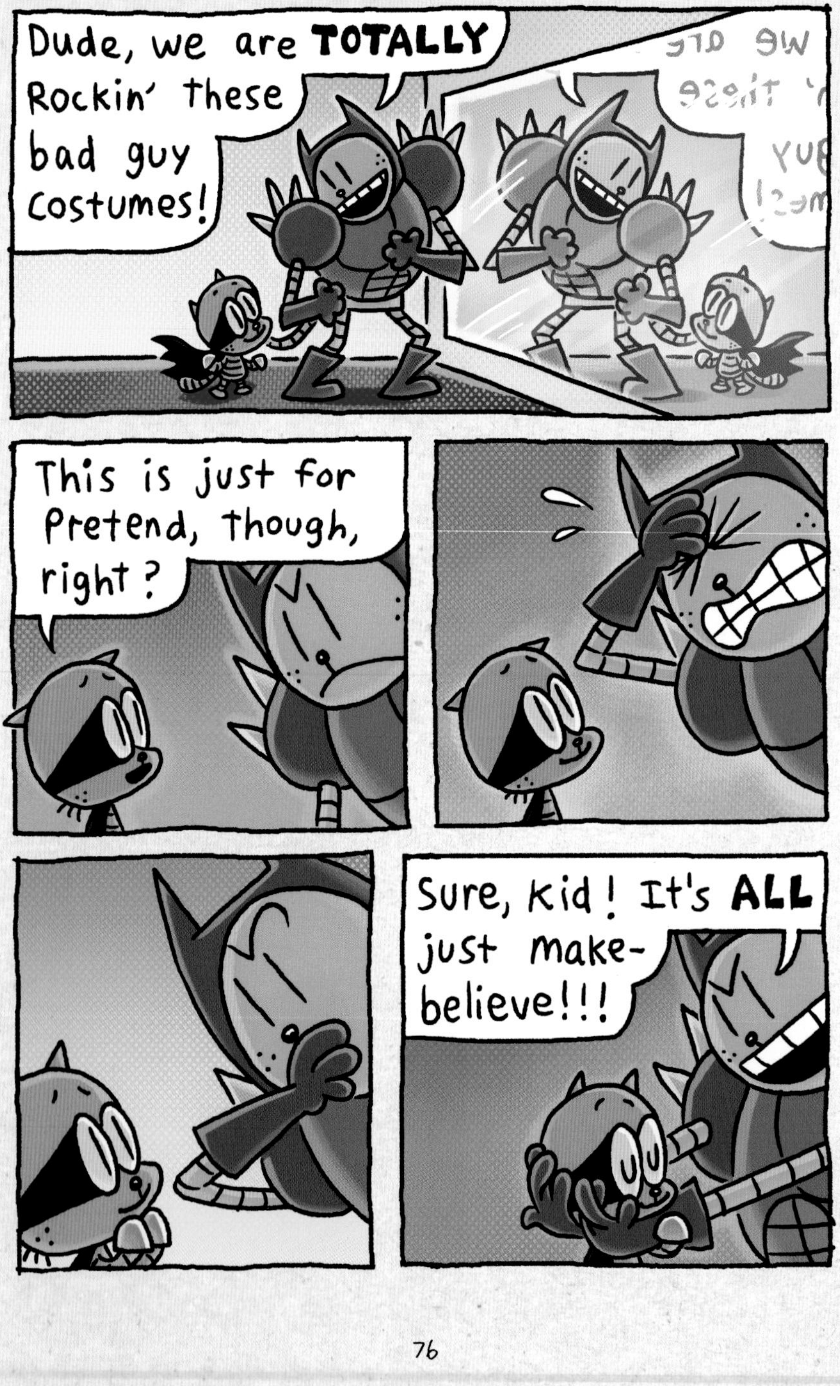
Dude, we are **TOTALLY** Rockin' these bad guy costumes!
This is just for Pretend, though, right?
Sure, kid! It's **ALL** just make-believe!!!

CHAPTER 5

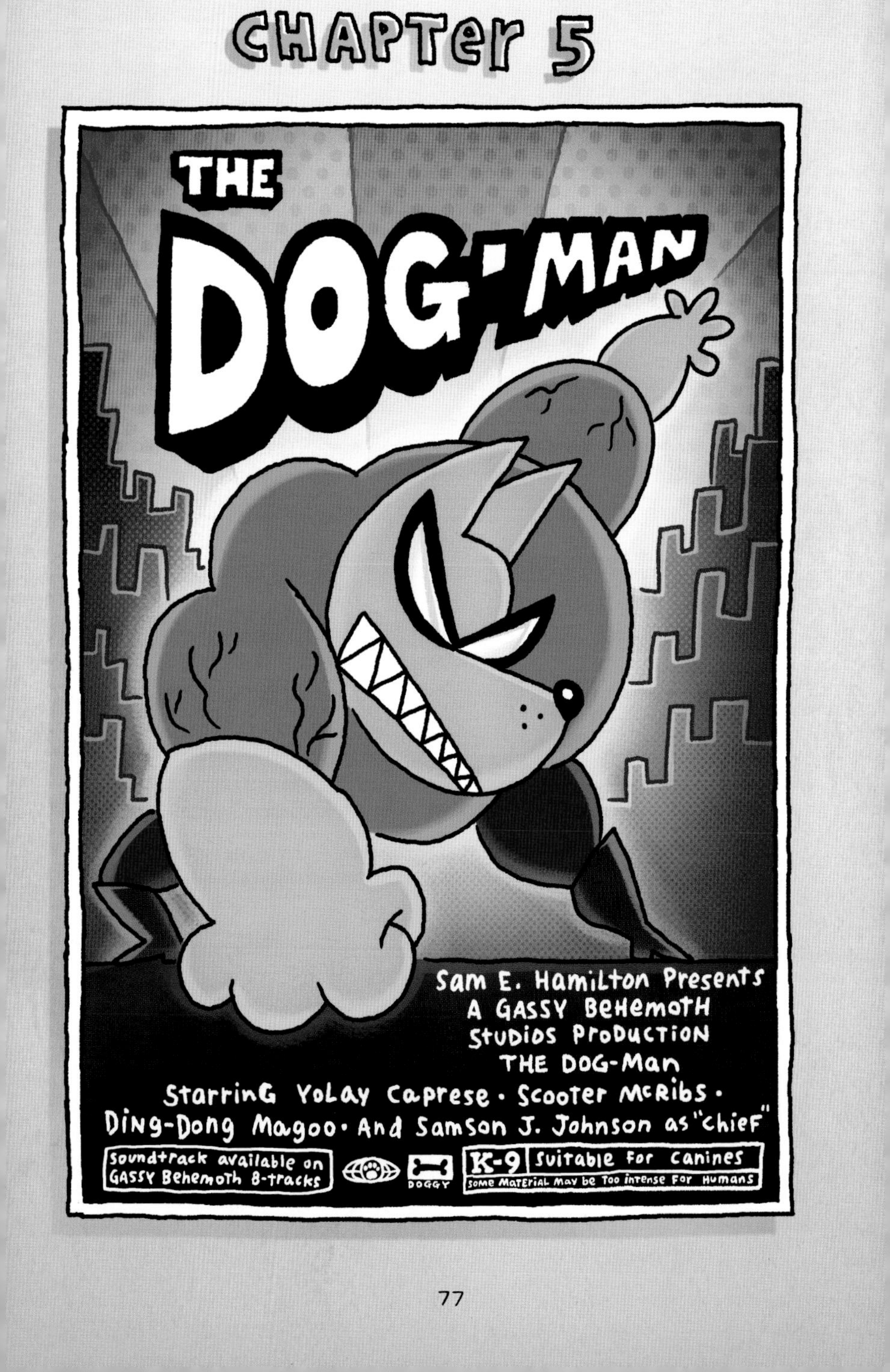
THE DOG-MAN
Sam E. Hamilton Presents
A GASSY Behemoth
Studios Production
THE DOG-Man
Starring Yolay Caprese • Scooter McRibs •
Ding-Dong Magoo • And Samson J. Johnson as "chief"
soundtrack available on GASSY Behemoth 8-tracks
DOGGY
K-9 suitable for canines
some material may be too intense for humans

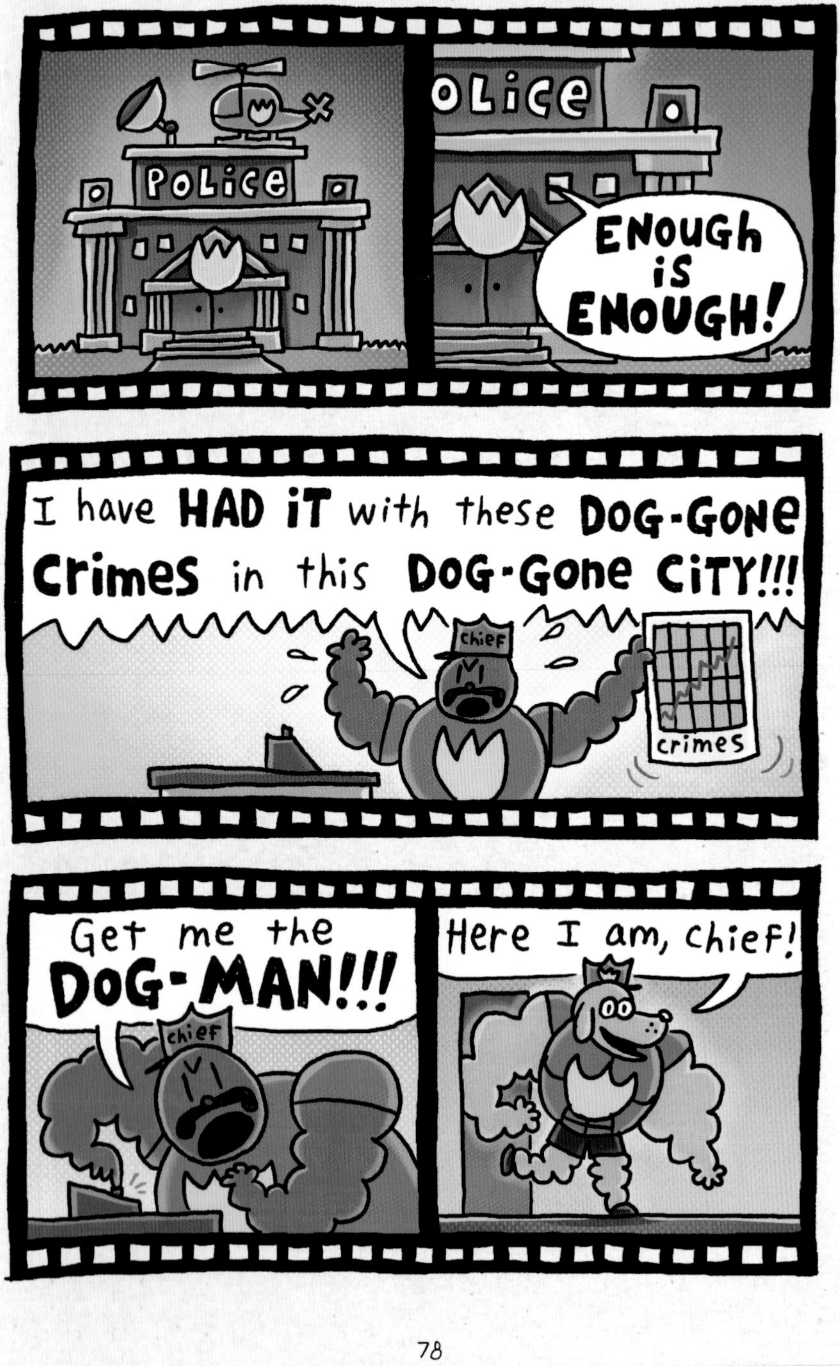

POLICE
OLICE
ENOUGH IS ENOUGH!
I have HAD iT with these DOG-GONE Crimes in this DOG-Gone CiTY!!!
chief
crimes
Get me the DOG-MAN!!!
chief
Here I am, chief!

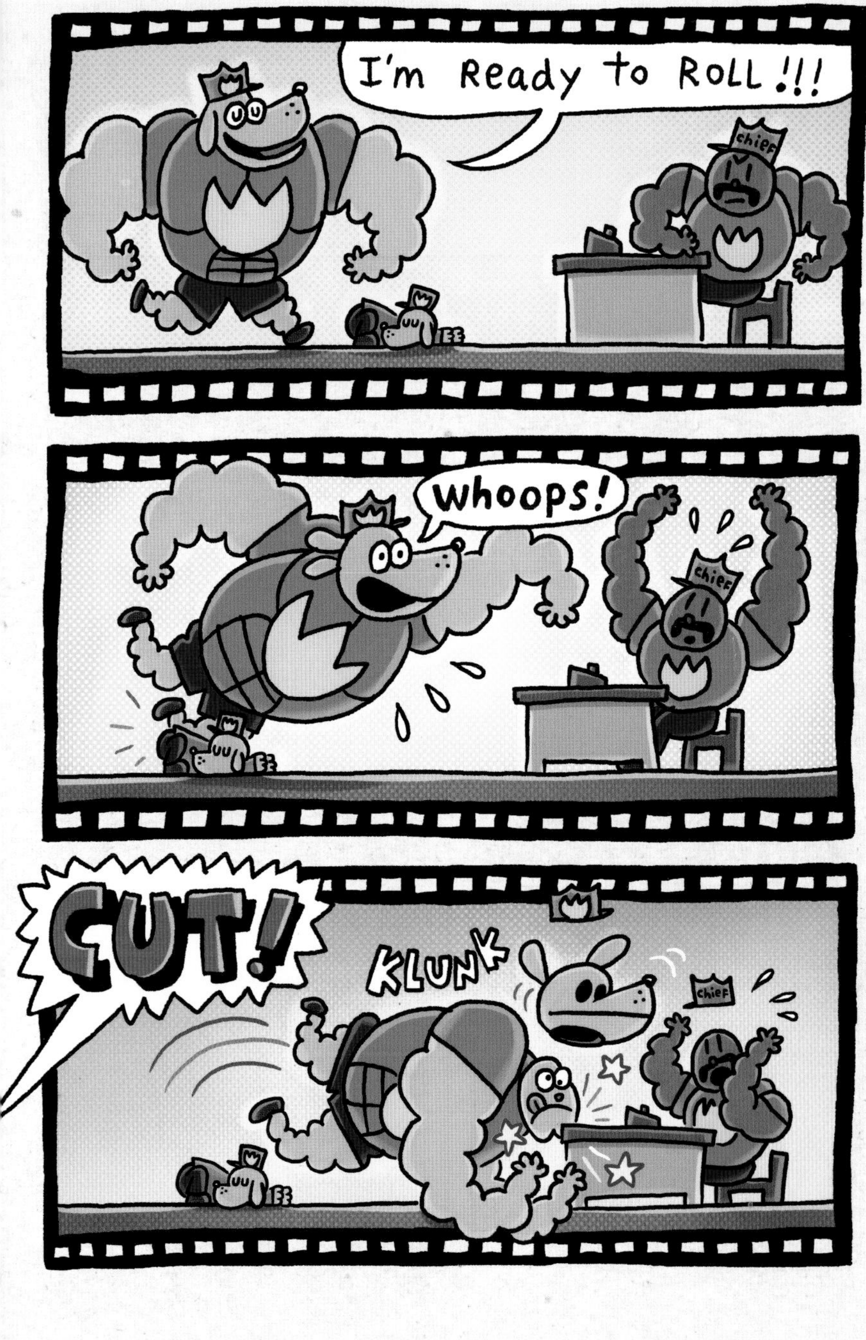

I'm Ready to ROLL!!!
chief
Whoops!
chief
CUT!
KLUNK
chief

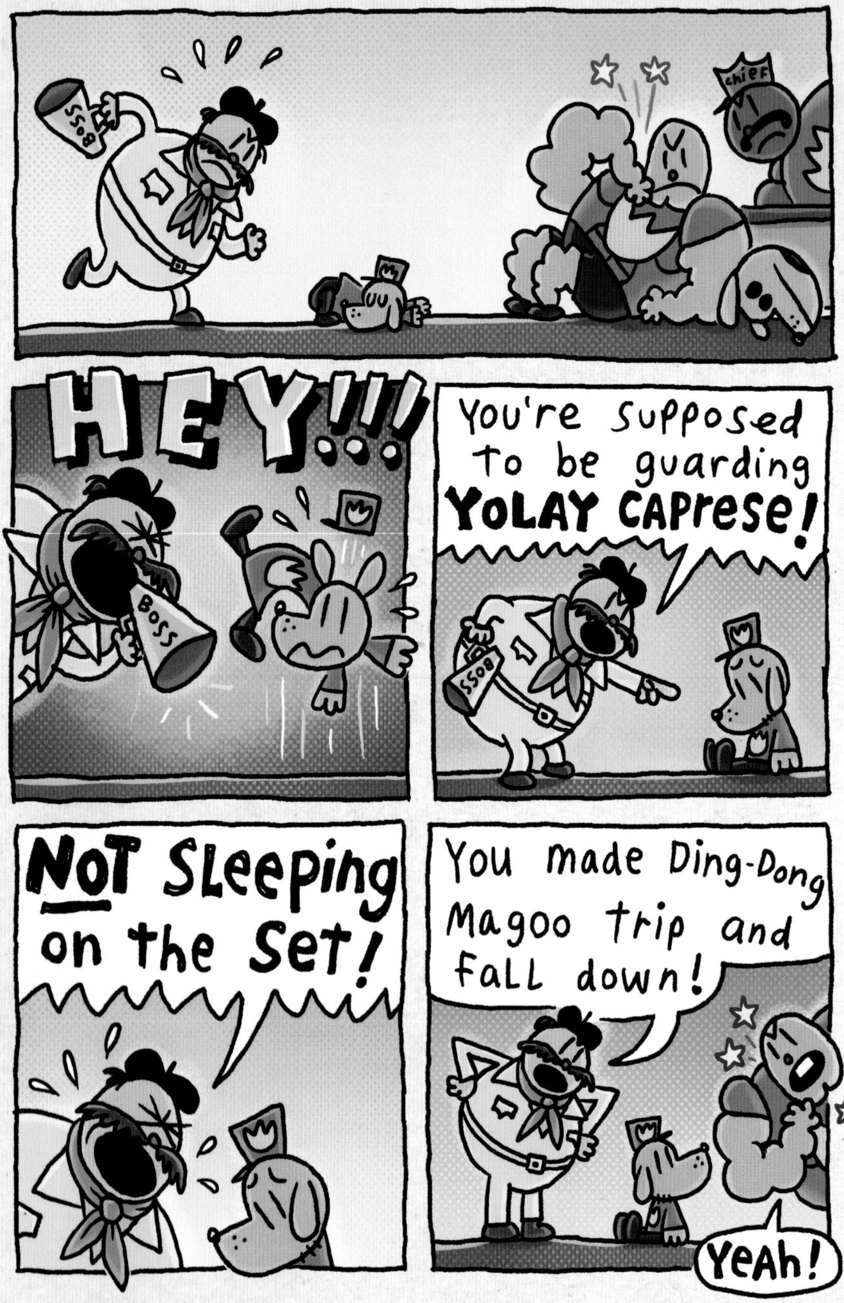

BOSS
CHIEF
HEY!!!
BOSS
You're supposed to be guarding YOLAY CAPRESE!
BOSS
NOT Sleeping on the Set!
You made Ding-Dong Magoo trip and fall down!
YeAh!

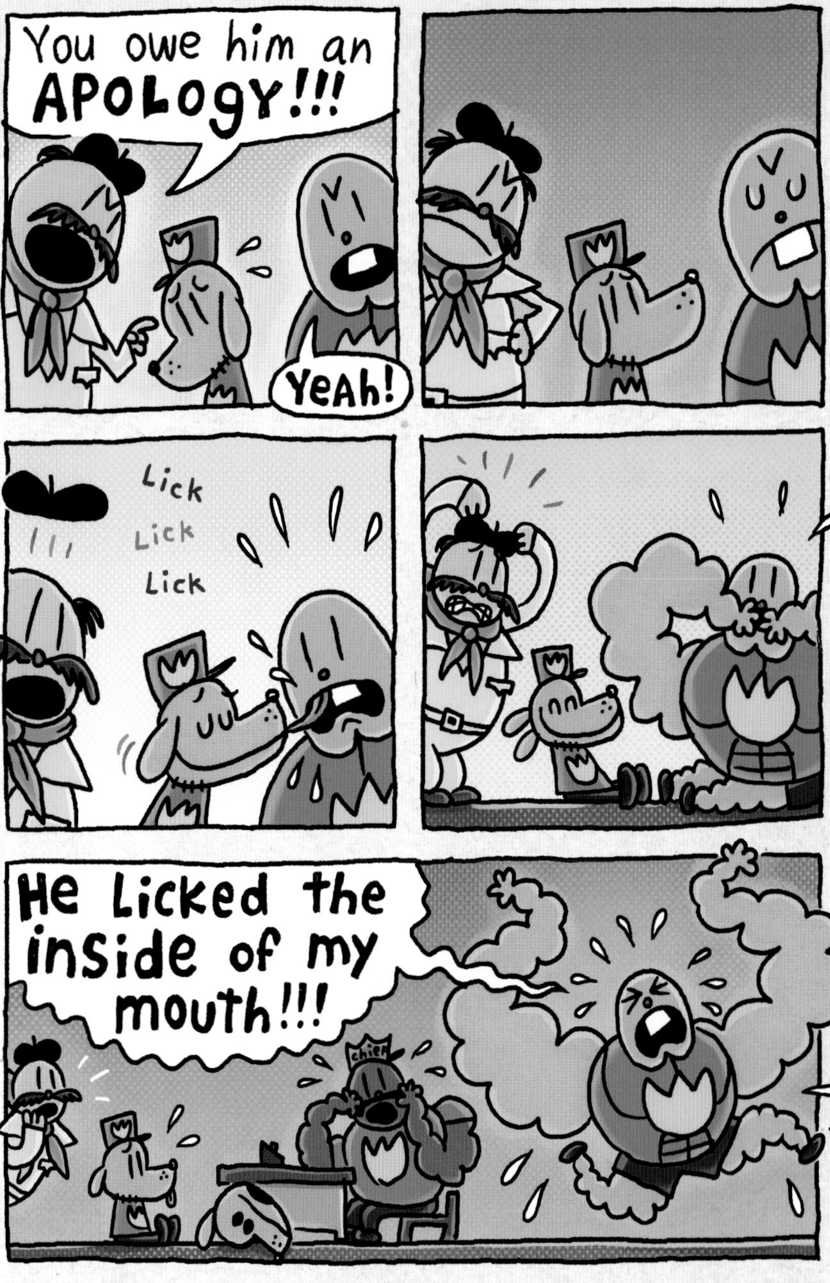
You owe him an APOLOGY!!!
YEAh!
Lick
Lick
Lick
He Licked the inside of my mouth!!!
CHIEF

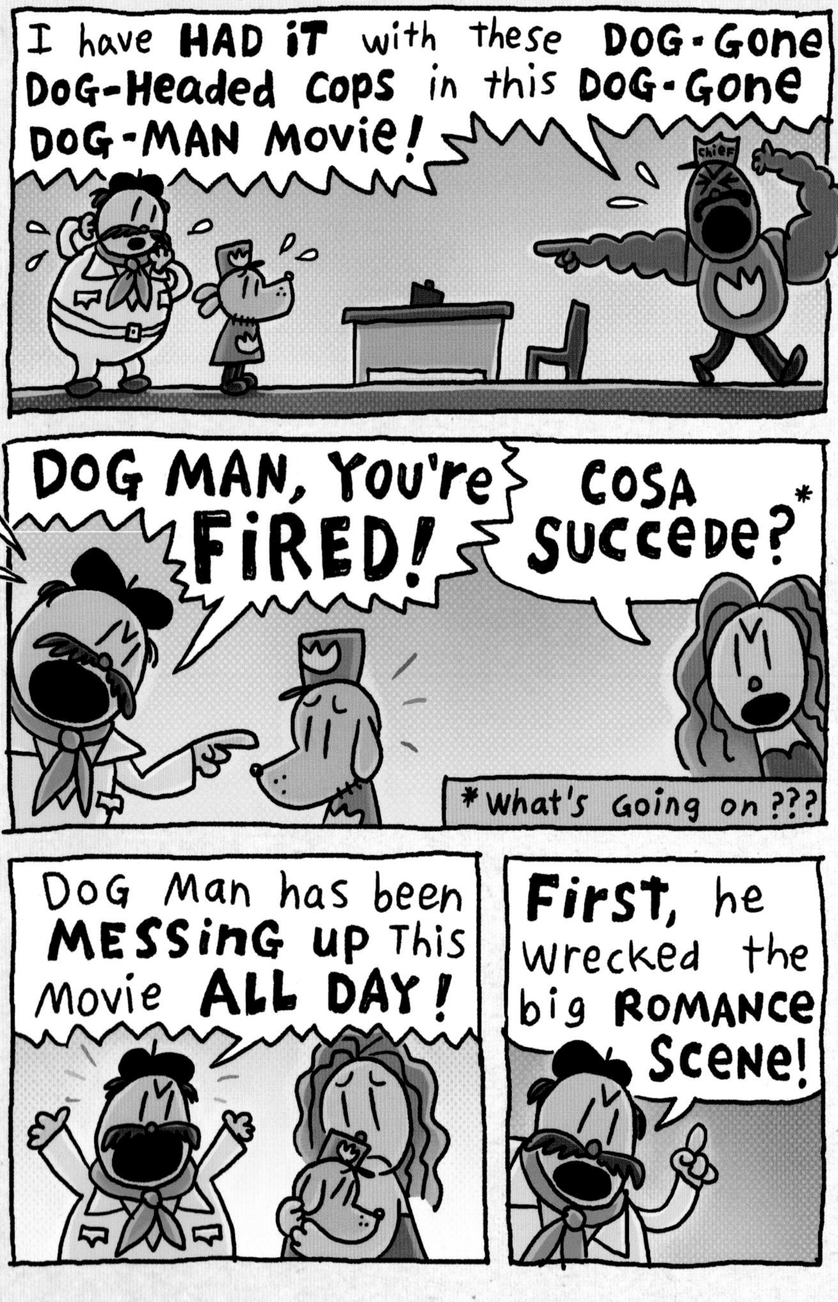
I have HAD iT with these DOG-Gone DOG-Headed COPS in this DOG-Gone DOG-MAN Movie!
CHIEF
DOG MAN, You're FiRED!
COSA SUCCEDE?*
*What's Going on???
DOG Man has been MESSinG up This Movie ALL DAY!
First, he wrecked the big ROMANCE SCENE!

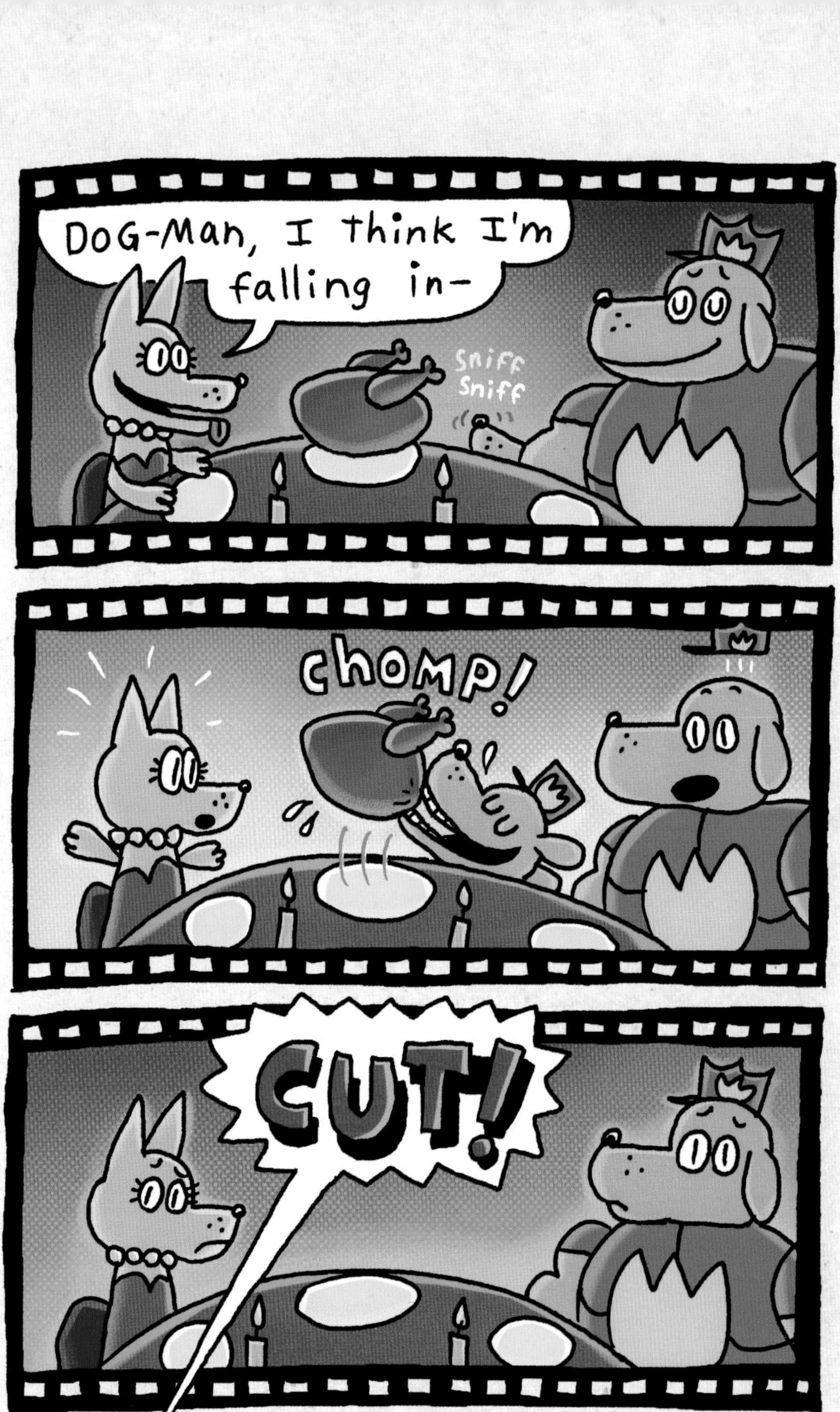
DOG-Man, I think I'm falling in-
Sniff Sniff
chomp!
CUT!

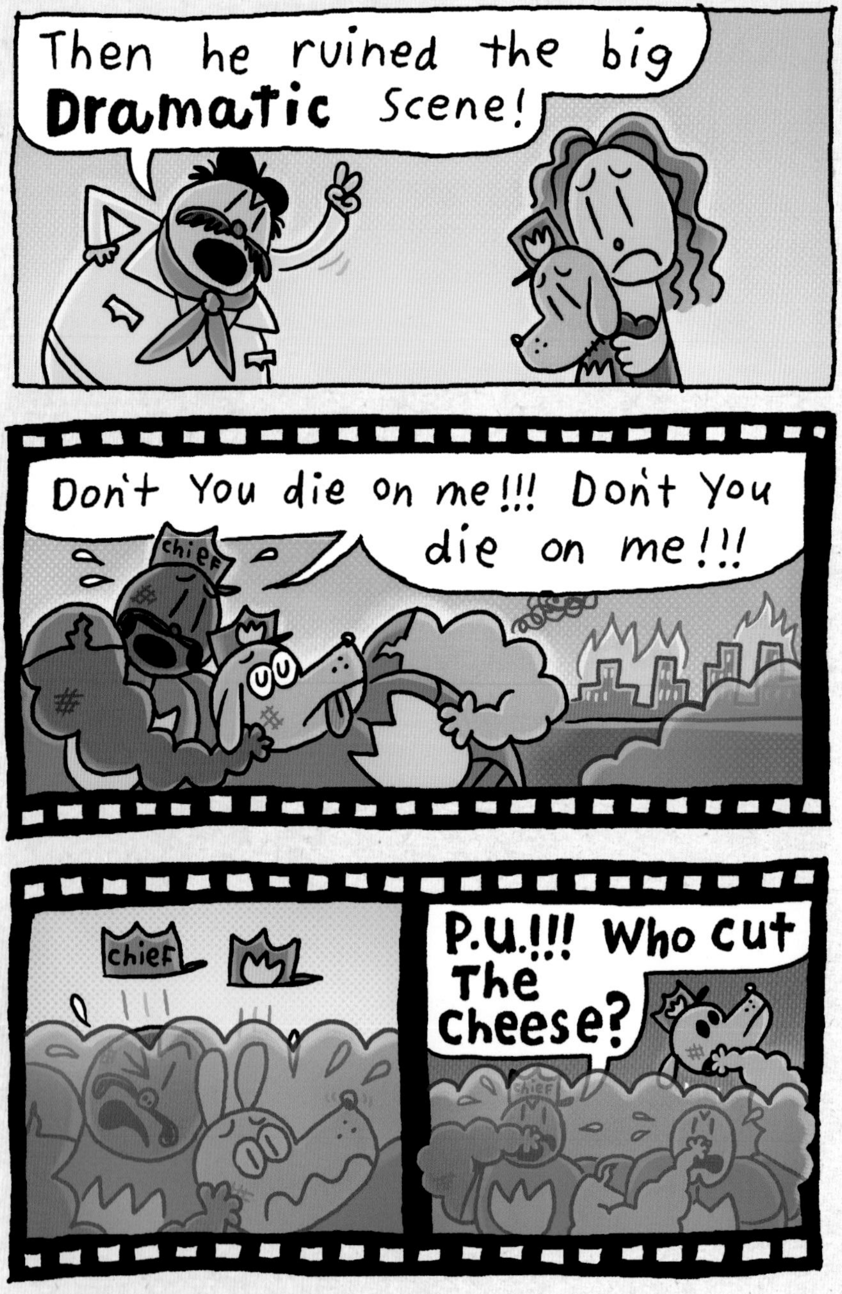
Then he ruined the big **Dramatic** Scene!
Don't You die on me!!! Don't You die on me!!!
chief
chief
P.U.!!! Who cut The cheese?
chief

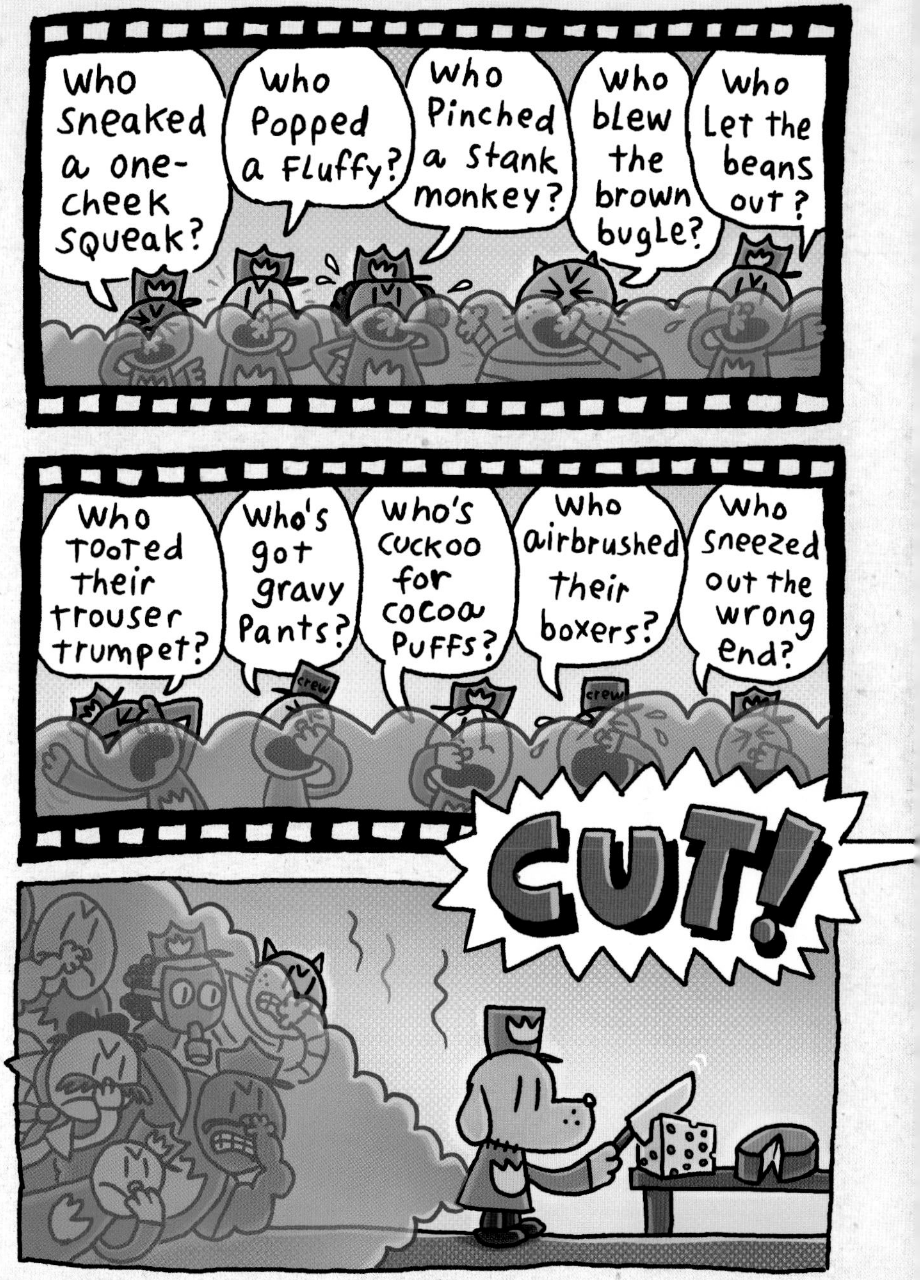

Who sneaked a one-cheek squeak?
Who popped a fluffy?
Who pinched a stank monkey?
Who blew the brown bugle?
Who let the beans out?
Who tooted their trouser trumpet?
Who's got gravy pants?
Who's cuckoo for cocoa puffs?
Who airbrushed their boxers?
Who sneezed out the wrong end?
crew
crew
crew
CUT!

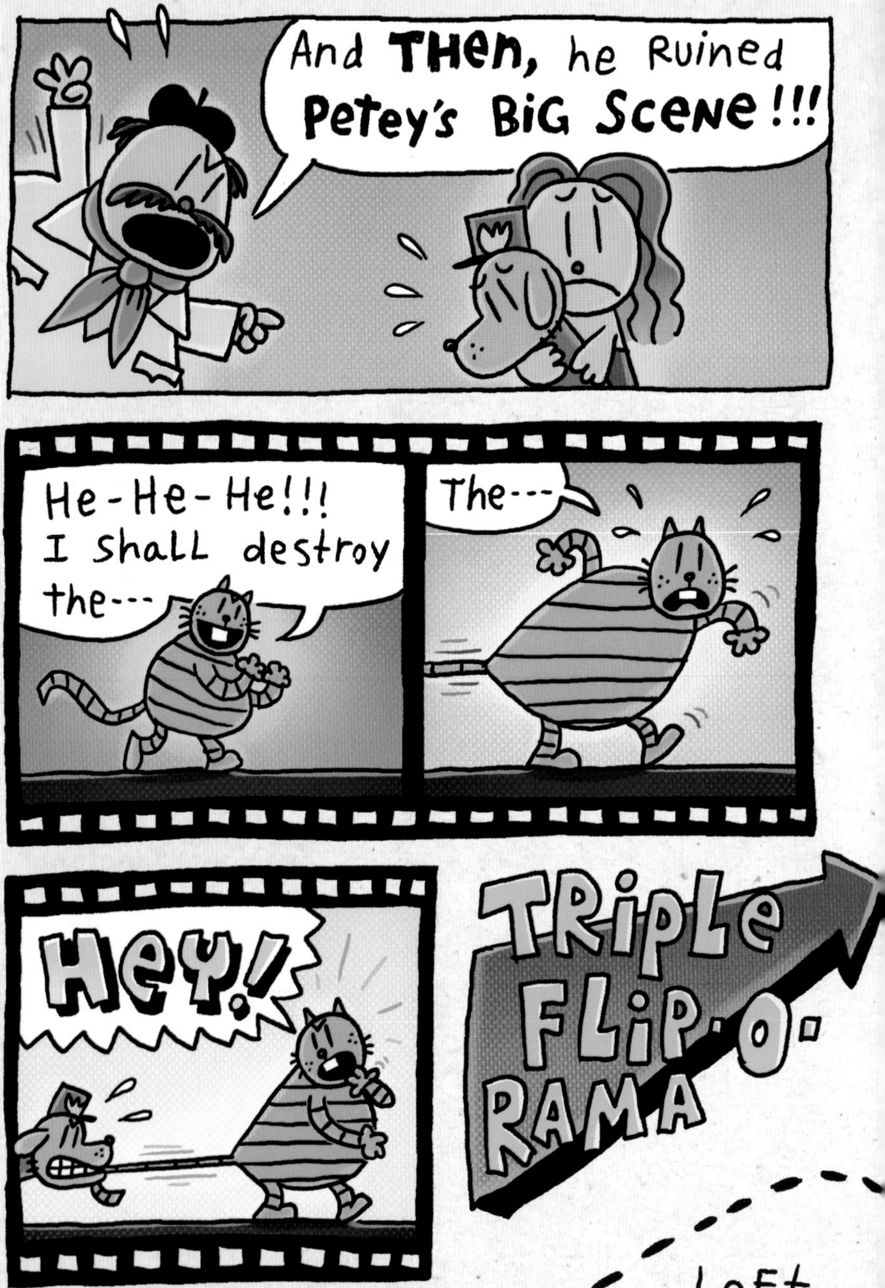
And THEn, he Ruined Petey's BiG Scene!!!
He-He-He!!! I shall destroy the---
The---
HEY!
TRIPLE FLIP-O-RAMA

Left hand here.

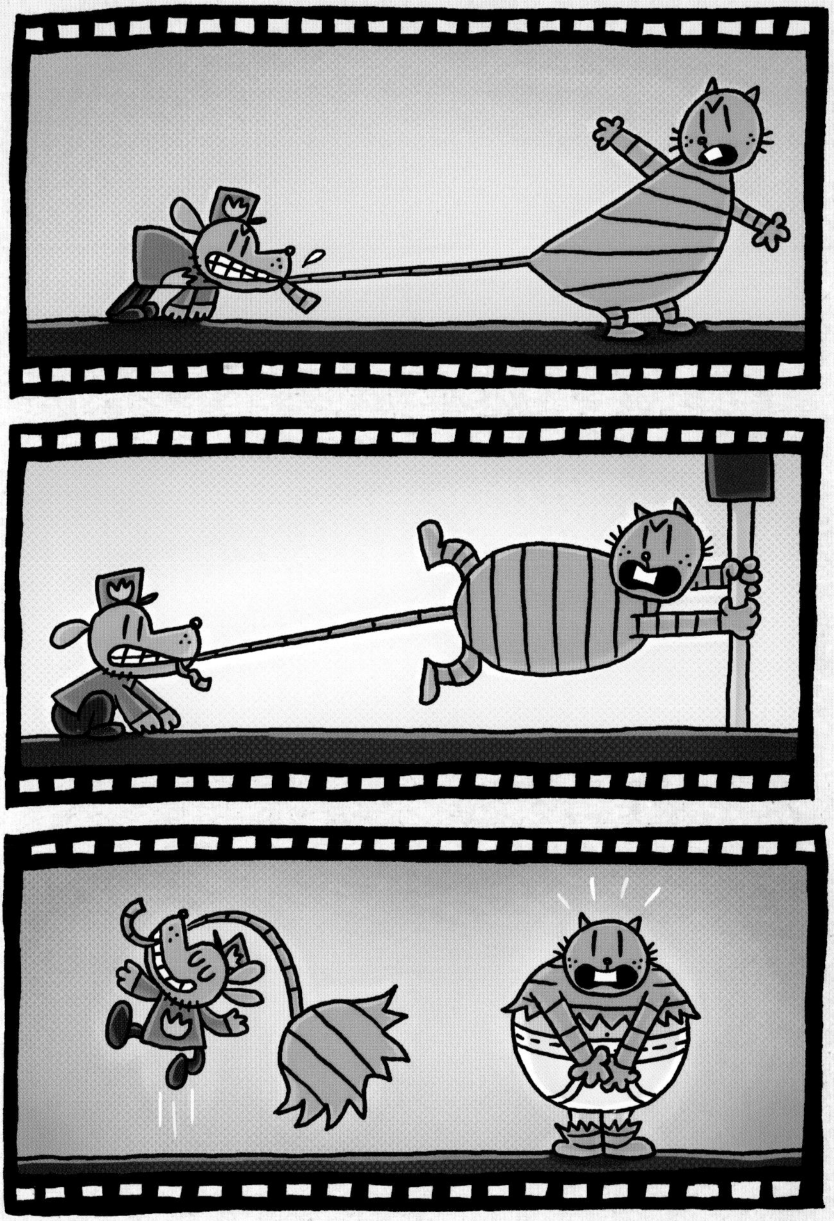

Right Thumb here.

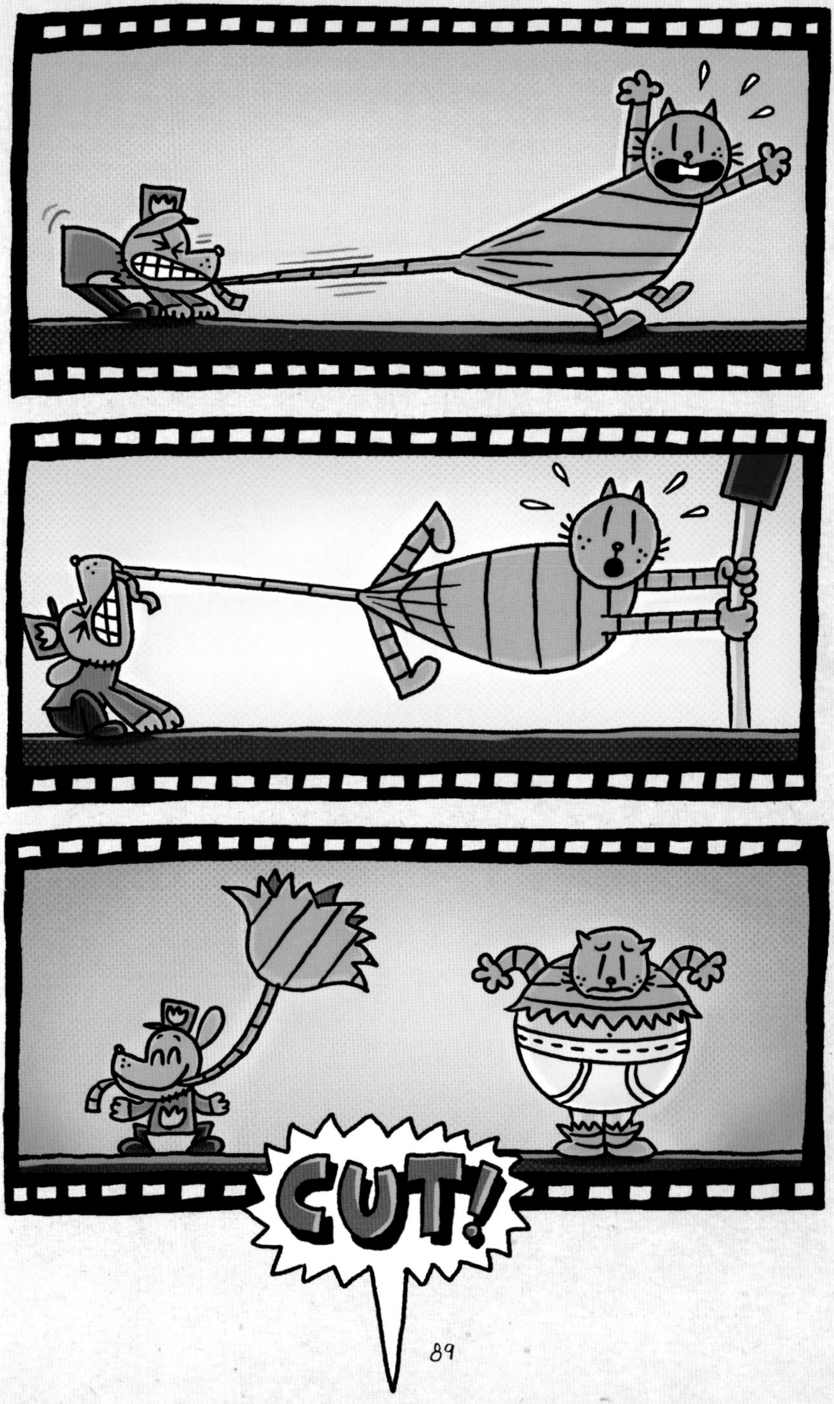
CUT!

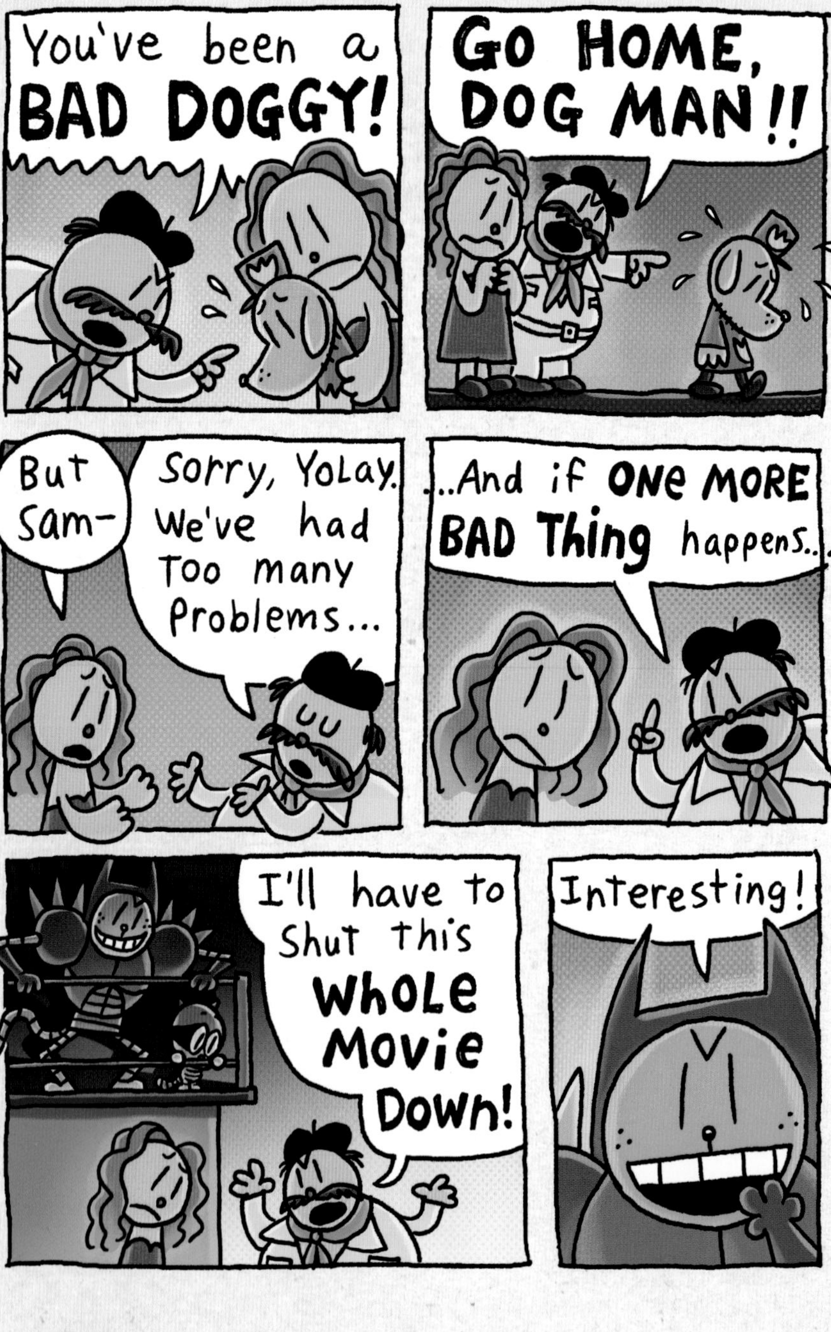
You've been a BAD DOGGY!
GO HOME, DOG MAN!!
But Sam-
Sorry, YoLay. We've had Too many Problems...
...And if ONE MORE BAD Thing happens...
I'll have to Shut this WhoLe Movie Down!
Interesting!

Chapter 6

THE BARK KNIGHT RISES

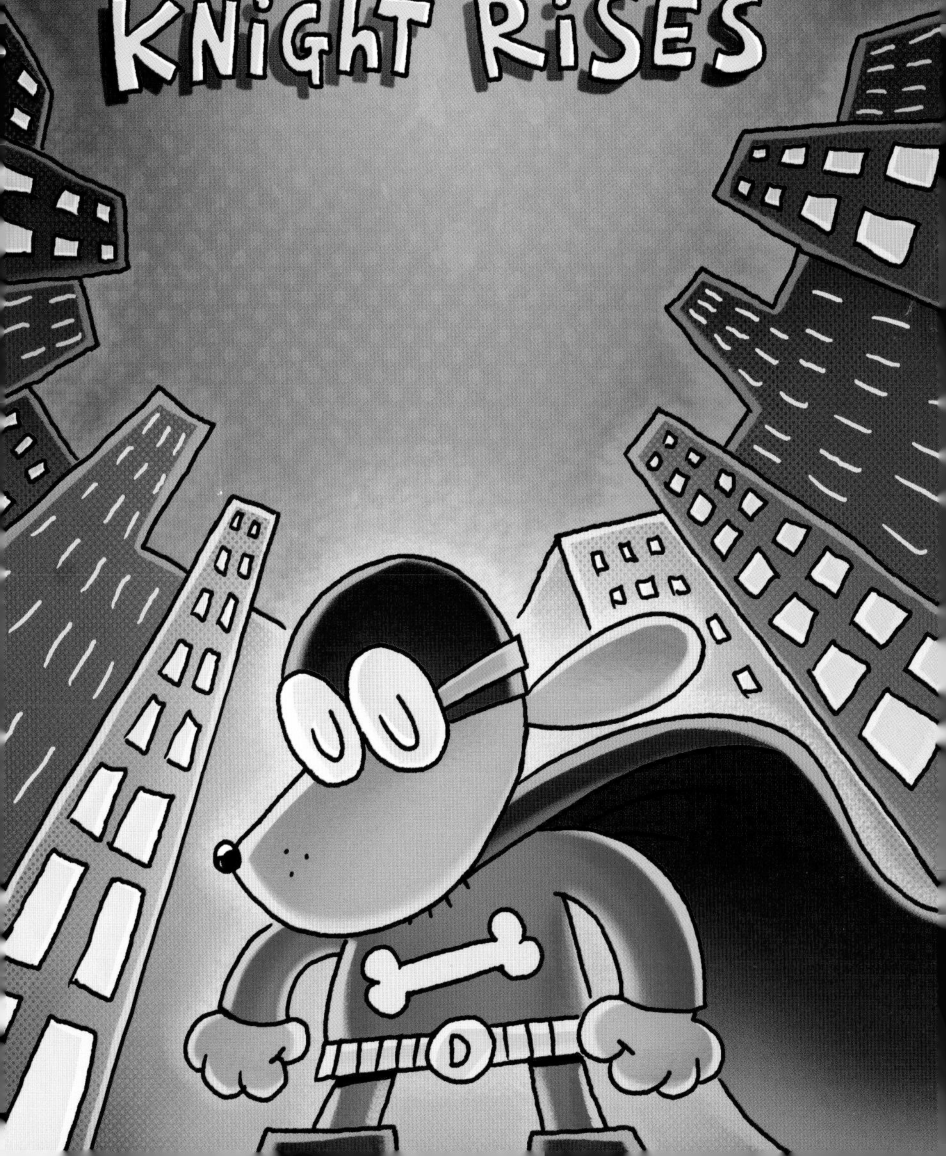

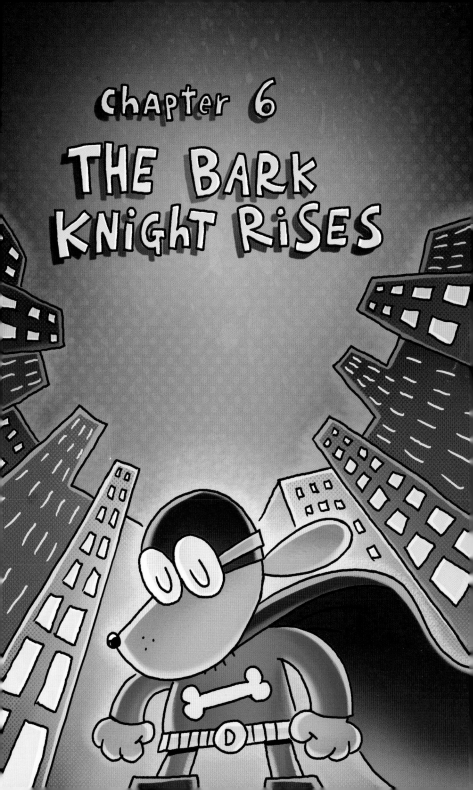

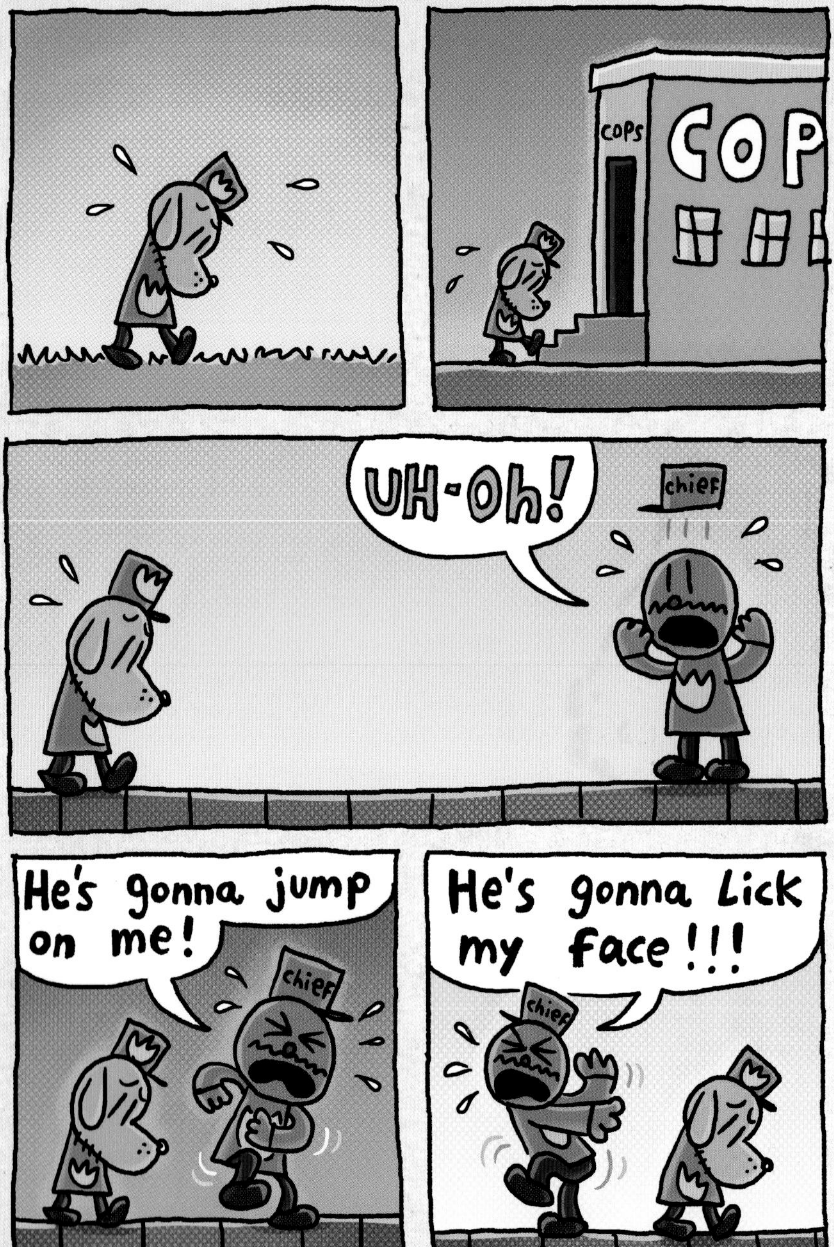
COPS
COP
UH-Oh!
chief
He's gonna jump on me!
chief
He's gonna Lick my face!!!
chief

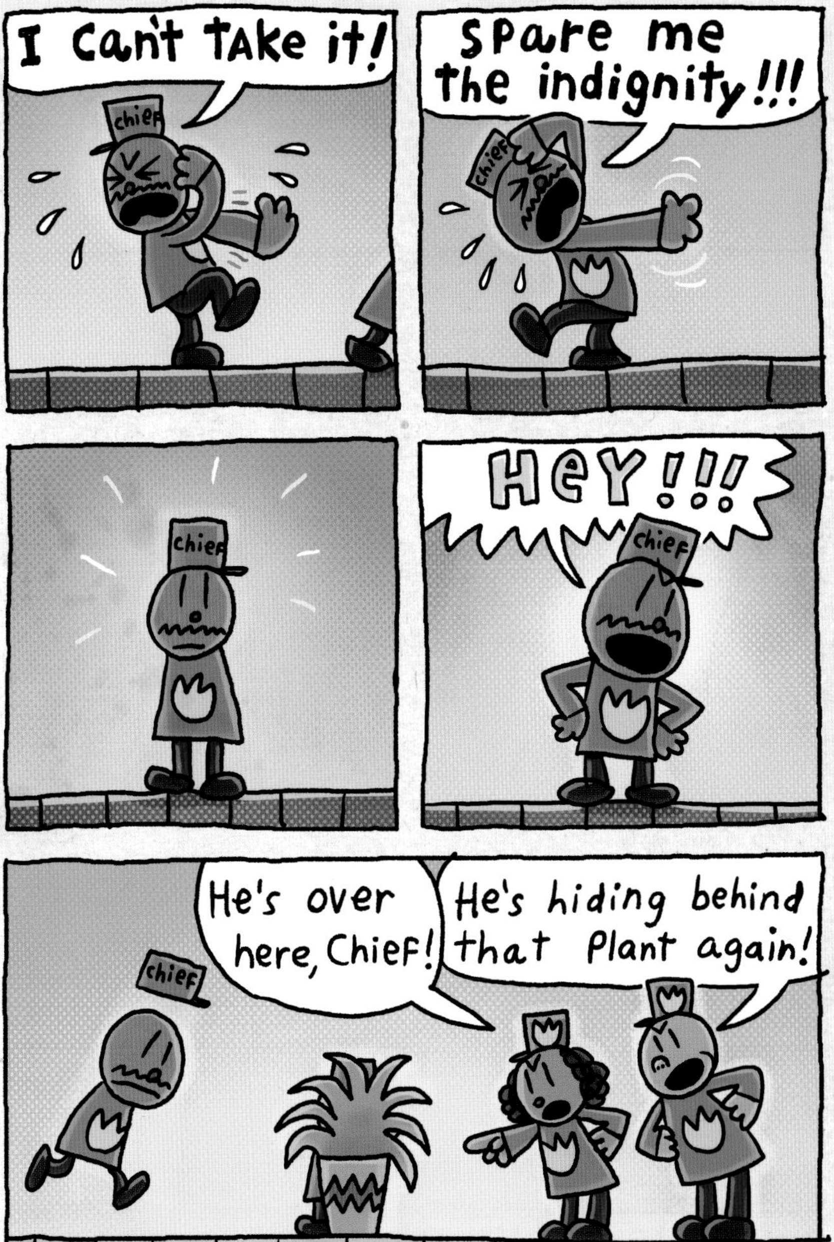
I can't take it!
Spare me the indignity!!!
chief
HEY!!!
He's over here, Chief!
He's hiding behind that plant again!

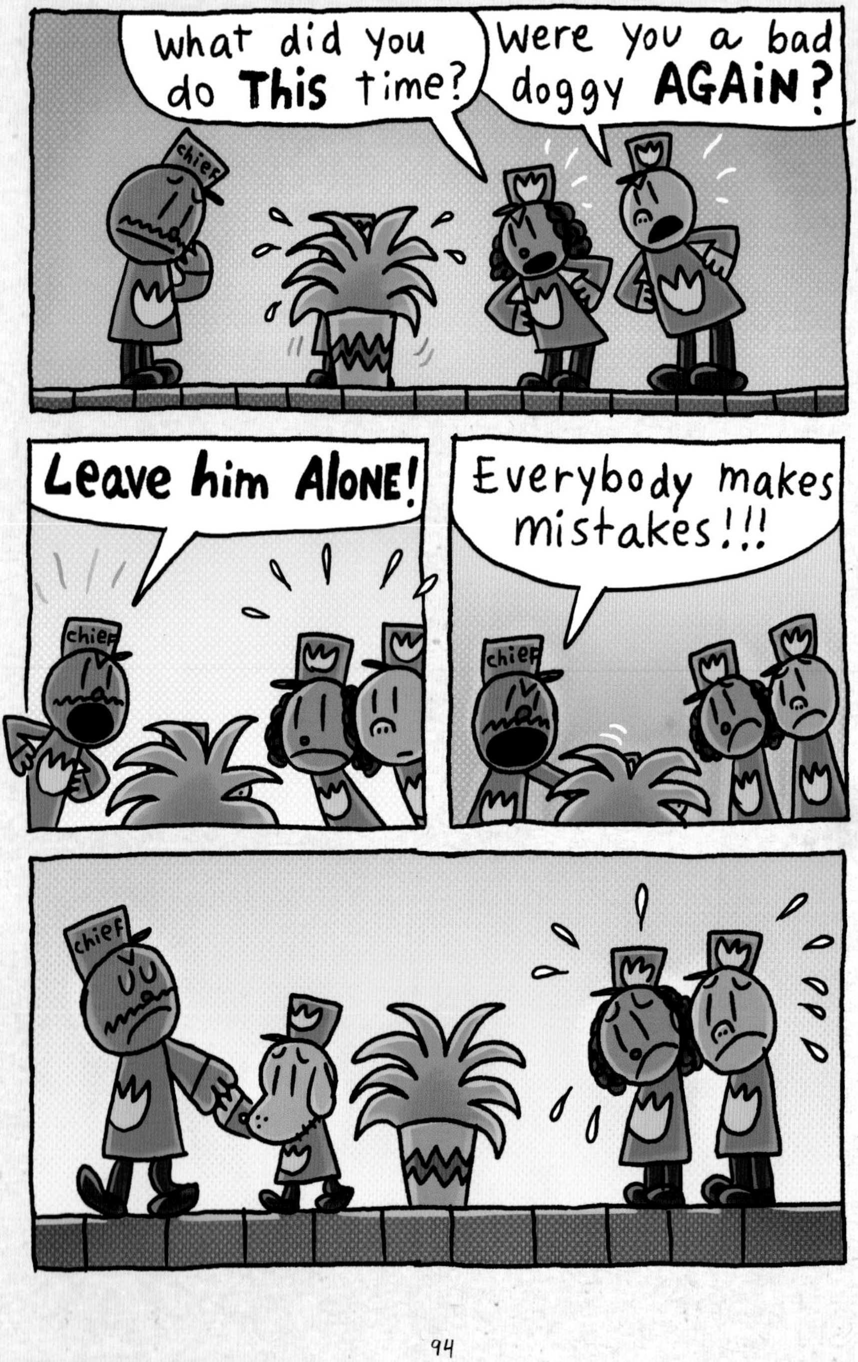
What did you do THIS time?
Were you a bad doggy AGAIN?
chief
Leave him ALONE!
chief
Everybody makes mistakes!!!
chief
chief

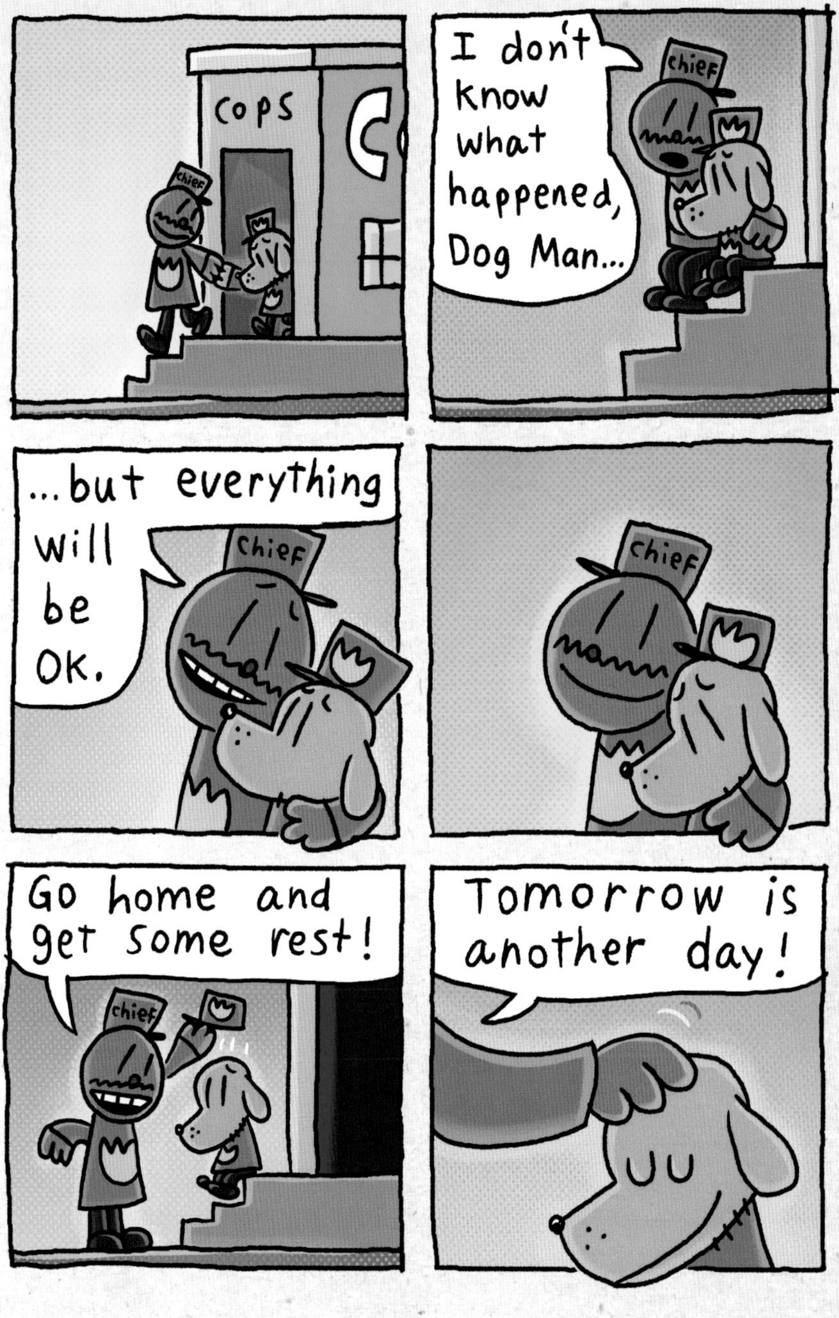
COPS
chief
I don't know what happened, Dog Man...
chief
...but everything will be OK.
chief
chief
Go home and get some rest!
chief
Tomorrow is another day!

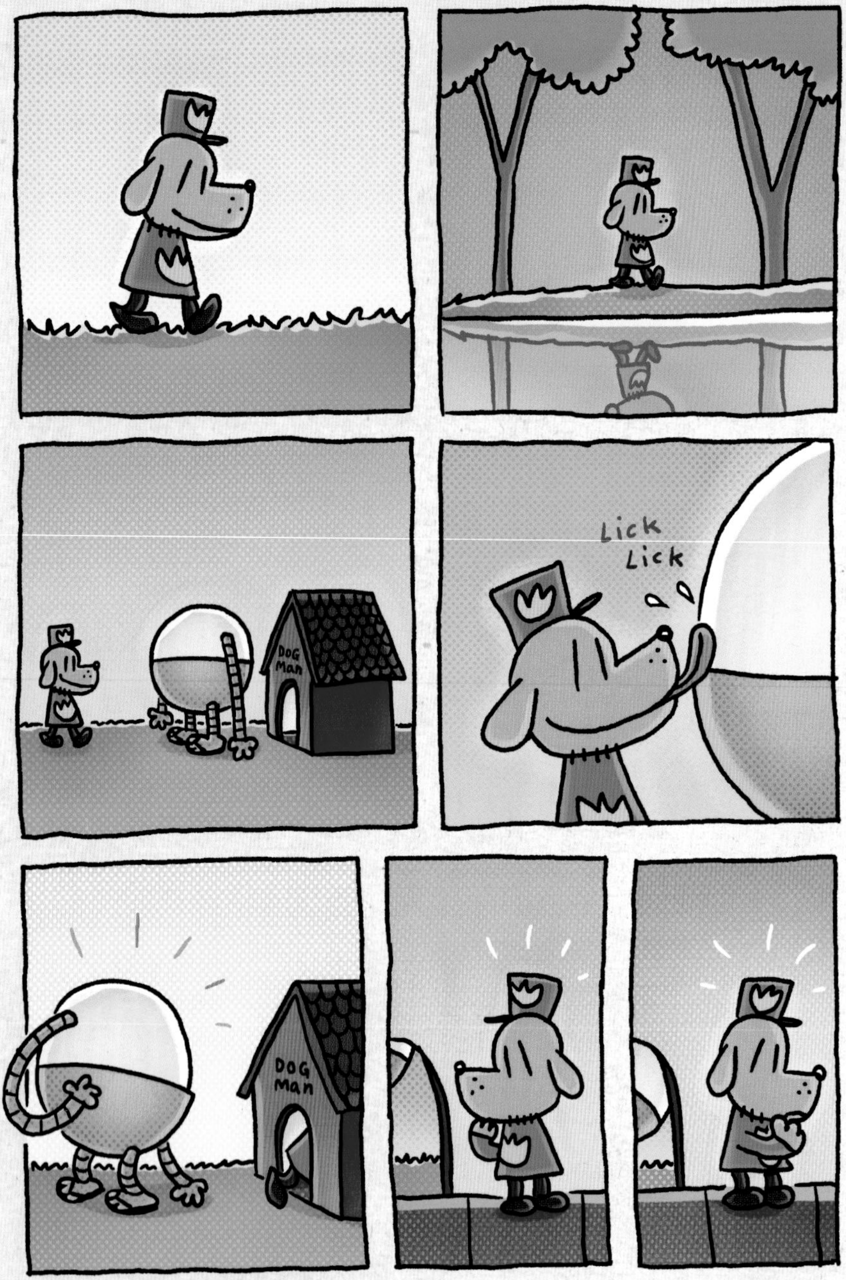
DOG Man
Lick
Lick
DOG Man

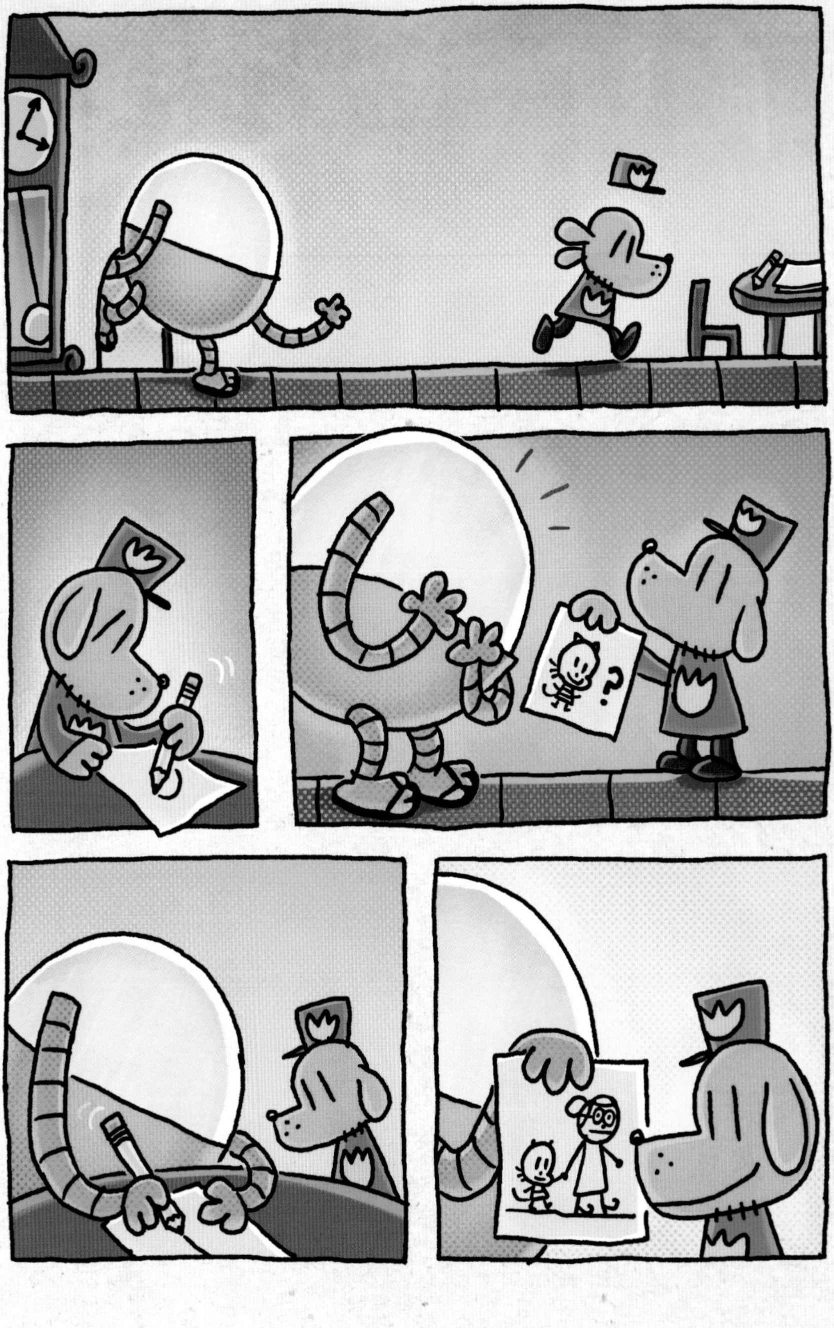
?

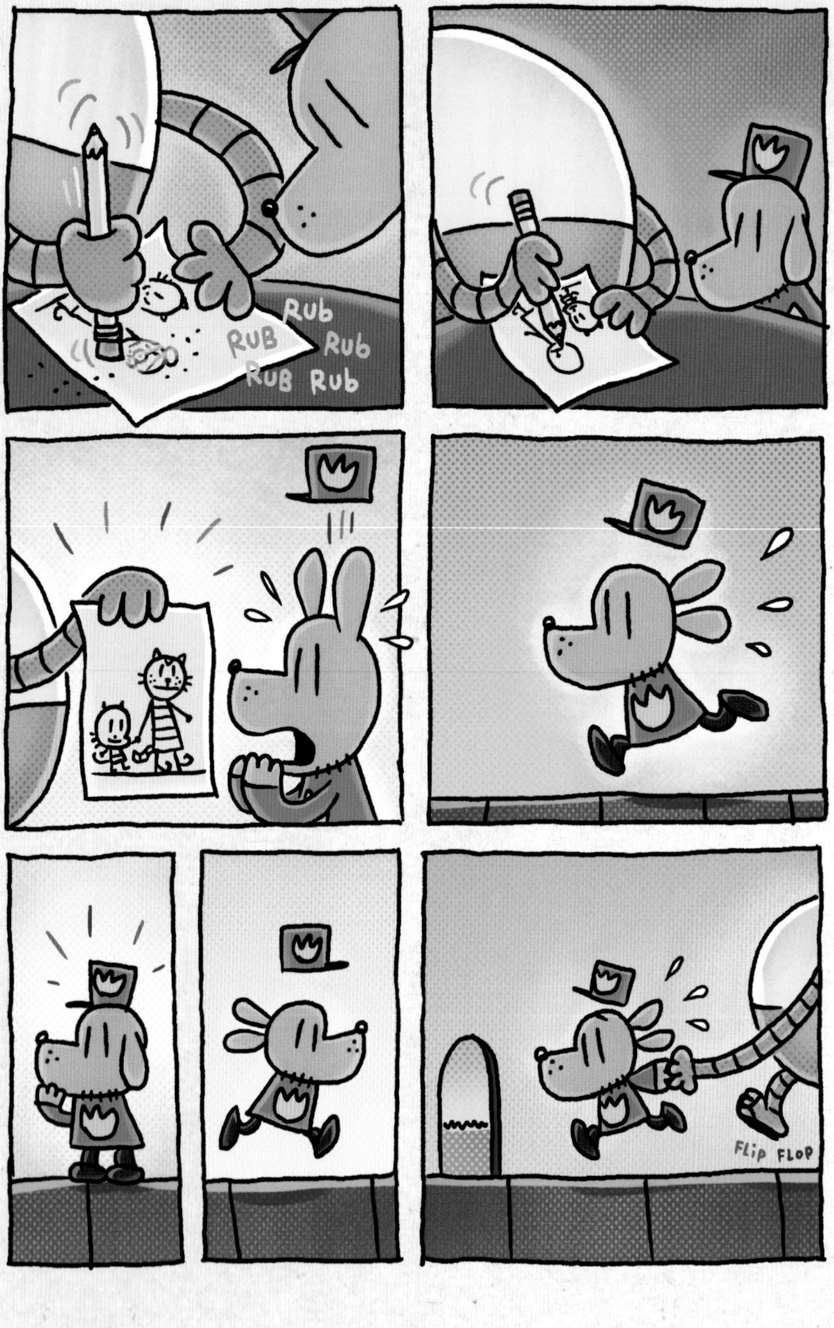
Rub
RUB
Rub
RUB Rub
Flip FLOP

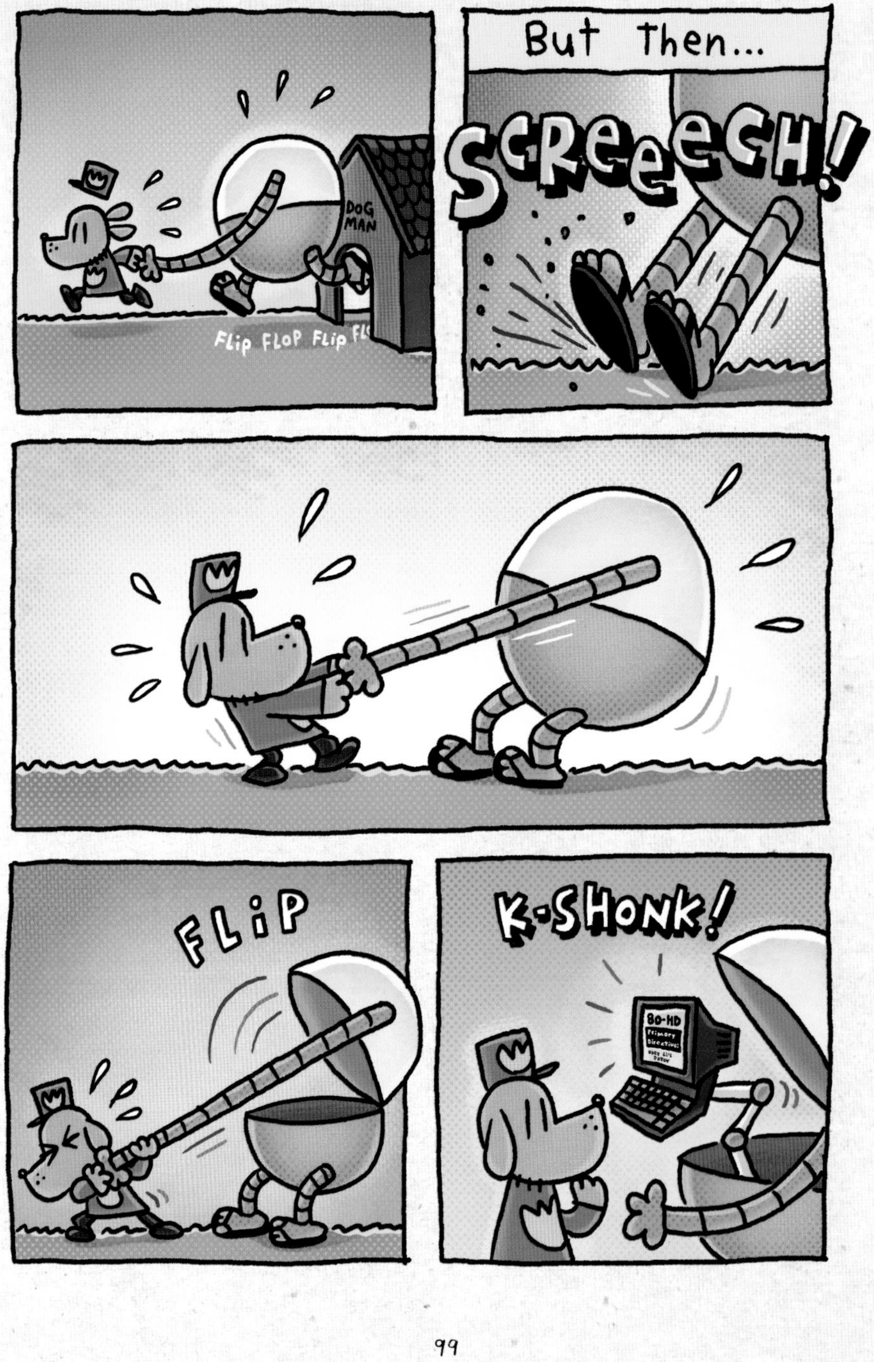
FLIP FLOP FLIP FL
DOG MAN
But Then...
SCREEECH!
FLIP
K-SHONK!
80-HD
Primary Directives

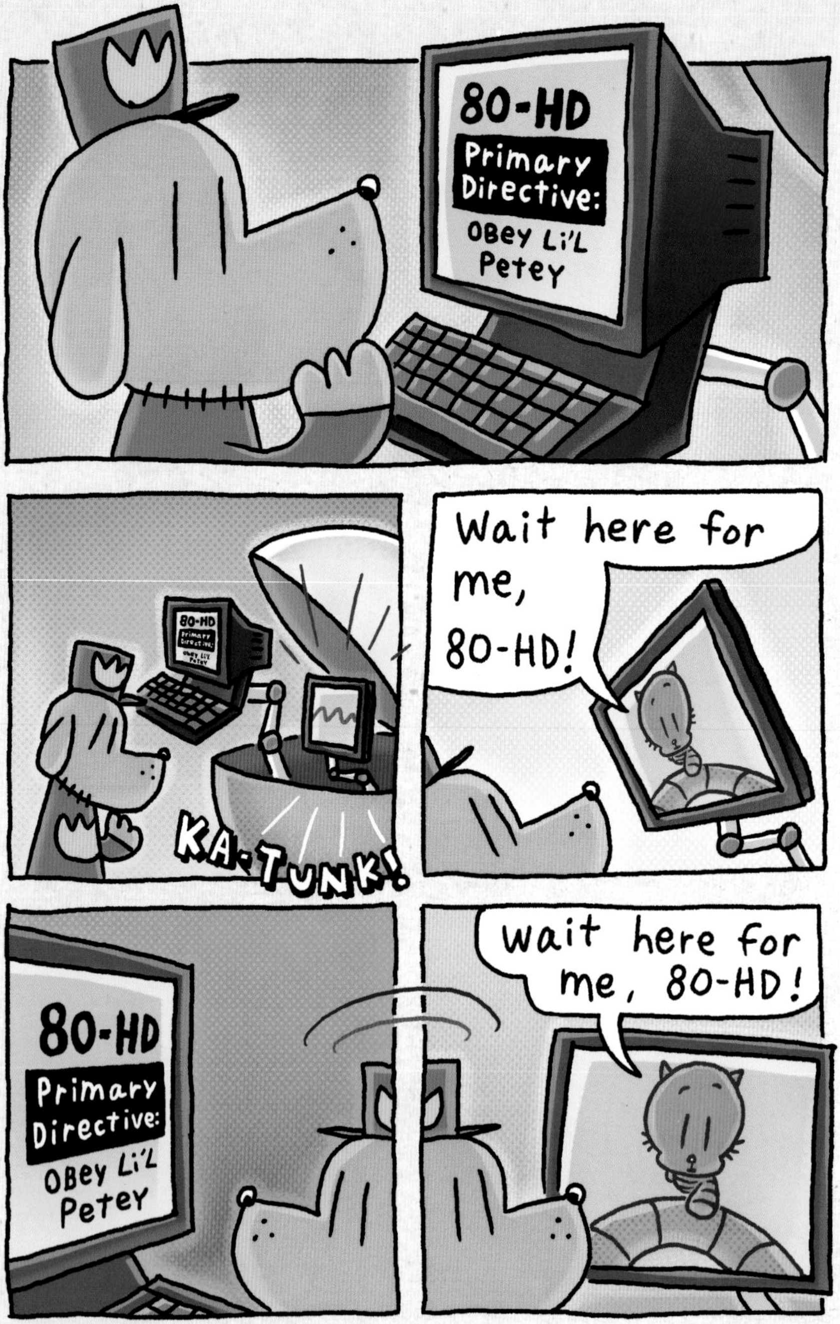
80-HD
Primary Directive:
OBey Li'L Petey
KA-TUNK!
Wait here for me, 80-HD!
80-HD
Primary Directive:
OBey Li'L Petey
wait here for me, 80-HD!

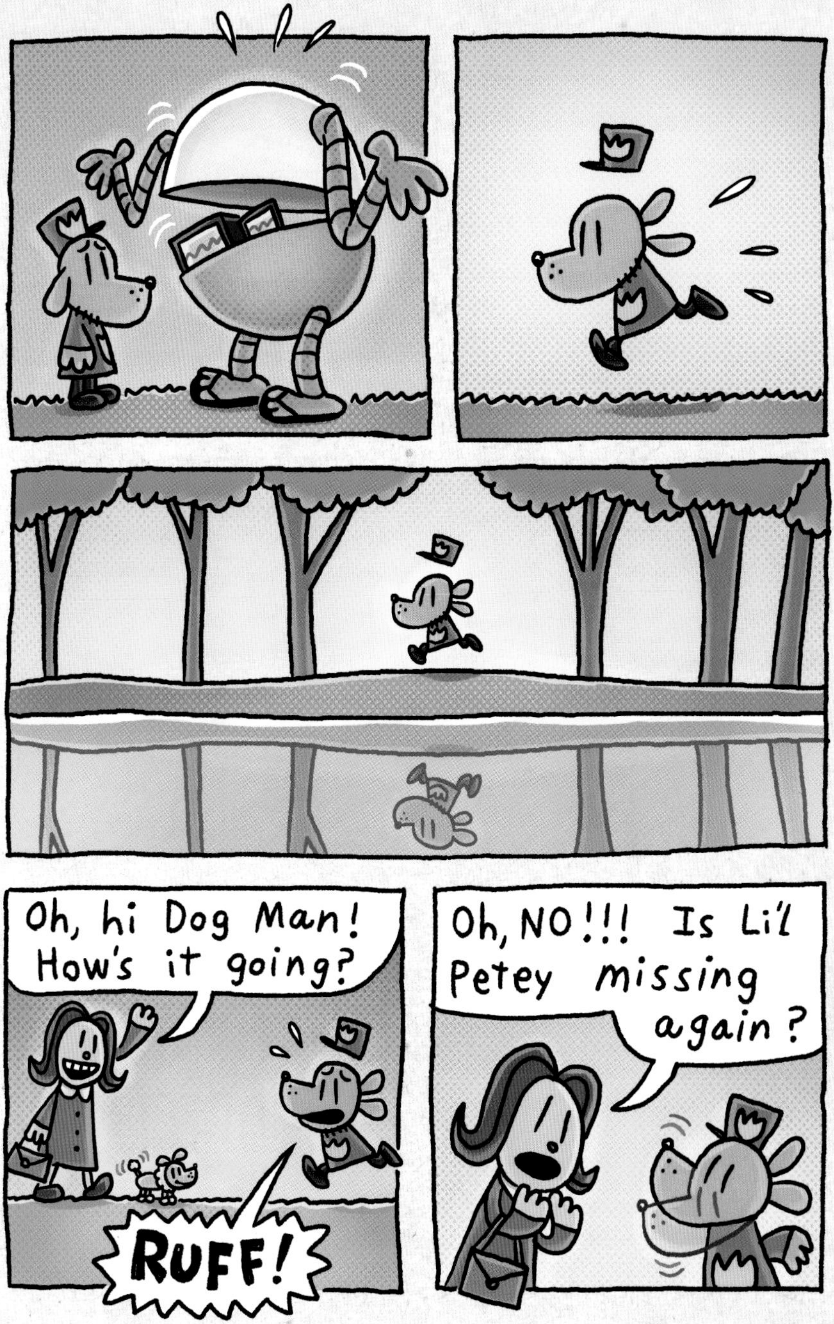
Oh, hi Dog Man! How's it going?
RUFF!
Oh, NO!!! Is Li'l Petey missing again?

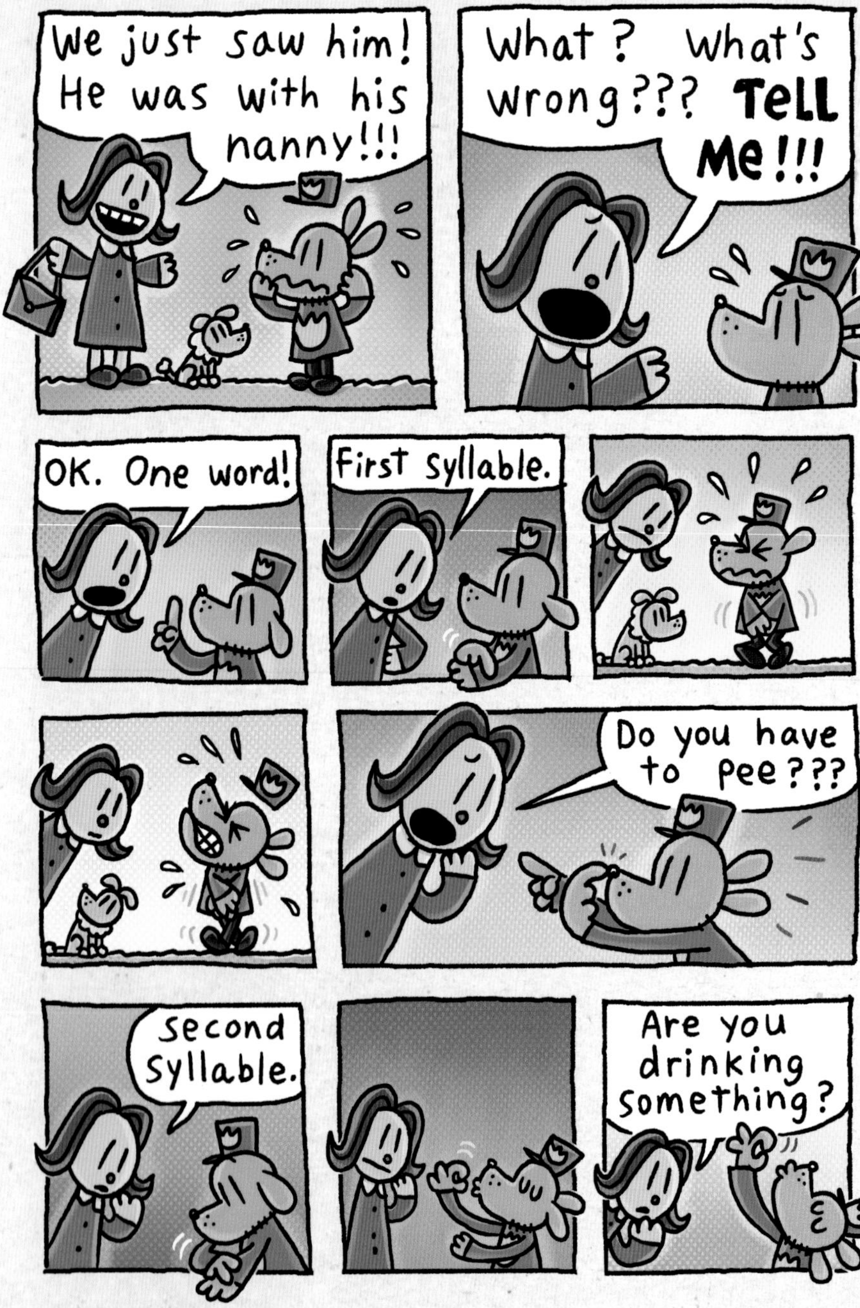
We just saw him! He was with his nanny!!!
What? What's wrong??? TELL ME!!!
OK. One word!
First syllable.
Do you have to pee???
Second syllable.
Are you drinking something?

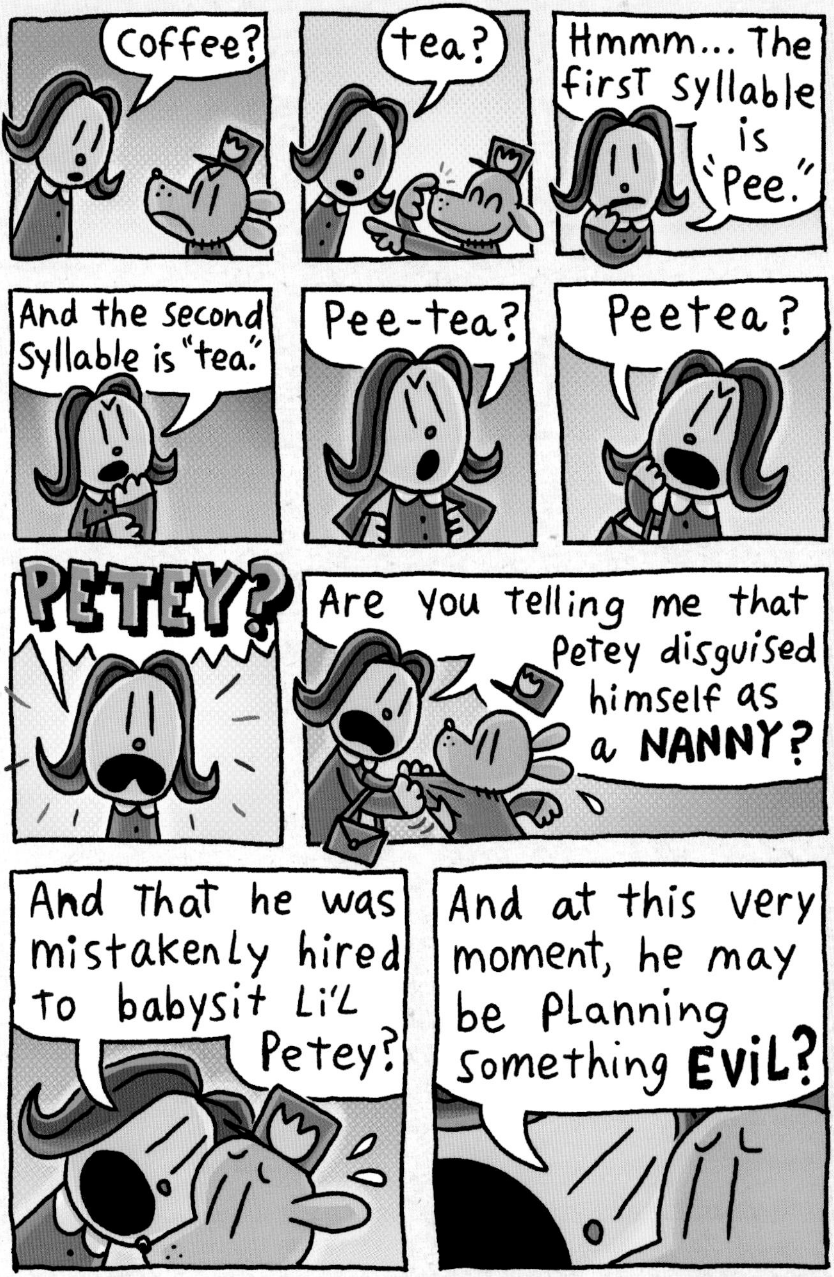
Coffee?
tea?
Hmmm... The first syllable is "Pee."
And the second syllable is "tea."
Pee-tea?
Peetea?
PETEY?
Are you telling me that Petey disguised himself as a NANNY?
And That he was mistakenLy hired to babysit Li'L Petey?
And at this very moment, he may be PLanning Something EViL?

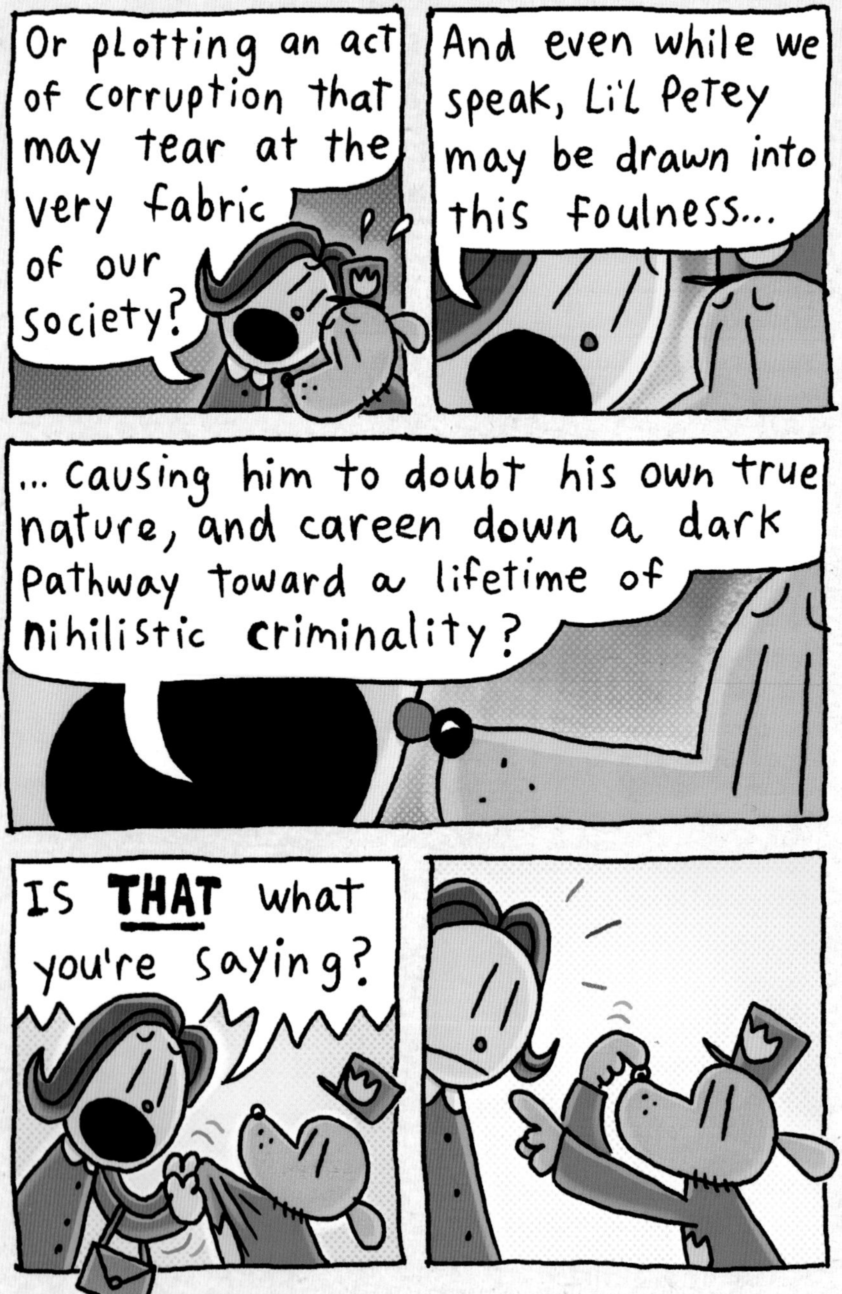
Or plotting an act of corruption that may tear at the very fabric of our society?
And even while we speak, Li'l Petey may be drawn into this foulness...
... causing him to doubt his own true nature, and careen down a dark pathway toward a lifetime of nihilistic criminality?
Is **THAT** what you're saying?

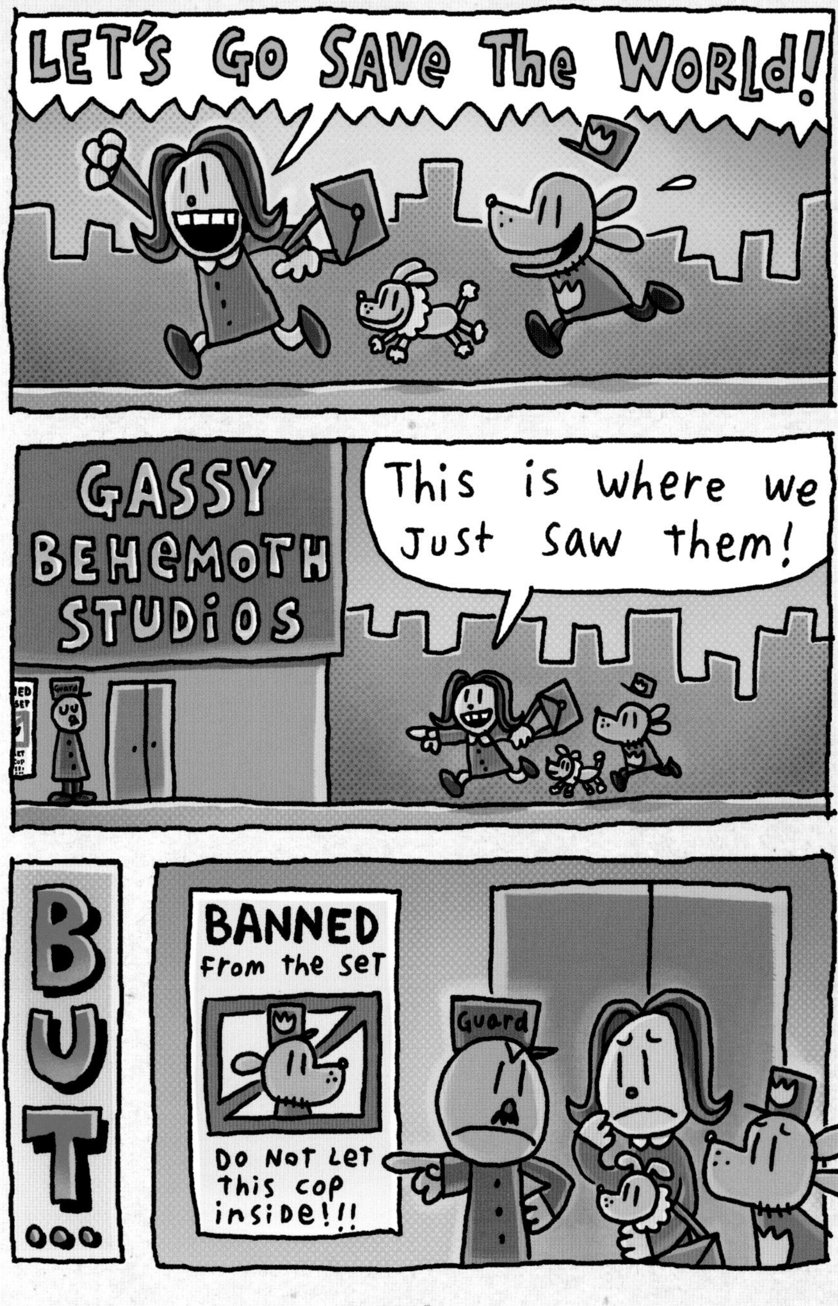
LET'S GO SAVE THE WORLD!
GASSY BEHEMOTH STUDIOS
This is where we just saw them!
BUT...
BANNED From the SET
DO NOT LET this cop inSIDE!!!
Guard

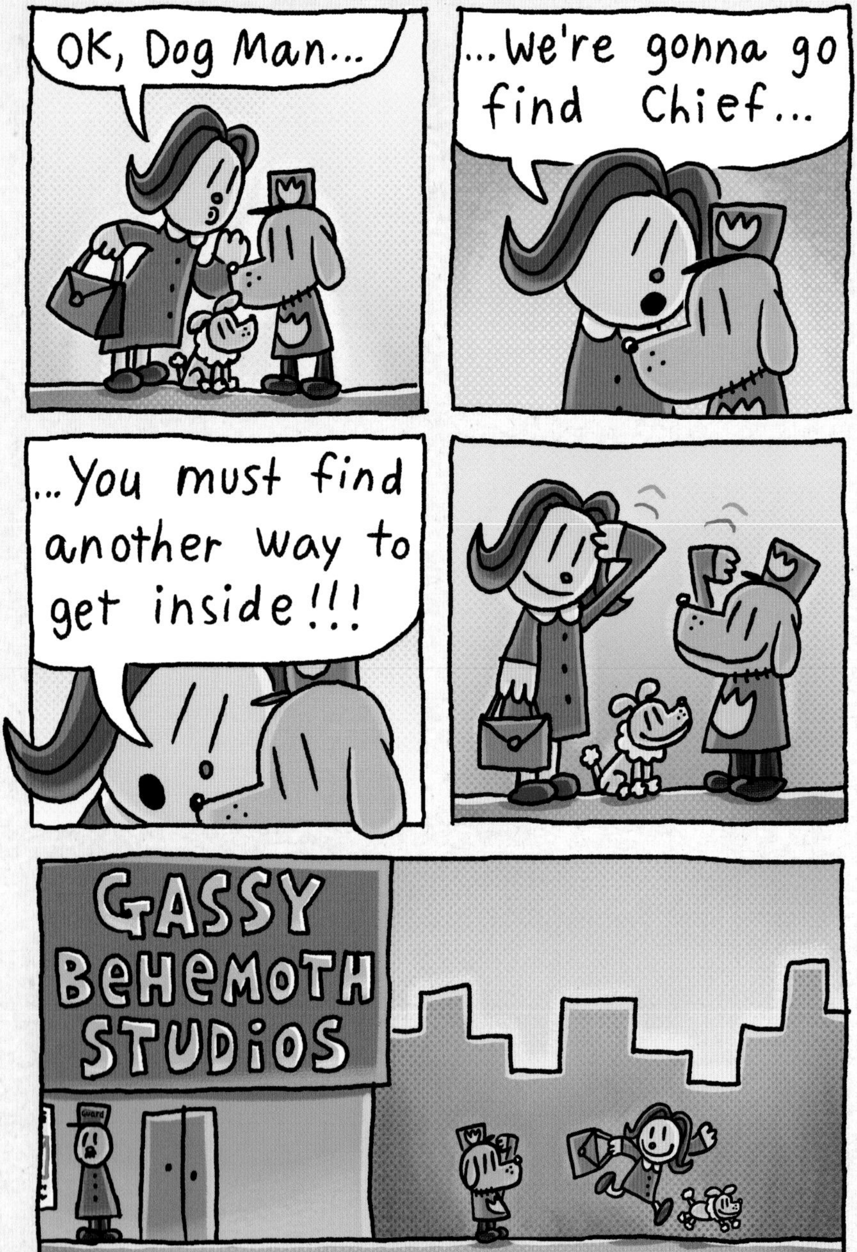
OK, Dog Man...
...We're gonna go find Chief...
...You must find another way to get inside!!!
GASSY BEHEMOTH STUDIOS
Guard

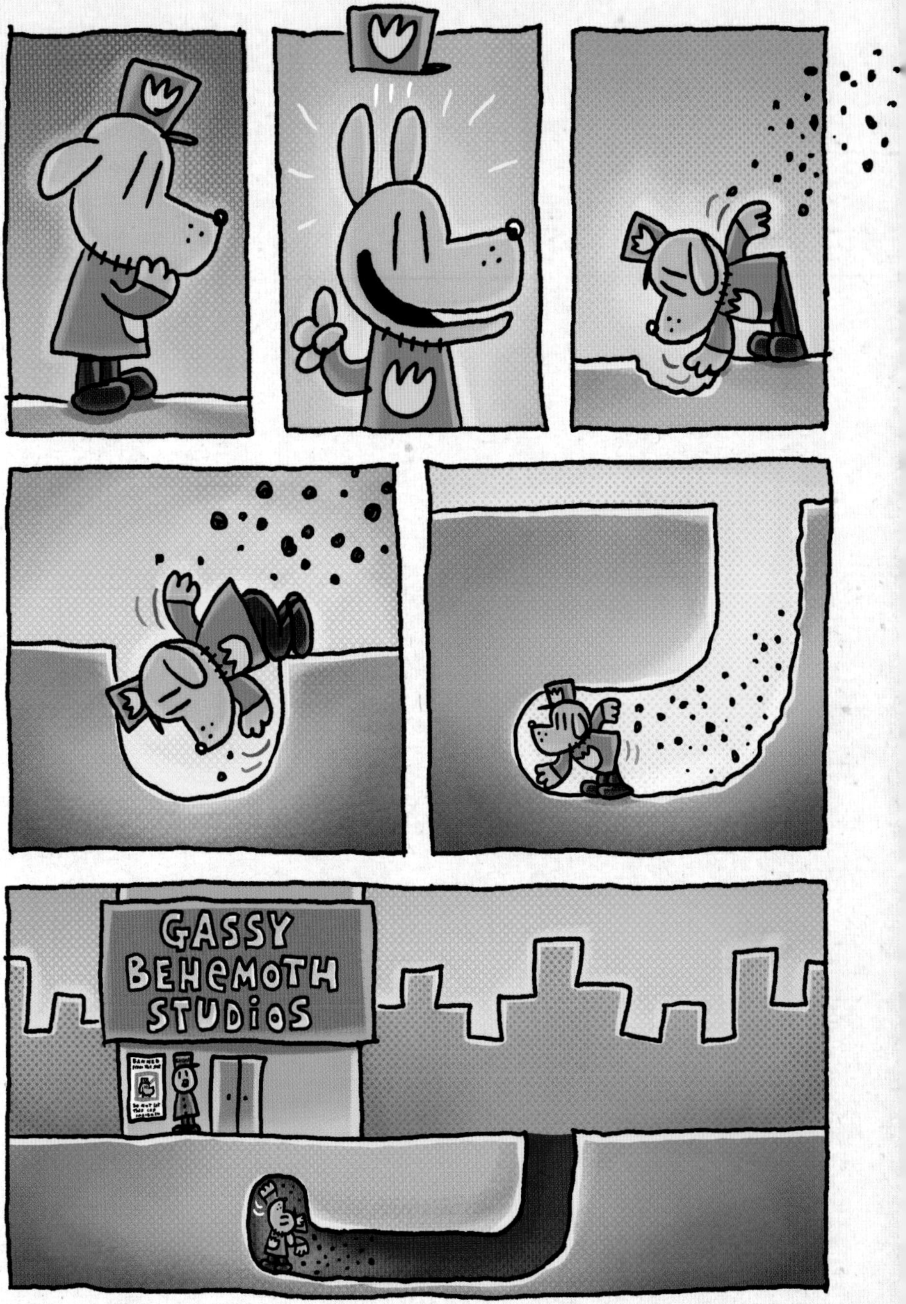

GASSY BEHEMOTH STUDIOS
BANNED

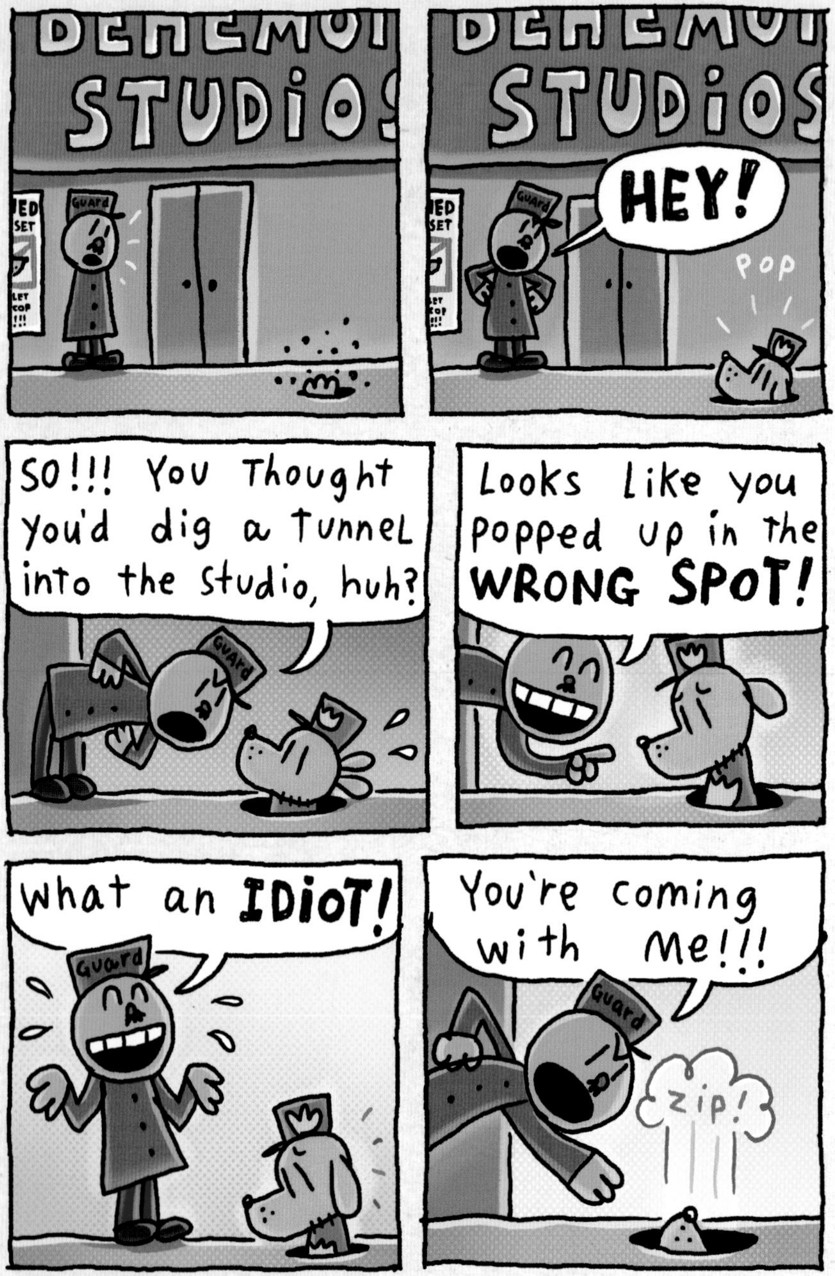
BEHEMOTH STUDIOS
HEY!
POP
SO!!! You Thought you'd dig a Tunnel into the Studio, huh?
Looks like you popped up in the WRONG SPOT!
What an IDIOT!
You're coming with Me!!!
Zip!

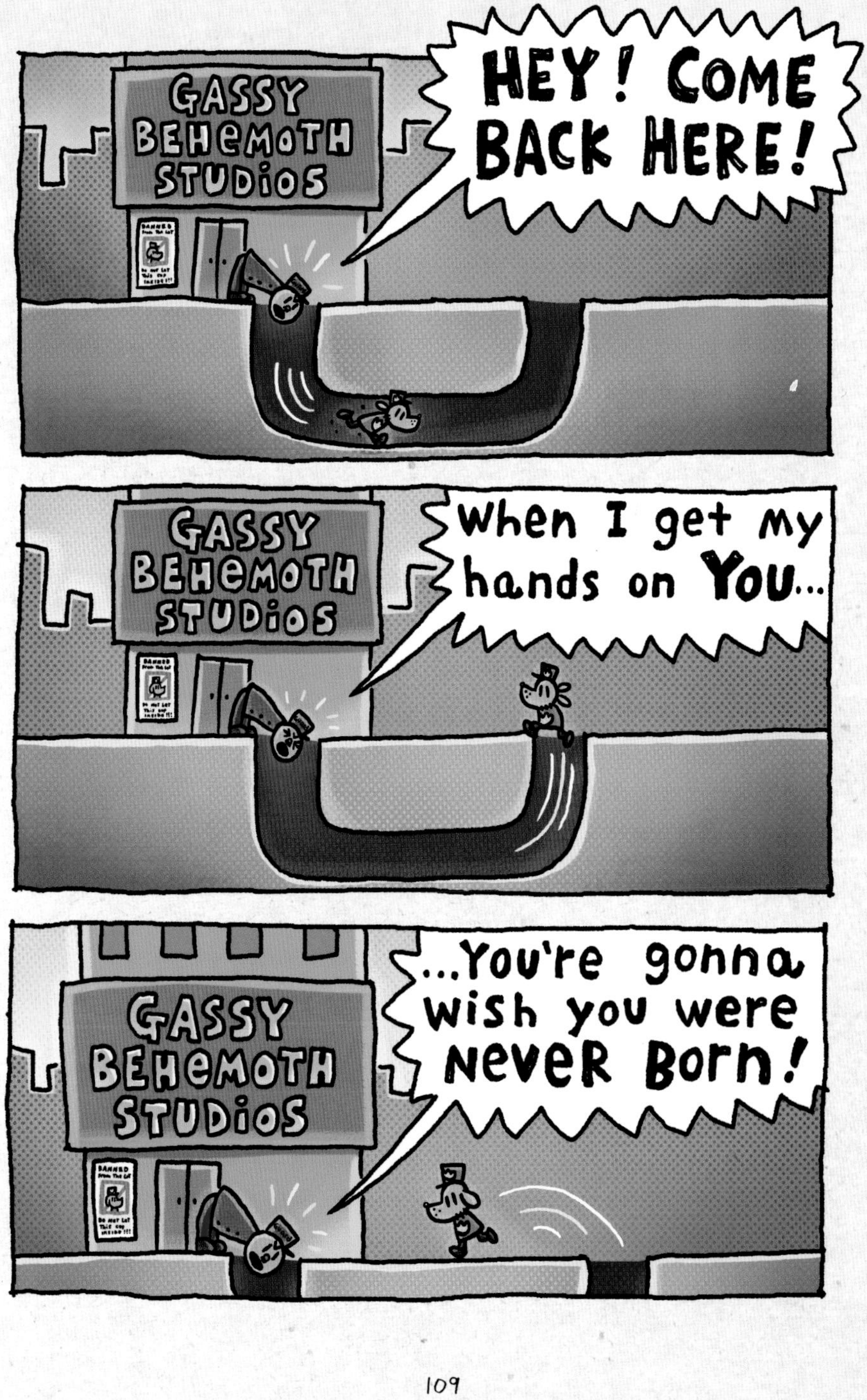
GASSY BEHEMOTH STUDIOS
HEY! COME BACK HERE!
GASSY BEHEMOTH STUDIOS
When I get my hands on YOU...
GASSY BEHEMOTH STUDIOS
...You're gonna wish you were NEVER Born!

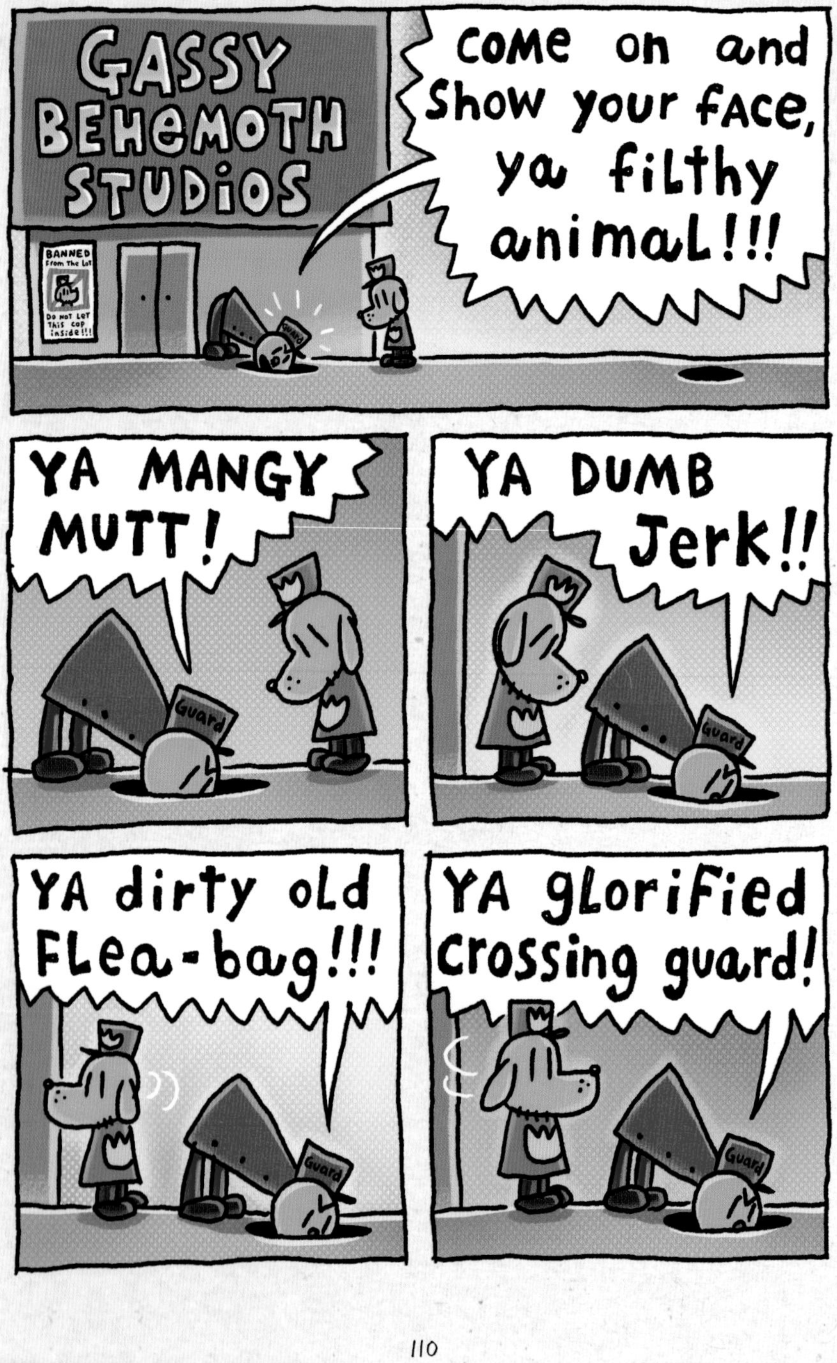
GASSY BEHEMOTH STUDIOS
BANNED From The Lot
Do NOT Let This cop inside!!!
Guard
COME on and Show your FACE, ya filthy animaL!!!
YA MANGY MUTT!
Guard
YA DUMB Jerk!!
Guard
YA dirty oLd FLea-bag!!!
Guard
YA gLorified crossing guard!
Guard

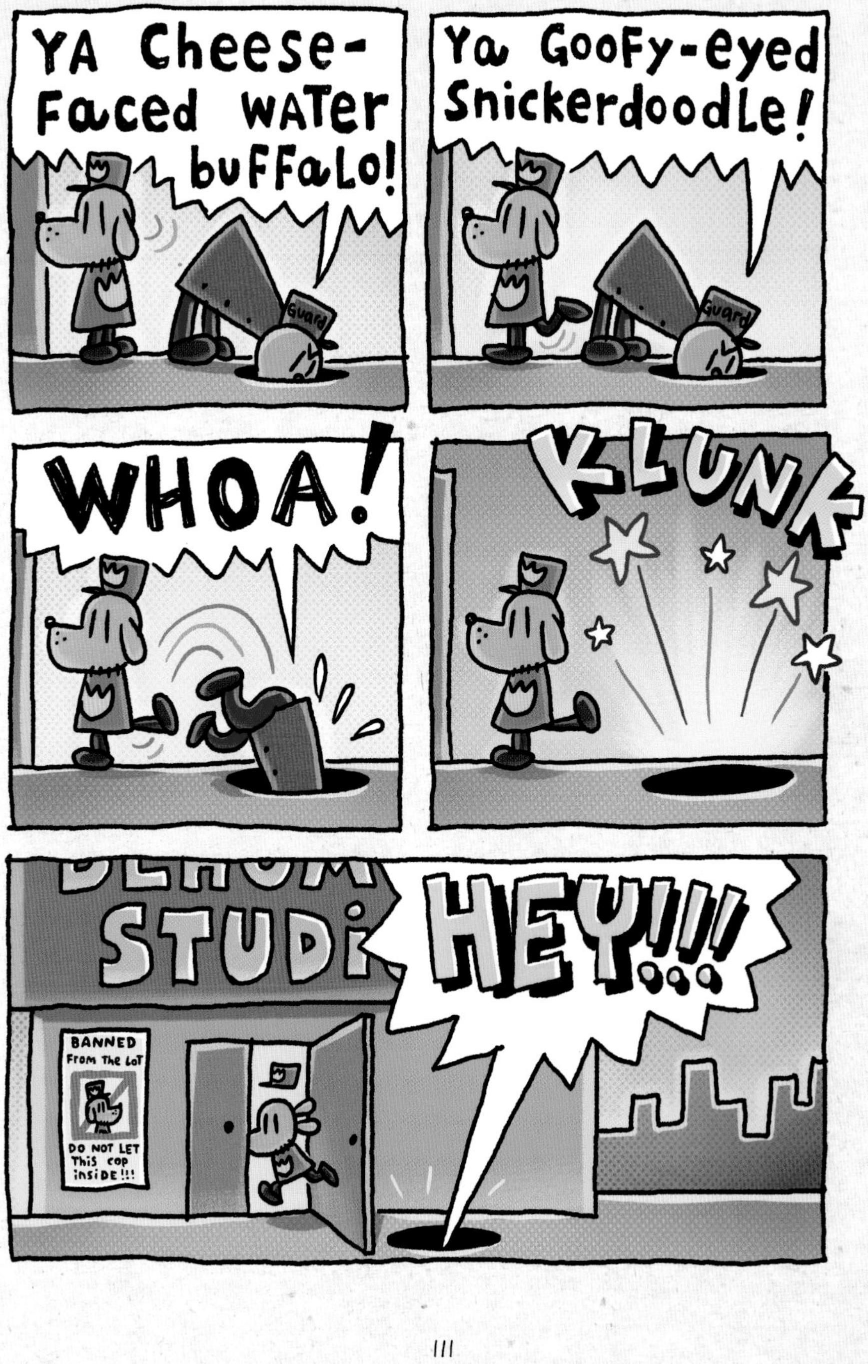
YA Cheese-Faced WATer buFFaLo!
Guard
Ya GooFy-eyed SnickerdoodLe!
Guard
WHOA!
KLUNK
STUDI
HEY!!!!
BANNED From The LoT
DO NOT LET This cop inSIDE!!!

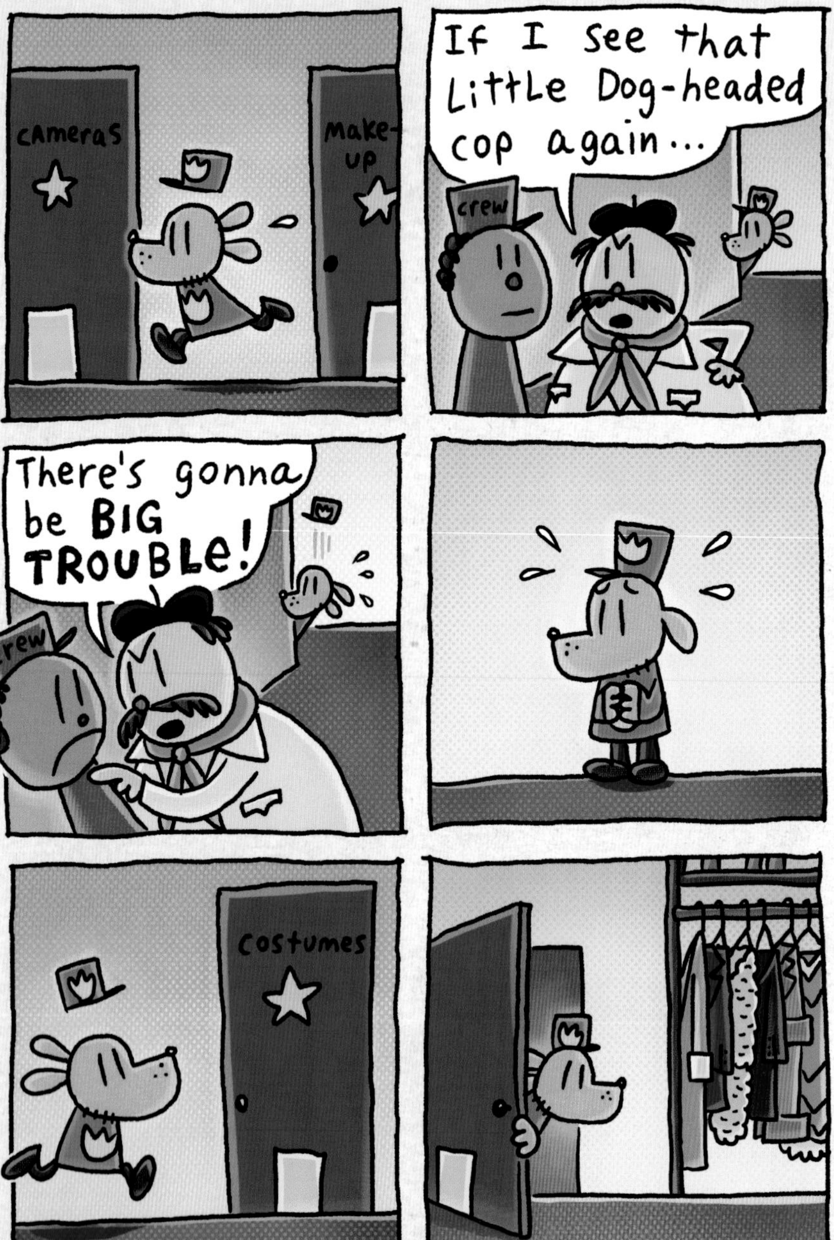

Cameras
Make-up
If I see that Little Dog-headed cop again...
crew
There's gonna be **BIG TROUBLE!**
crew
Costumes

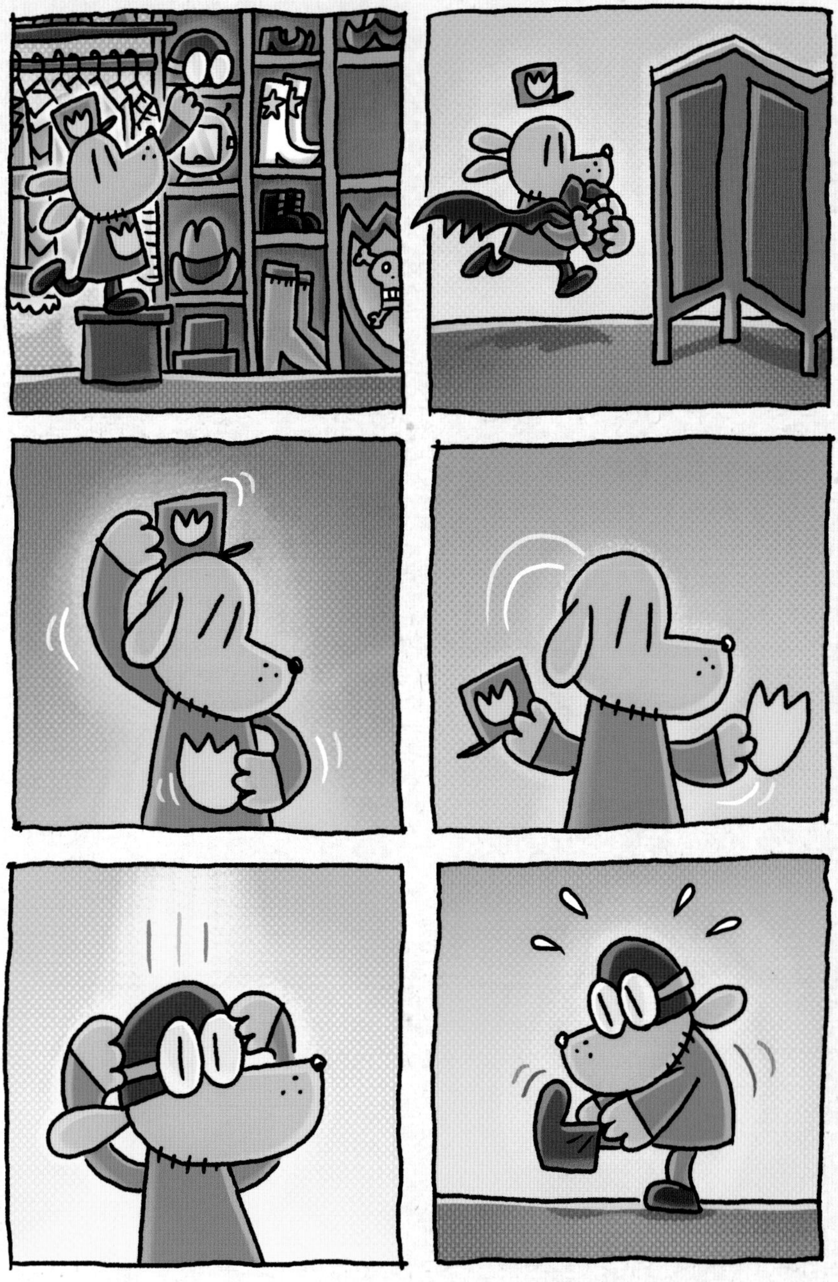

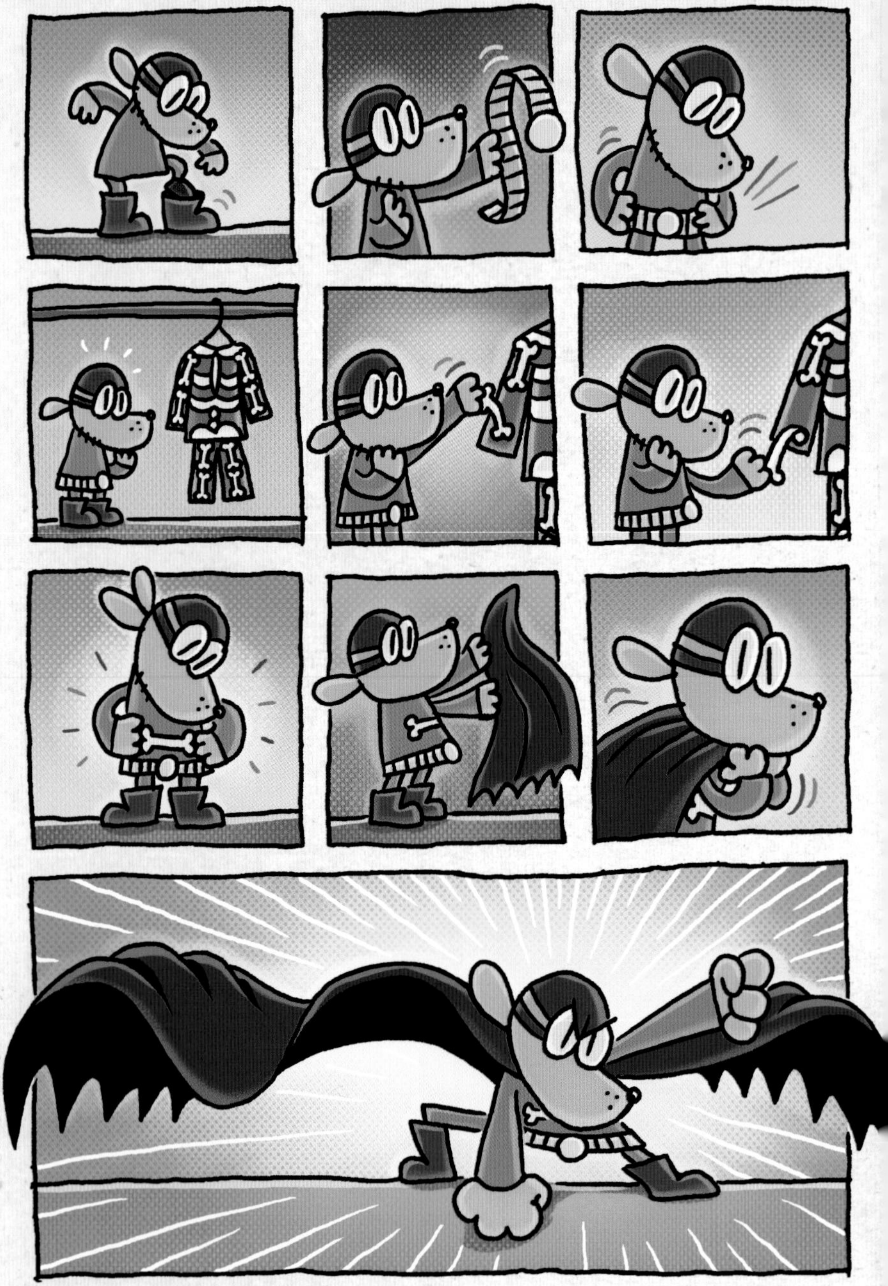

Chapter 7
A Buncha Stuff That Happened Next

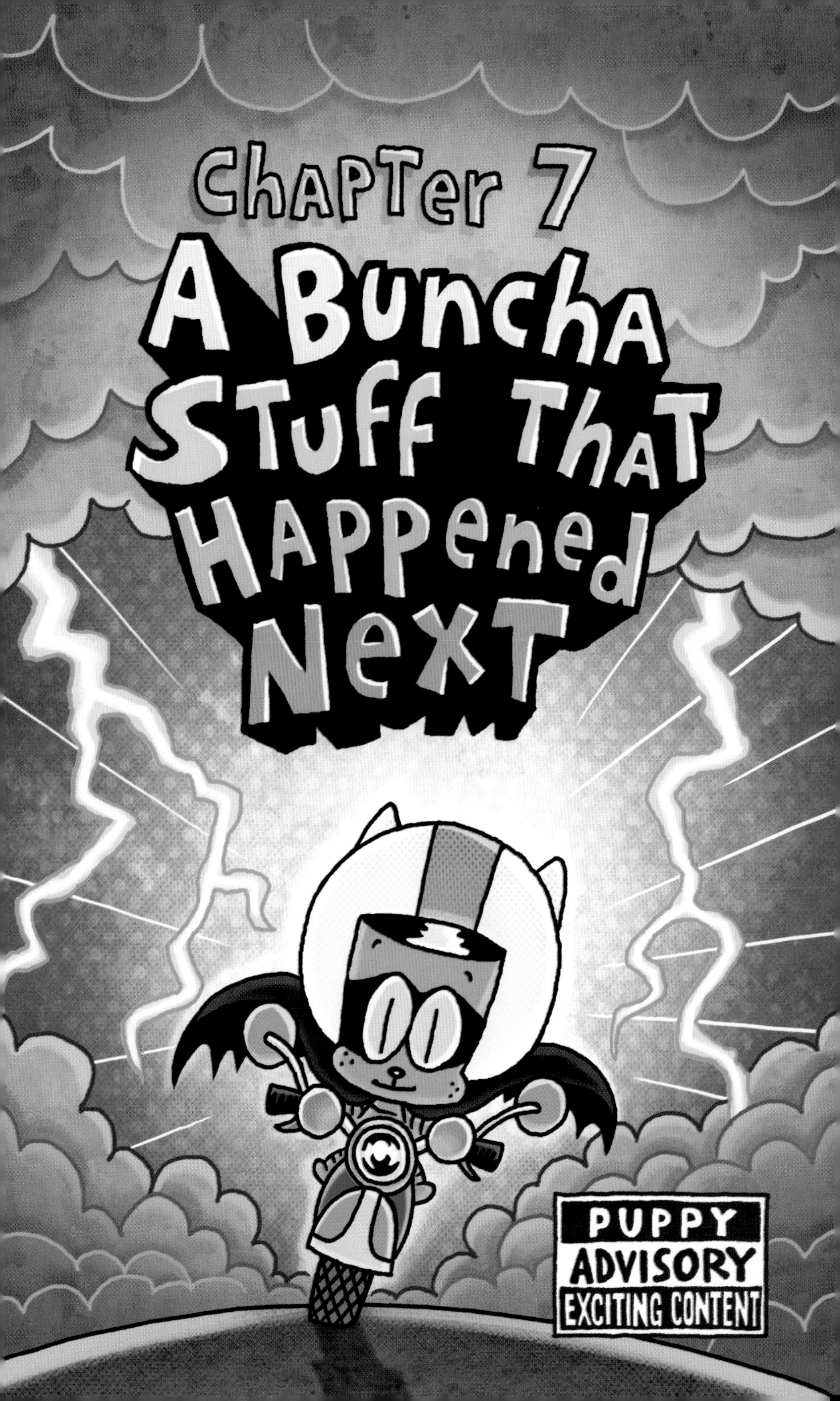
PUPPY
ADVISORY
EXCITING CONTENT

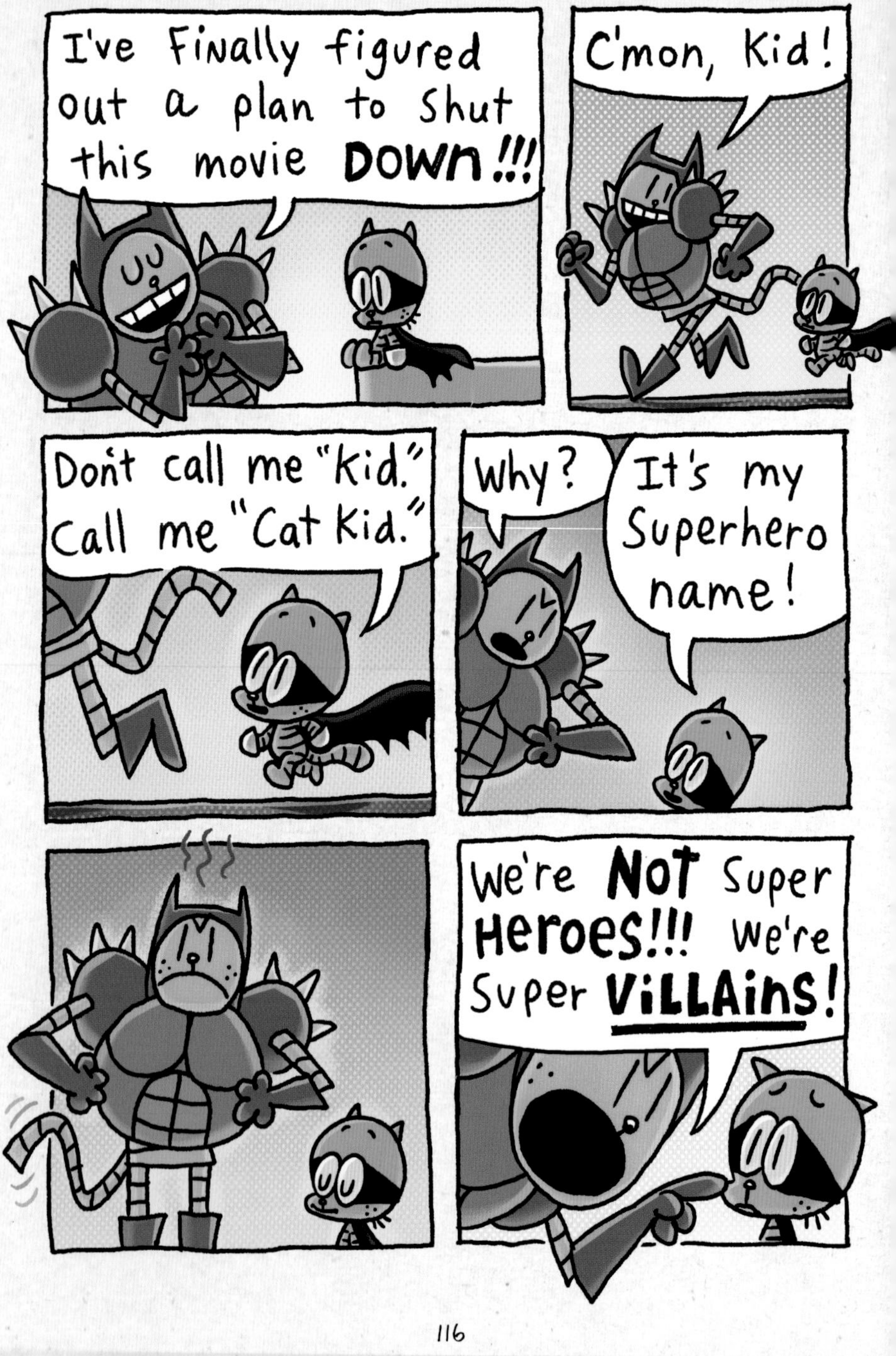
I've Finally figured out a plan to Shut this movie **DOWN**!!!
C'mon, Kid!
Don't call me "kid." Call me "Cat Kid."
Why?
It's my Superhero name!
We're **NOT** Super **HEROES**!!! We're Super **VILLAINS**!

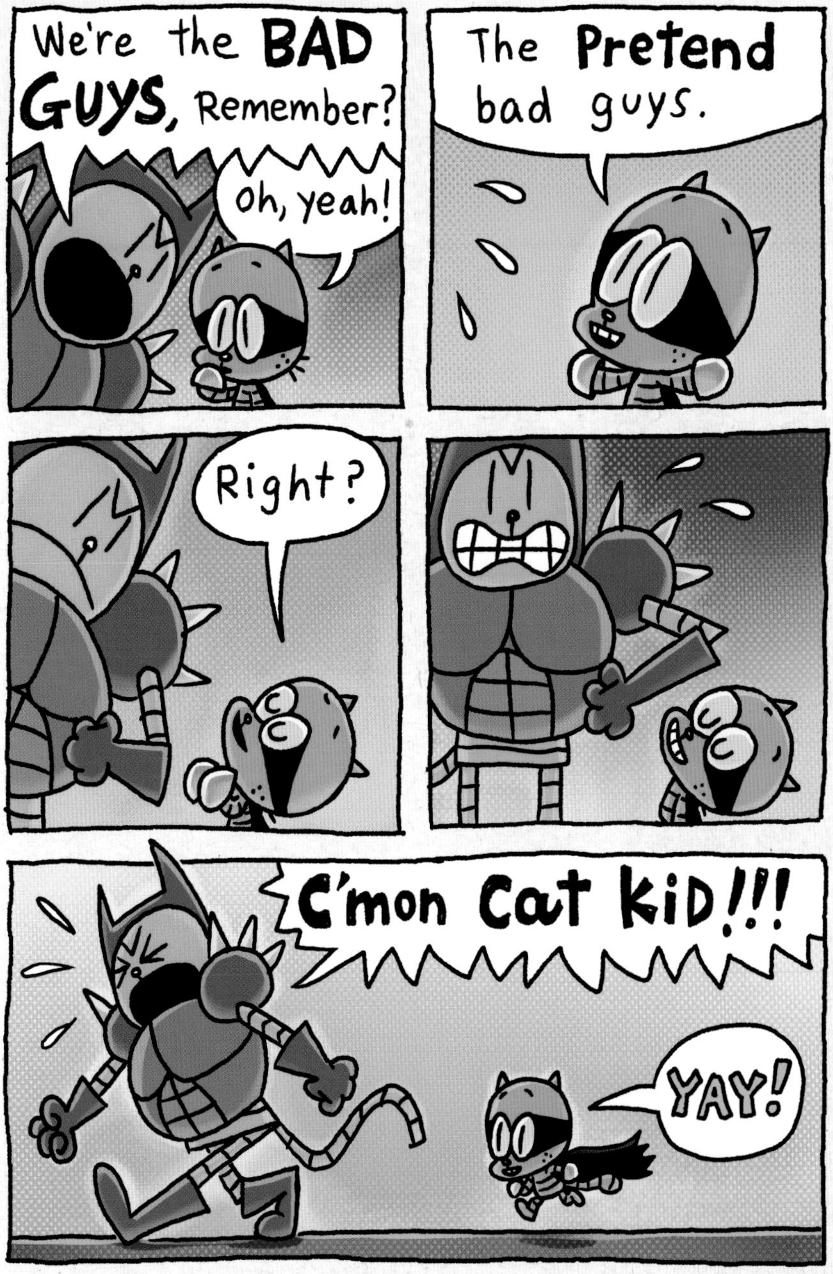
We're the BAD GUYS, Remember?
Oh, yeah!
The Pretend bad guys.
Right?
C'mon Cat KiD!!!
YAY!

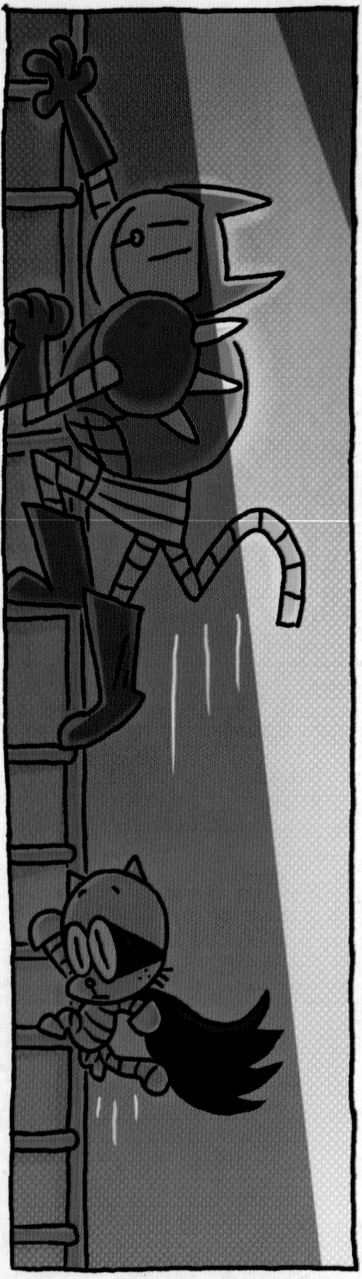

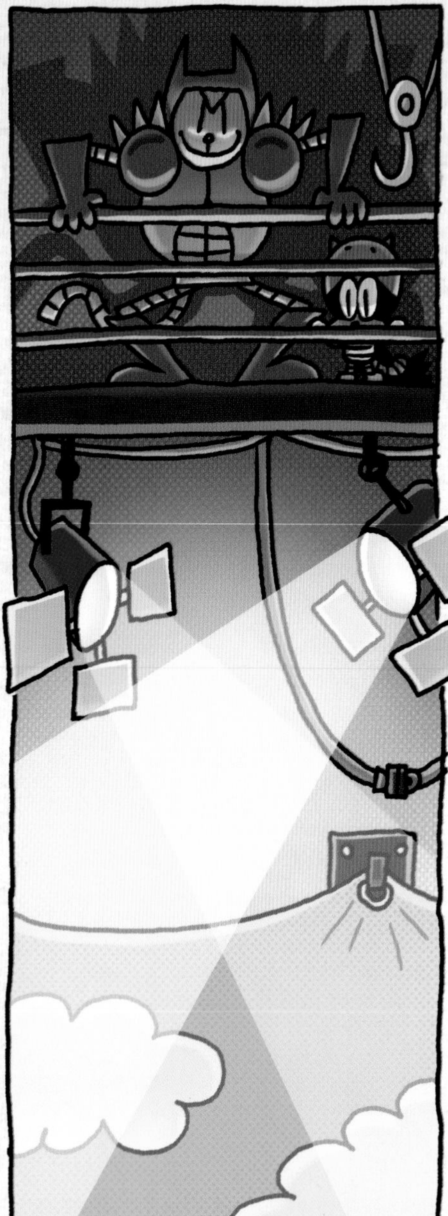

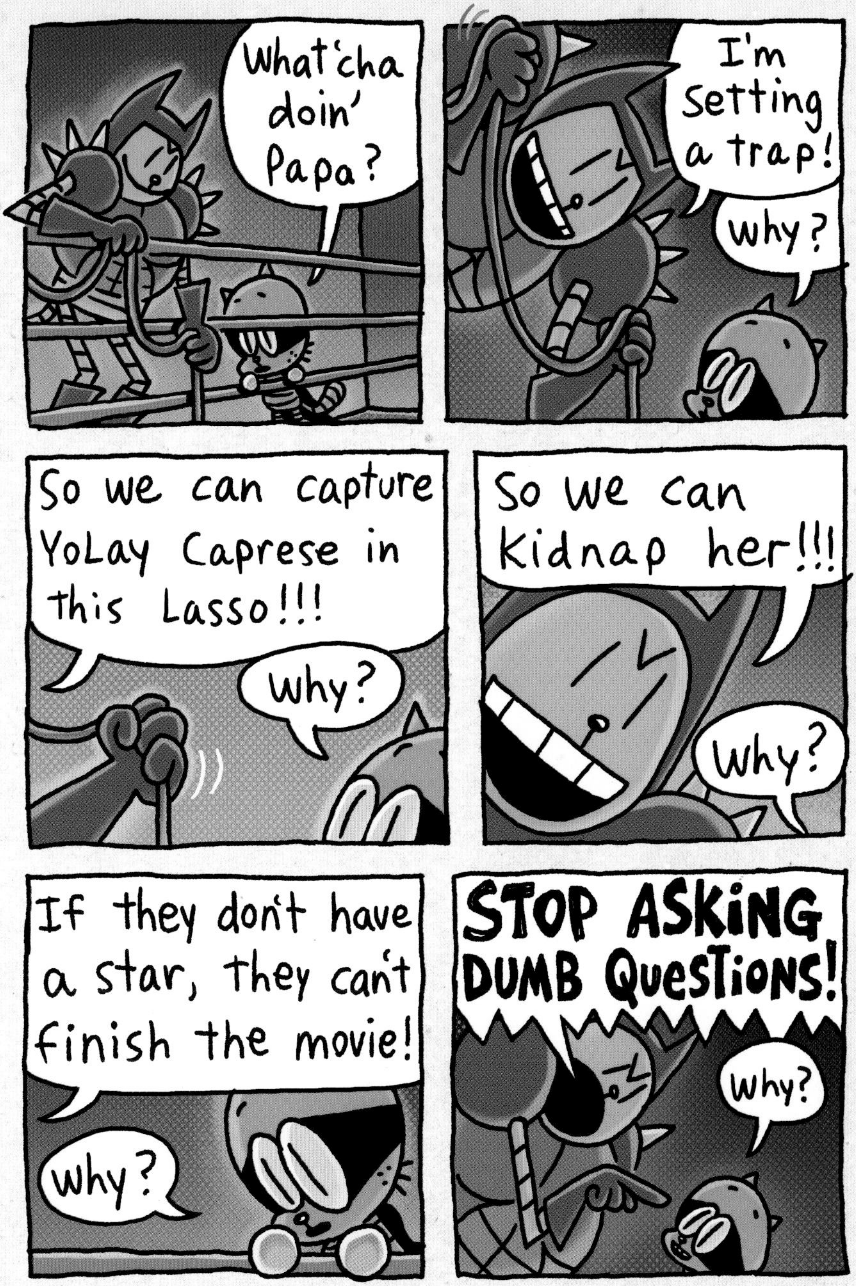
What'cha doin' Papa?
I'm setting a trap!
Why?
So we can capture YoLay Caprese in this Lasso!!!
Why?
So we can Kidnap her!!!
Why?
If they don't have a star, they can't finish the movie!
Why?
STOP ASKING DUMB QUESTIONS!
Why?

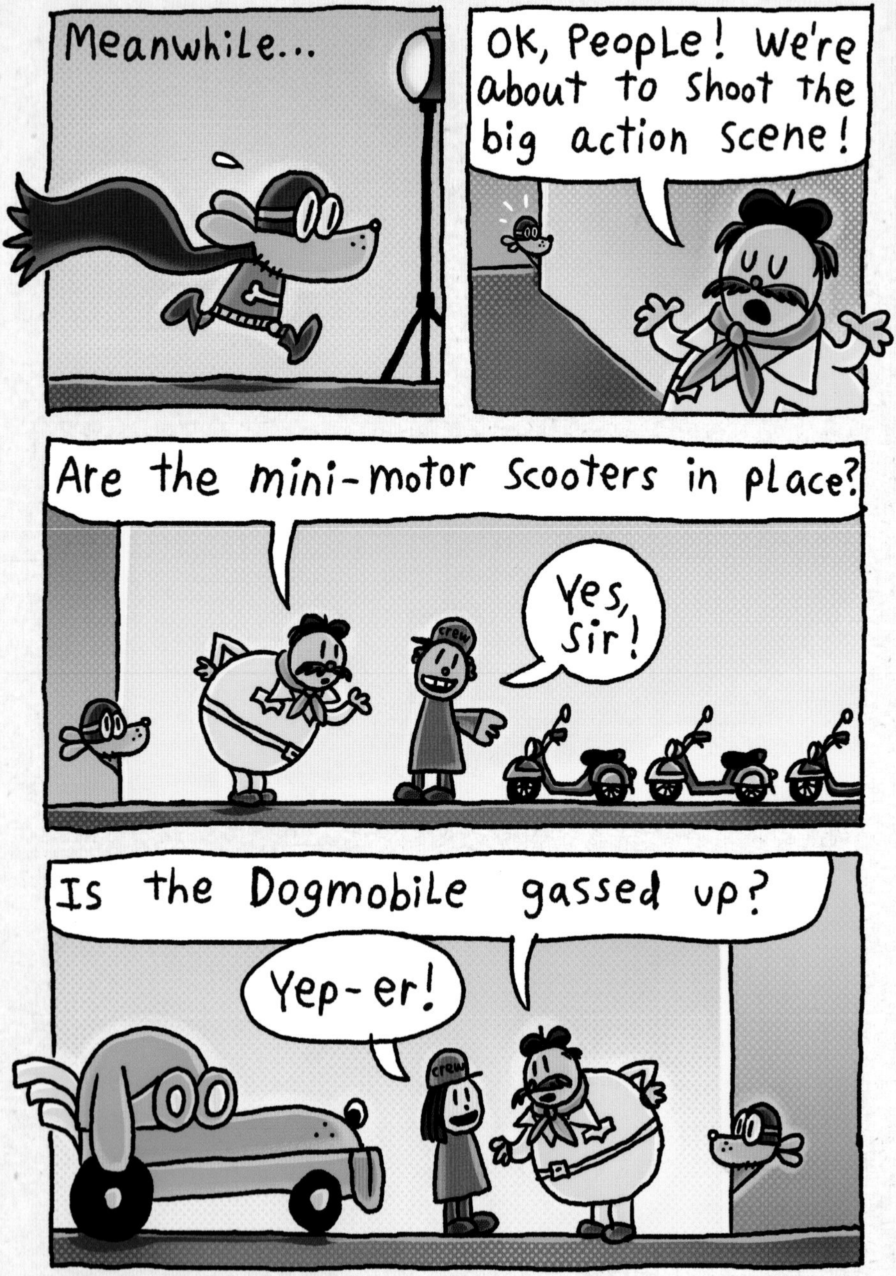
Meanwhile...
OK, People! We're about to Shoot the big action Scene!
Are the mini-motor Scooters in place?
Yes, Sir!
Is the Dogmobile gassed up?
Yep-er!
crew
crew

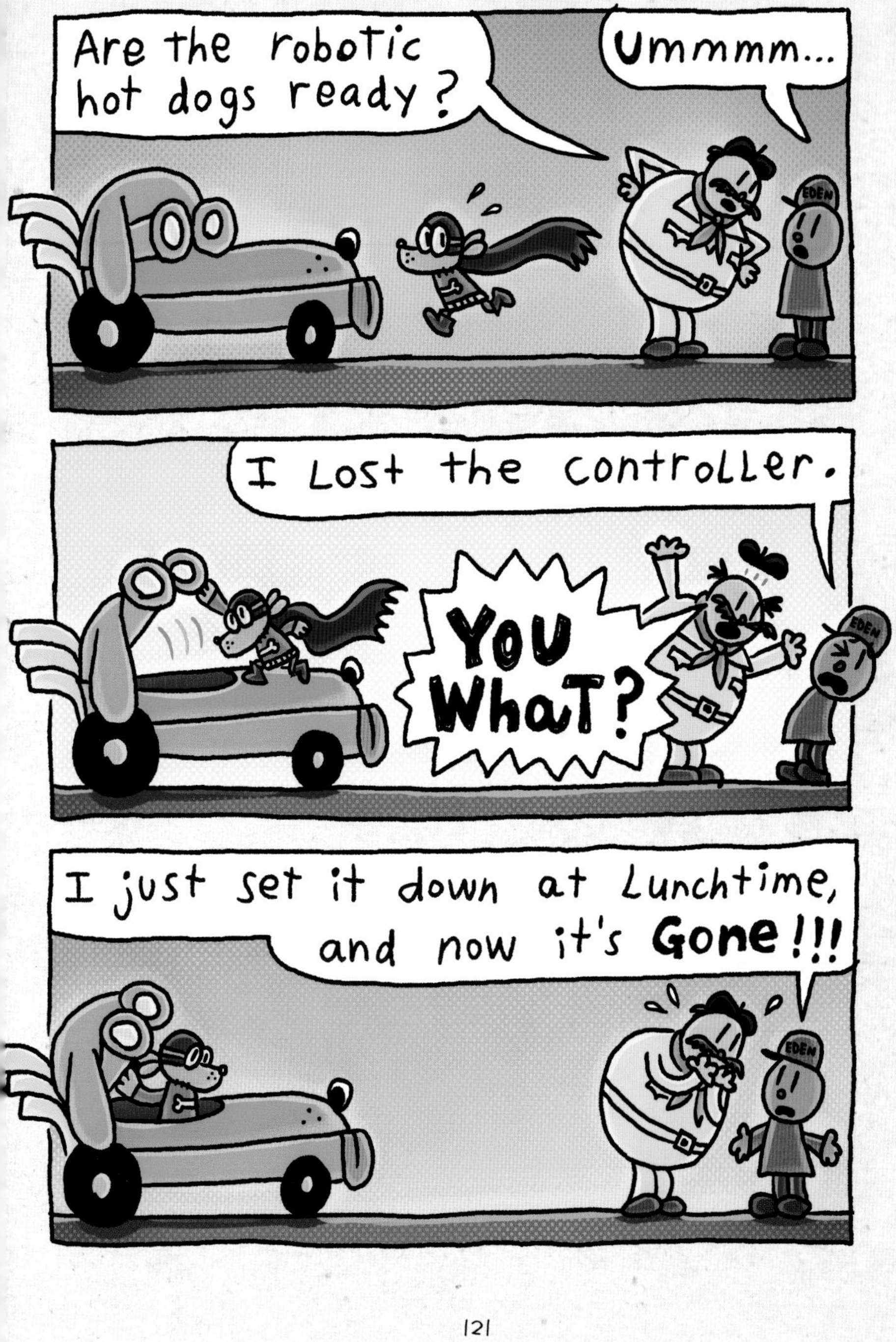
Are the robotic hot dogs ready?
Ummmm...
EDEN
I Lost the controller.
YOU WhaT?
EDEN
I just set it down at Lunchtime, and now it's **Gone**!!!
EDEN

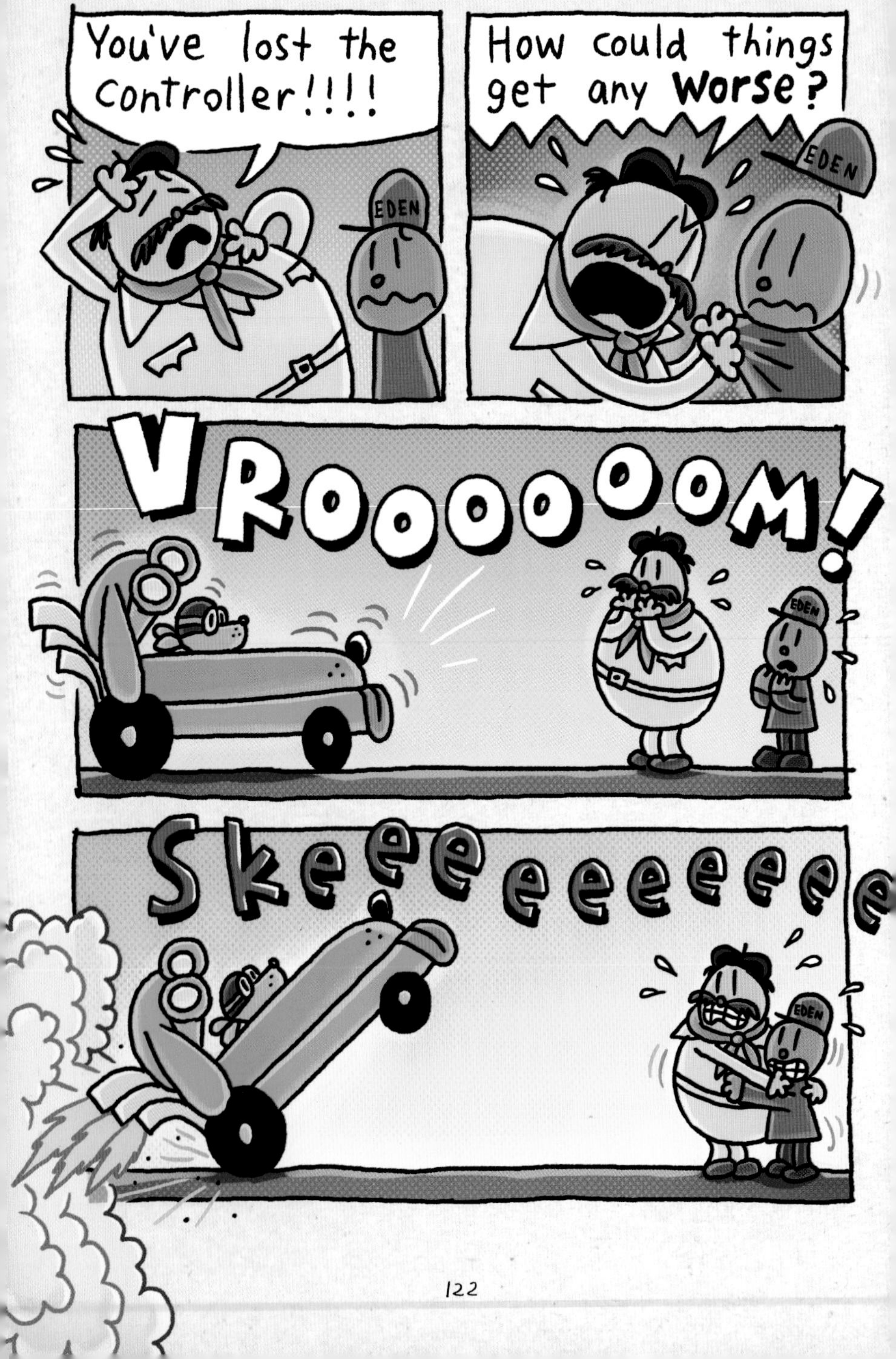

You've lost the controller!!!!
How could things get any **worse**?
EDEN
VROOOOOOM!
SKEEEEEEEEE

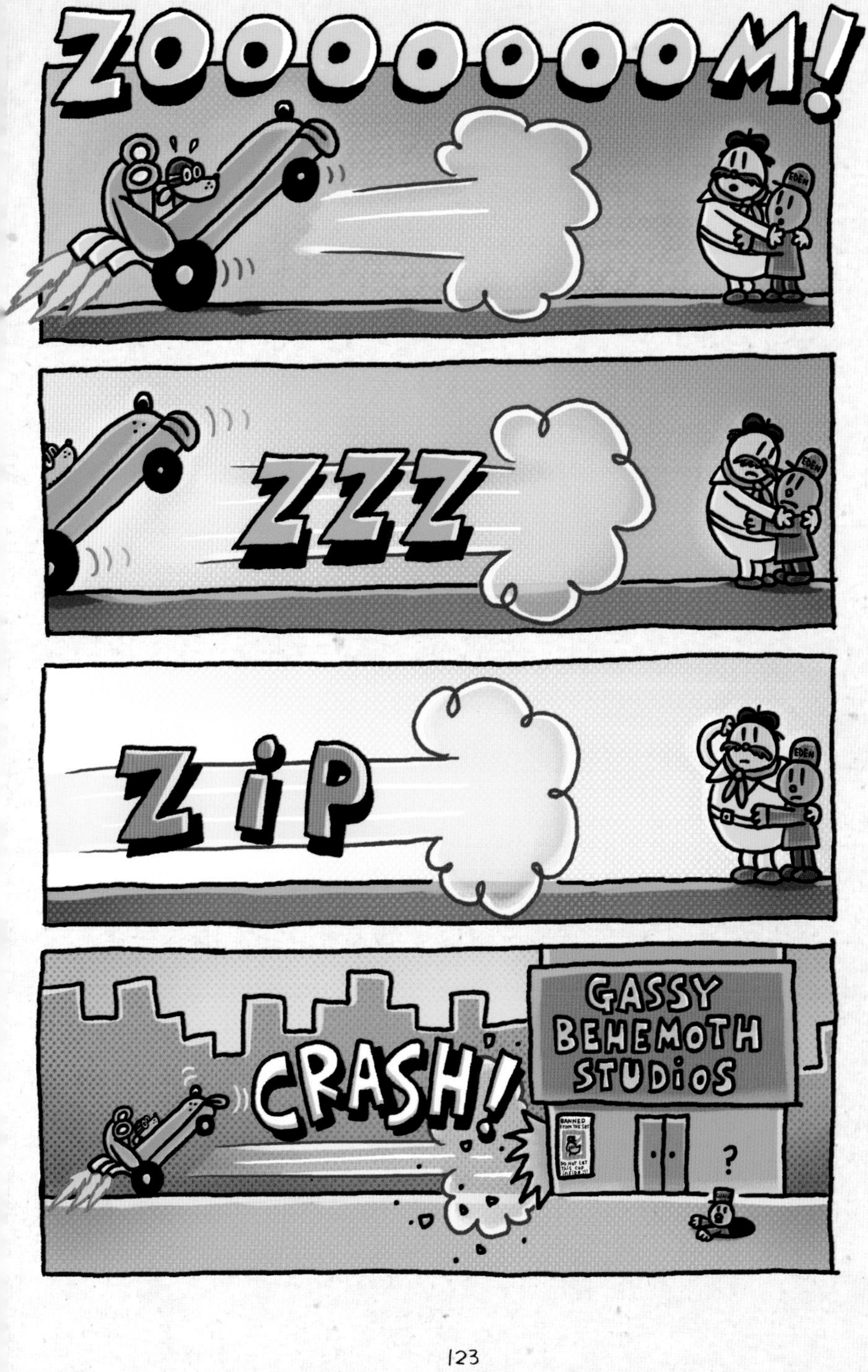
ZOOOOOOOM!
EDEN
ZZZ
EDEN
ZiP
EDEN
GASSY BEHEMOTH STUDIOS
CRASH!
?

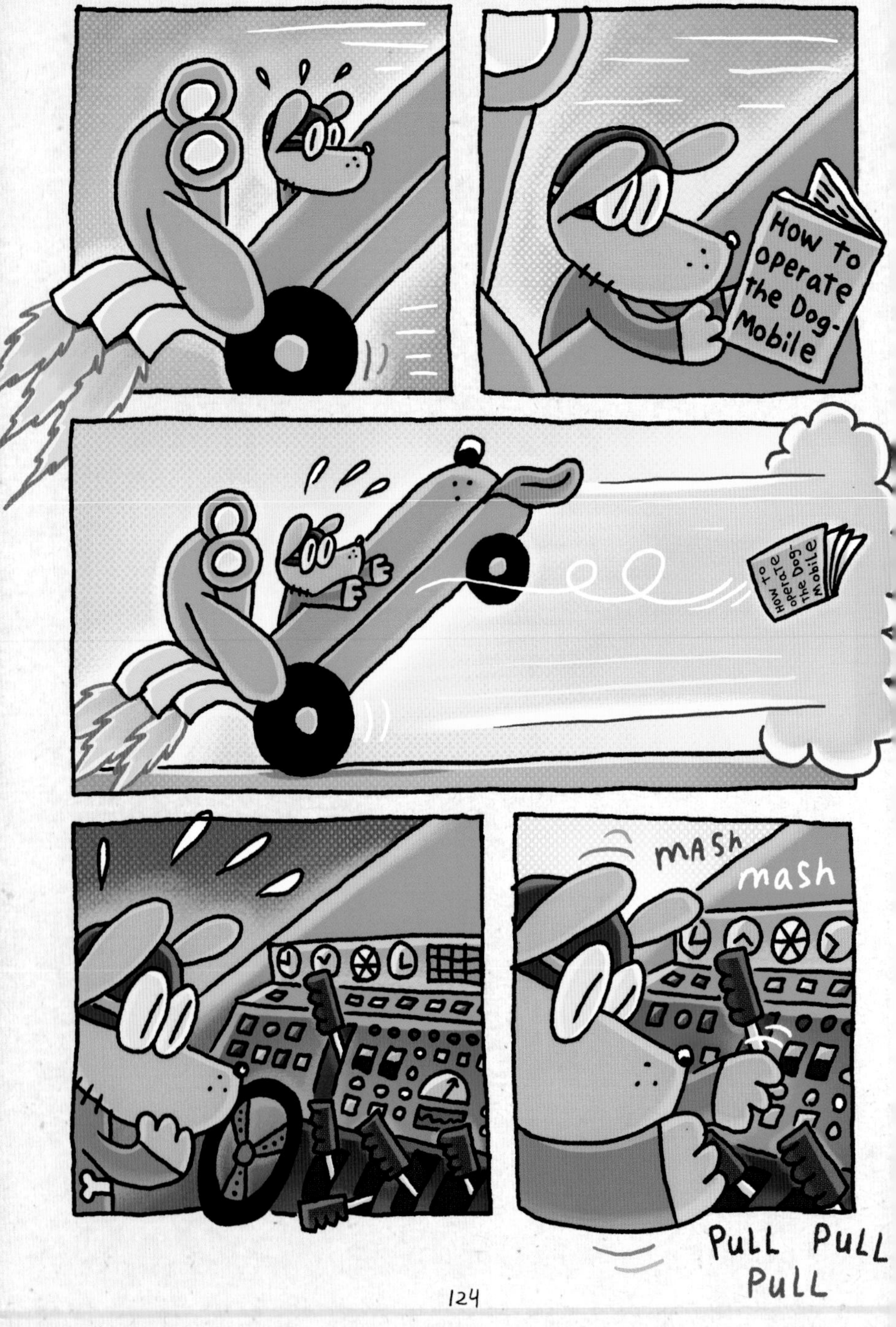
How to operate the Dog-Mobile
How to operate the Dog-Mobile
MASh
mash
PULL PULL
PULL

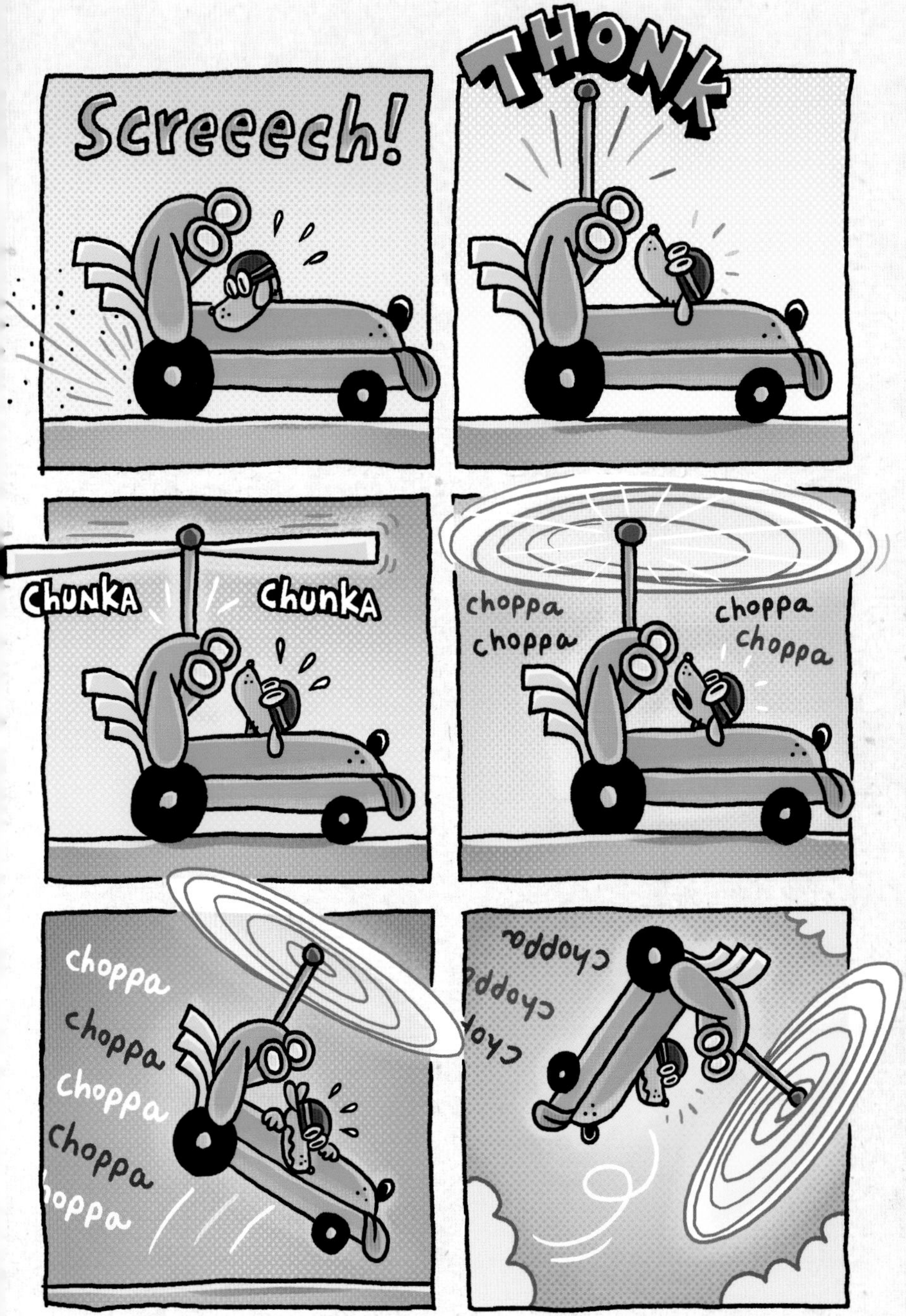
Screeech!
THONK
CHUNKA
CHUNKA
choppa
choppa
choppa
choppa
choppa
choppa
choppa
choppa
choppa
oppa
choppa
choppa
chop

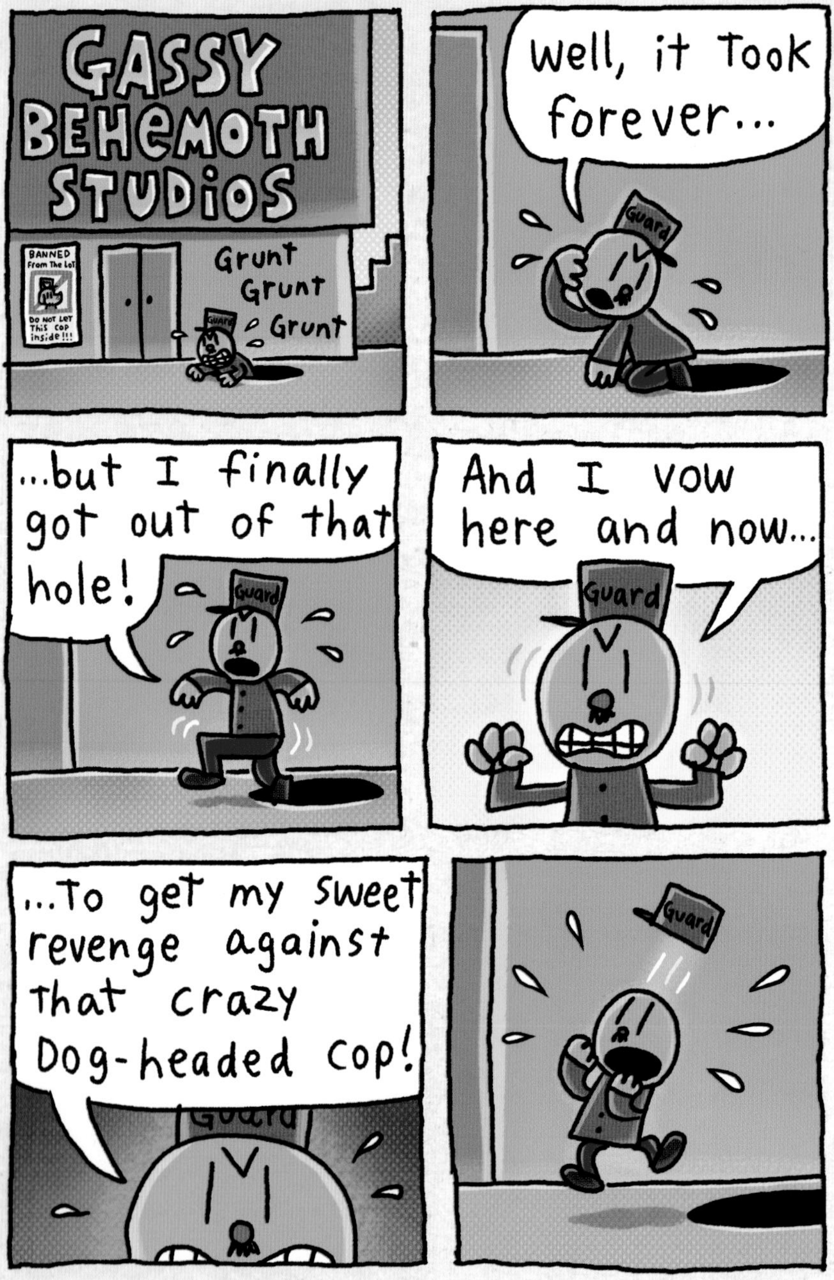
GASSY BEHEMOTH STUDIOS
BANNED From The Lot
DO NOT LET THIS COP inside!!!
Guard
Grunt
Grunt
Grunt
Well, it Took forever...
Guard
...but I finally got out of that hole!
Guard
And I vow here and now...
Guard
...To get my sweet revenge against That crazy Dog-headed cop!
Guard

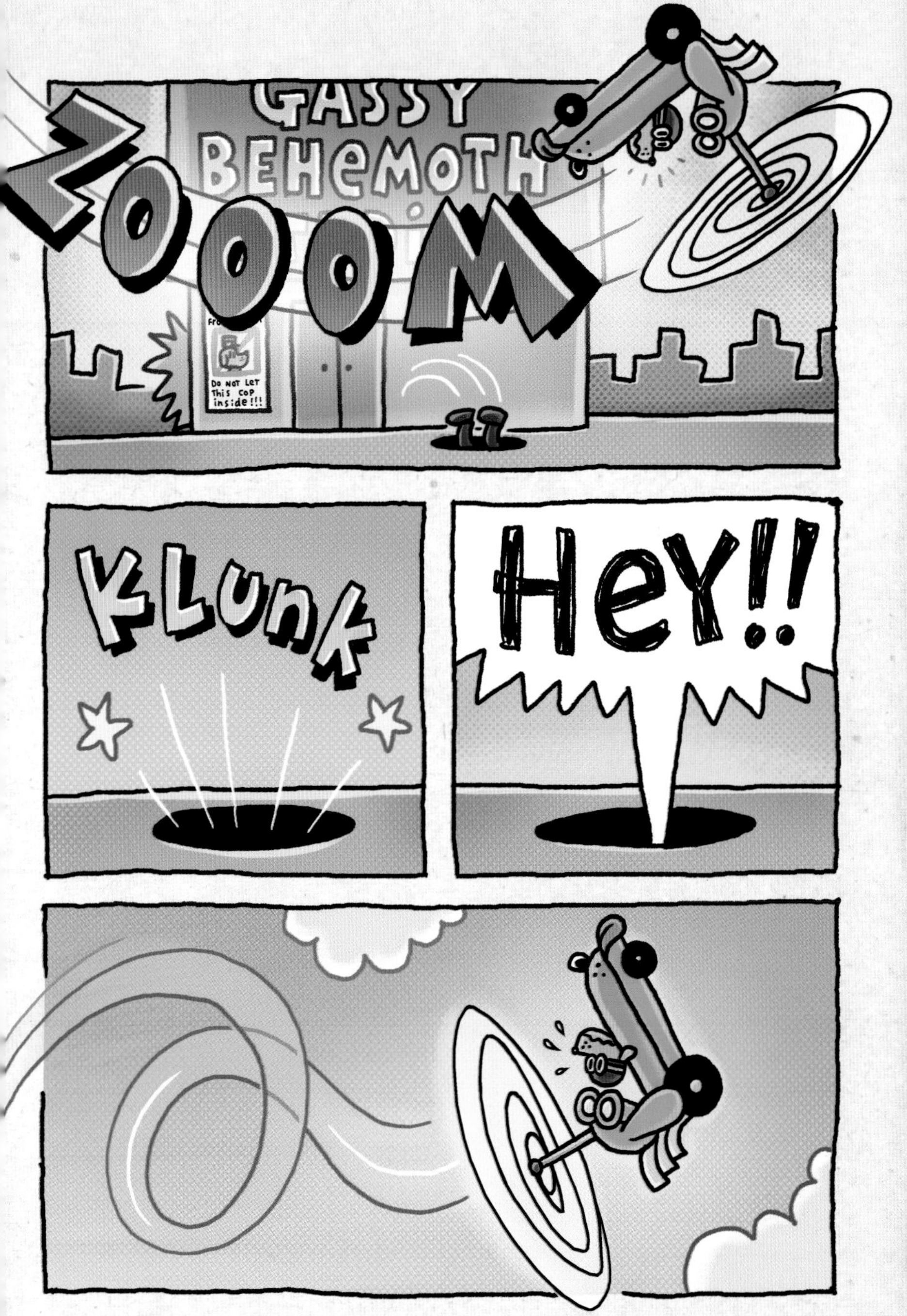
GASSY
BEHEMOTH
Do Not Let This cop inside!!!
ZOOOM
KLUNK
HEY!!

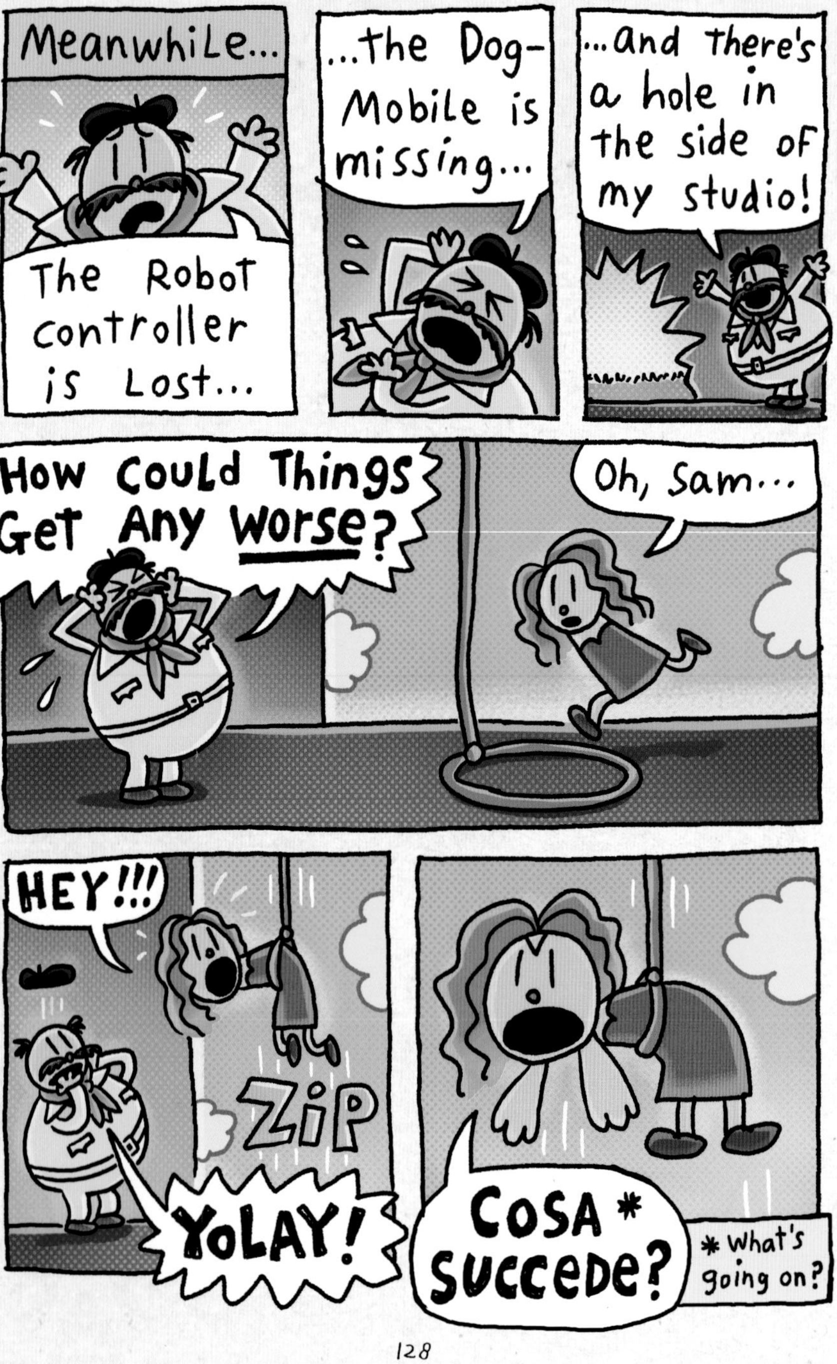

Meanwhile...
The Robot controller is Lost...
...the Dog-Mobile is missing...
...and there's a hole in the side of my studio!
How Could Things Get Any Worse?
Oh, Sam...
HEY!!!
ZIP
YOLAY!
COSA* SUCCEDE?
* What's going on?

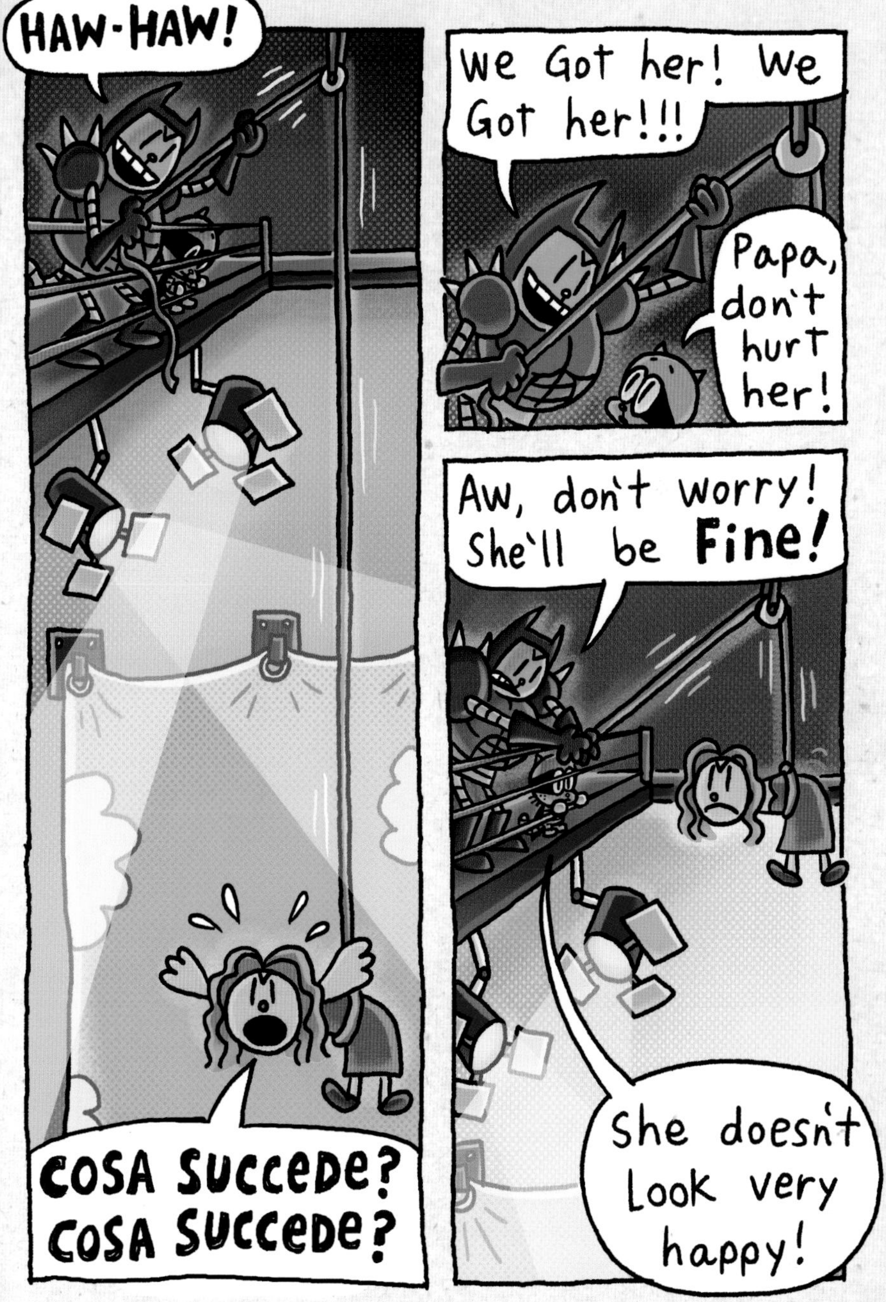
HAW-HAW!
COSA SUCCEDE? COSA SUCCEDE?
We Got her! We Got her!!!
Papa, don't hurt her!
Aw, don't worry! She'll be **Fine!**
She doesn't Look very happy!

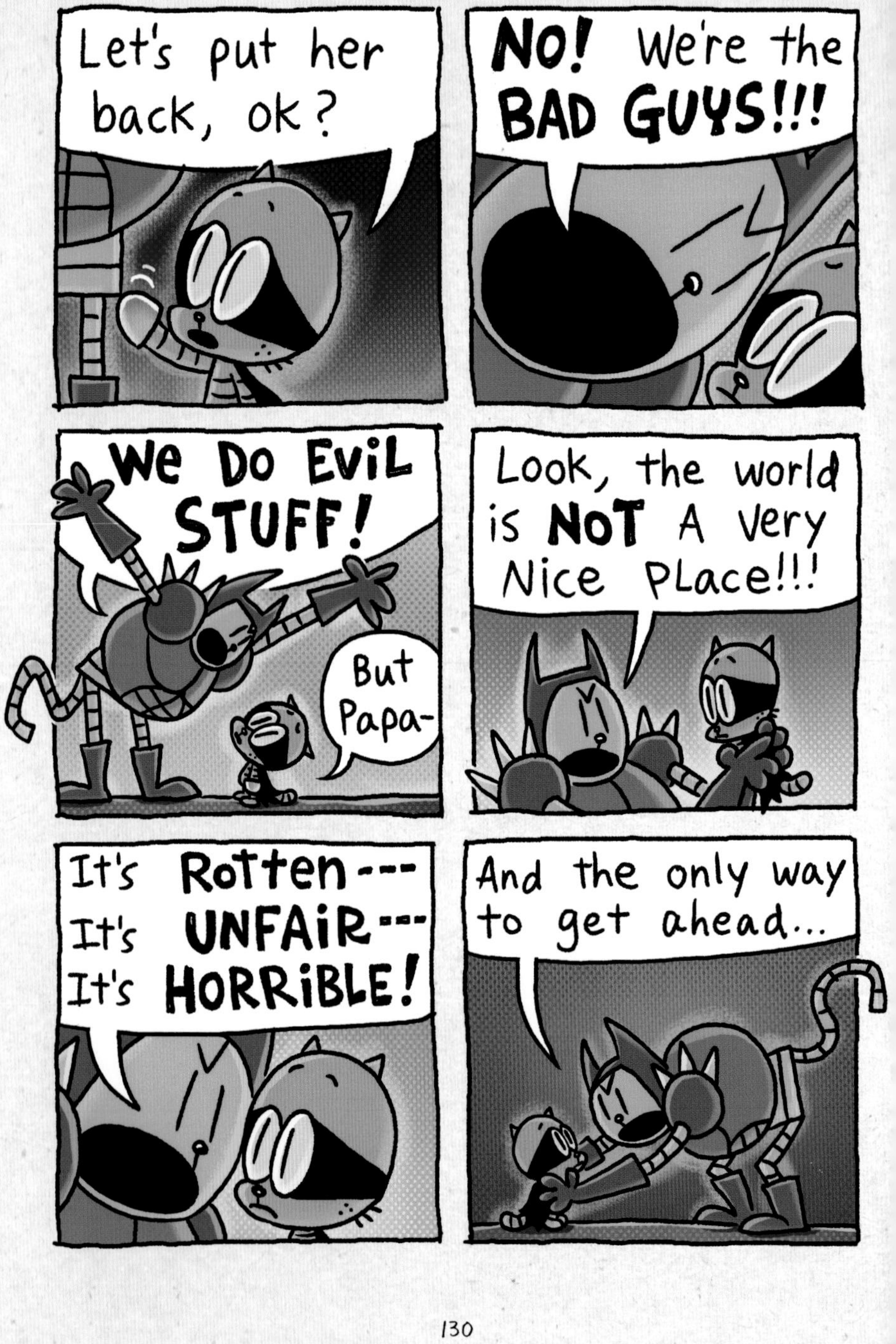
Let's put her back, ok?
NO! We're the BAD GUYS!!!
WE DO EVIL STUFF!
But Papa-
Look, the world is NOT A very Nice Place!!!
It's Rotten--- It's UNFAIR--- It's HORRIBLE!
And the only way to get ahead...

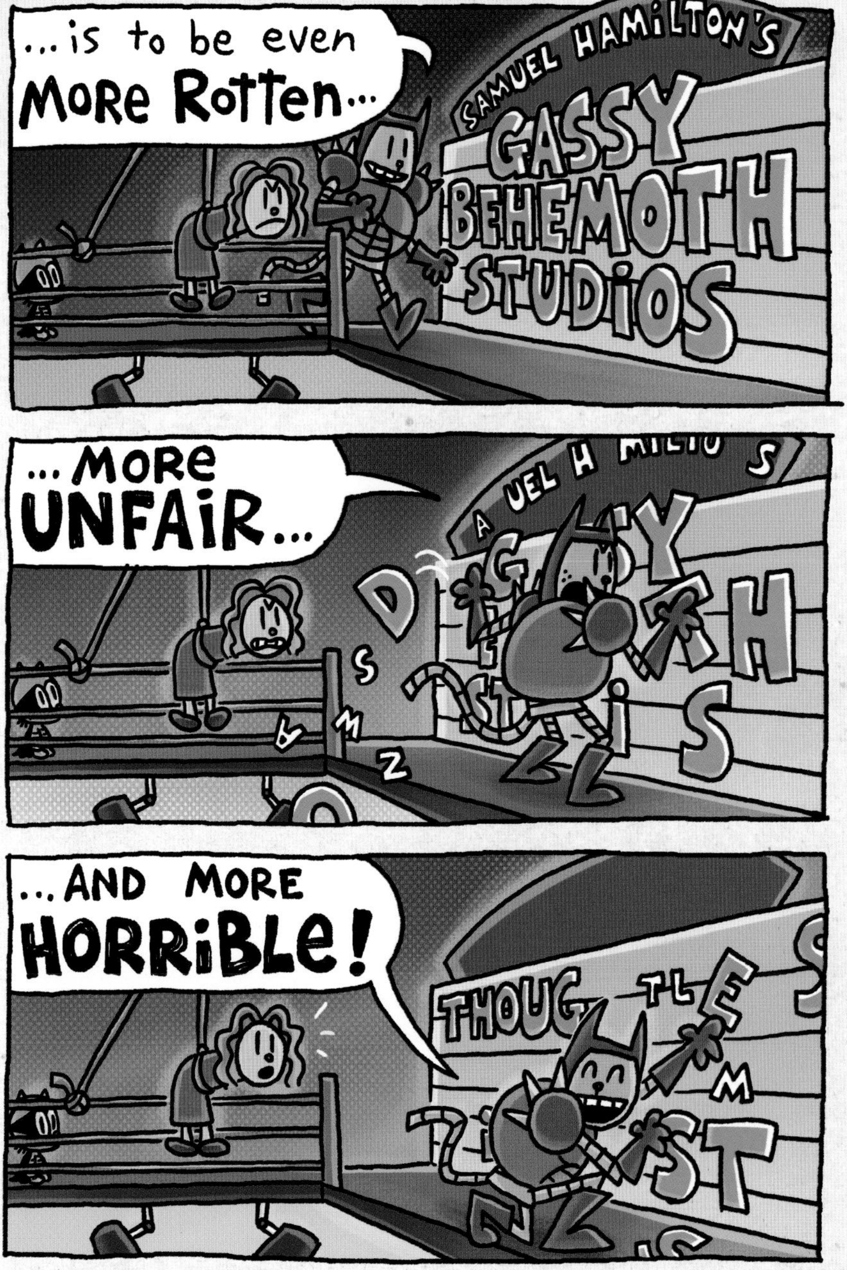

...is to be even
More Rotten...
SAMUEL HAMILTON'S
GASSY
BEHEMOTH
STUDIOS
...MORE
UNFAIR...
...AND MORE
HORRIBLE!

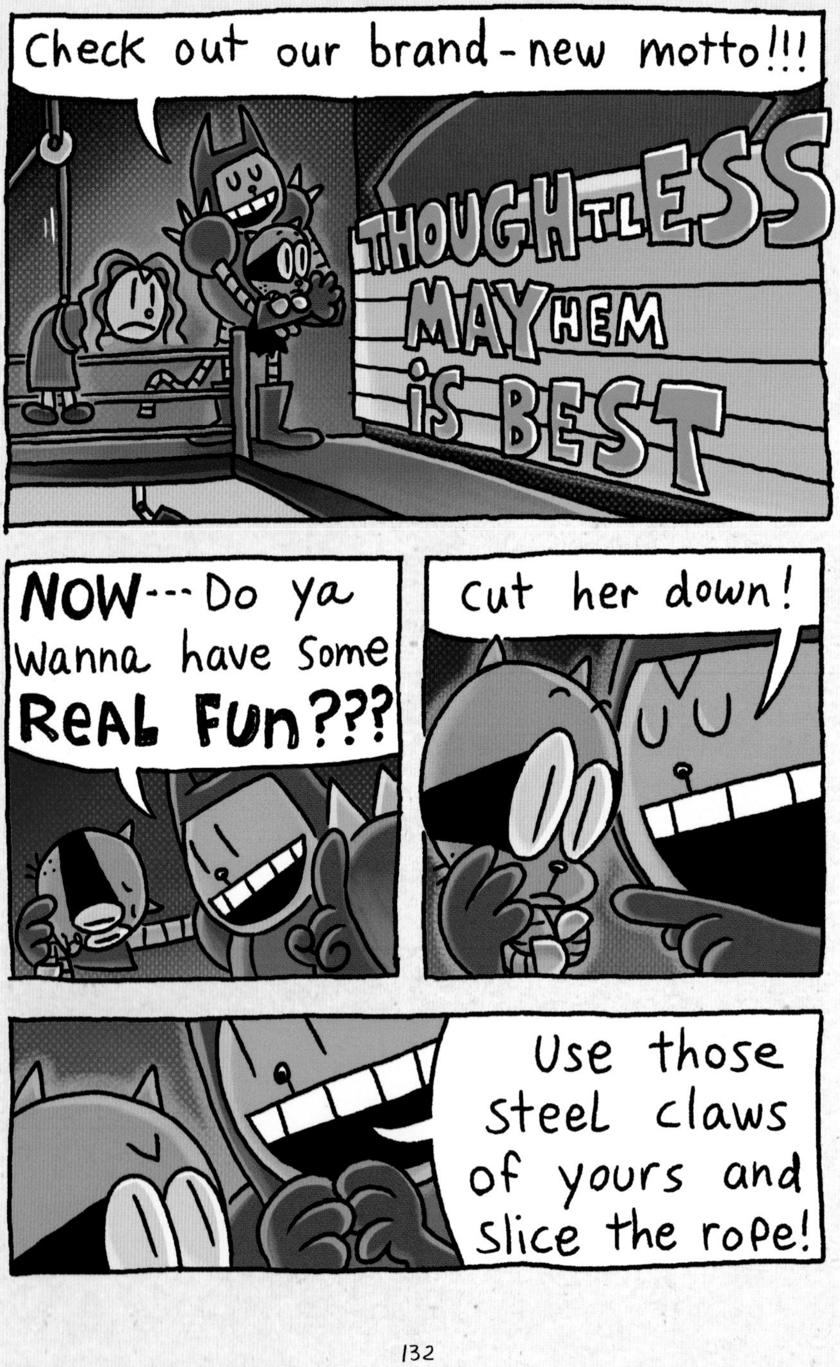

Check out our brand-new motto!!!
THOUGHTLESS MAYHEM iS BEST
NOW--- Do ya wanna have some REAL FUN???
cut her down!
Use those steel claws of yours and slice the rope!

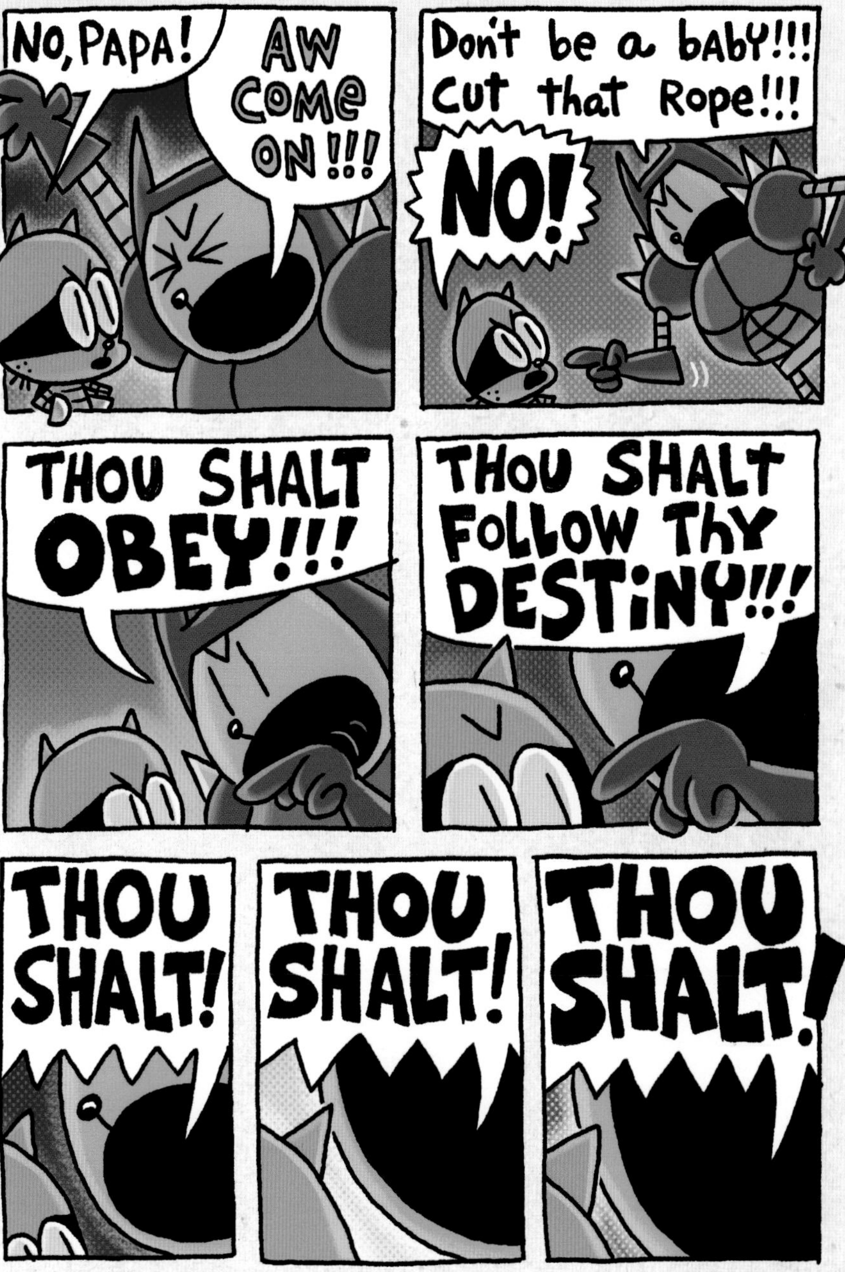
NO, PAPA!
AW COME ON!!!
Don't be a baby!!! Cut that Rope!!!
NO!
THOU SHALT OBEY!!!
THOU SHALT FOLLOW THY DESTINY!!!
THOU SHALT!
THOU SHALT!
THOU SHALT!

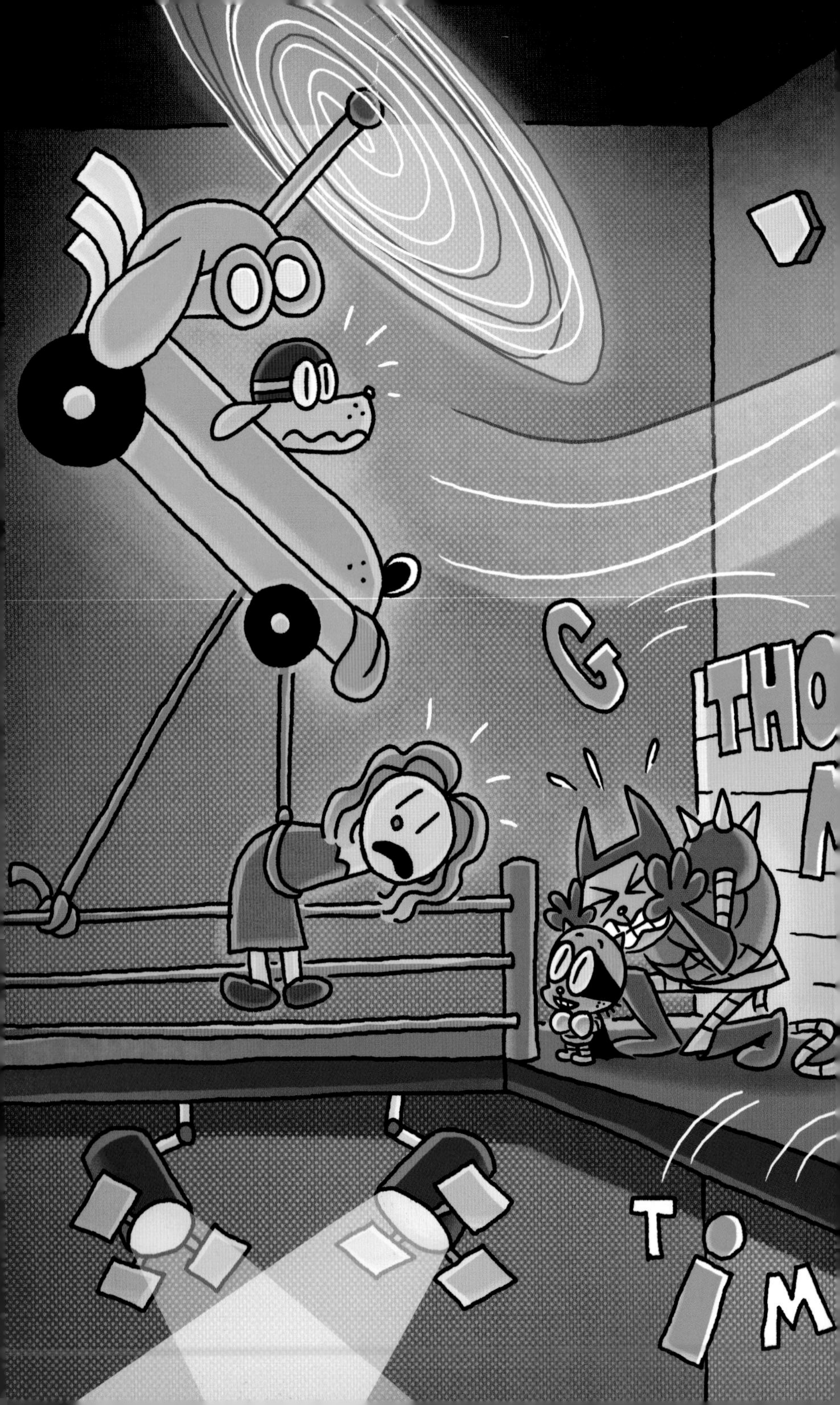
G
THO
T
i
M

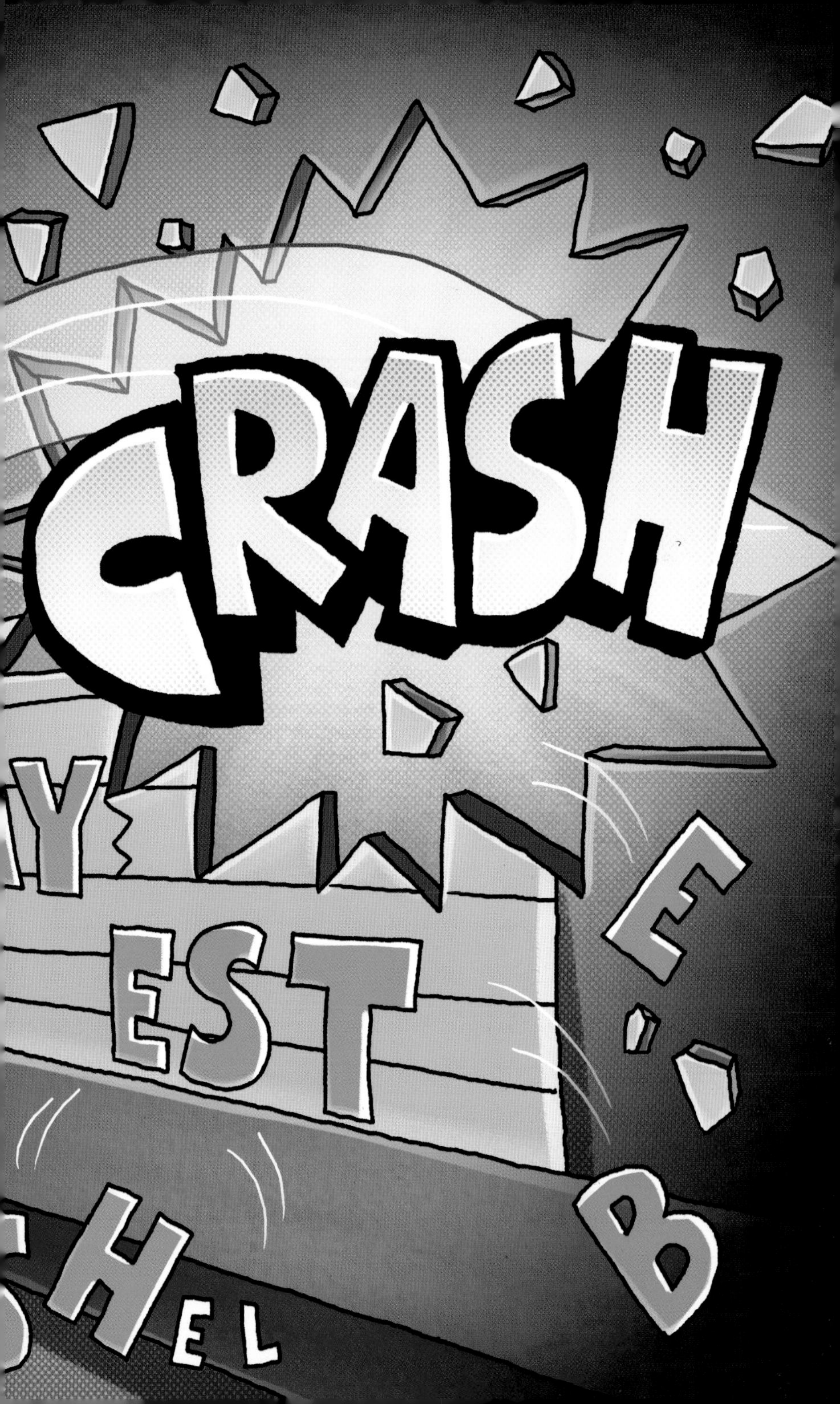
CRASH

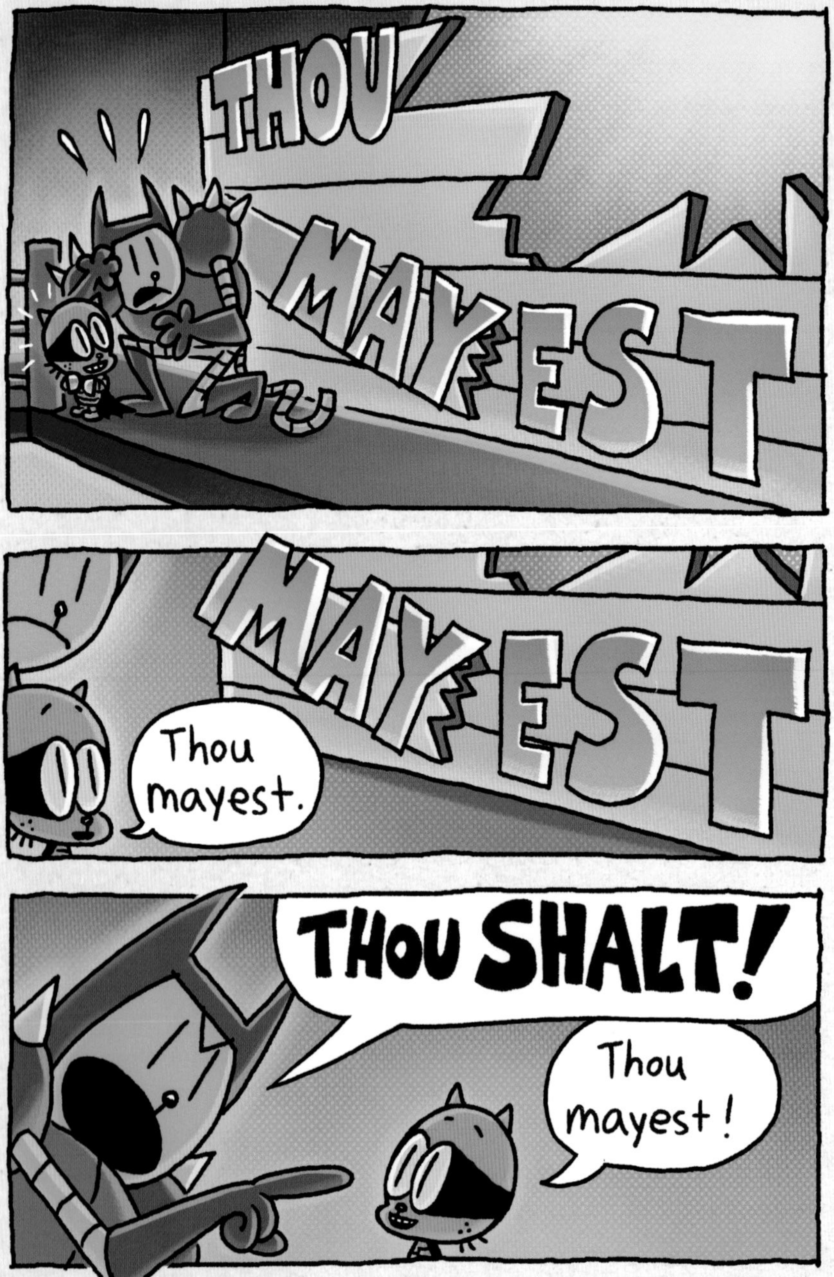
THOU
MAYEST
MAYEST
Thou mayest.
THOU SHALT!
Thou mayest!

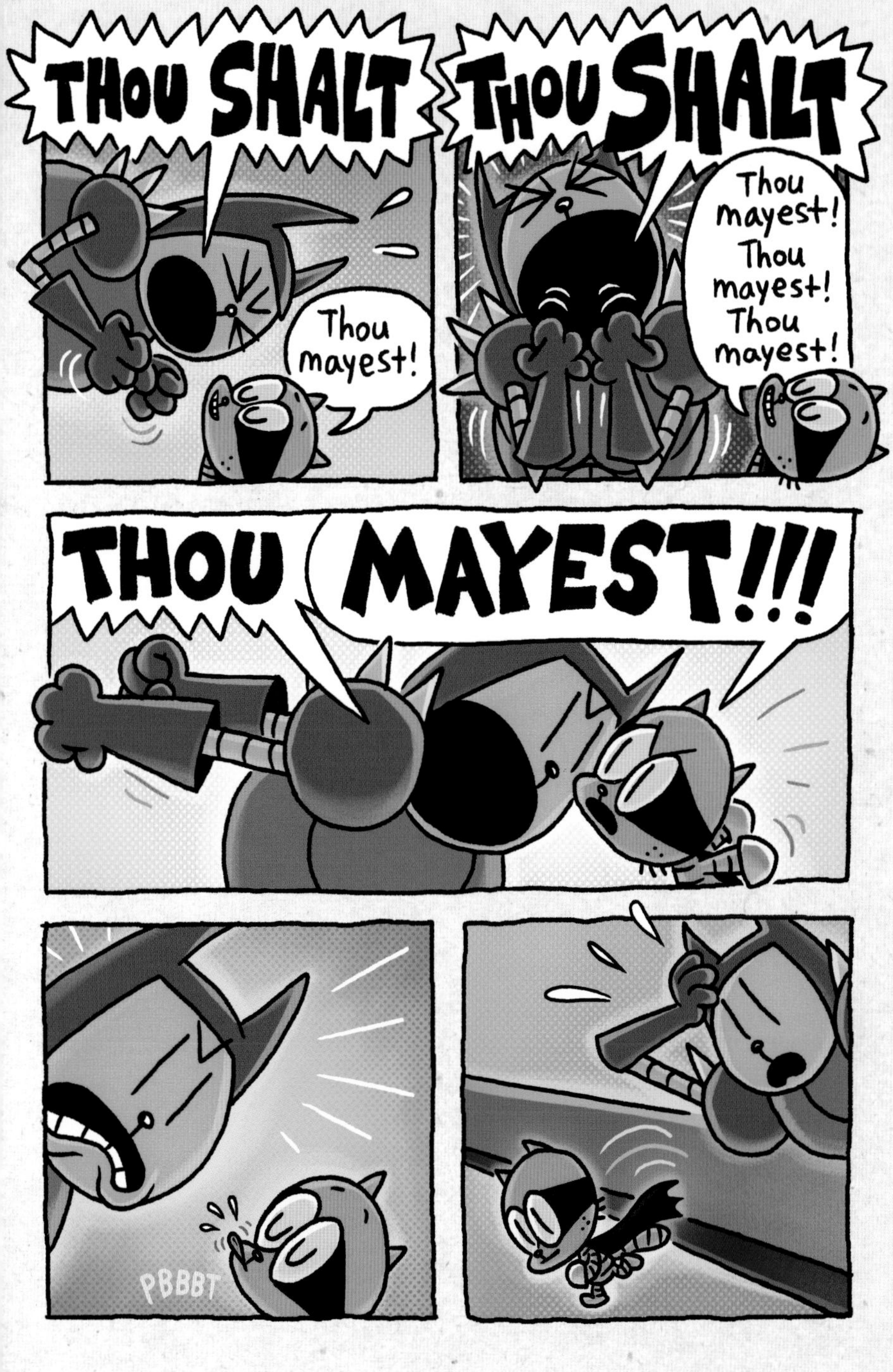
THOU SHALT
Thou mayest!
THOU SHALT
Thou mayest! Thou mayest! Thou mayest!
THOU
MAYEST!!!
PBBBT

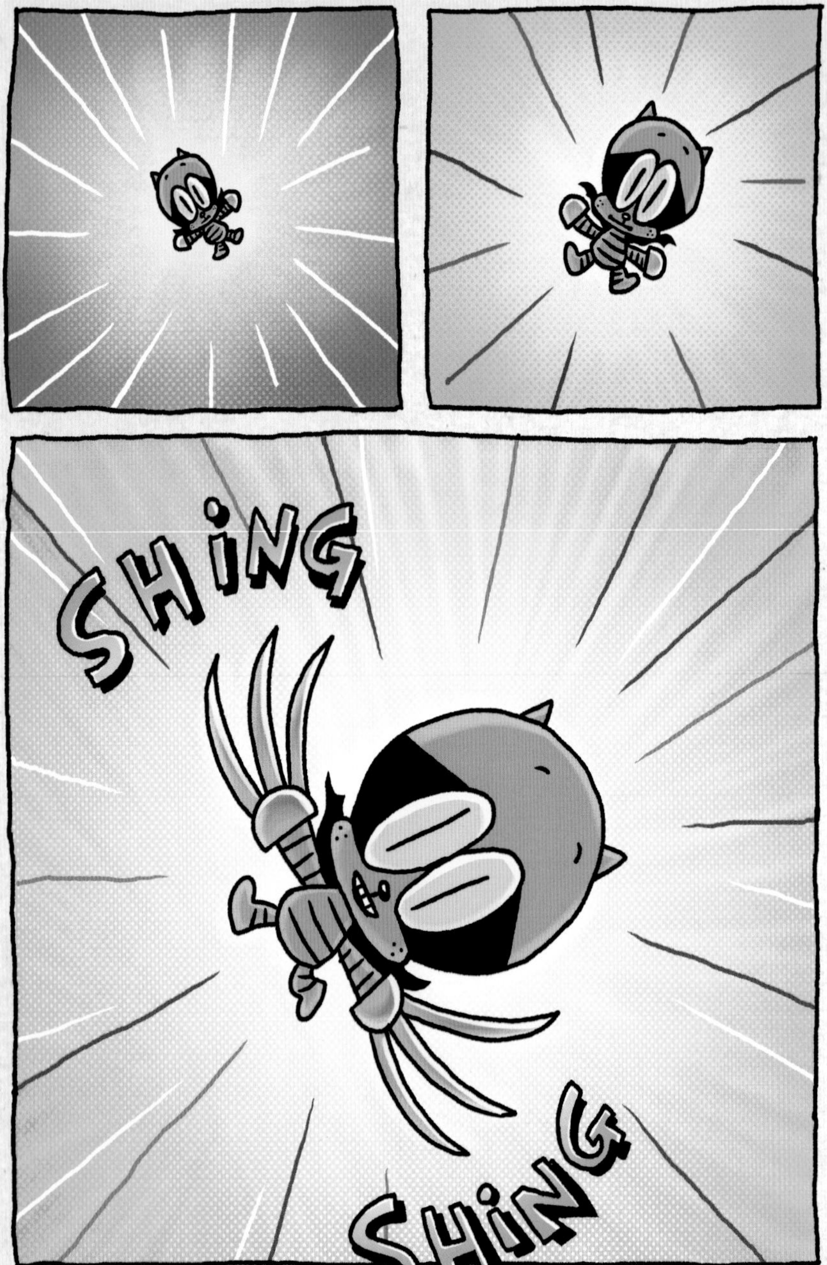
SHING
SHING

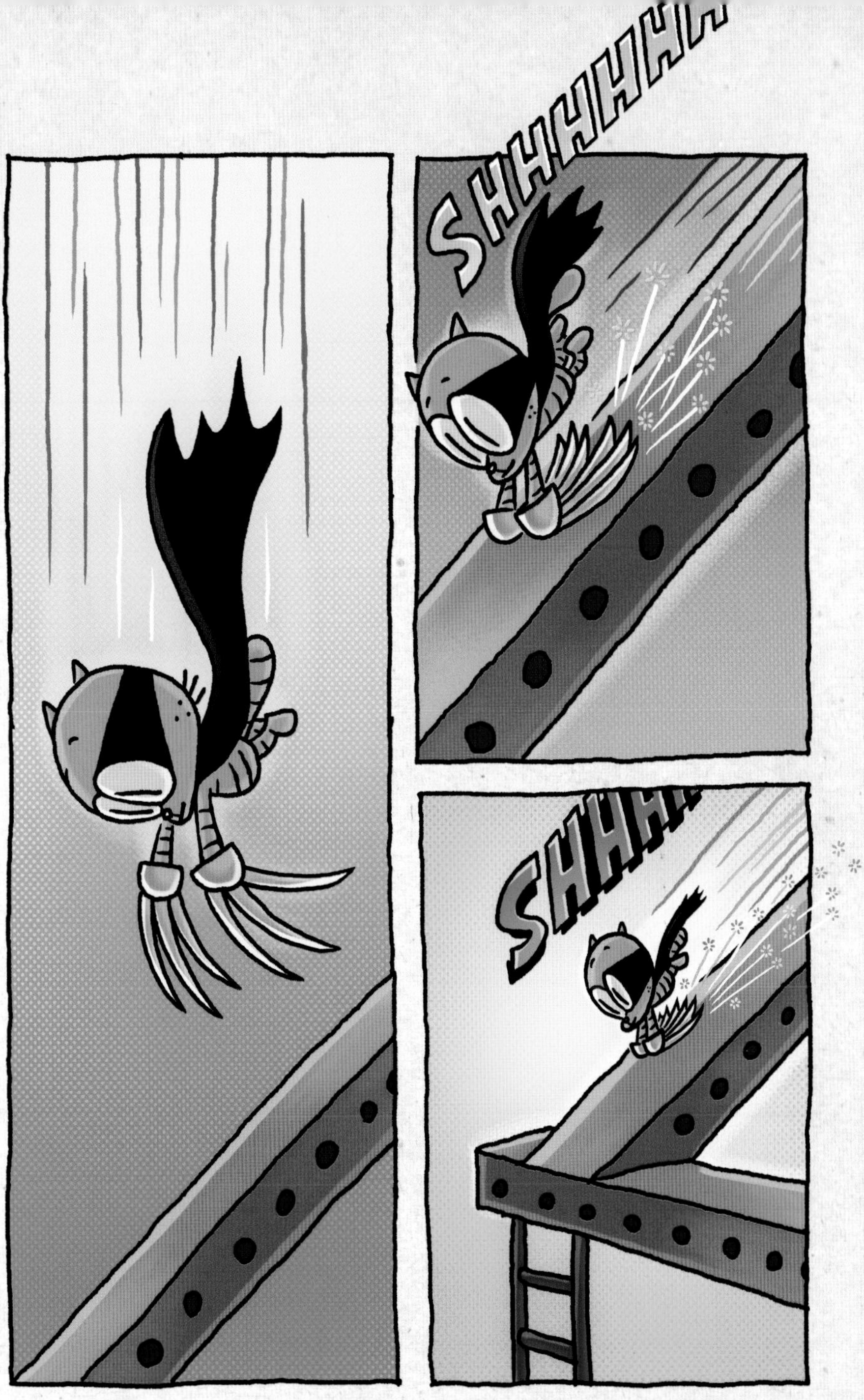
SHHHHHH
SHHHH

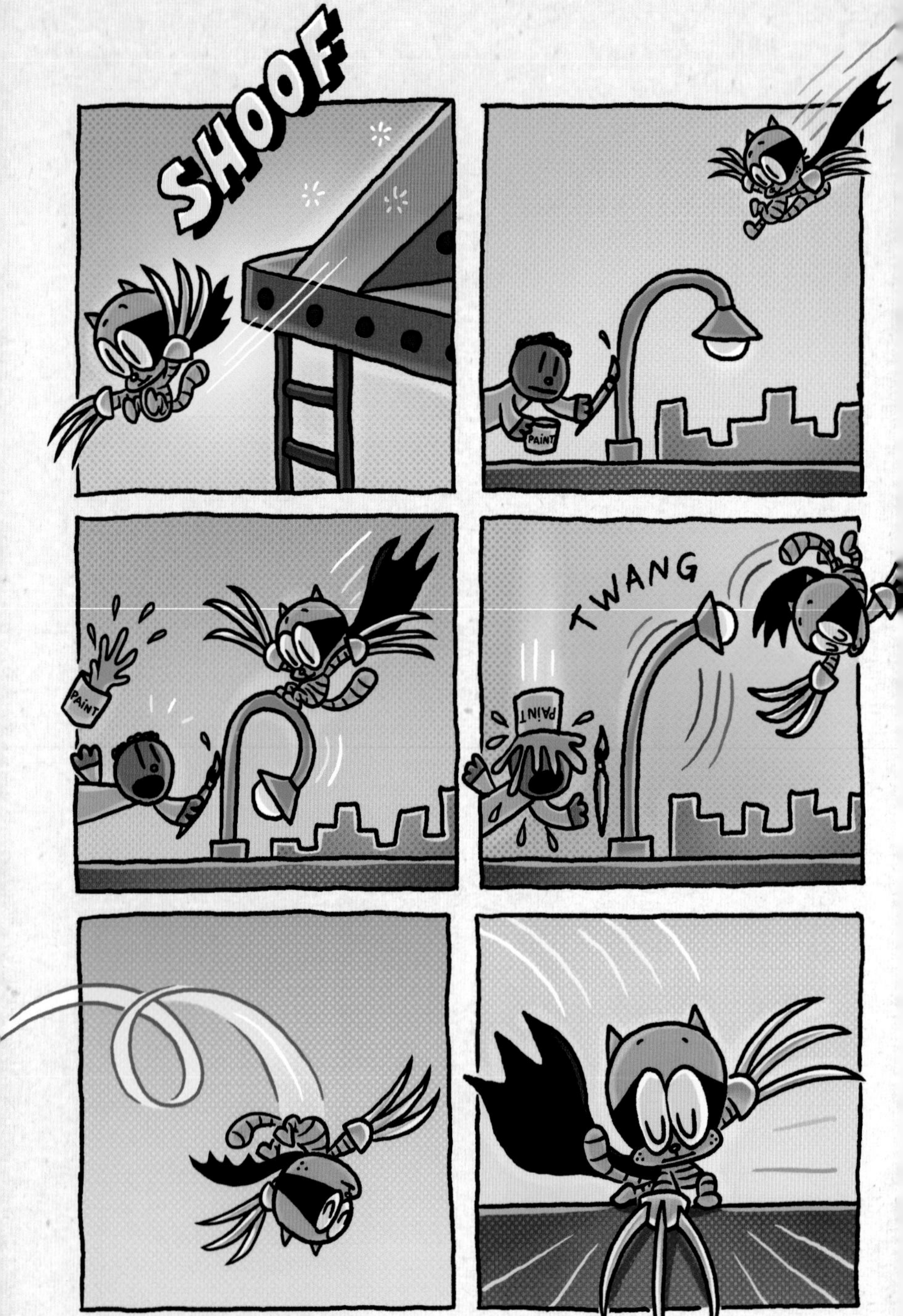
SHOOF
PAINT
PAINT
TWANG
PAINT

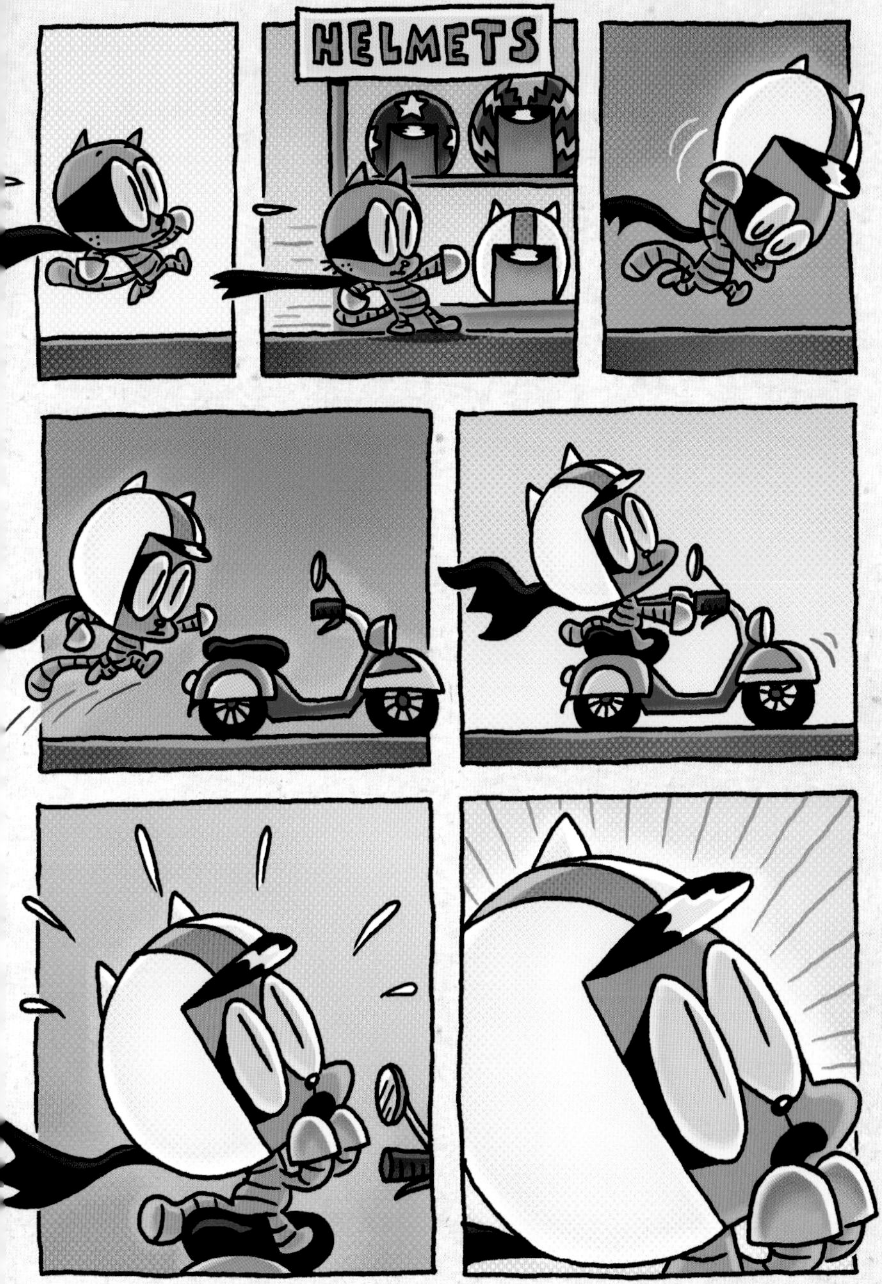
HELMETS

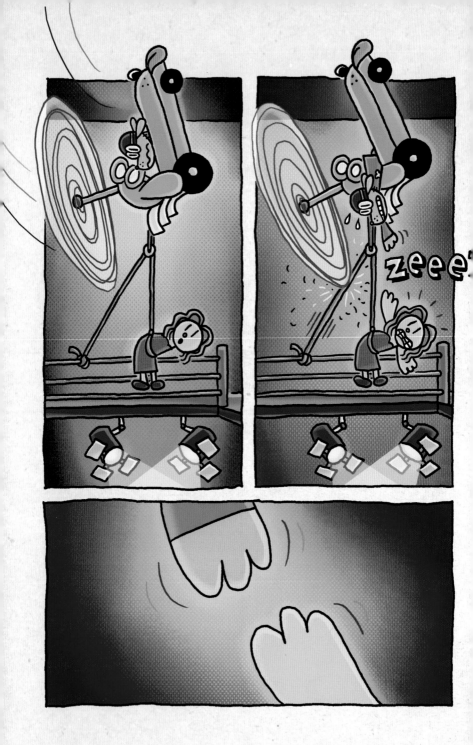

zeeee

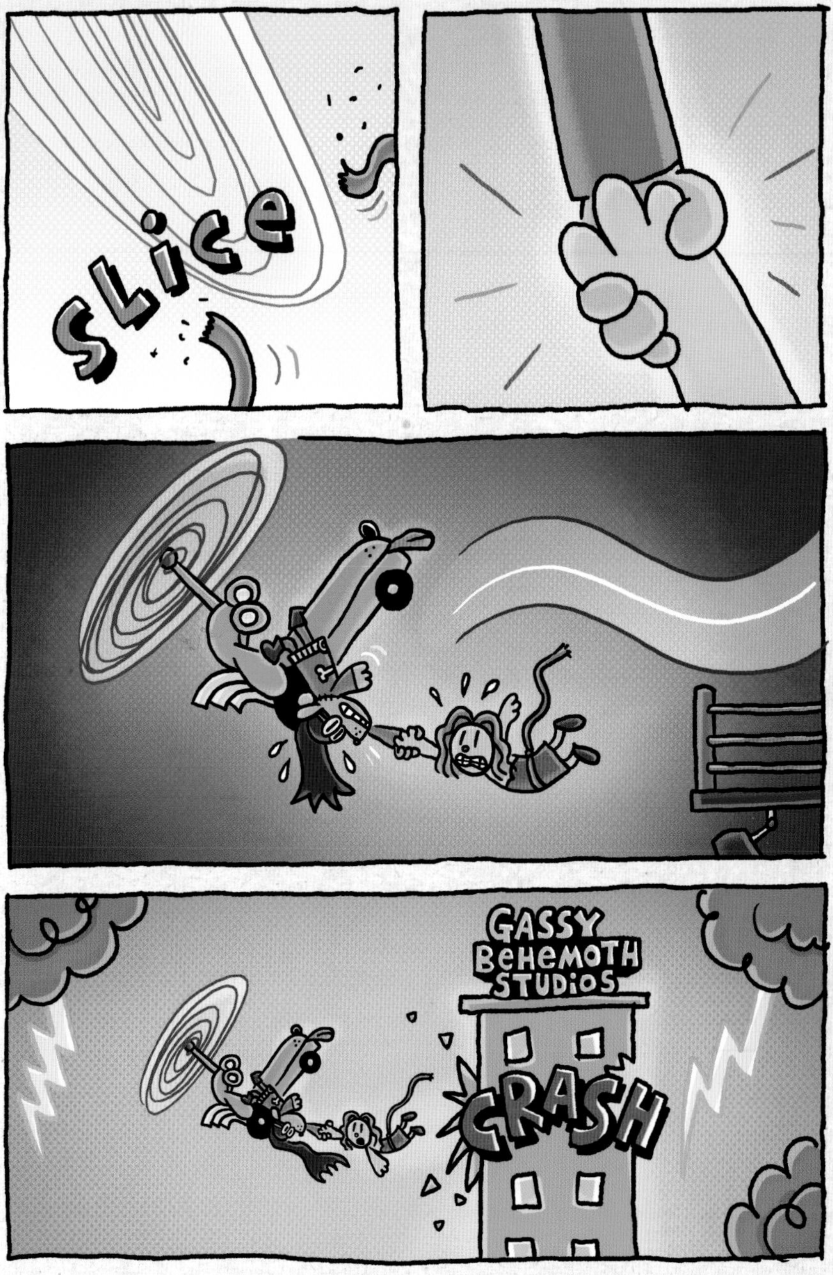
SLICE
GASSY BEHEMOTH STUDIOS
CRASH

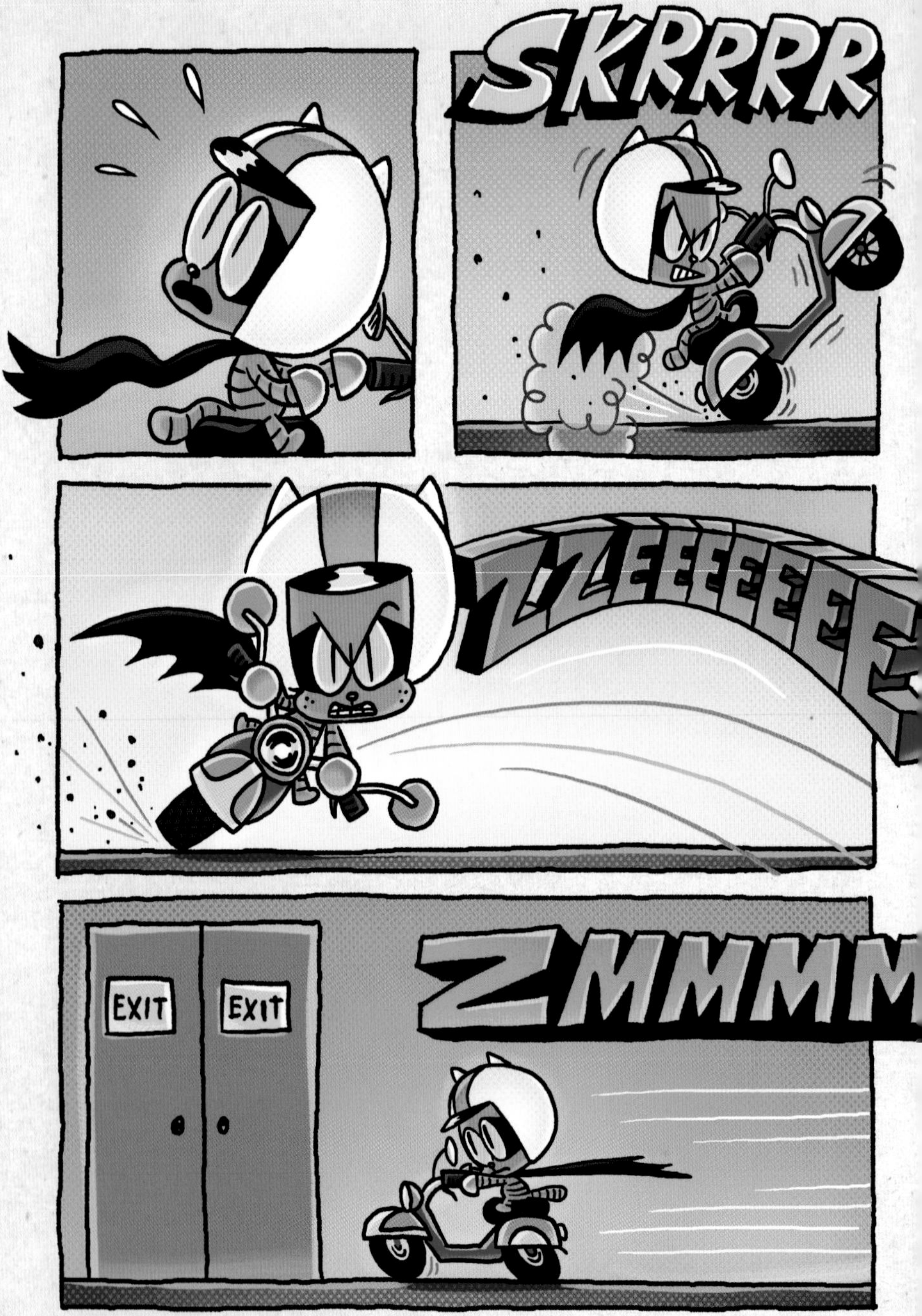
SKRRRR
ZZEEEEEEEE
EXIT
EXIT
ZMMMMM

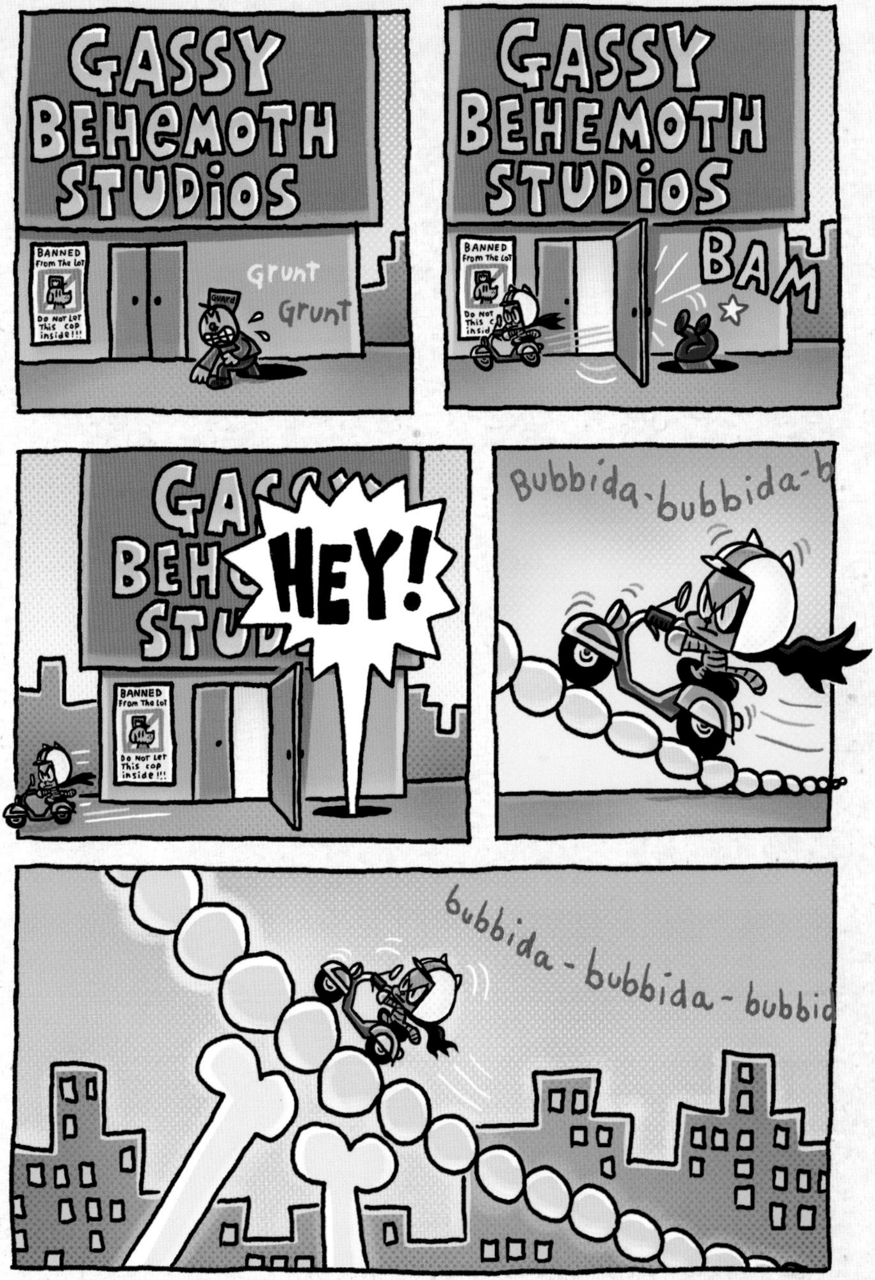

GASSY BEHEMOTH STUDIOS
BANNED From The Lot
Do NOT LET This cop inside!!!
GUARD
Grunt
Grunt
GASSY BEHEMOTH STUDIOS
BANNED From The Lot
BAM
HEY!
BANNED From The Lot
Do NOT LET This cop inside!!!
Bubbida-bubbida-b
bubbida-bubbida-bubbid

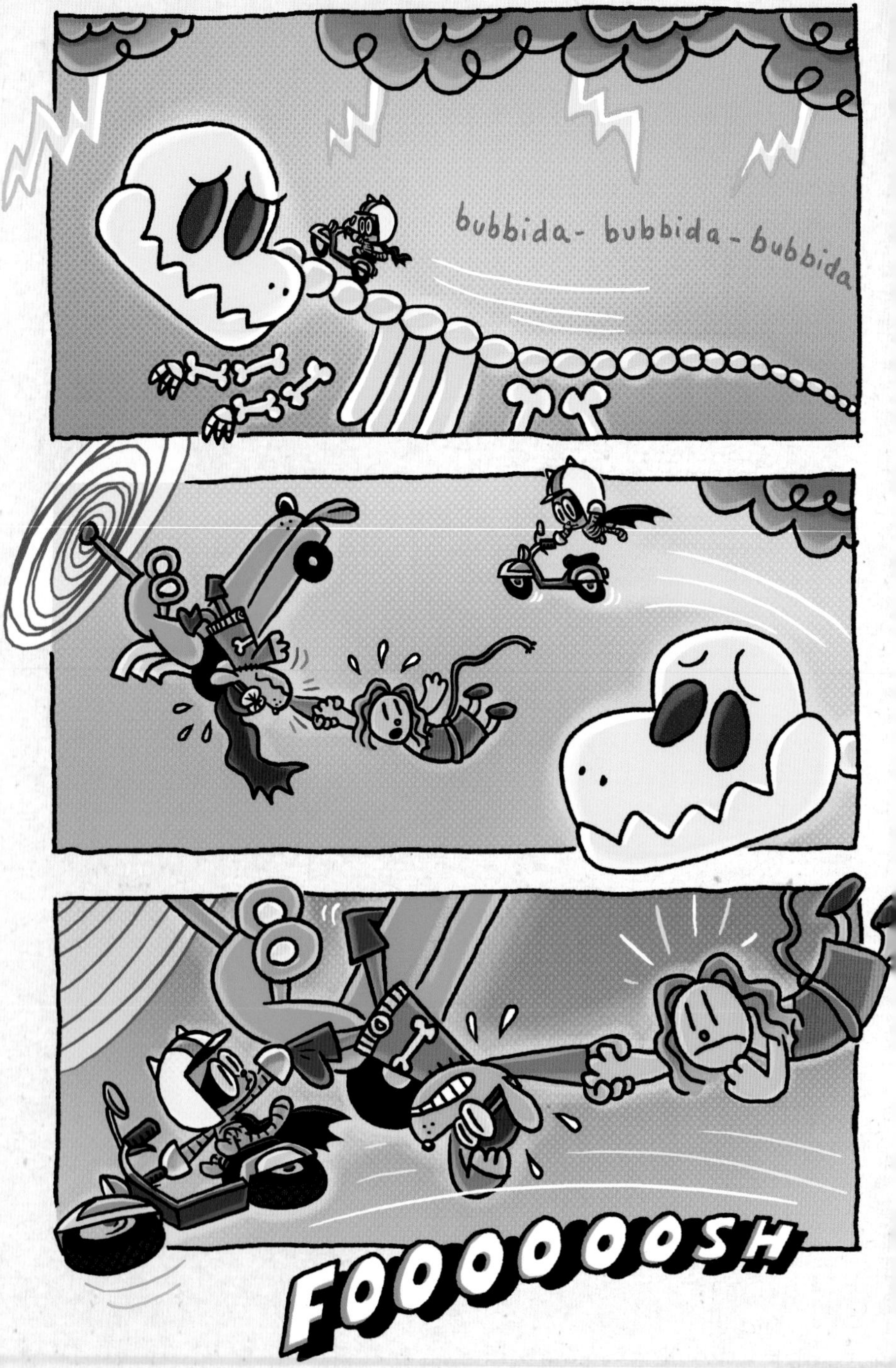
bubbida- bubbida- bubbida
FOOOOOOOSH

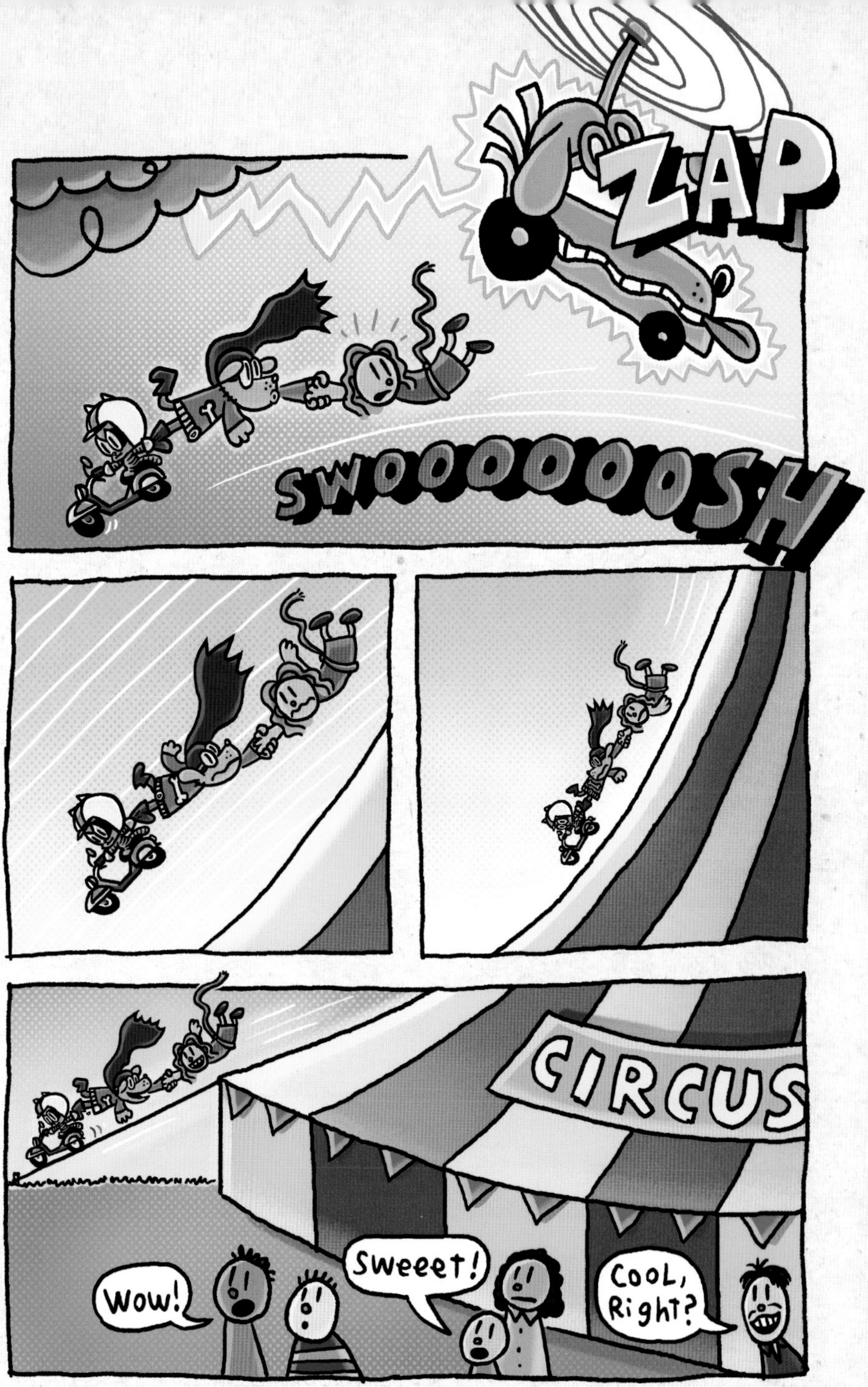
ZAP
SWOOOOOOOSH
CIRCUS
Wow!
Sweeet!
Cool, Right?

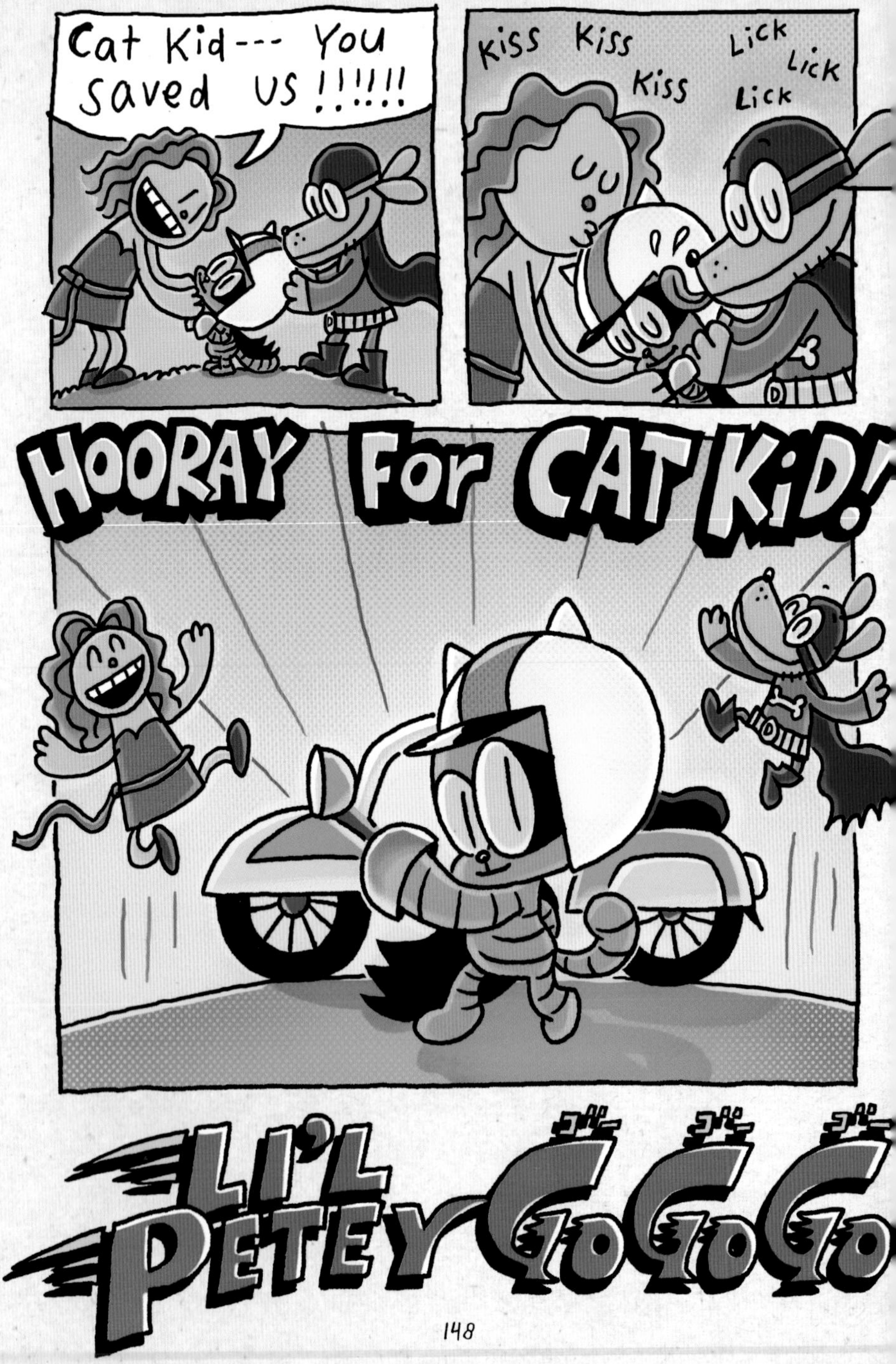

Cat Kid--- You saved us!!!!!!
Kiss Kiss Kiss
Lick Lick Lick
HOORAY For CAT KiD!
LI'L PETEY GO GO GO

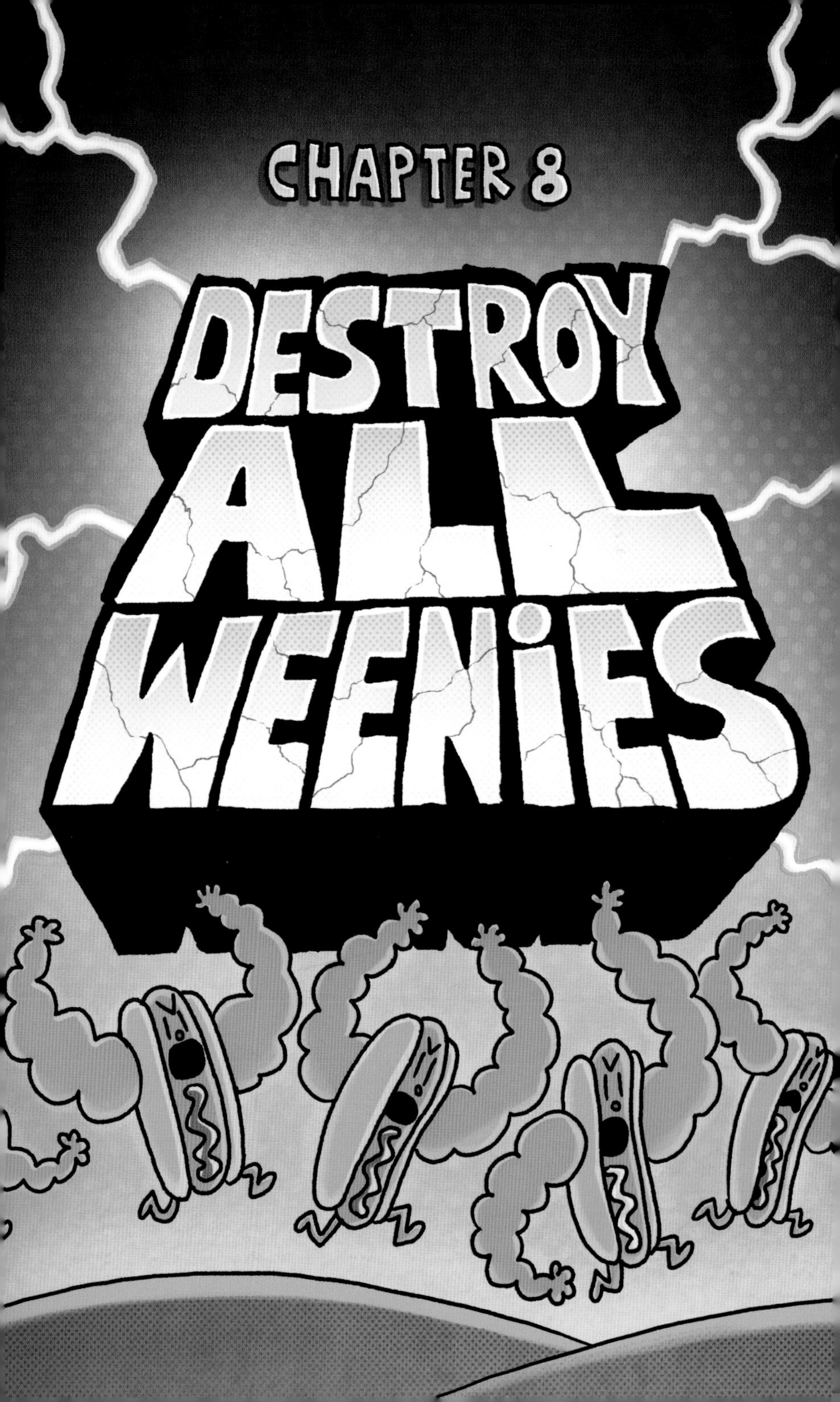
CHAPTER 8
DESTROY ALL WEENIES

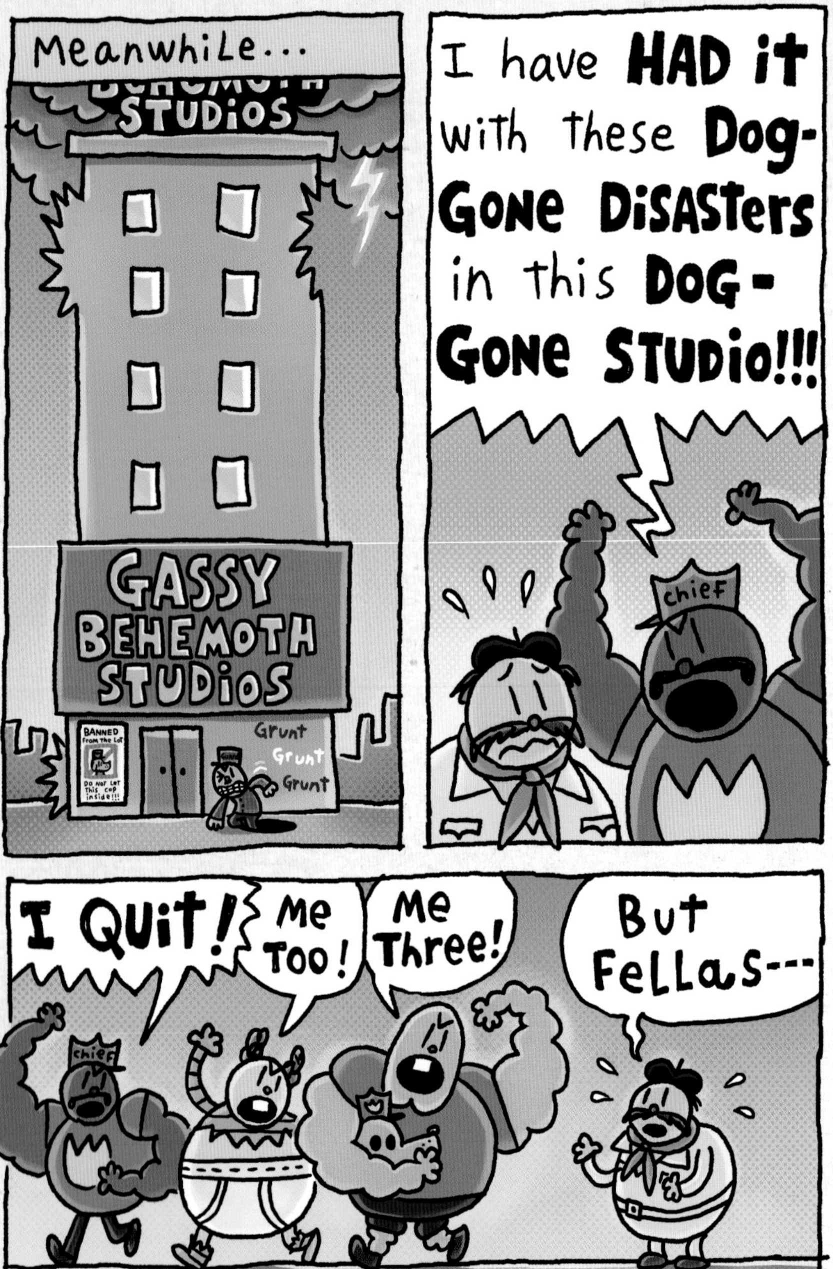
Meanwhile...
STUDIOS
GASSY BEHEMOTH STUDIOS
BANNED From the Lot
Do Not Let This cop inside!!!
Grunt
Grunt
Grunt
I have HAD it with these Dog-Gone DiSASTers in this DOG-Gone STUDio!!!
chief
I Quit!
Me Too!
Me Three!
But Fellas---
chief

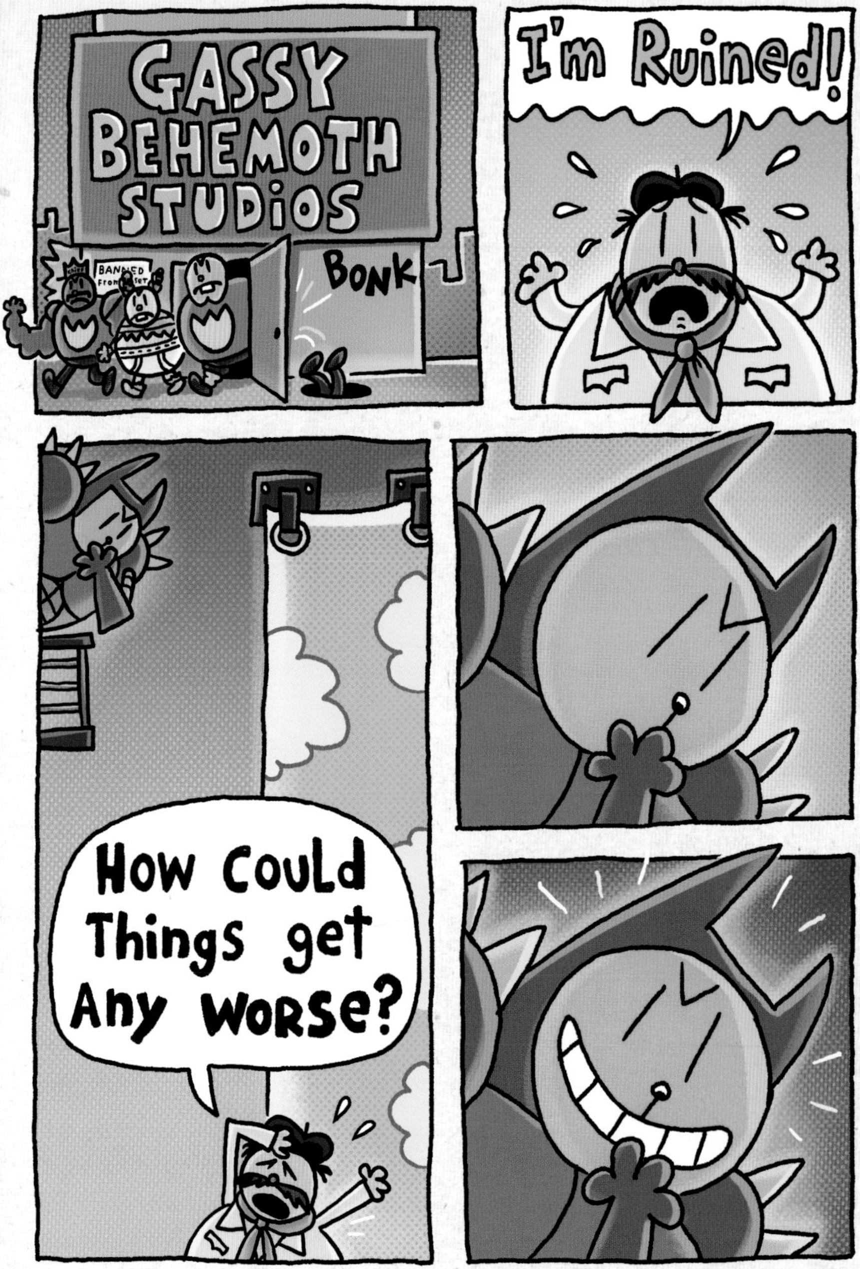
GASSY BEHEMOTH STUDIOS
BONK
I'm Ruined!
How Could Things get Any Worse?

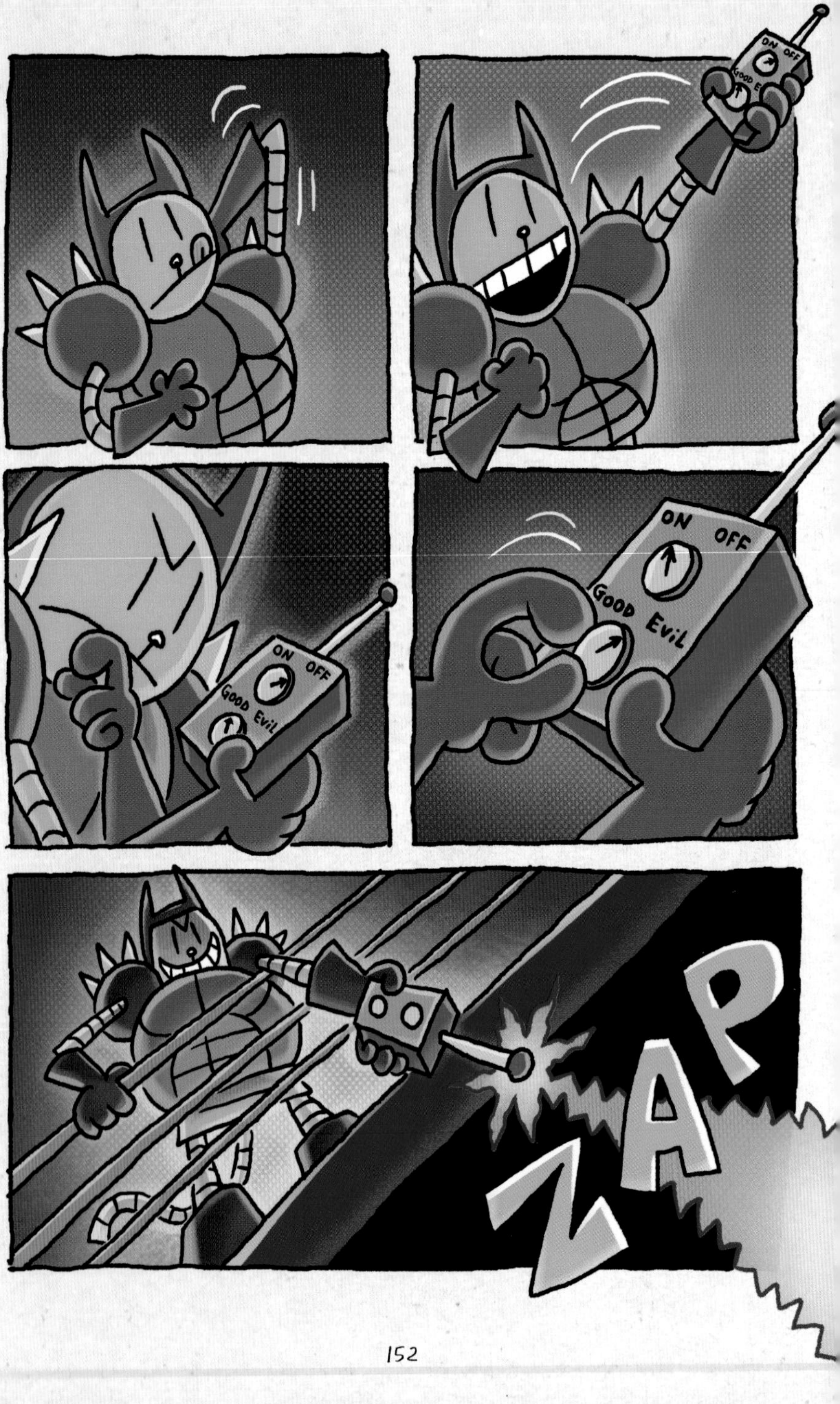
ON OFF
GOOD E
ON OFF
GOOD EVIL
ON OFF
GOOD EVIL
ZAP

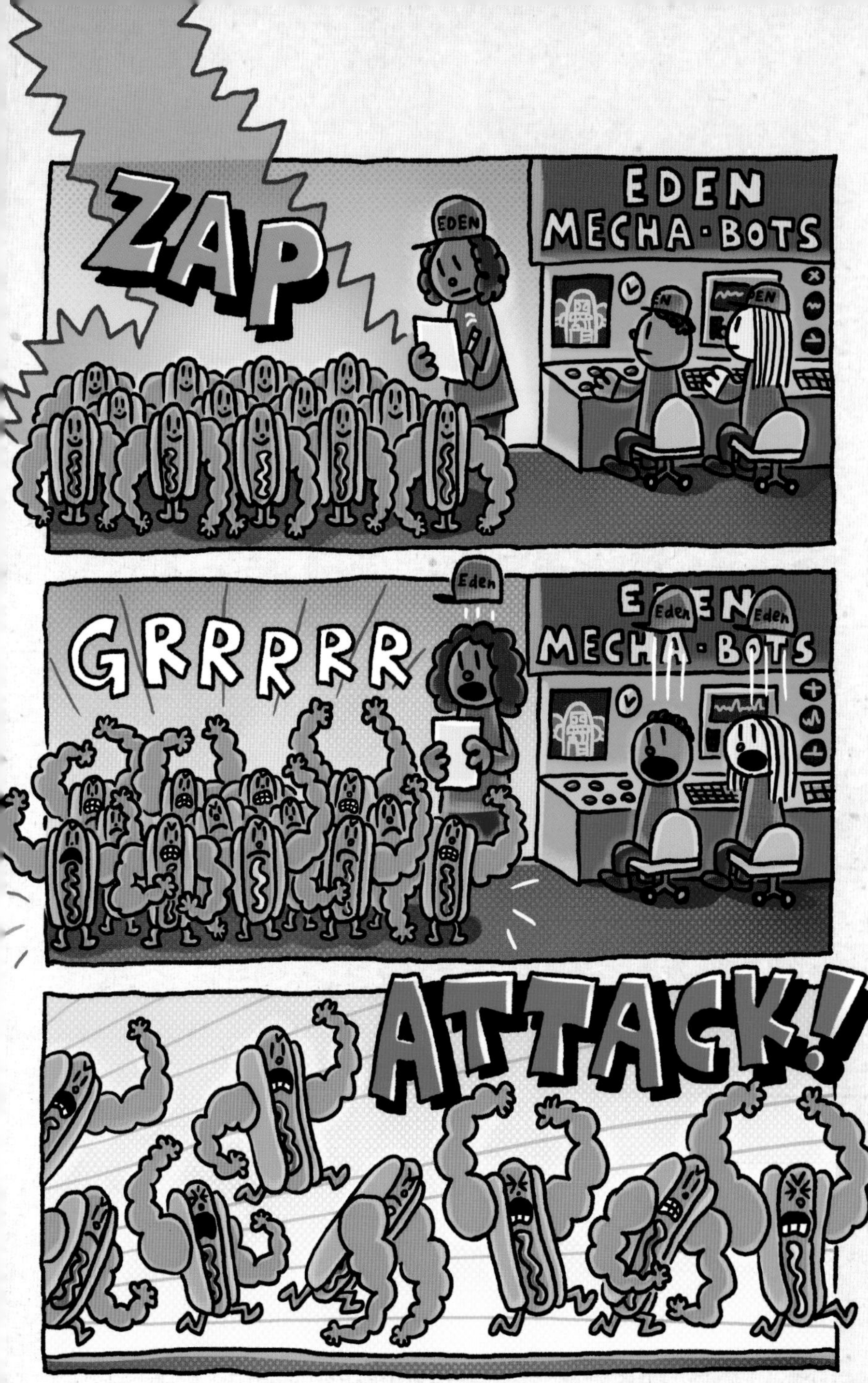
ZAP
EDEN
EDEN MECHA-BOTS
EN
EN
GRRRRR
Eden
EDEN MECHA-BOTS
Eden
Eden
ATTACK!

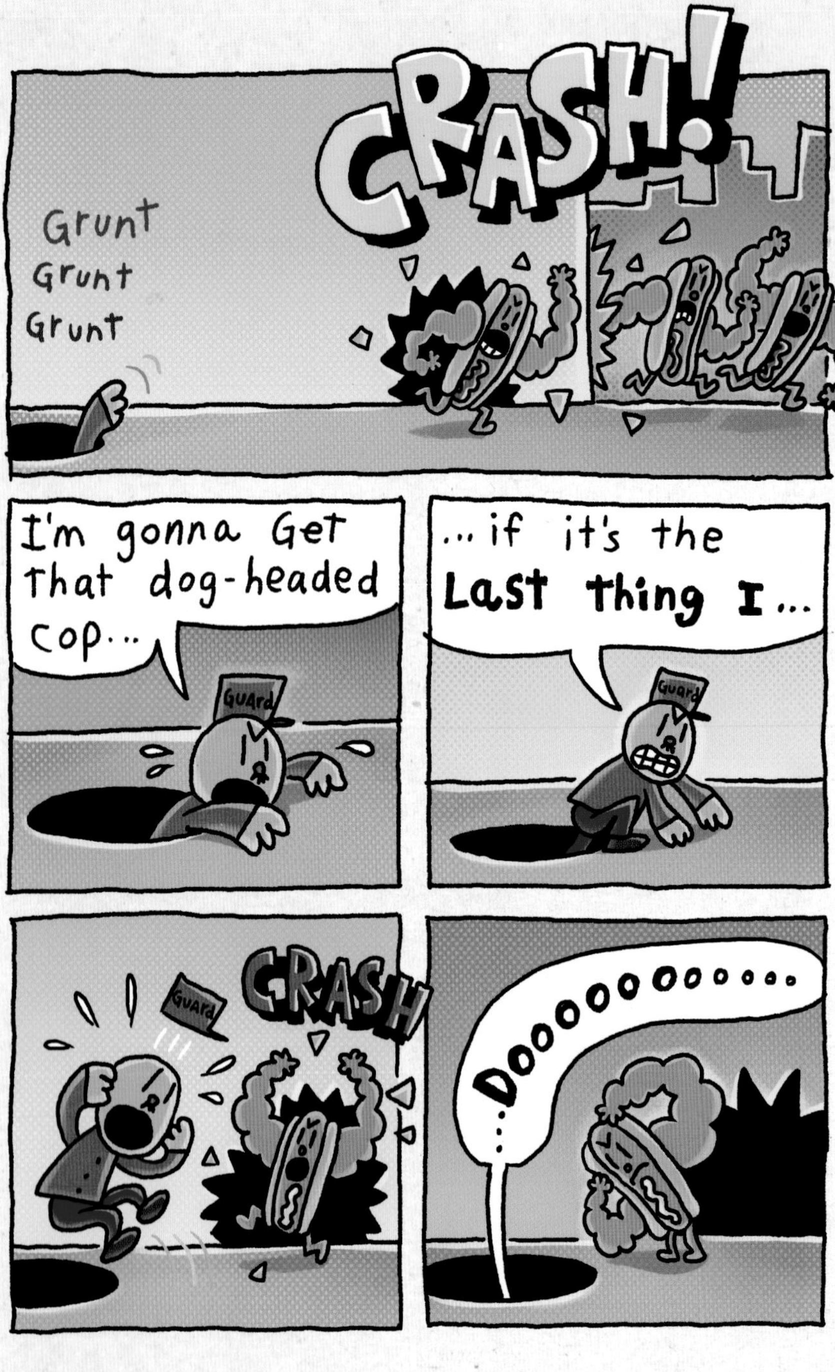
CRASH!
Grunt
Grunt
Grunt
I'm gonna Get that dog-headed cop...
Guard
...if it's the Last thing I...
Guard
Guard
CRASH
...Doooooooooo...

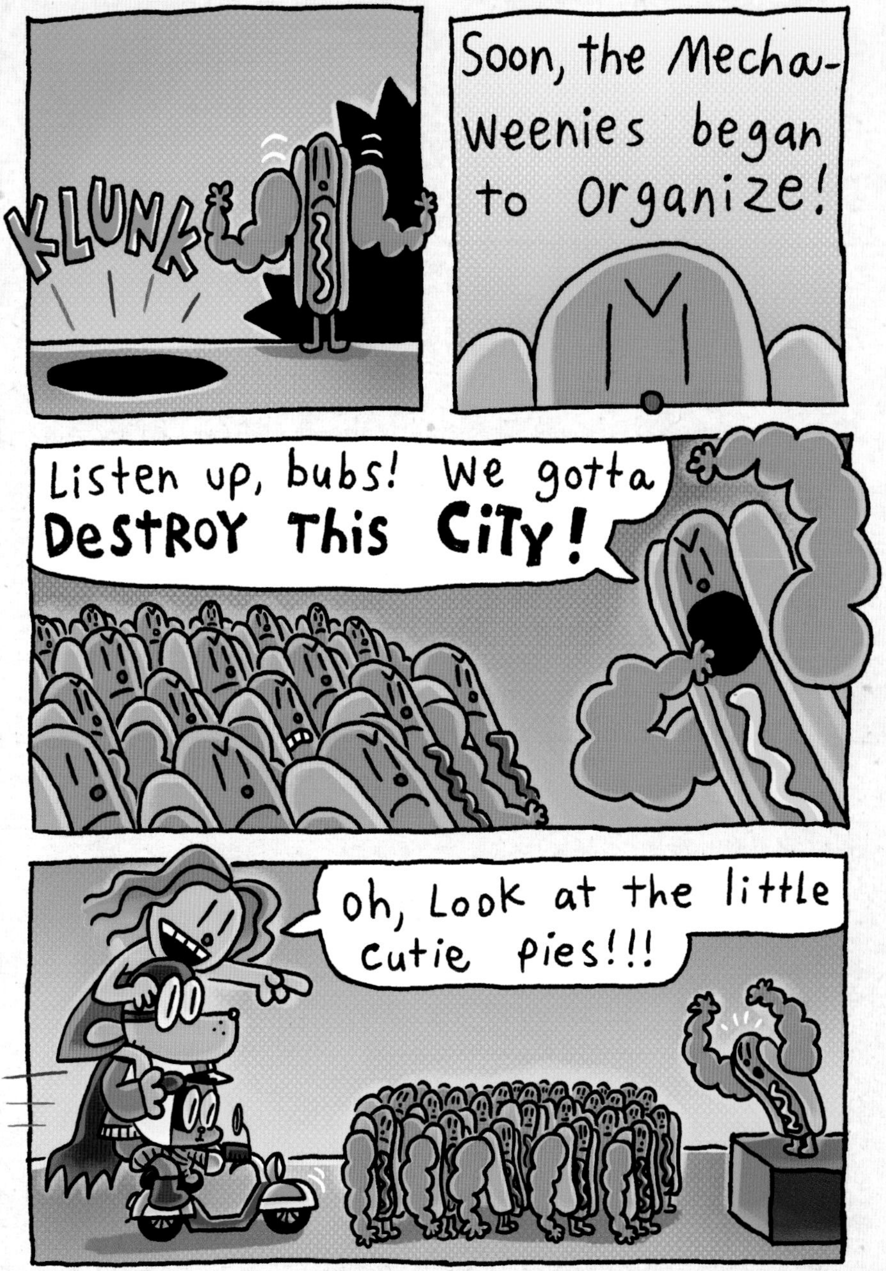
KLUNK
Soon, the Mecha-weenies began to Organize!
Listen up, bubs! We gotta DESTROY This CiTy!
Oh, Look at the little cutie pies!!!

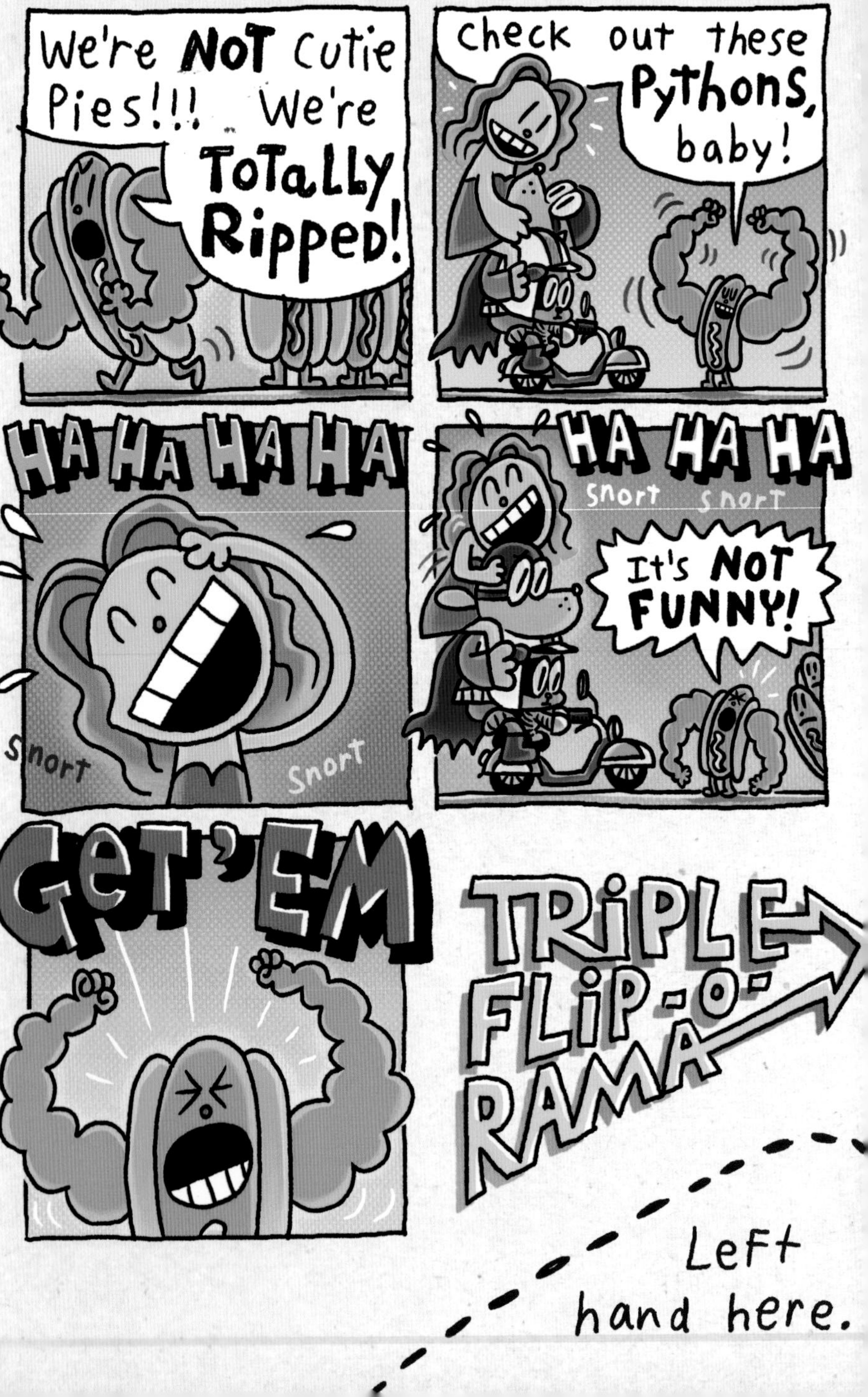

We're NOT cutie Pies!!! We're TOTALLY RIPPED!
Check out these Pythons, baby!
HA HA HA HA HA
Snort
Snort
HA HA HA
Snort
Snort
It's NOT FUNNY!
GET 'EM
TRIPLE FLIP-O-RAMA
Left hand here.

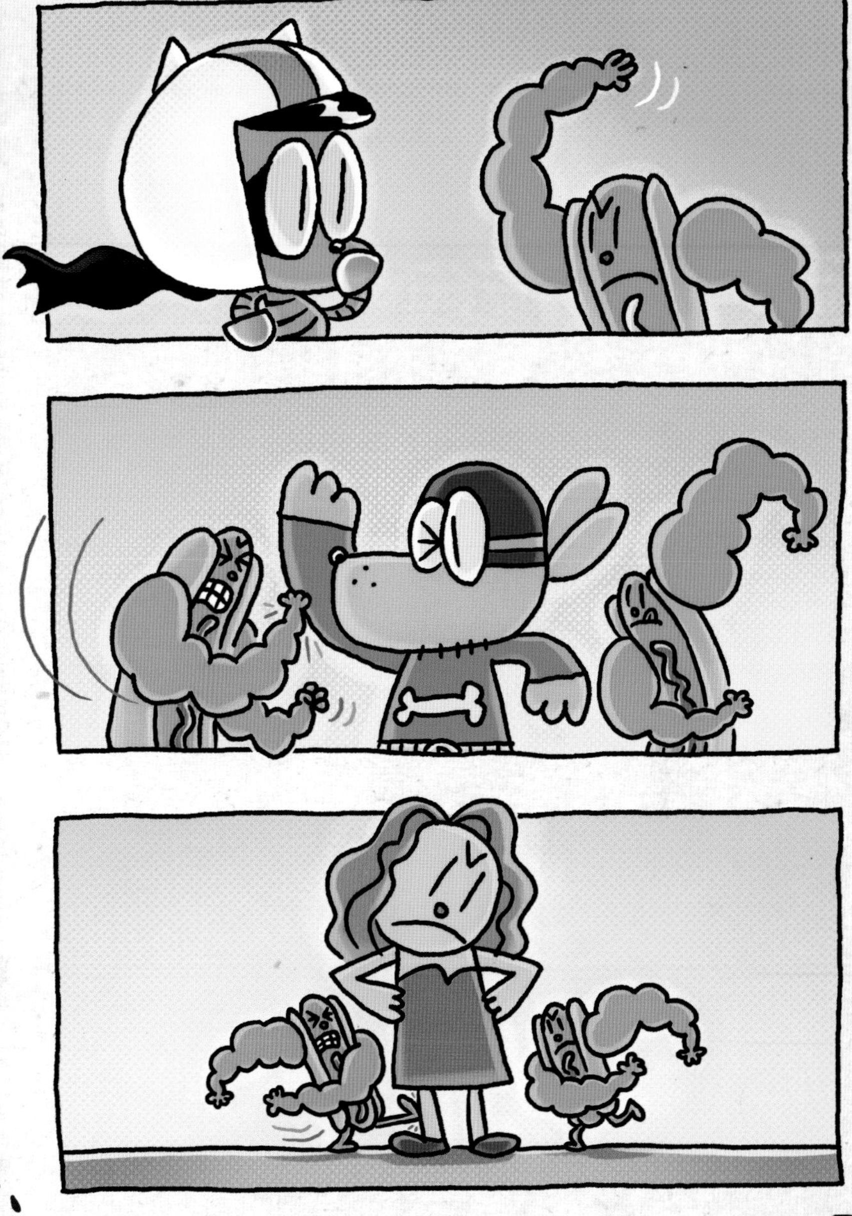

Right Thumb here.

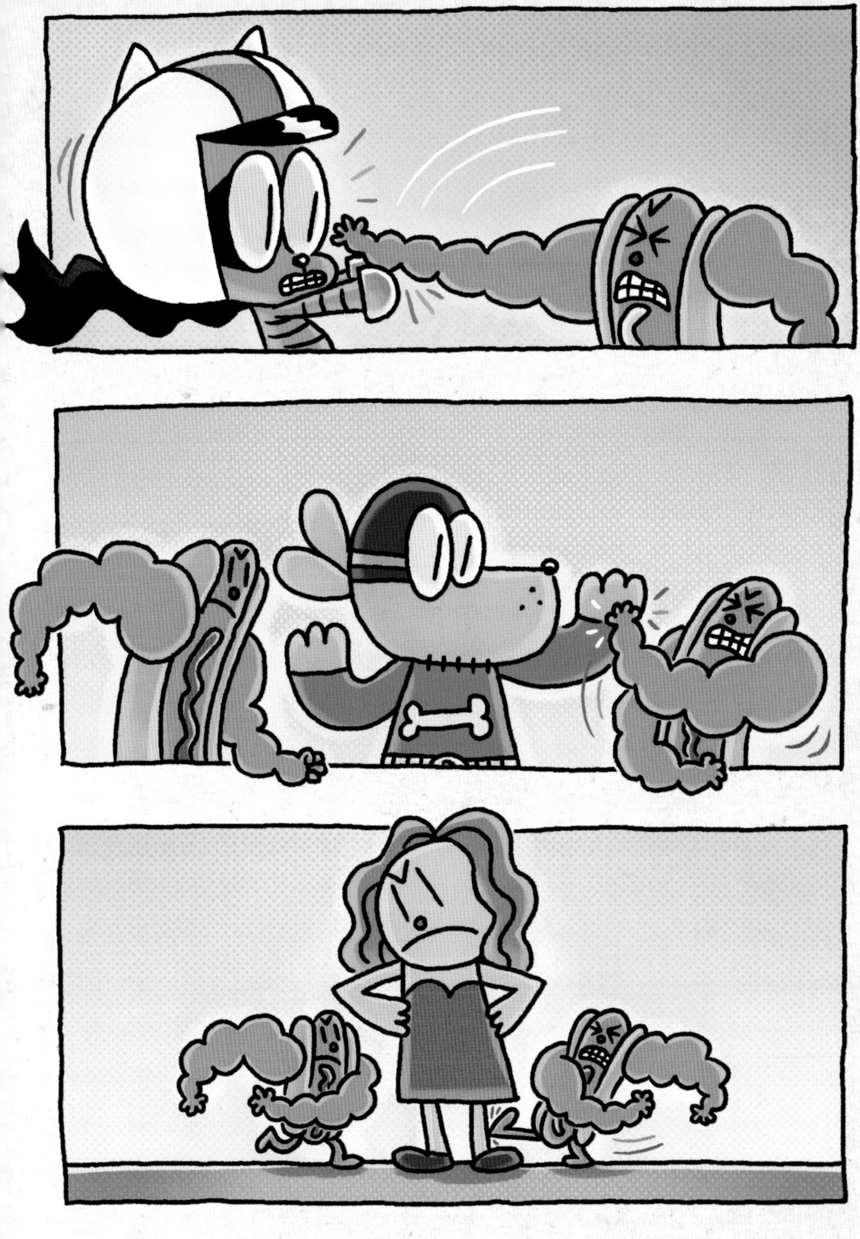

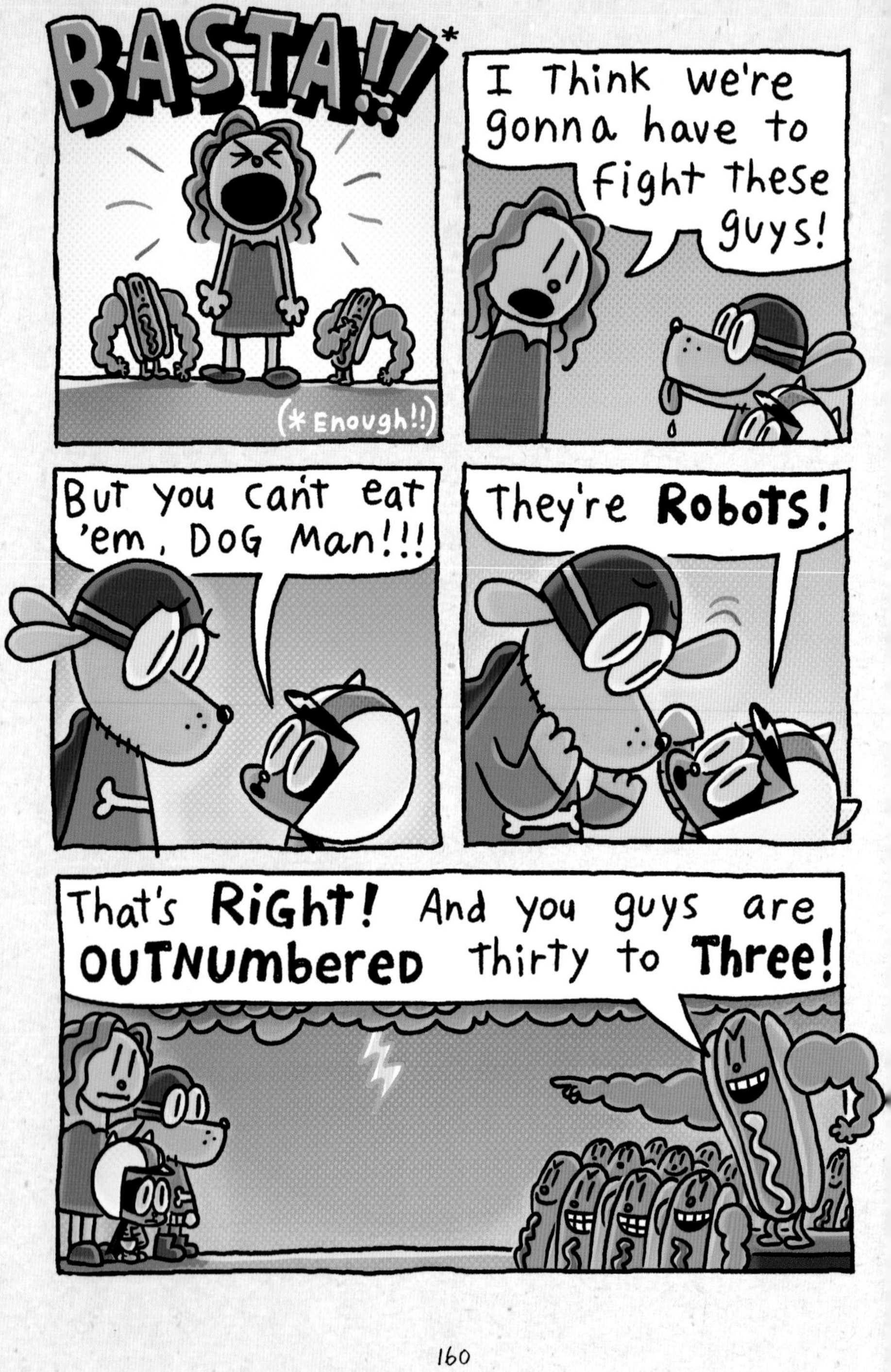
BASTA!!*
(*Enough!!)
I Think we're gonna have to fight these guys!
But you can't eat 'em, DOG Man!!!
They're Robots!
That's RiGht! And you guys are OUTNUMBERED thirty to Three!

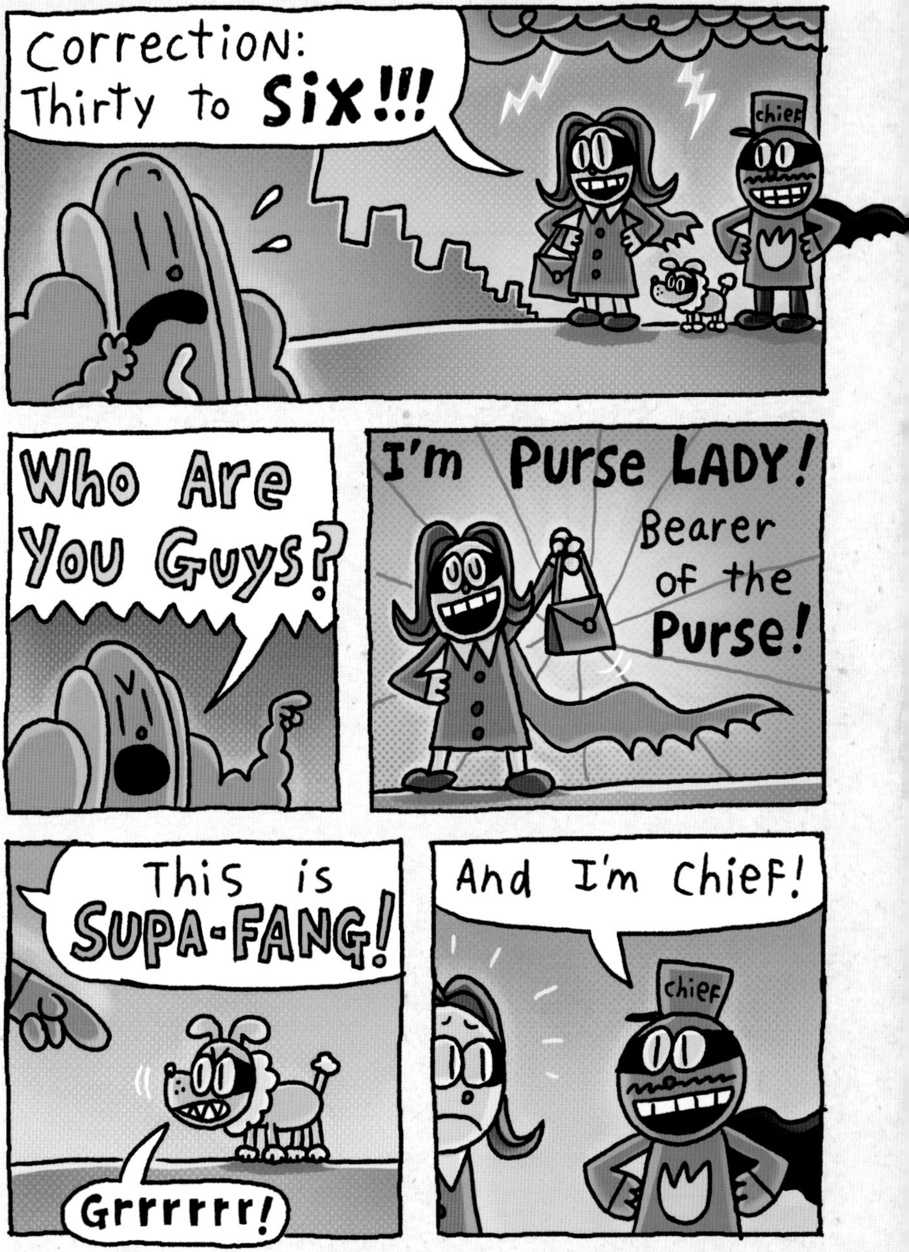
Correction: Thirty to SIX!!!
Who Are You Guys?
I'm Purse LADY!
Bearer of the Purse!
This is SUPA-FANG!
Grrrrrr!
And I'm Chief!
chief
chief

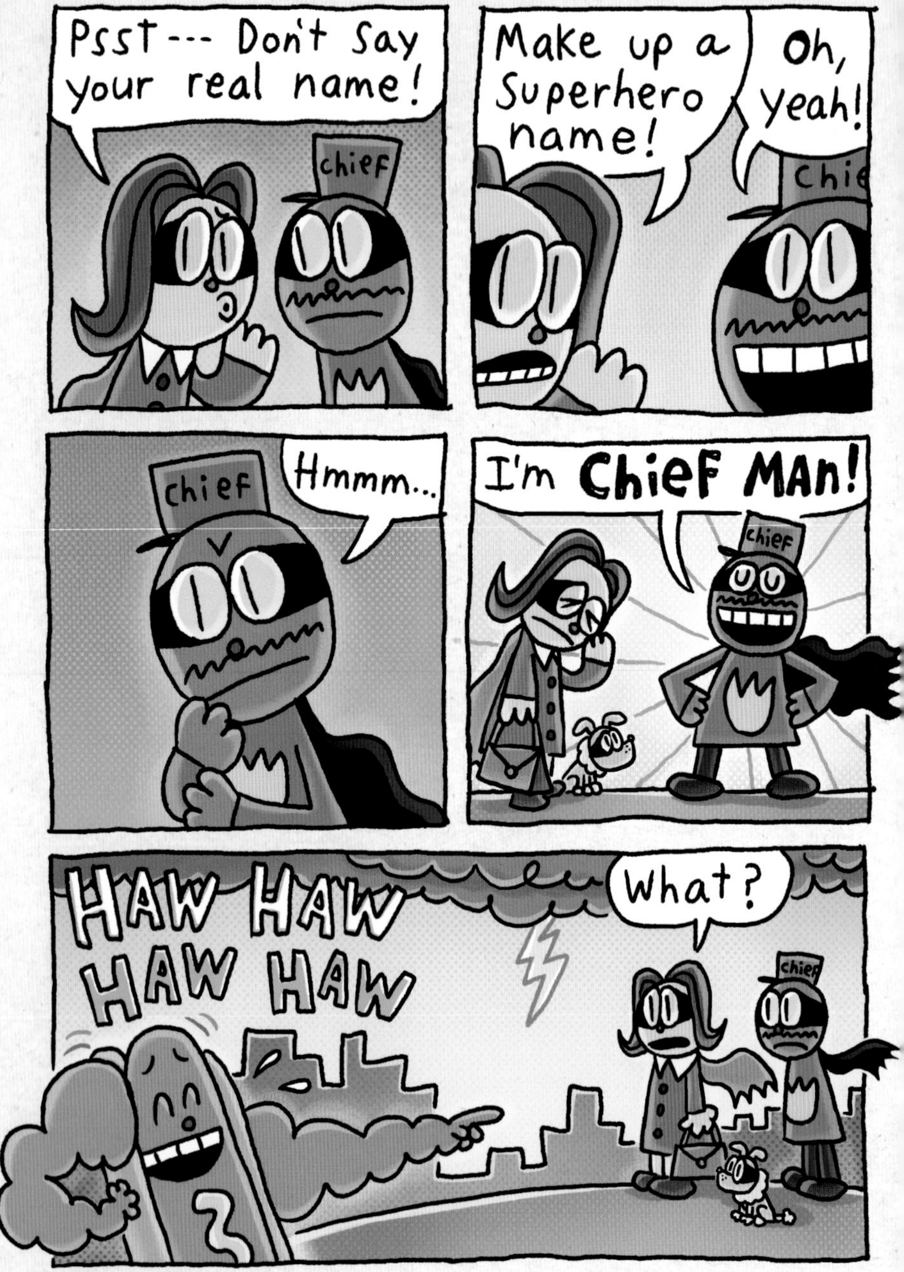
Psst--- Don't say your real name!
chief
Make up a Superhero name!
Oh, yeah!
chief
Hmmm...
I'm **Chief MAN!**
chief
HAW HAW HAW HAW
What?
chief

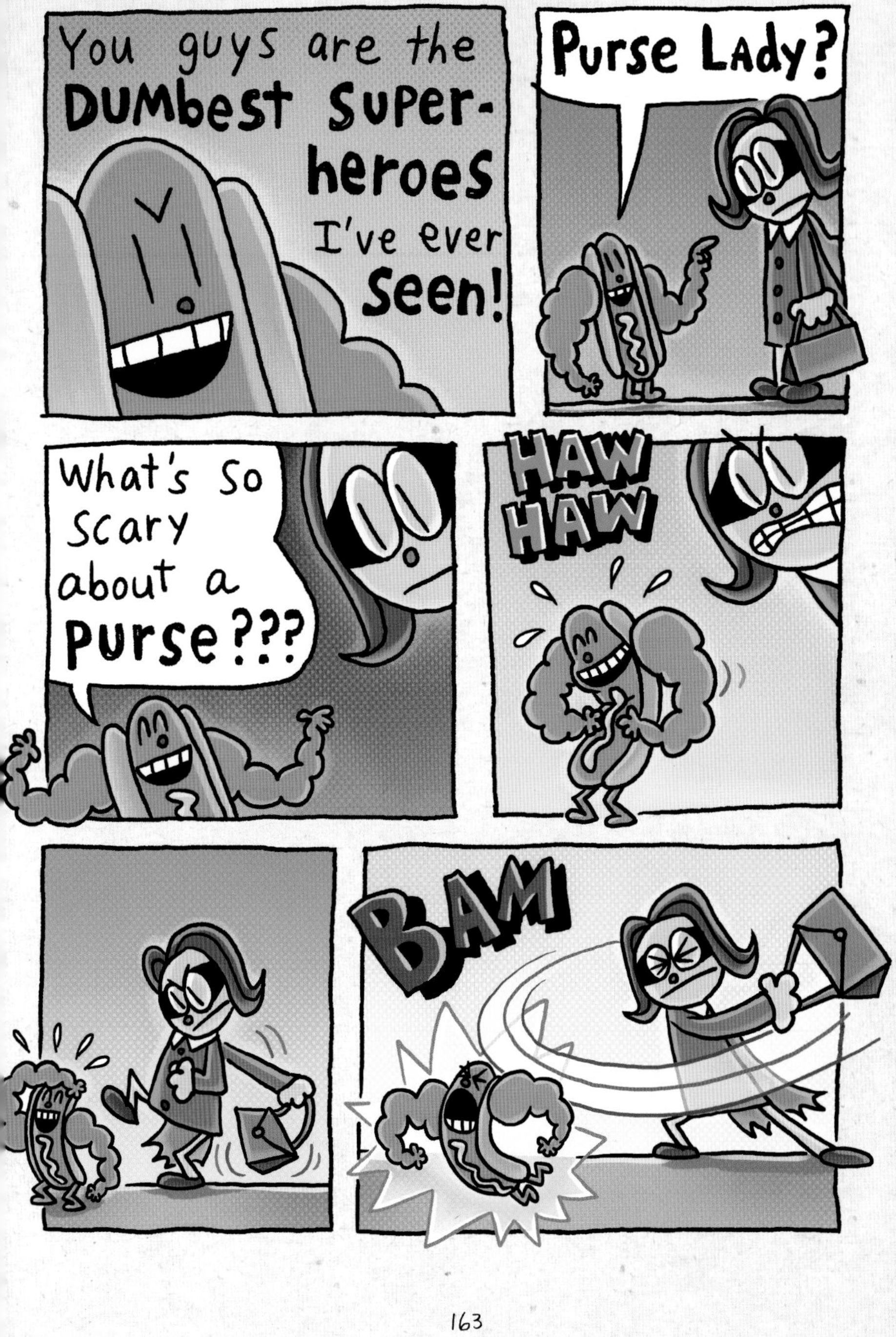
You guys are the DUMbest Super-heroes I've ever Seen!
Purse LAdy?
What's So Scary about a PUrSe???
HAW HAW
BAM!

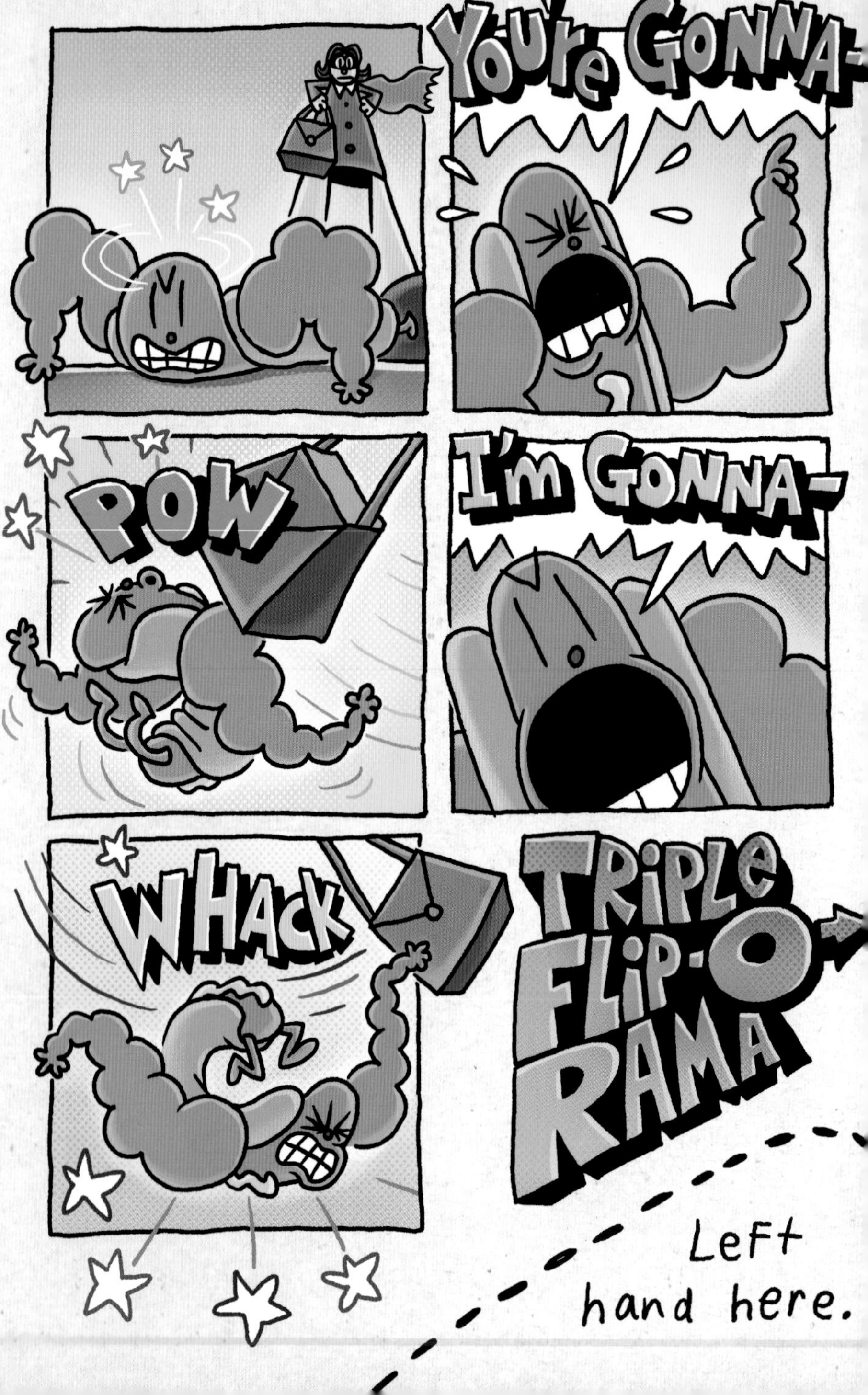

YOU'RE GONNA-
POW
I'M GONNA-
WHACK
TRIPLE FLIP-O-RAMA
Left hand here.

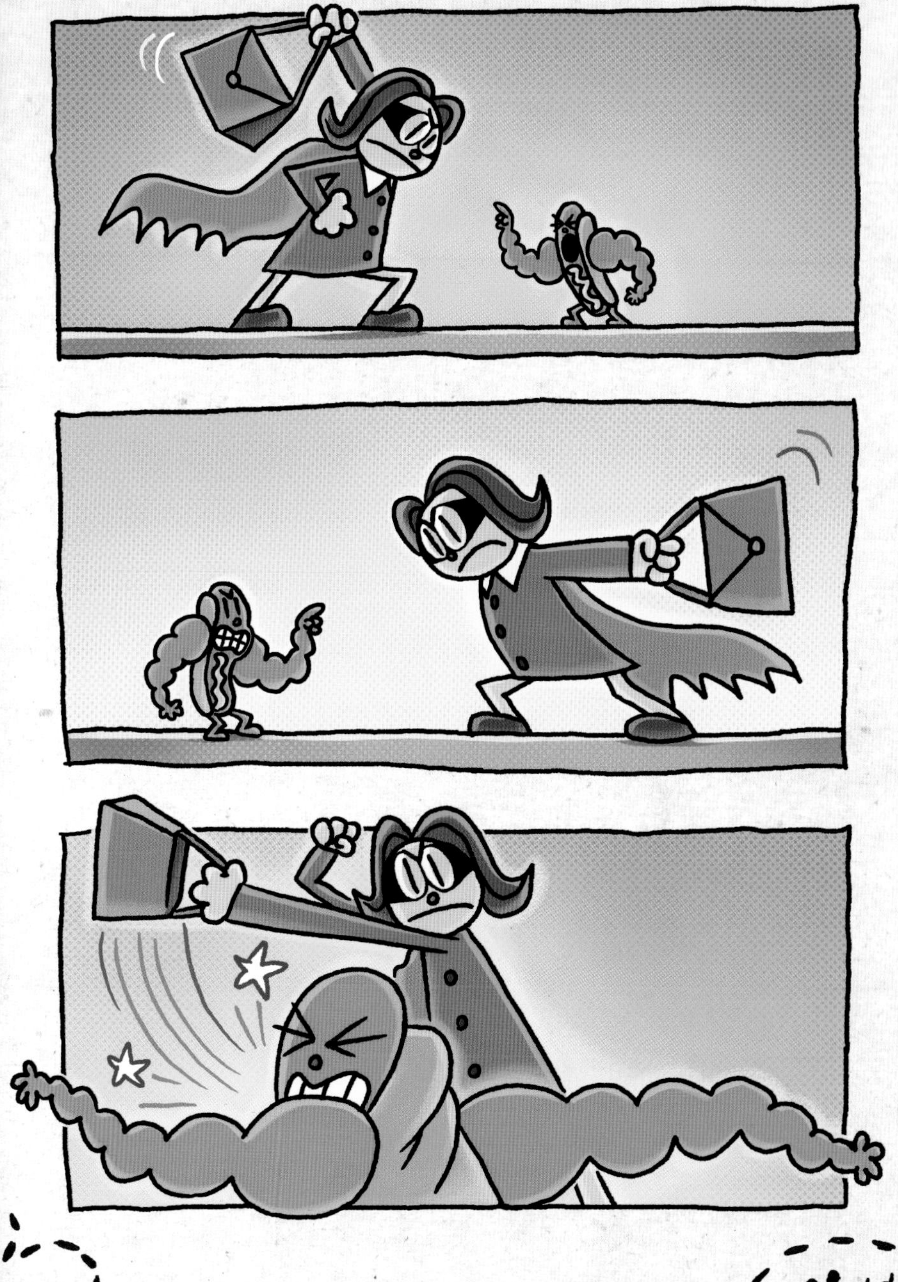

Right Thumb here.

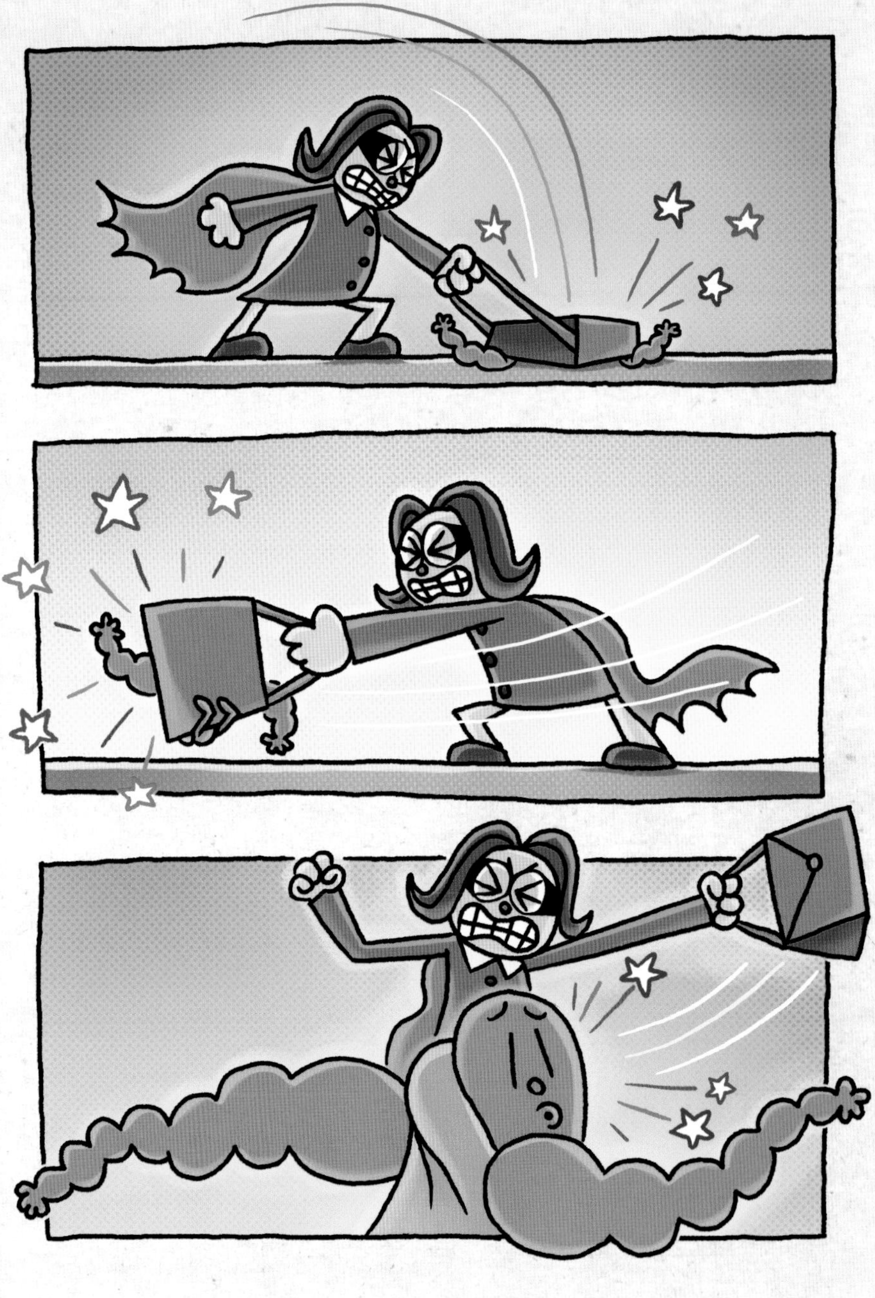

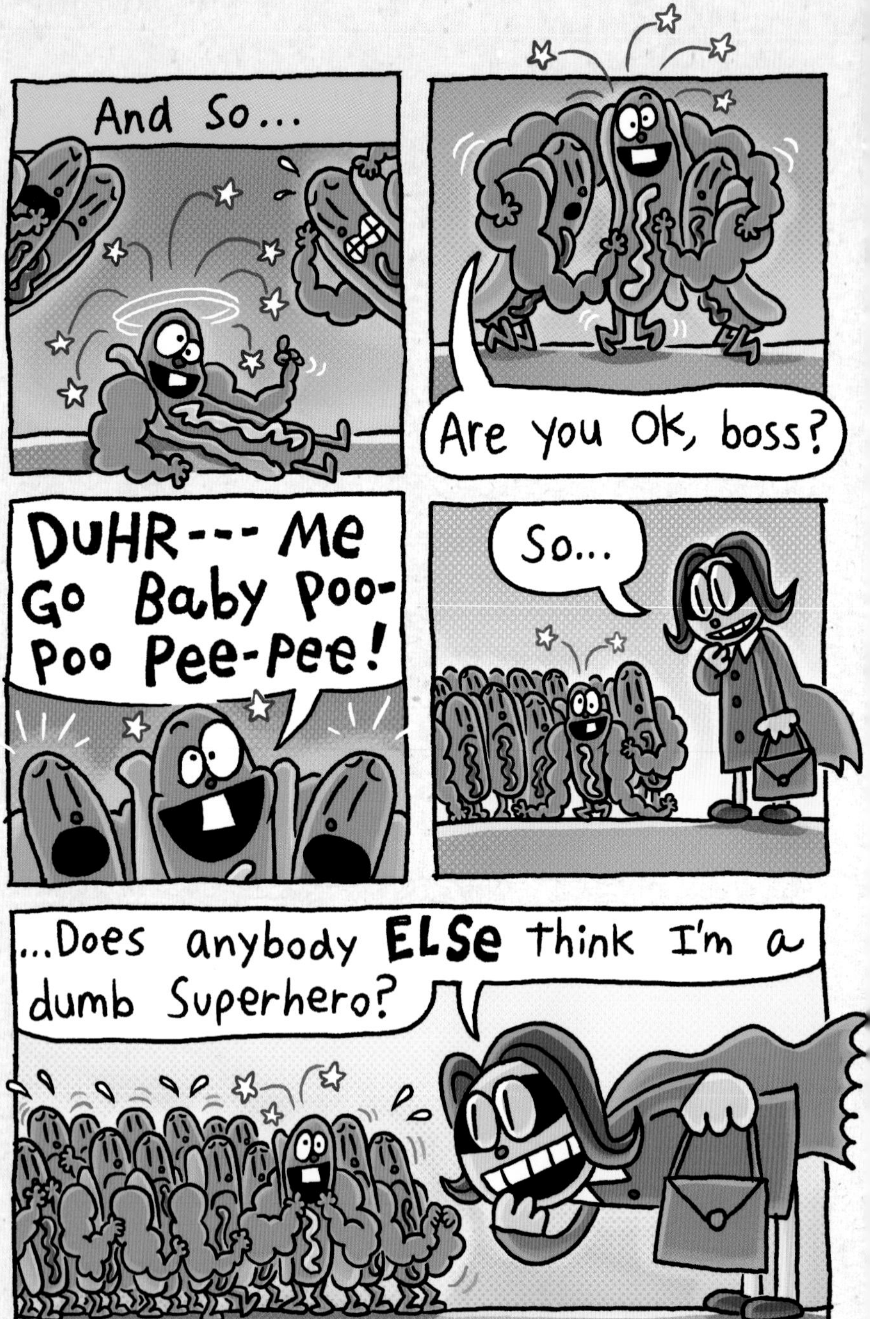
And So...
Are you OK, boss?
DUHR--- Me Go Baby Poo-Poo Pee-Pee!
So...
...Does anybody ELSe think I'm a dumb Superhero?

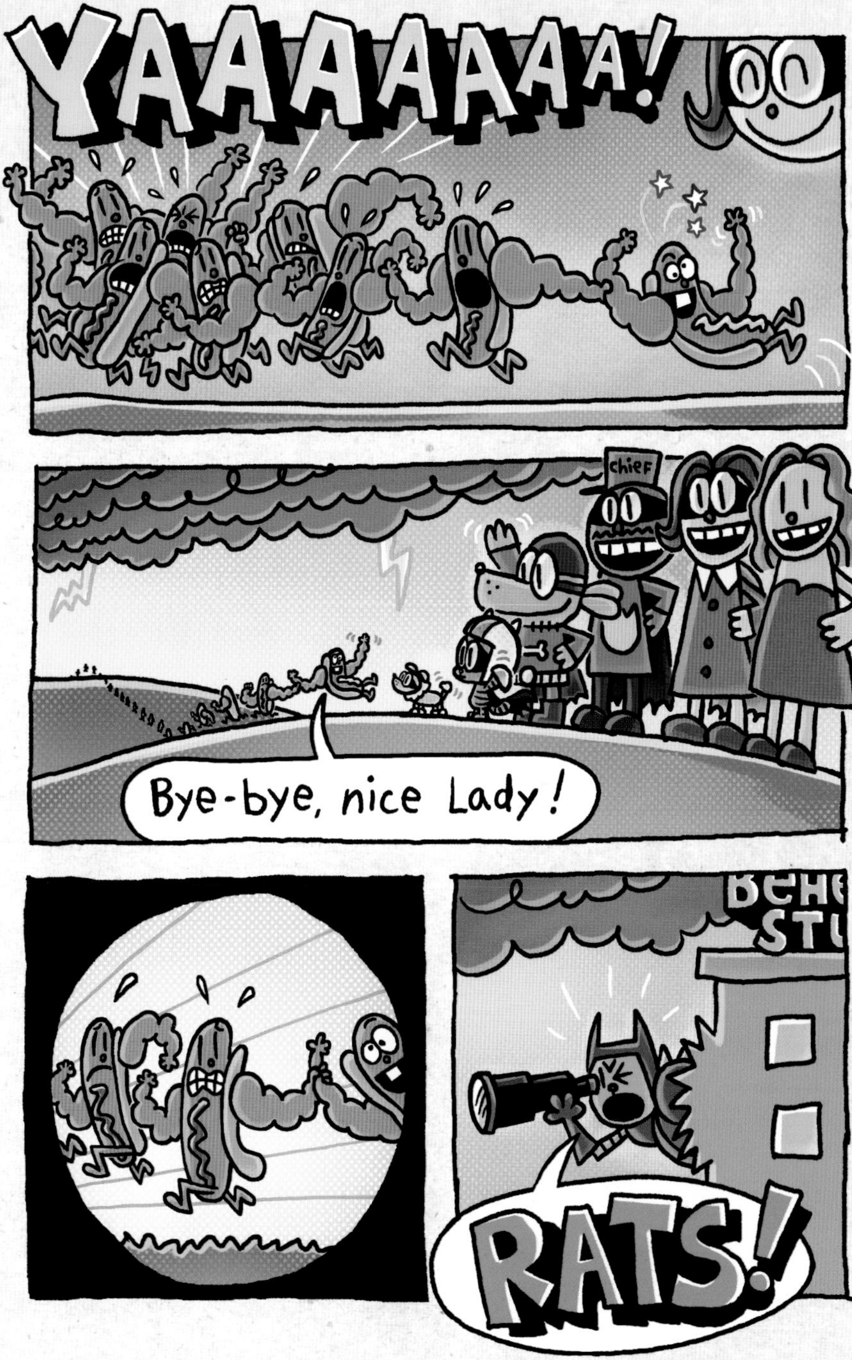

YAAAAAAA!
chief
Bye-bye, nice Lady!
RATS!

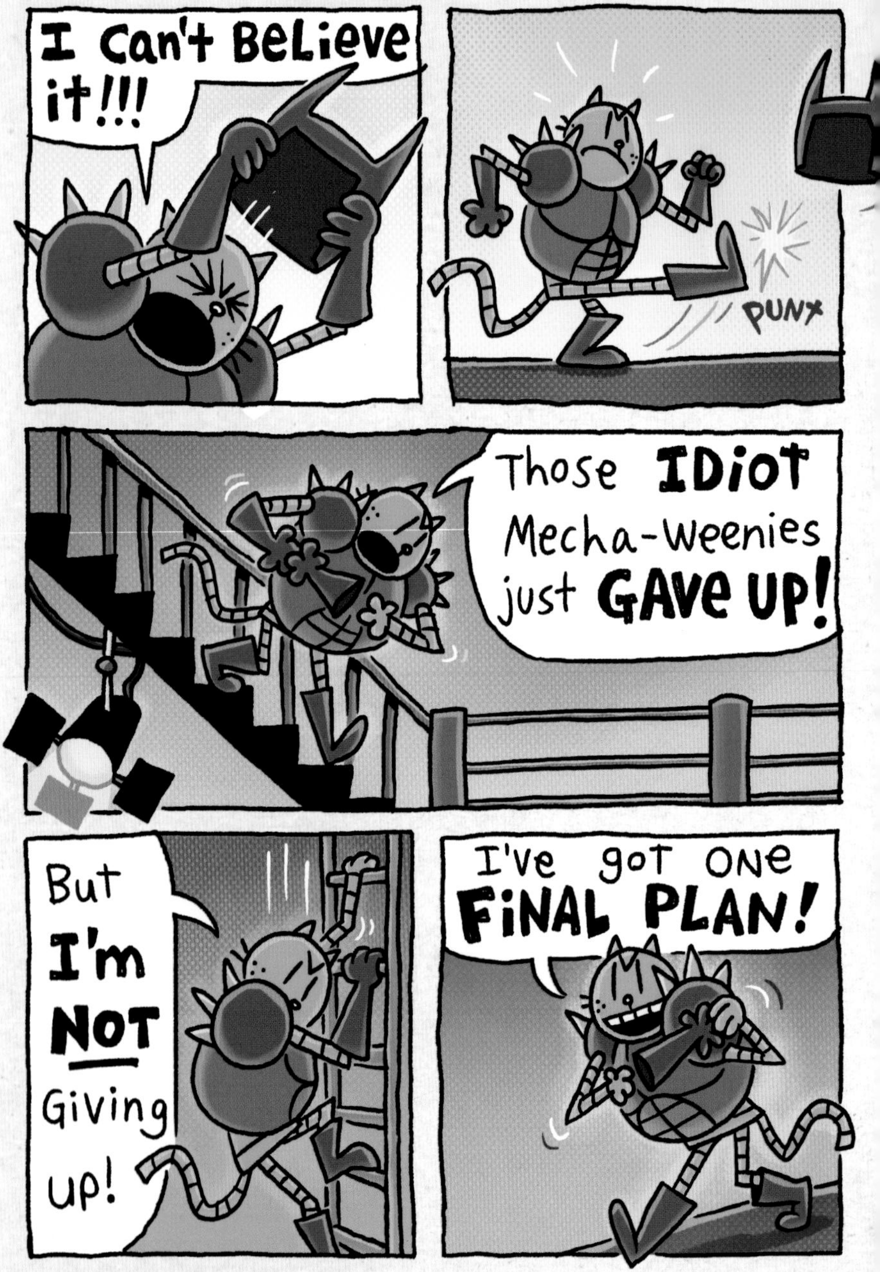
I Can't BeLieve it!!!
PUNT
Those IDioT Mecha-Weenies just GAVE UP!
But I'm NOT Giving up!
I've got ONE FiNAL PLAN!

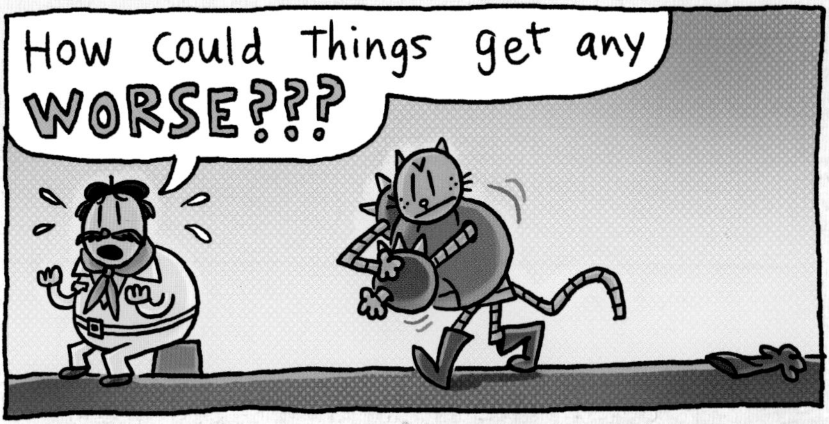
How could things get any WORSE???

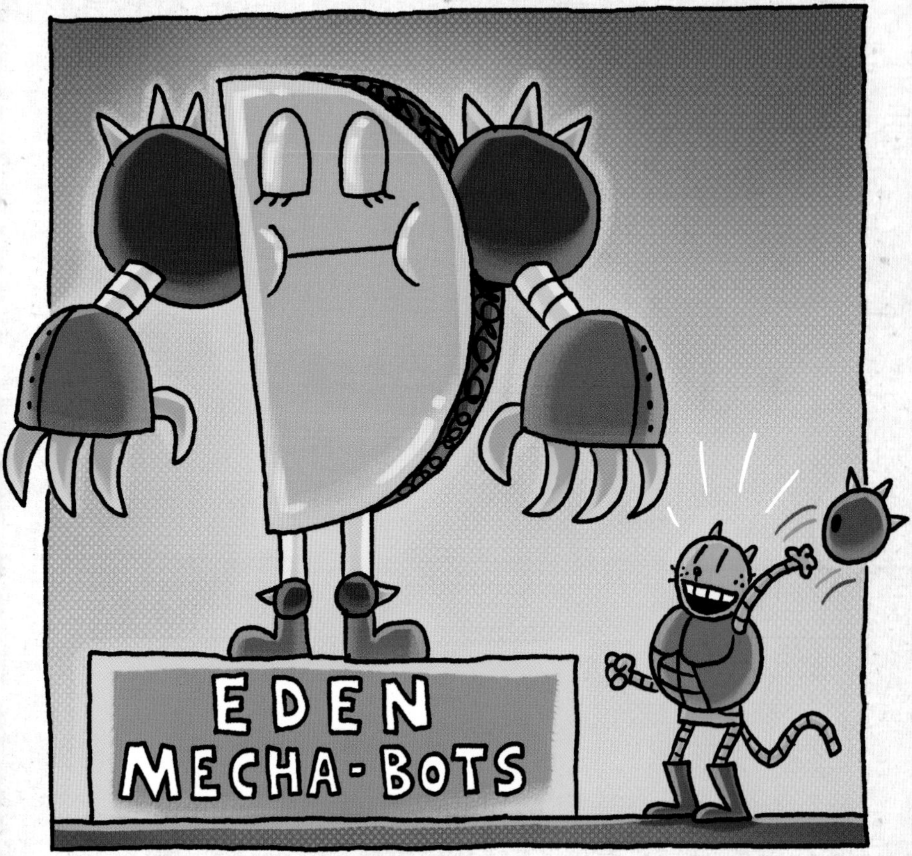
EDEN MECHA-BOTS

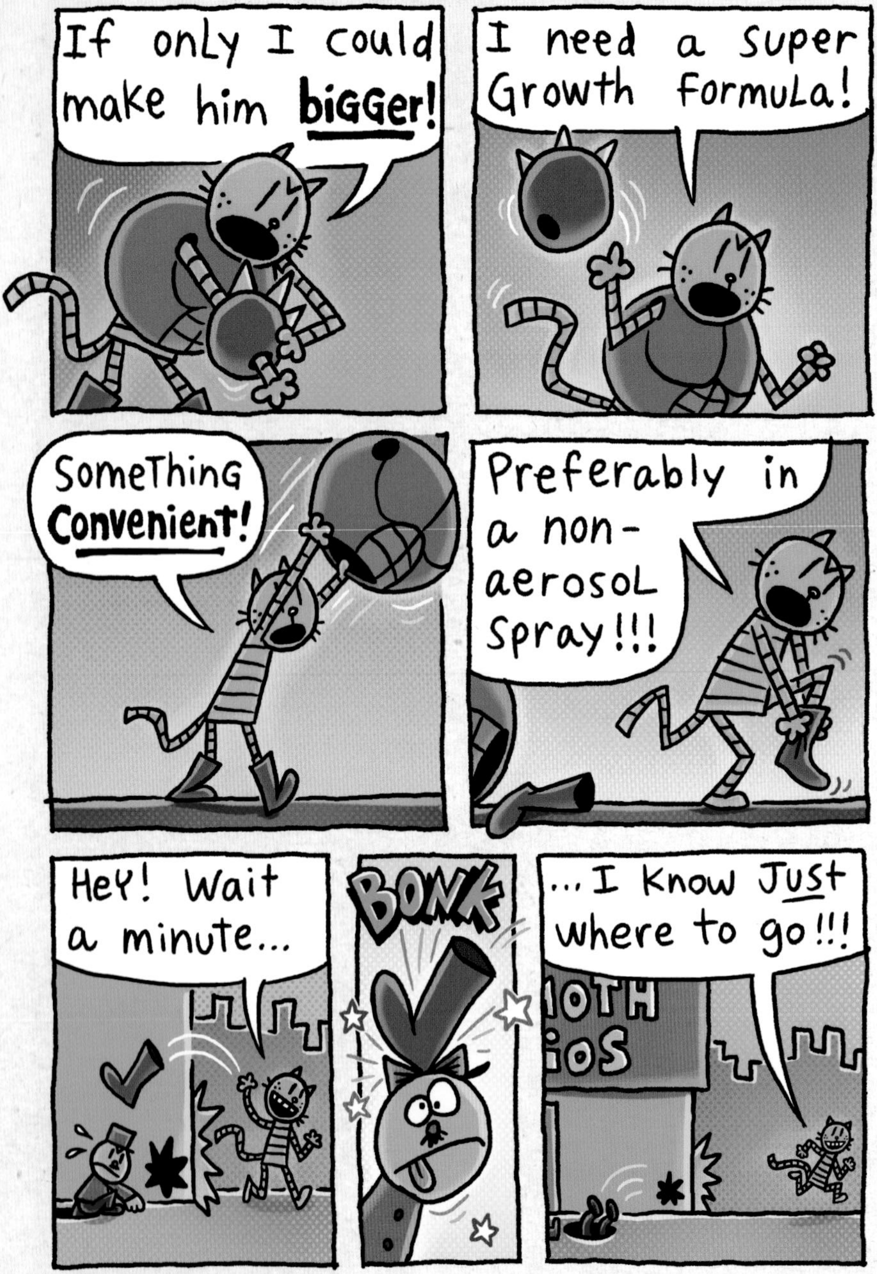
If only I could make him biGGer!
I need a Super Growth FormuLa!
SomeThinG Convenient!
Preferably in a non-aerosoL Spray!!!
Hey! Wait a minute...
BONK
...I know JUst where to go!!!
10TH
iOS

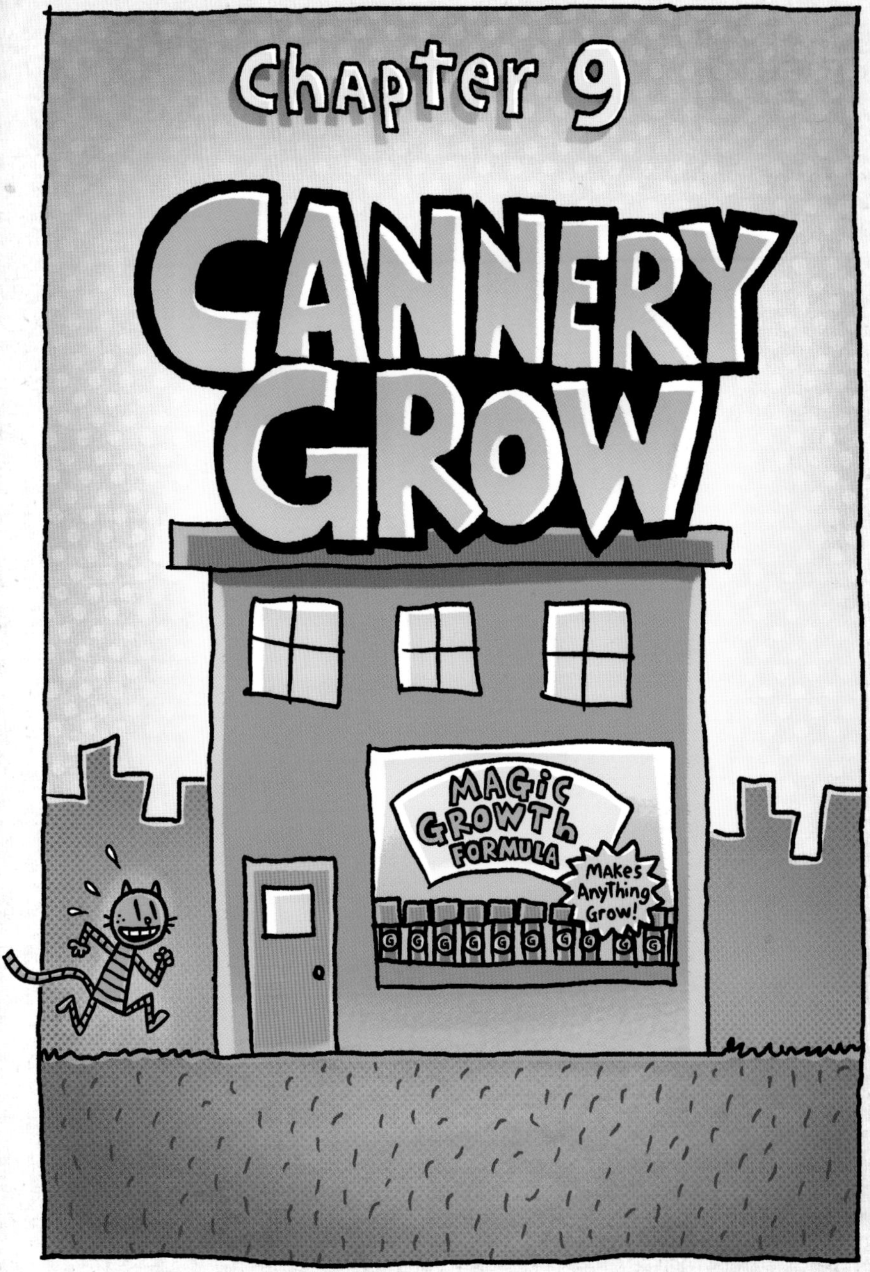
Chapter 9
CANNERY GROW
MAGIC GROWTH FORMULA
Makes Anything Grow!

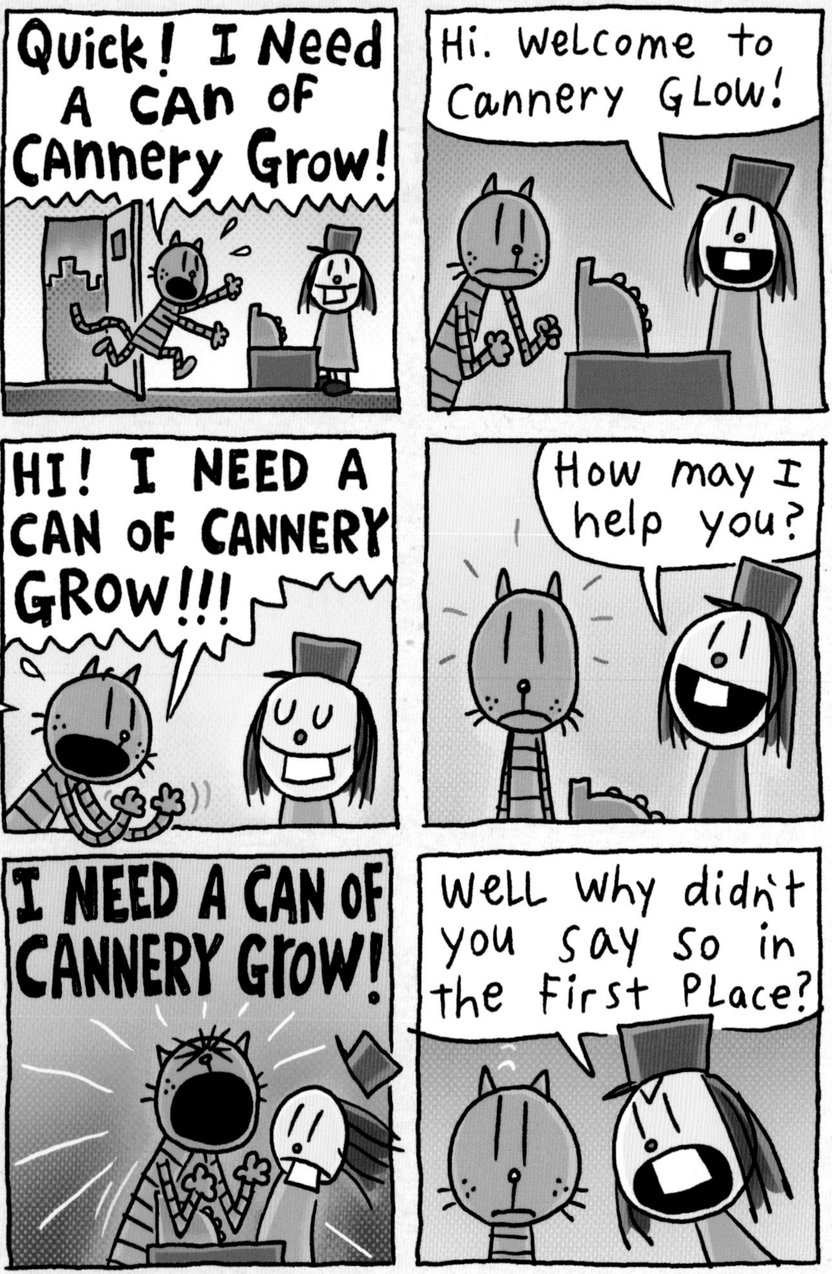

Quick! I Need A CAN OF CAnnery Grow!
Hi. Welcome to Cannery GLOW!
HI! I NEED A CAN OF CANNERY GROW!!!
How may I help you?
I NEED A CAN OF CANNERY Grow!
WeLL Why didn't you say so in the First PLace?

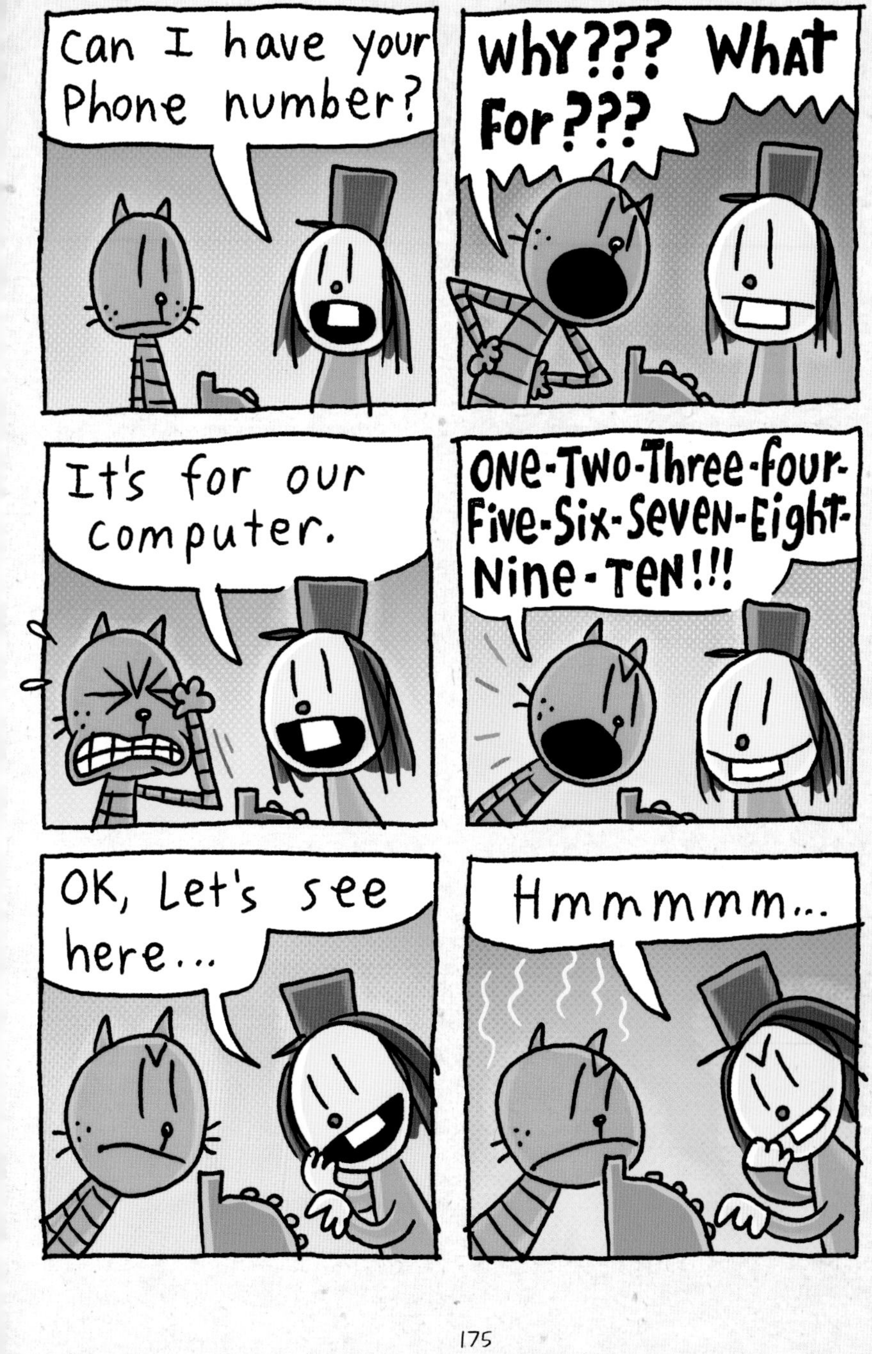
Can I have your Phone number?
WHY??? WHAT For???
It's for our computer.
ONE-Two-Three-four-Five-Six-Seven-Eight-Nine-TEN!!!
OK, Let's see here...
Hmmmmm...

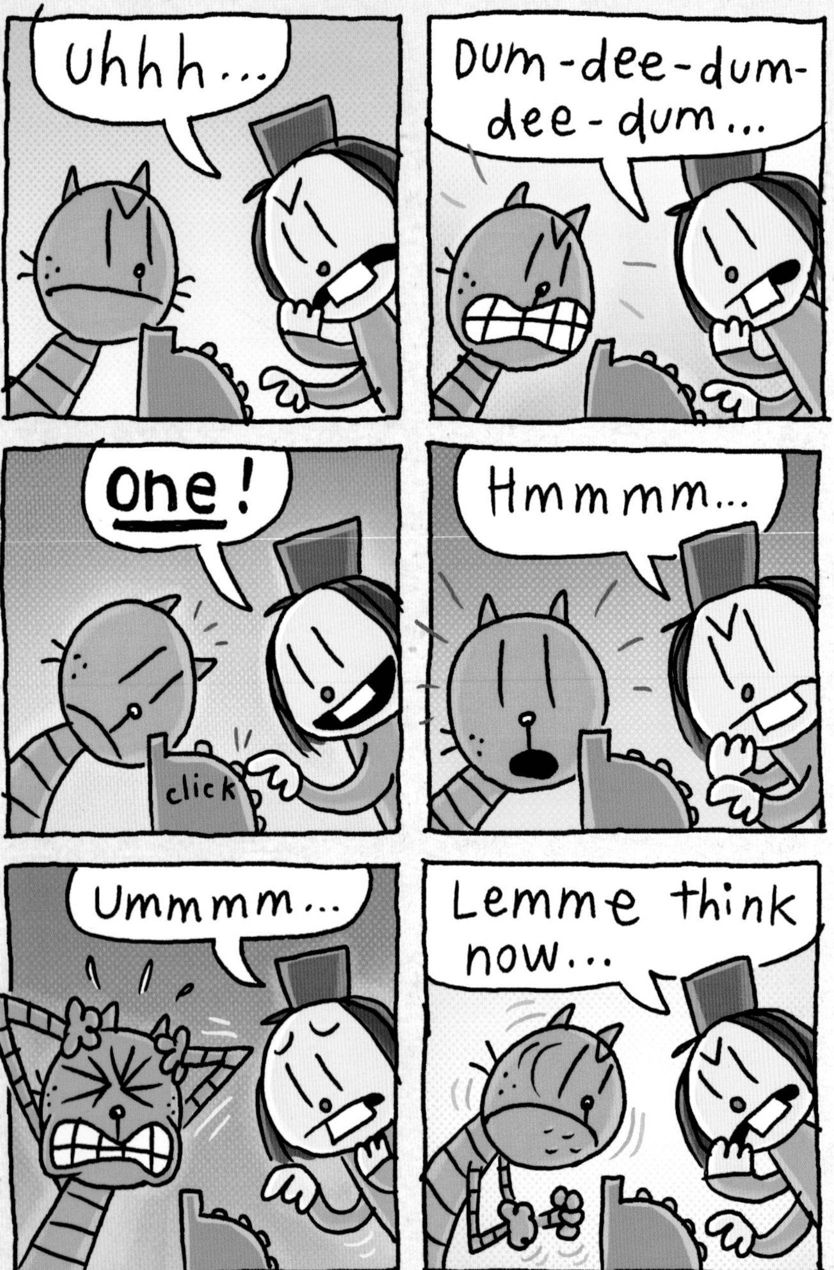
Uhhh...
Dum-dee-dum-dee-dum...
One!
click
Hmmmm...
Ummmm...
Lemme think now...

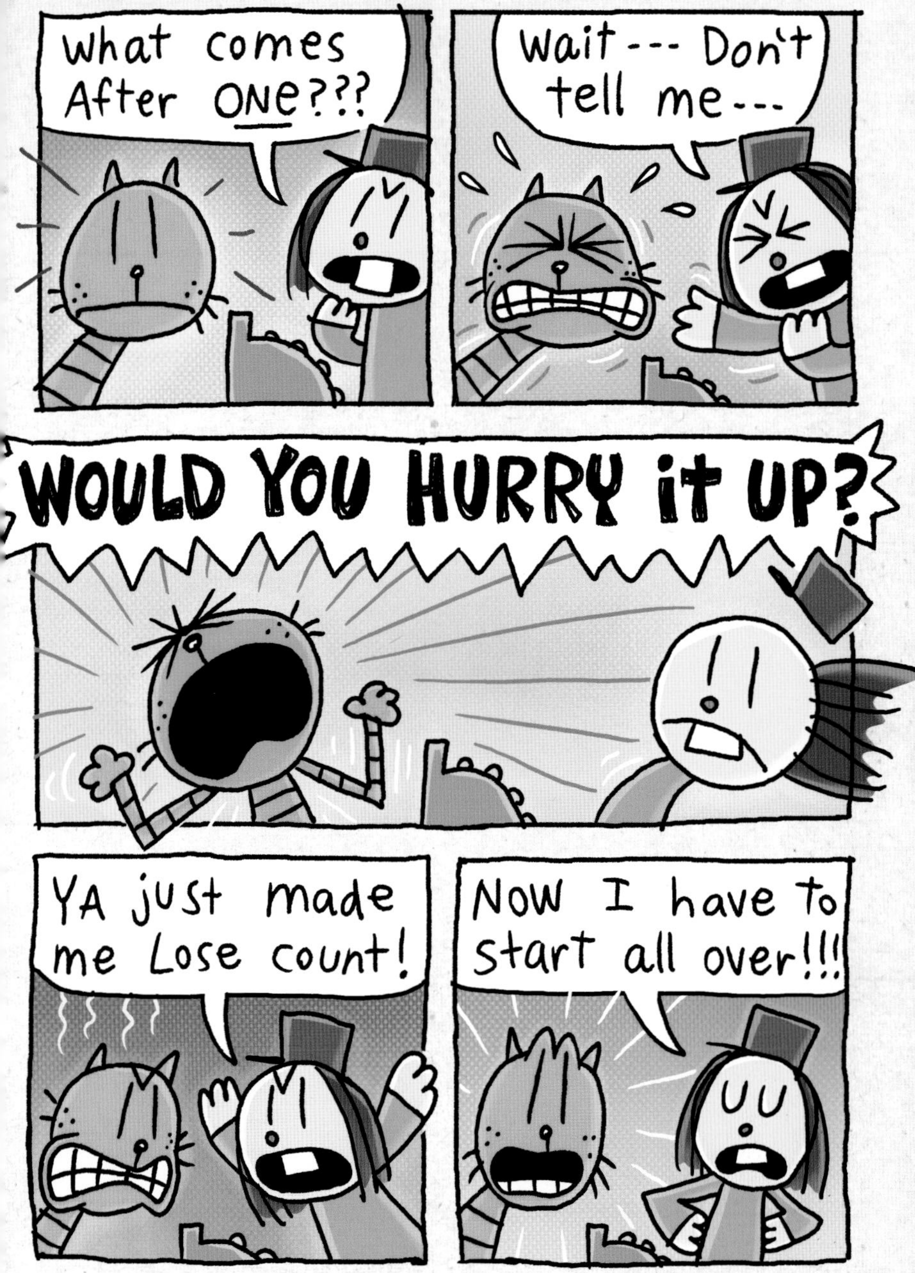

What comes After ONE???
Wait--- Don't tell me---
WOULD YOU HURRY it UP?
YA just made me Lose count!
Now I have to start all over!!!

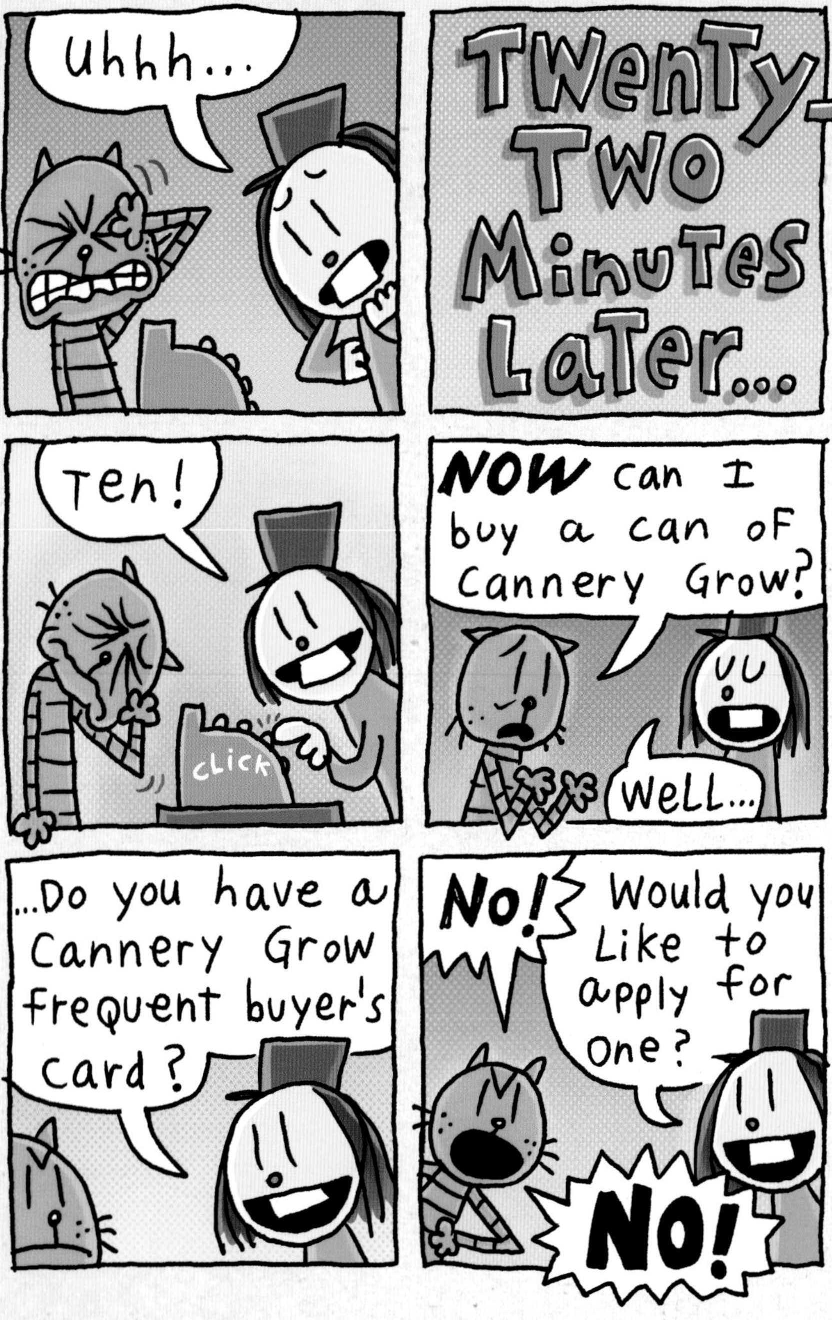
Uhhh...
TWENTY-TWO MINUTES LATER...
Ten!
CLICK
NOW can I buy a can of Cannery Grow?
WELL...
...Do you have a Cannery Grow frequent buyer's card?
No!
Would you Like to apply for one?
NO!

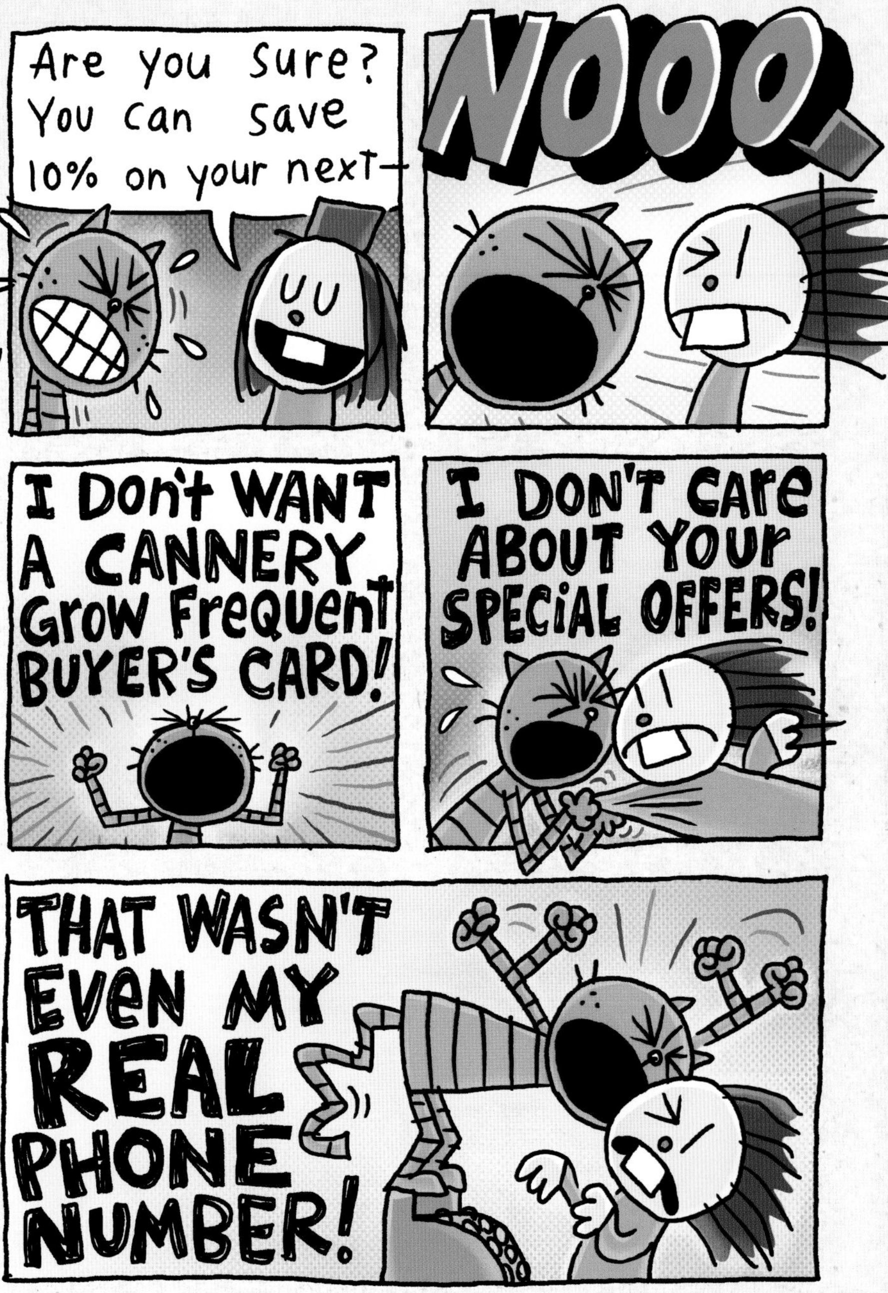

Are you sure? You can save 10% on your next—
NOOO
I DON'T WANT A CANNERY GROW FREQUENT BUYER'S CARD!
I DON'T CARE ABOUT YOUR SPECIAL OFFERS!
THAT WASN'T EVEN MY REAL PHONE NUMBER!

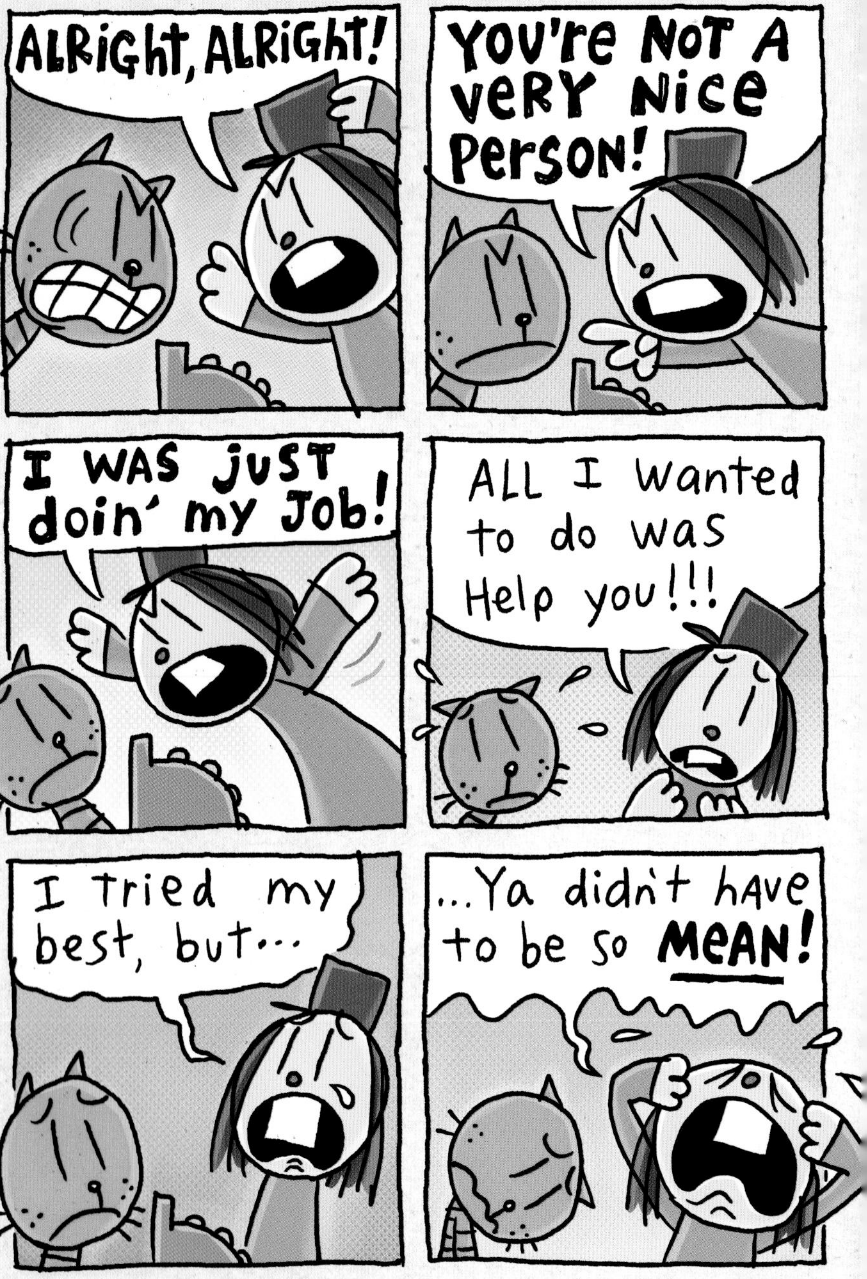
ALRIGHT, ALRIGHT!
YOU'RE NOT A VERY NICE PERSON!
I WAS JUST doin' my Job!
ALL I Wanted to do was Help you!!!
I tried my best, but...
...Ya didn't have to be so MEAN!

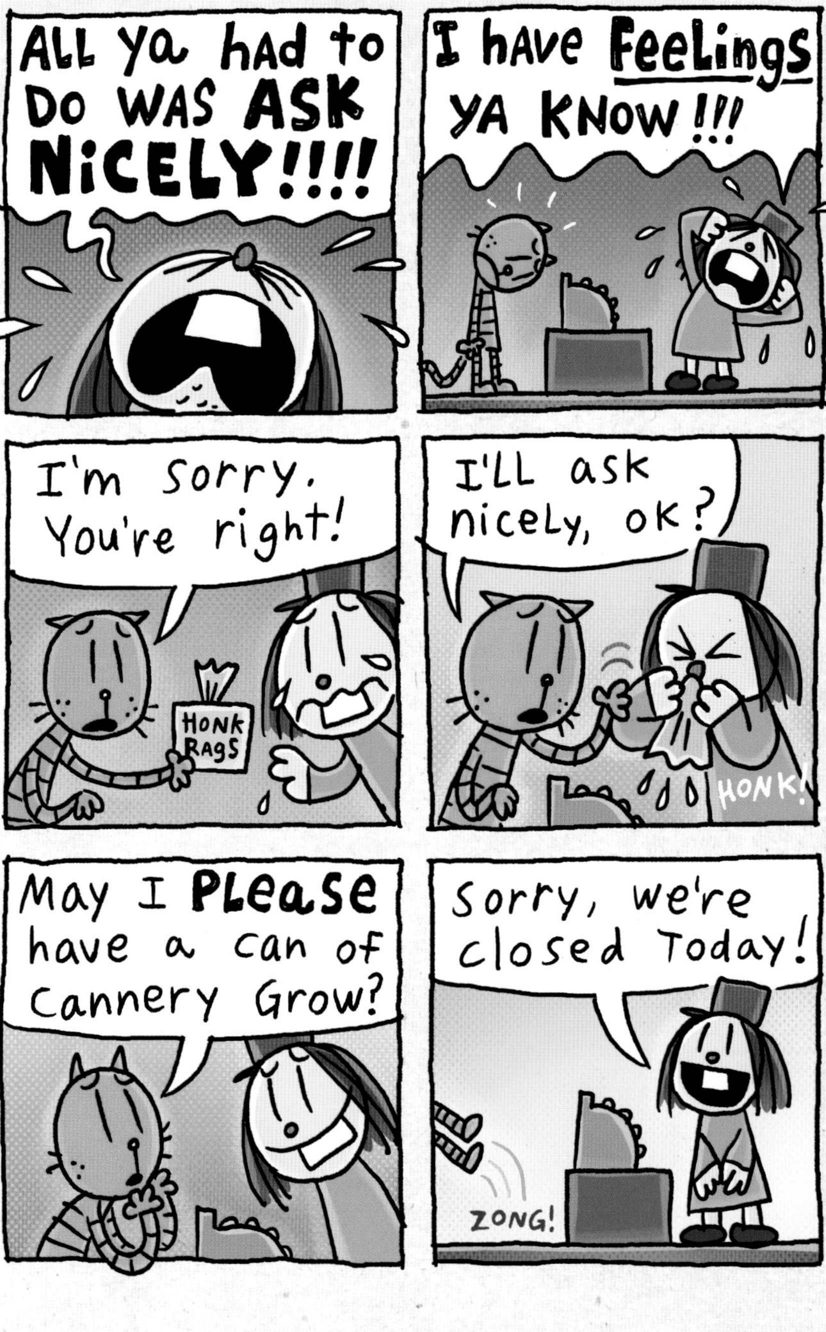
ALL ya had to DO WAS ASK NiCELY!!!!
I have FeeLings YA KNOW!!!
I'm Sorry. You're right!
HONK RAGS
I'LL ask nicely, ok?
HONK!
May I PLease have a can of cannery Grow?
Sorry, we're closed Today!
ZONG!

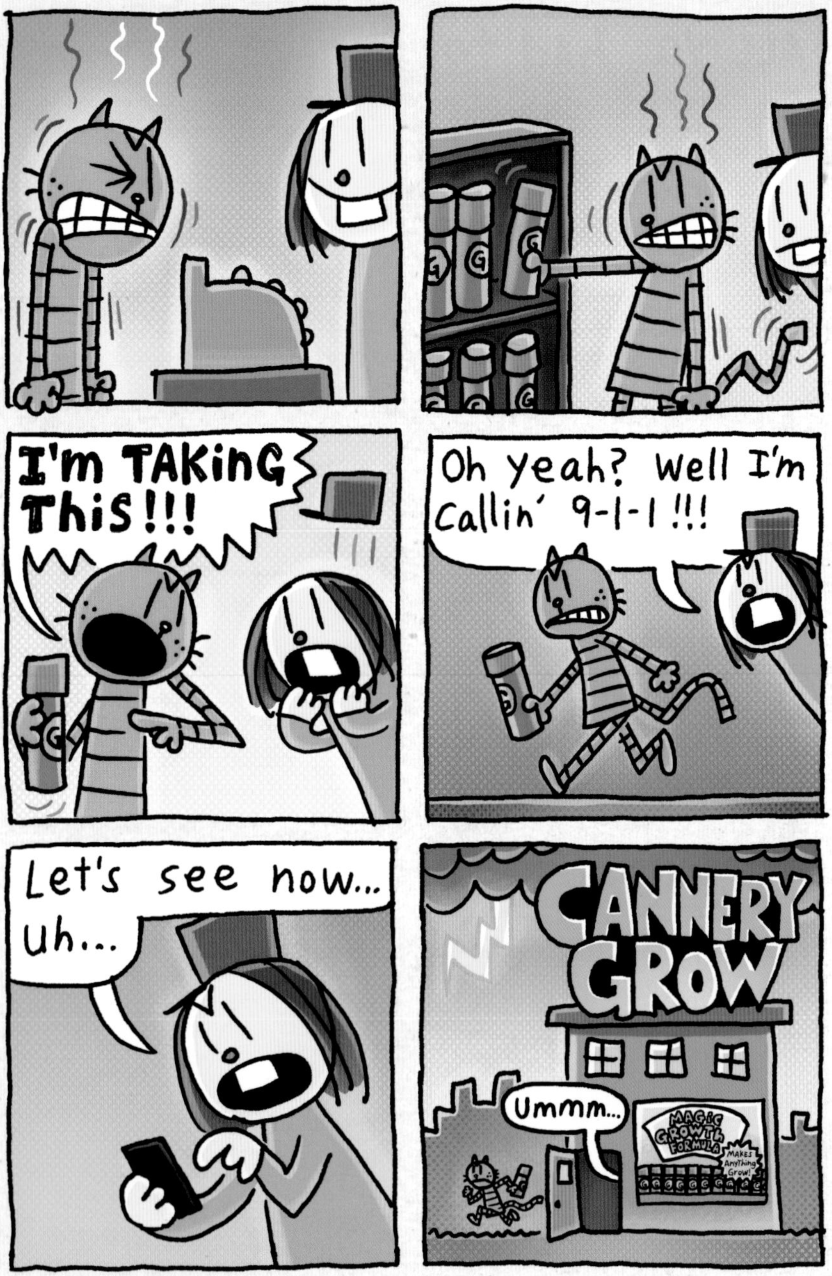
I'm TAKinG This!!!
Oh yeah? Well I'm Callin' 9-1-1!!!
Let's see now... uh...
CANNERY GROW
Ummm...
MAGIC GROWTH FORMULA
MAKES Anything Grow!

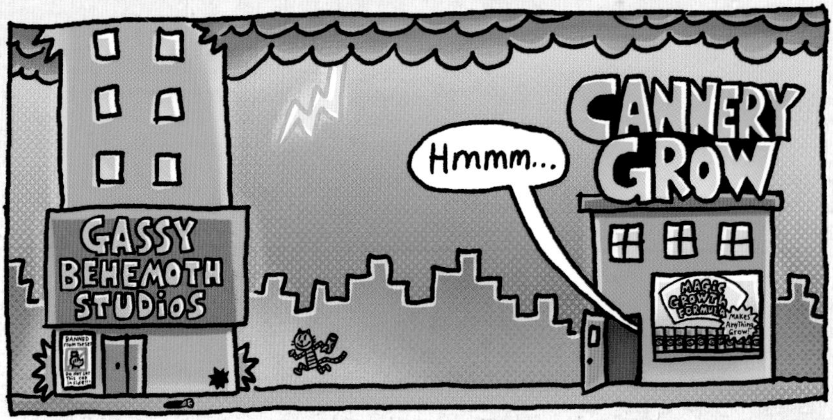
GASSY BEHEMOTH STUDIOS
BANNED FROM THE SET
DO NOT LET THIS CAT INSIDE!!!
CANNERY GROW
Hmmm...
MAGIC GROWTH FORMULA
MAKES ANYTHING GROW!

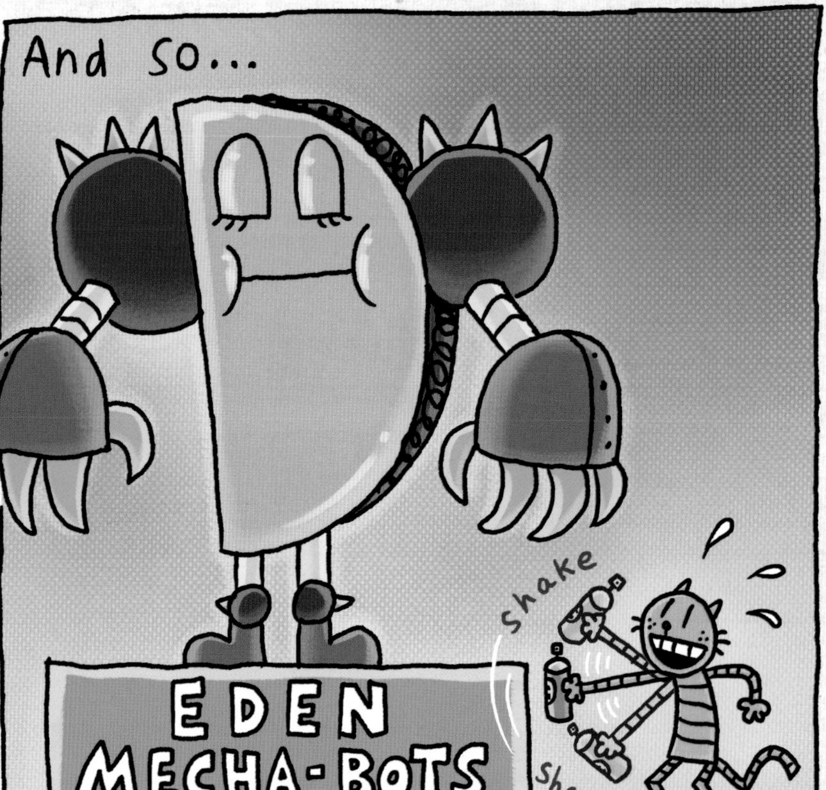
And so...
EDEN MECHA-BOTS
Shake
Shake

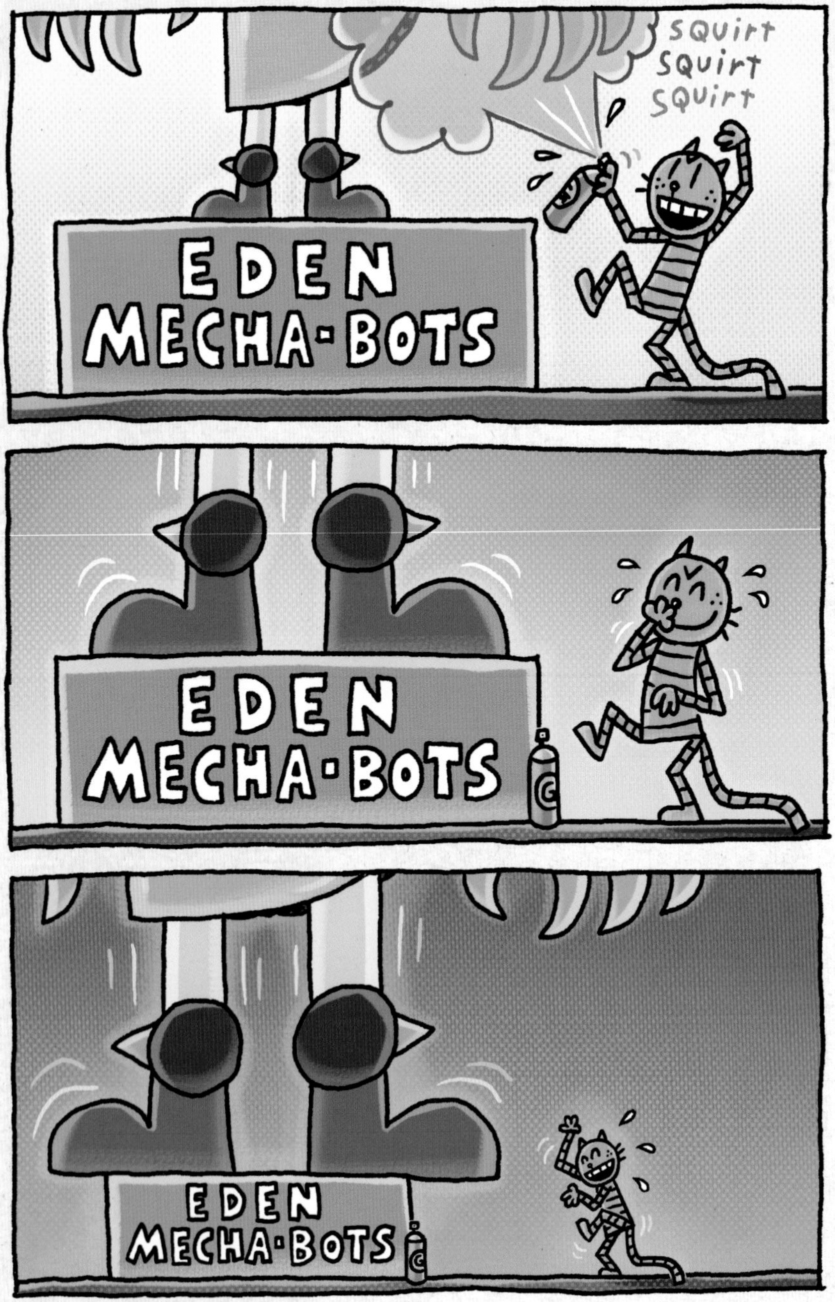
SQUIRT
SQUIRT
SQUIRT
EDEN
MECHA-BOTS
EDEN
MECHA-BOTS
EDEN
MECHA-BOTS

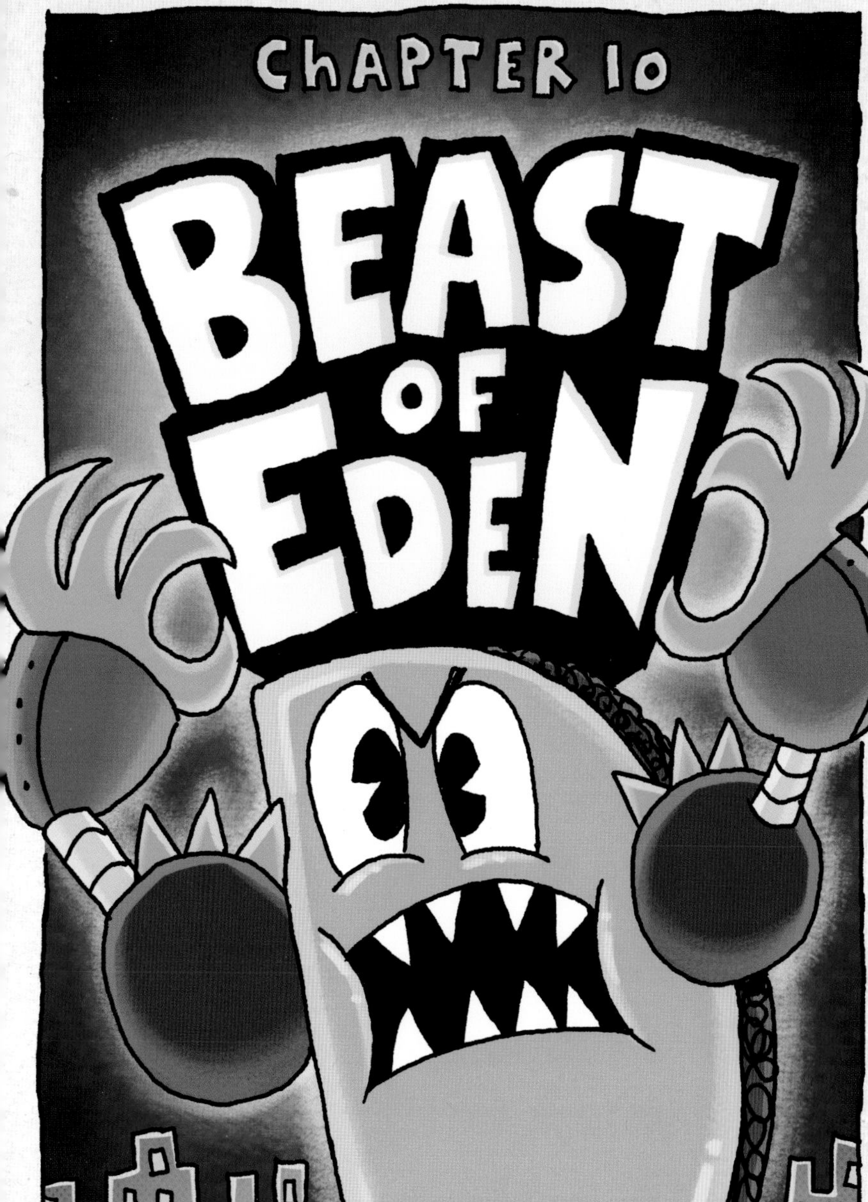
ChAPTER 10
BEAST OF EDEN

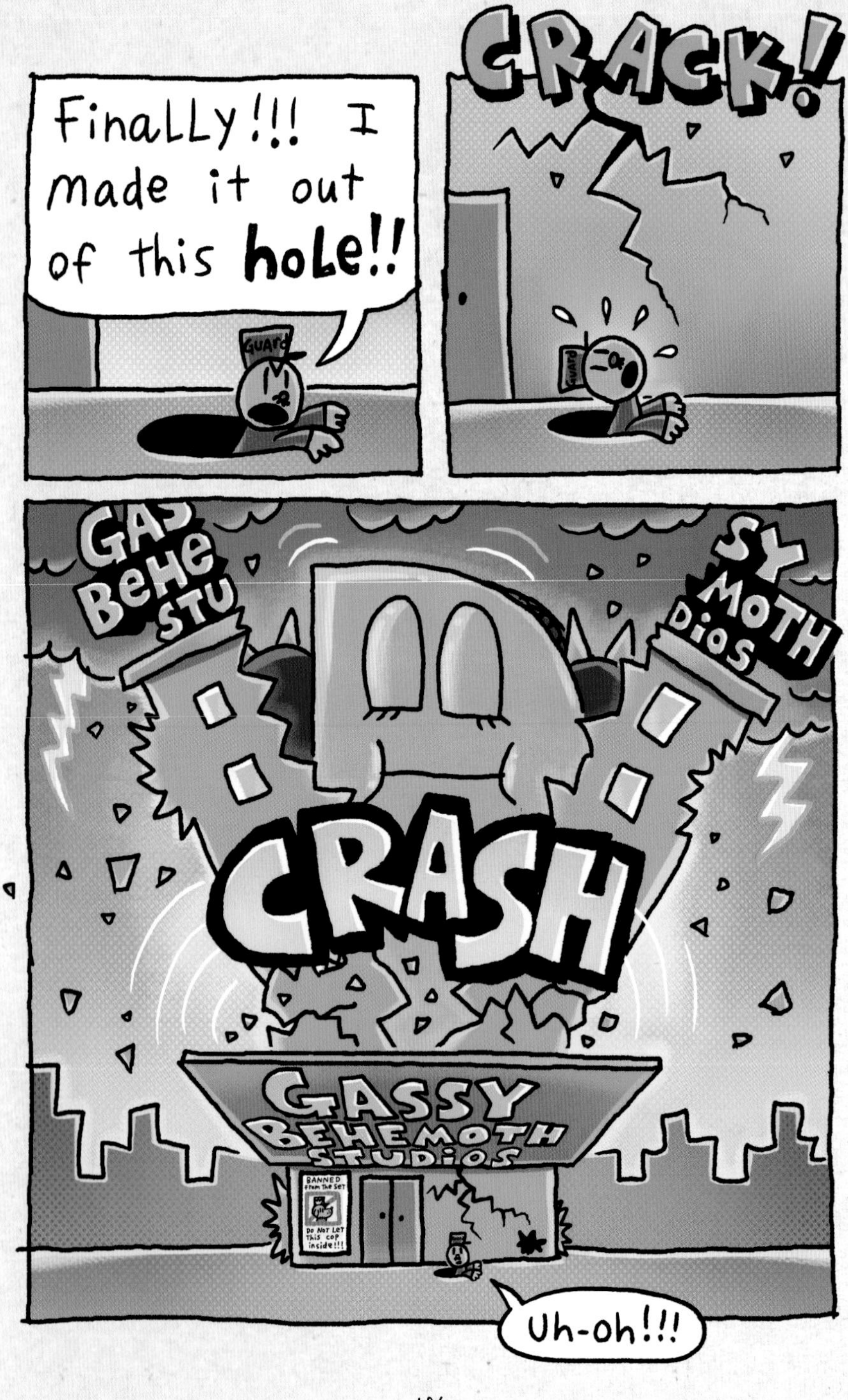
Finally!!! I made it out of this hole!!
GUARD
CRACK!
GUARD
GAS BeHe STU
SY MOTH DiOS
CRASH
GASSY BEHEMOTH STUDiOS
BANNED From The SET
Do NOT LET This cop inside!!!
Uh-oh!!!

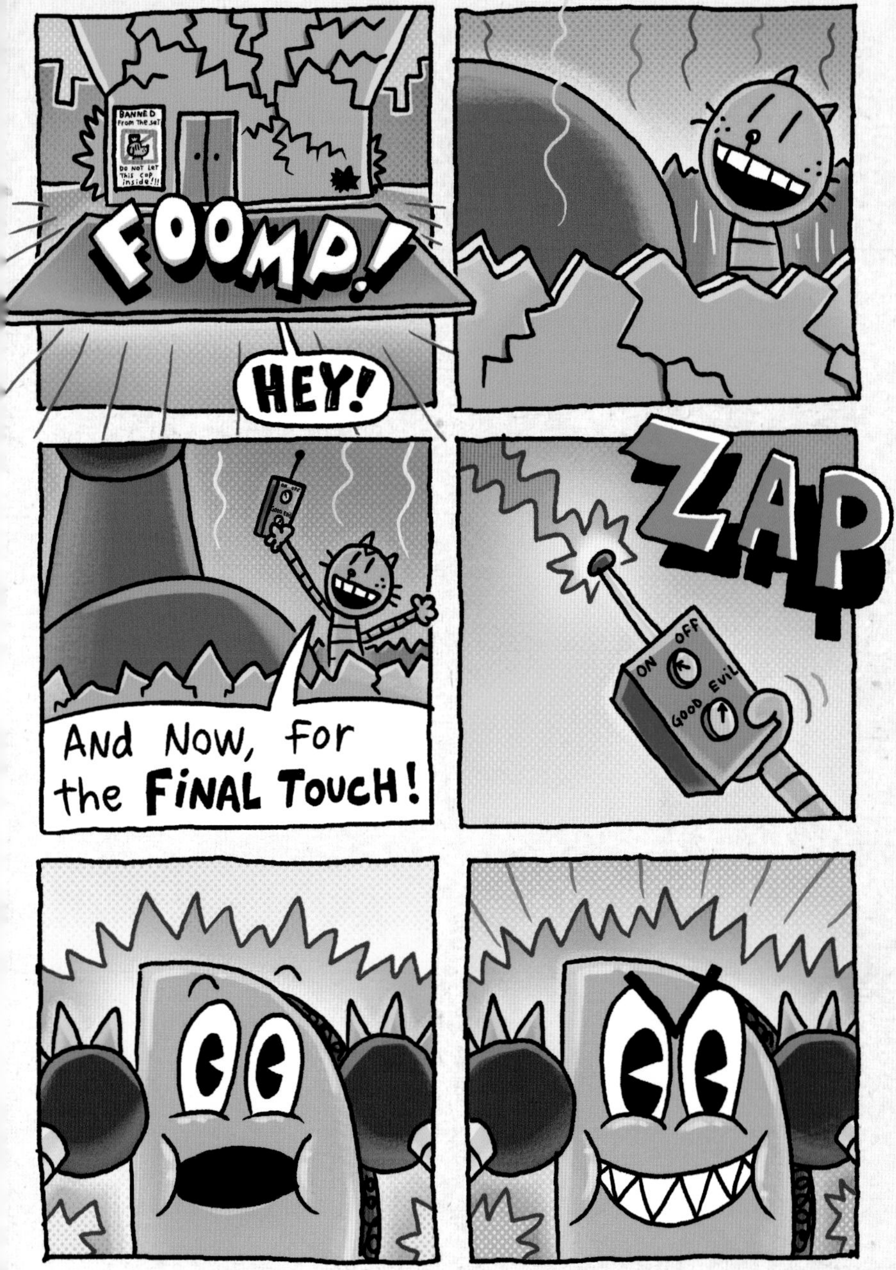

BANNED From the set
DO NOT LET THIS COP inside!!!
FOOMP!
HEY!
And Now, for the FINAL TOUCH!
ZAP
ON
OFF
GOOD
EVIL

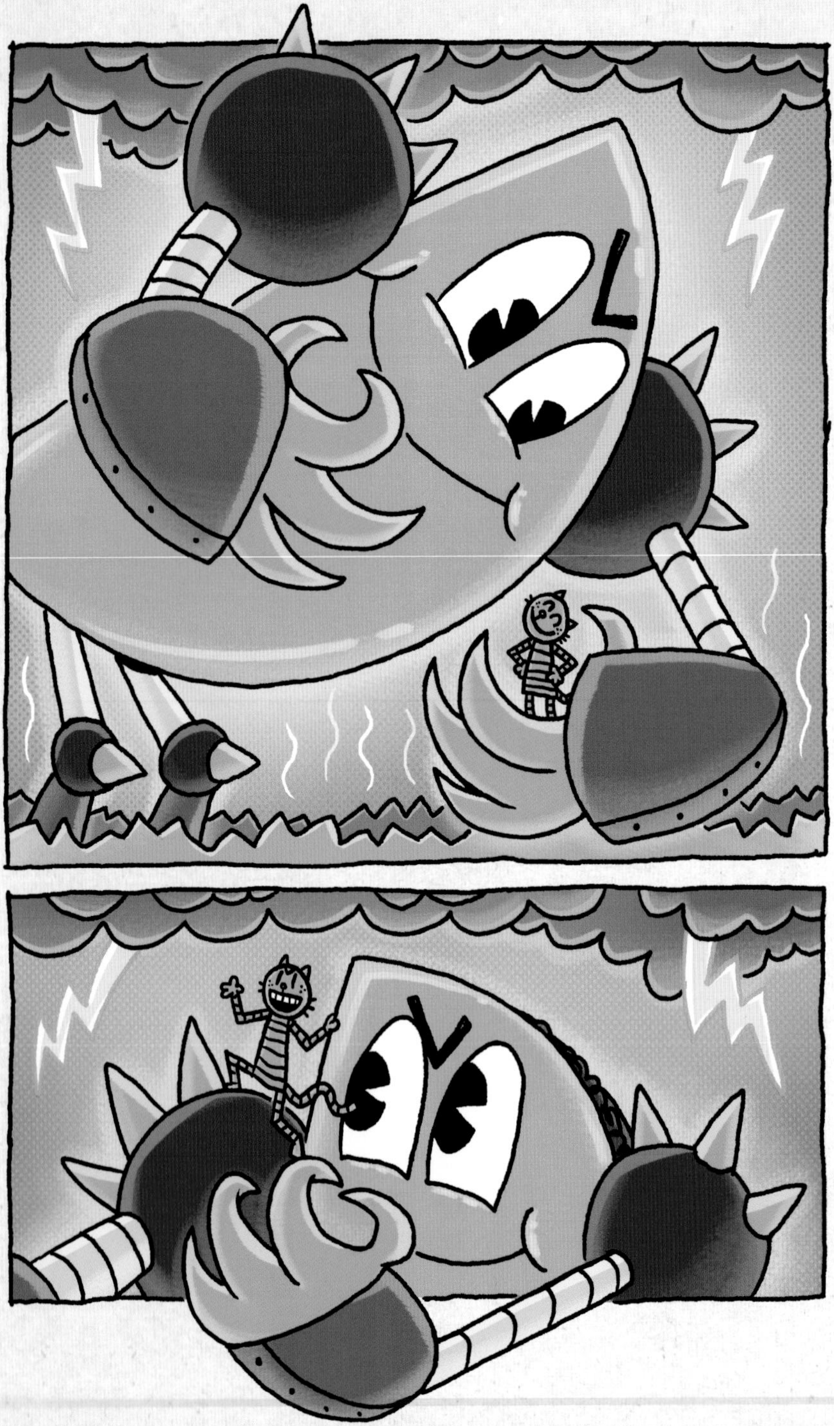

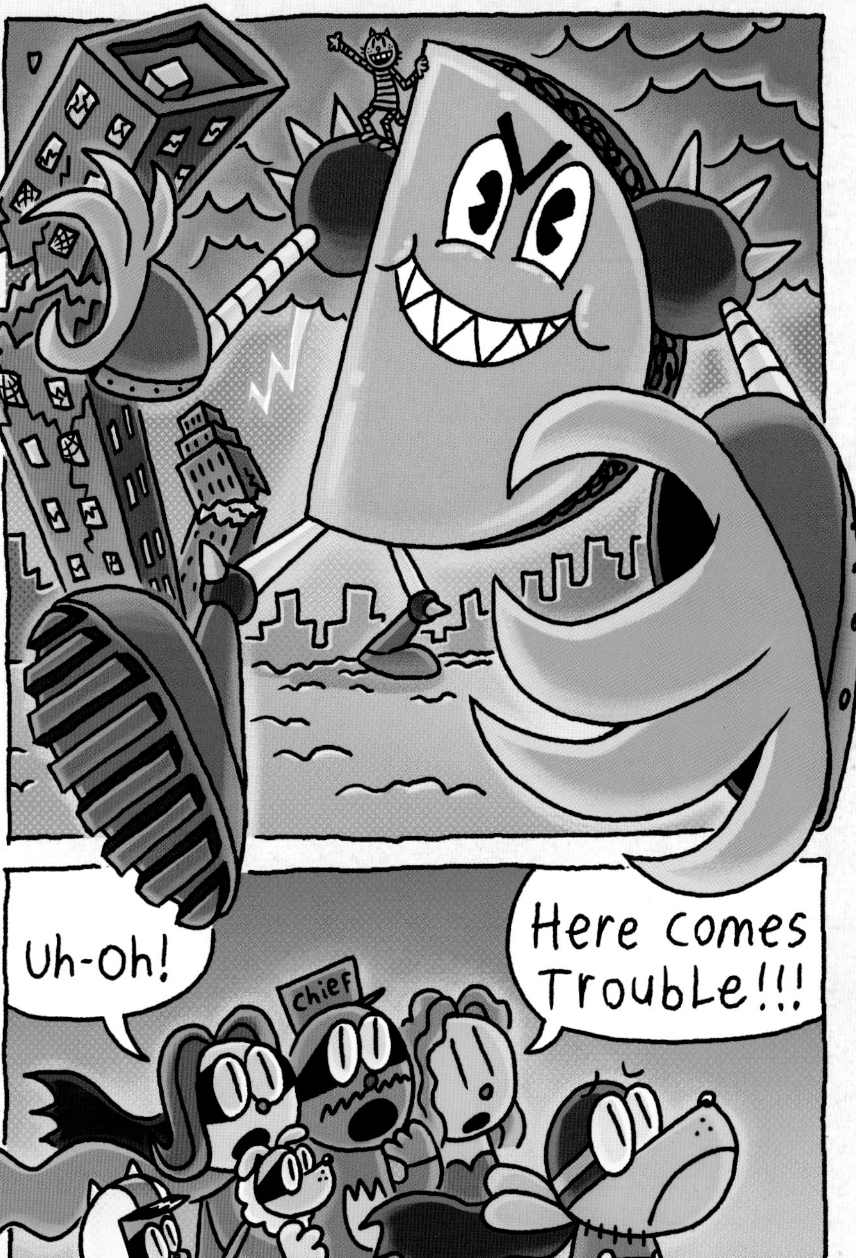
Uh-Oh!
Here comes Trouble!!!
Chief

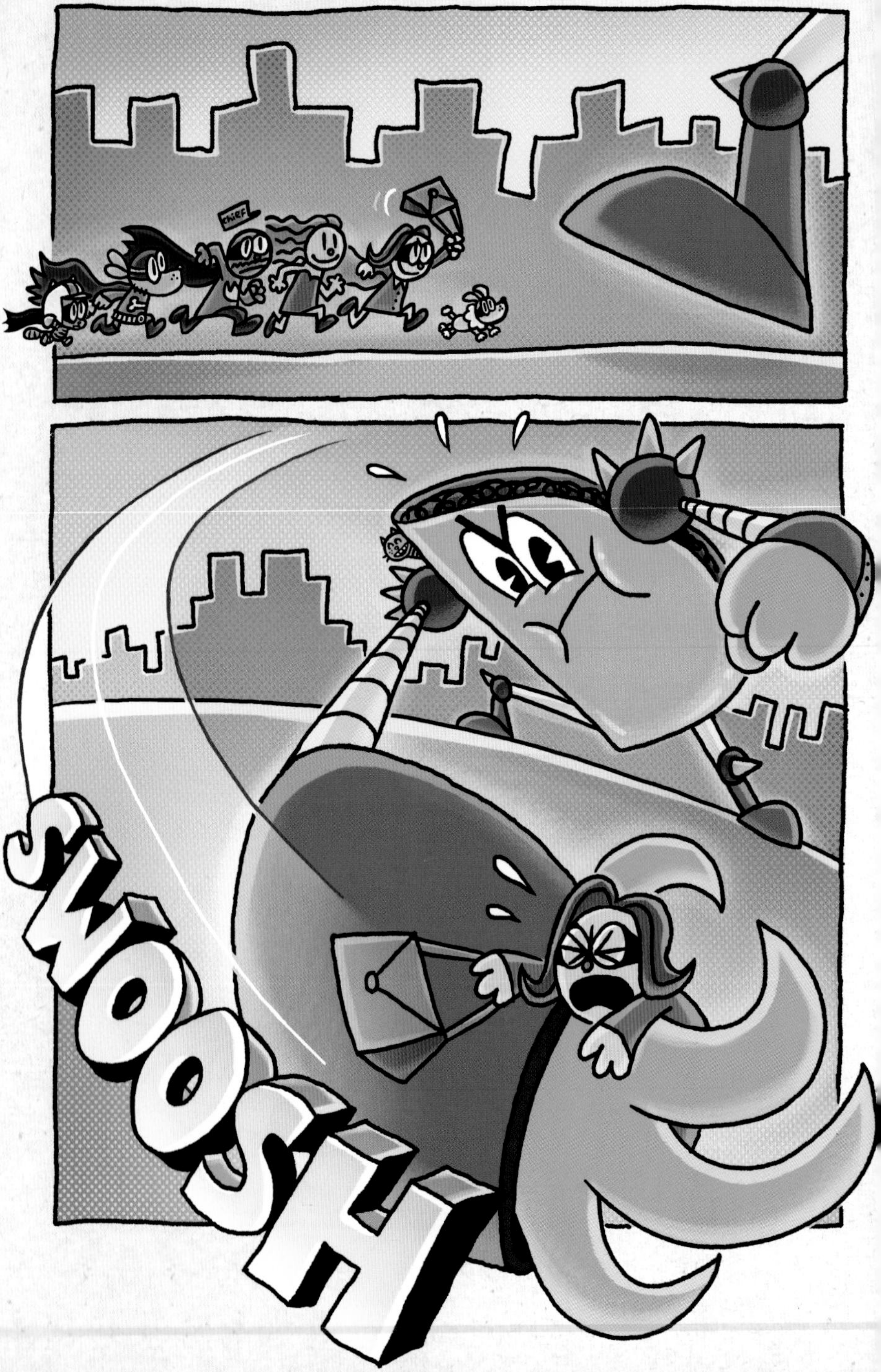
CHIEF
SWOOSH

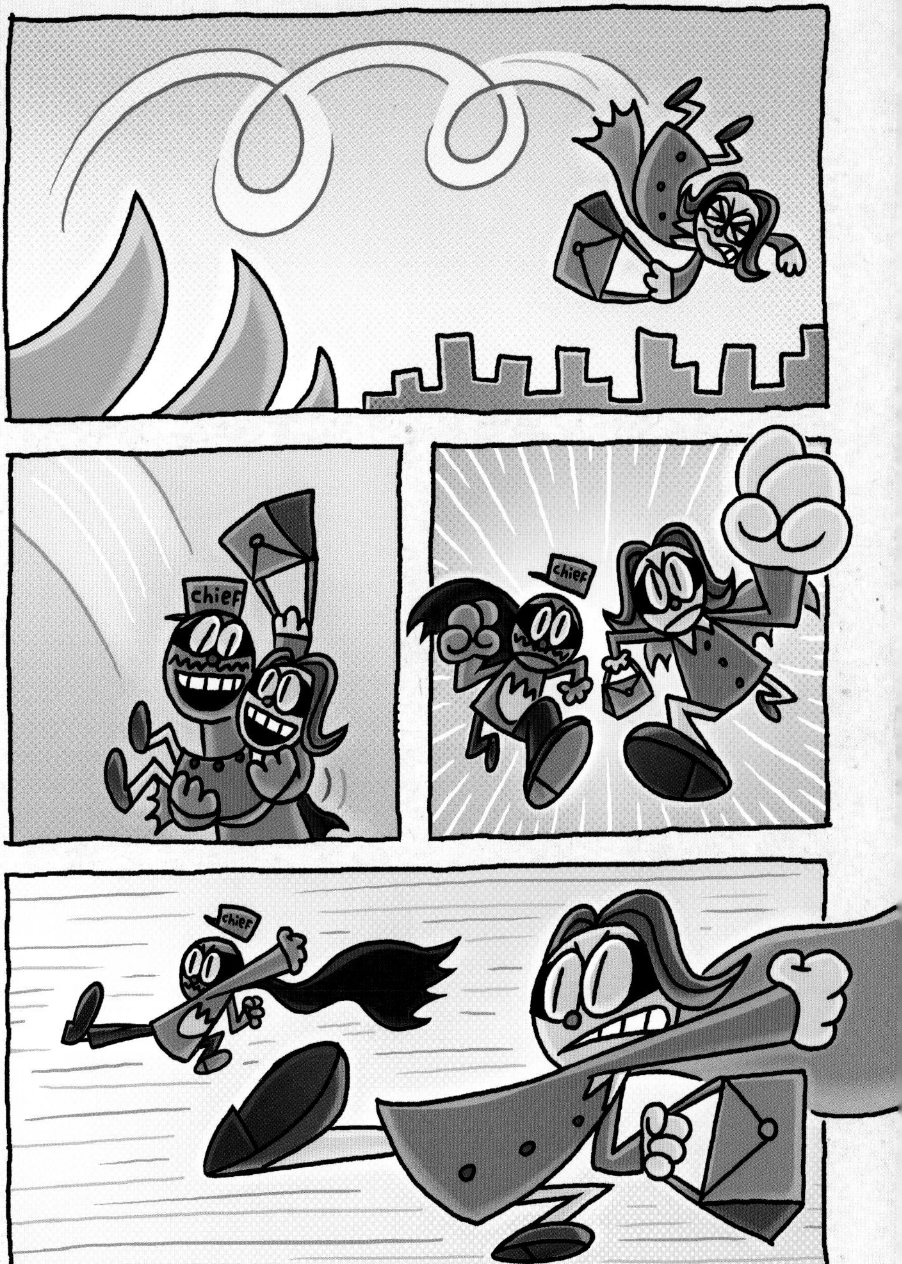
chief
chief
chief

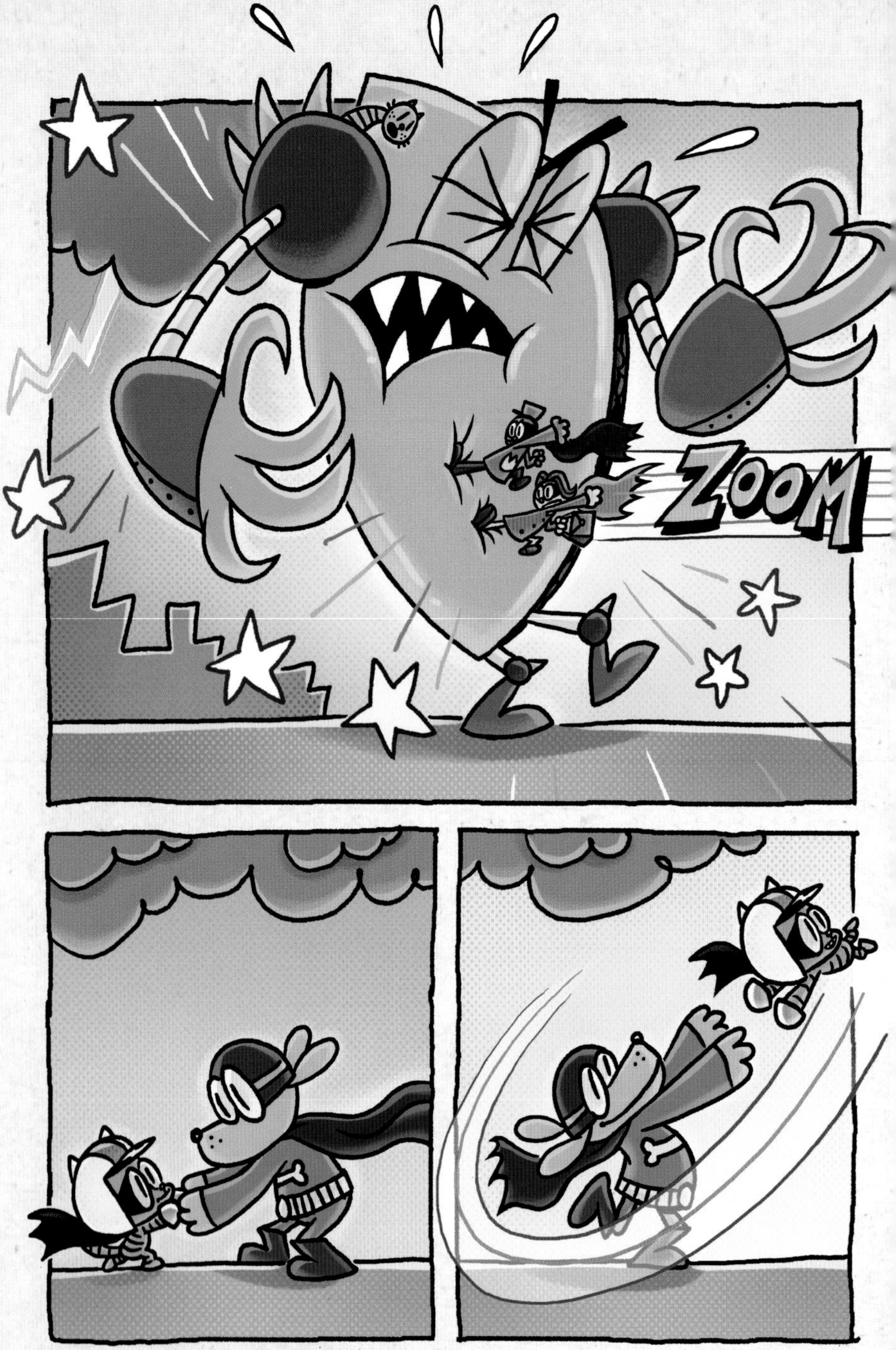
ZOOM

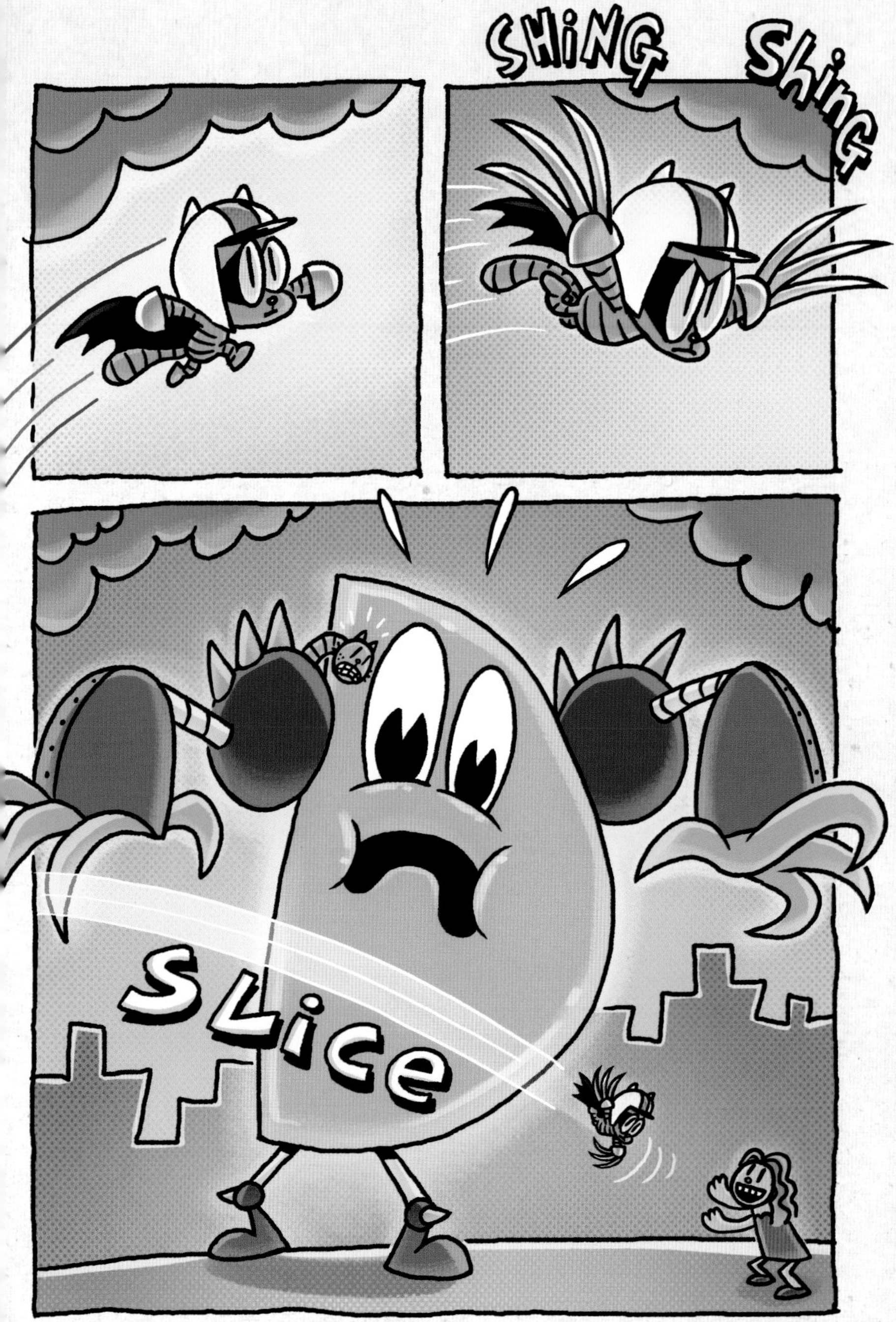
SHiNG
Shing
SLice

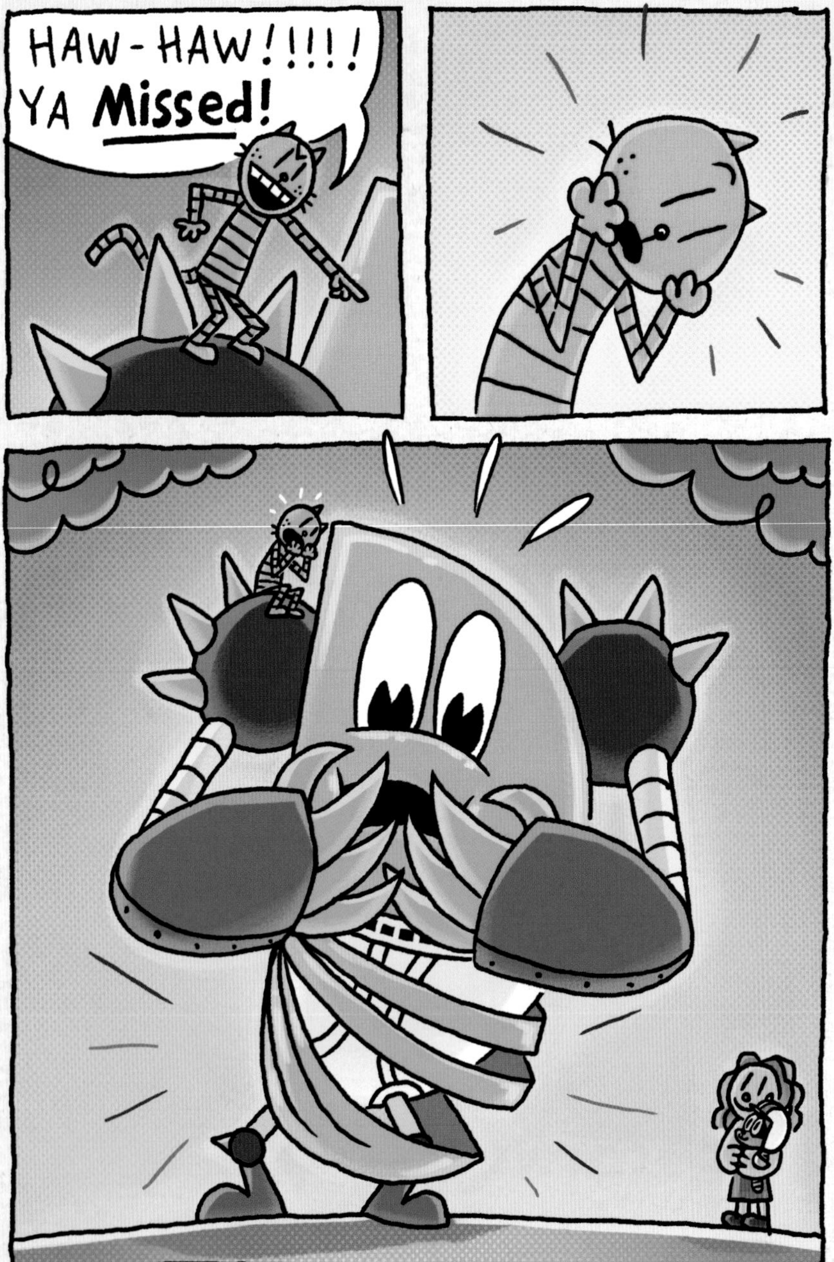
HAW-HAW!!!!!
YA **Missed!**

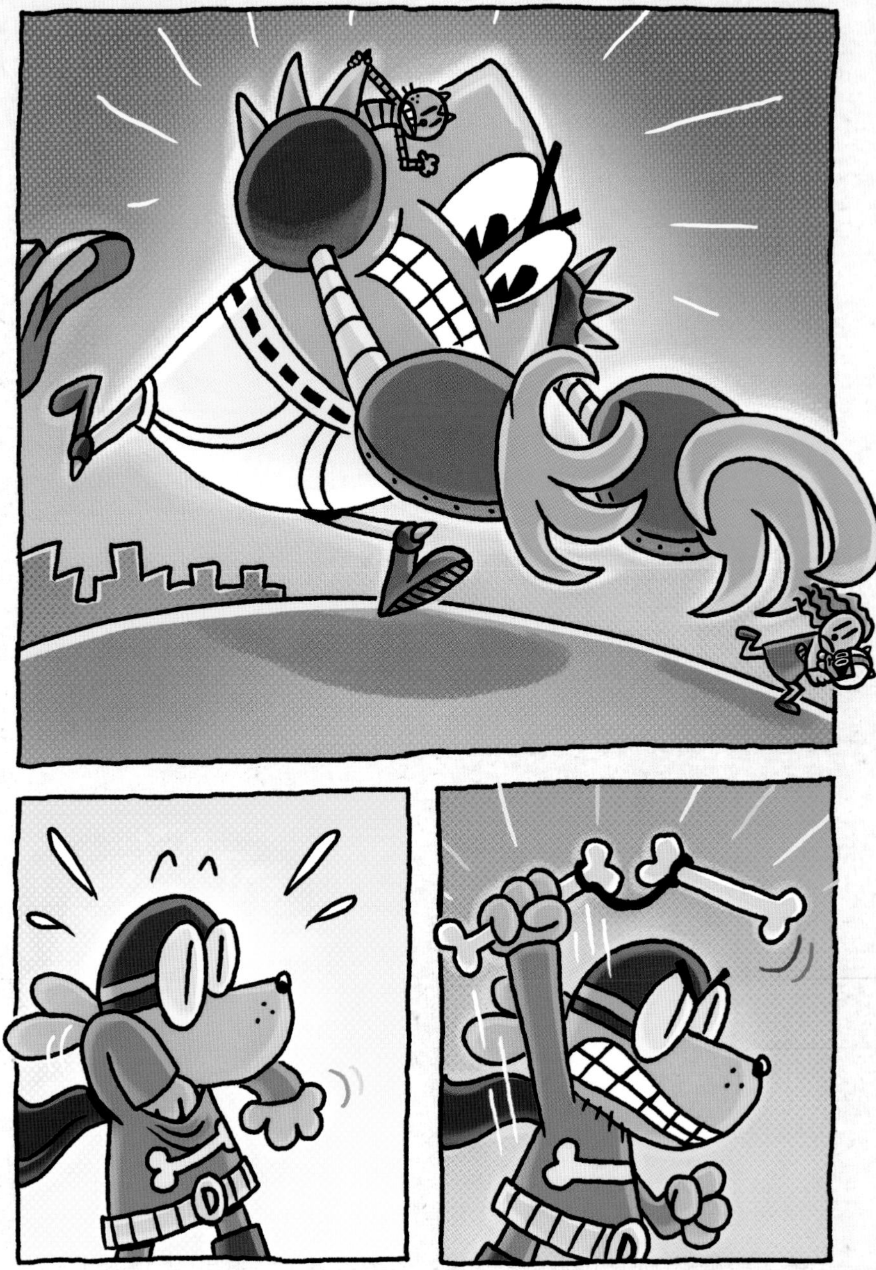

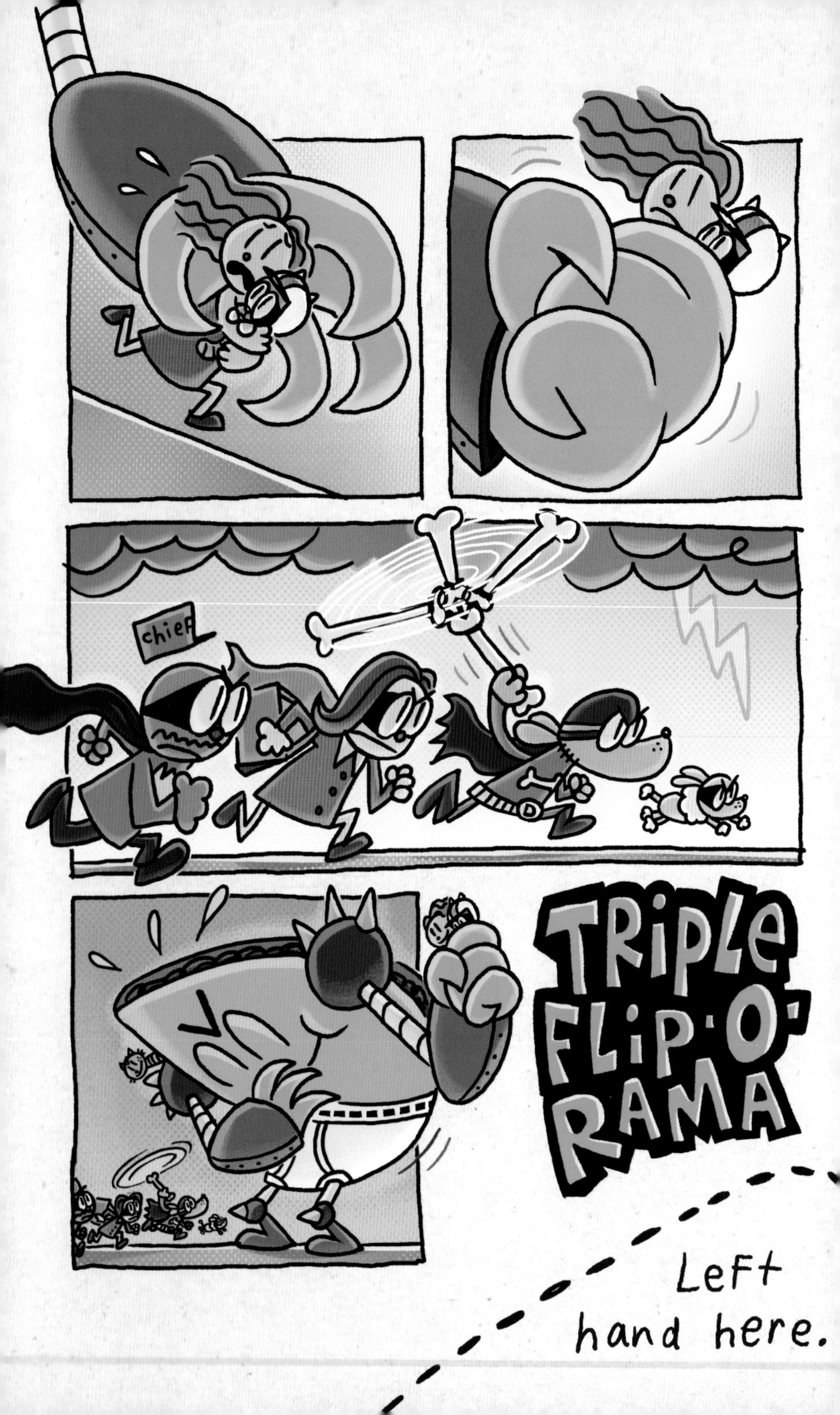
chief
TRIPLE FLIP-O-RAMA
Left hand here.

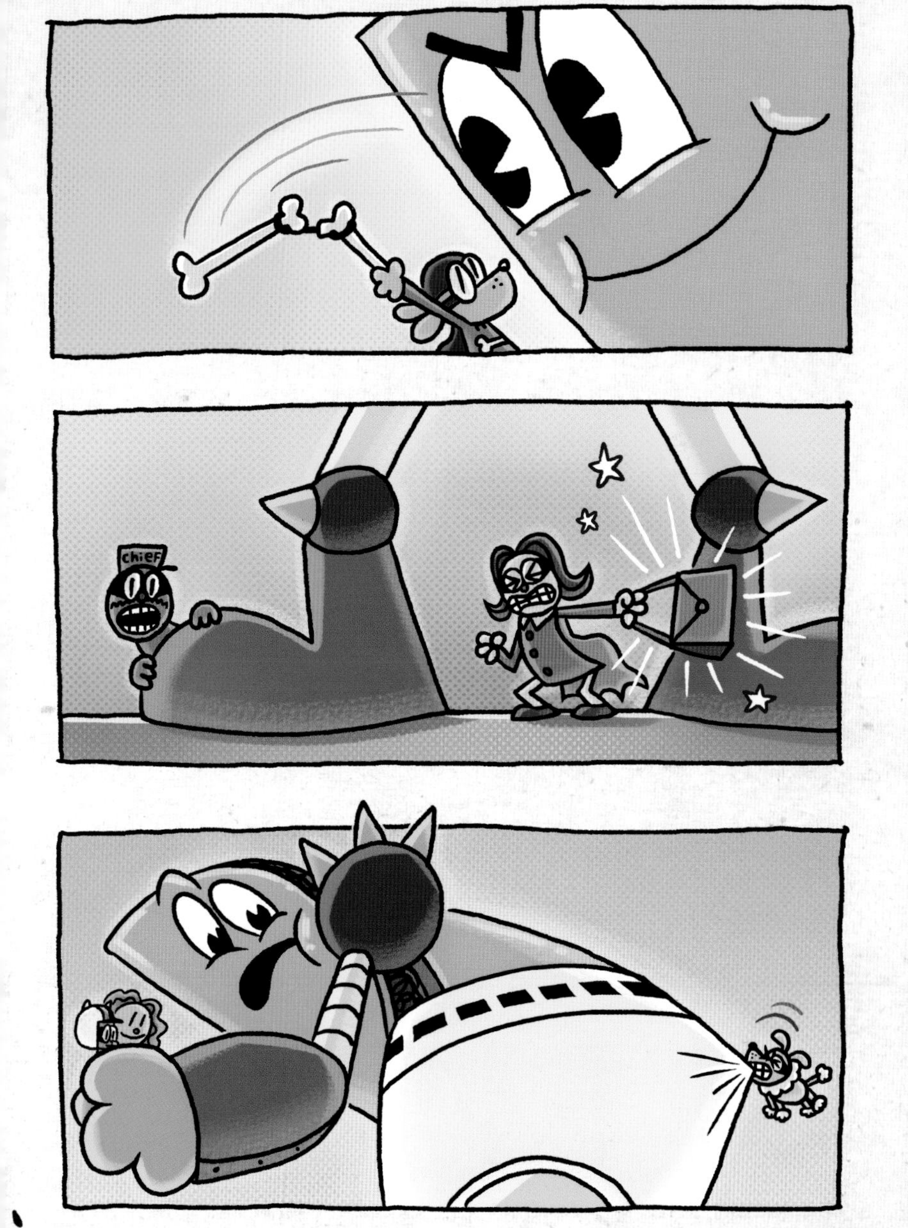
chief

Right Thumb here.

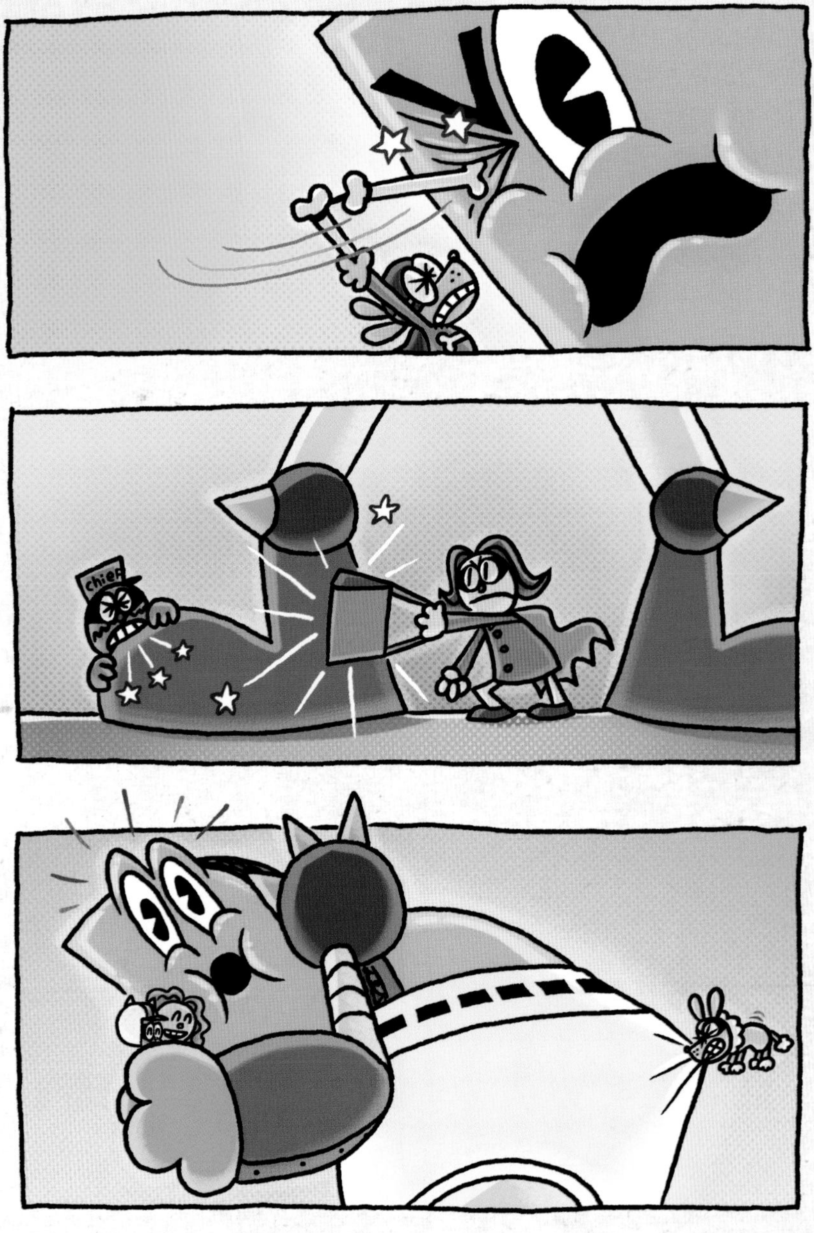
chief

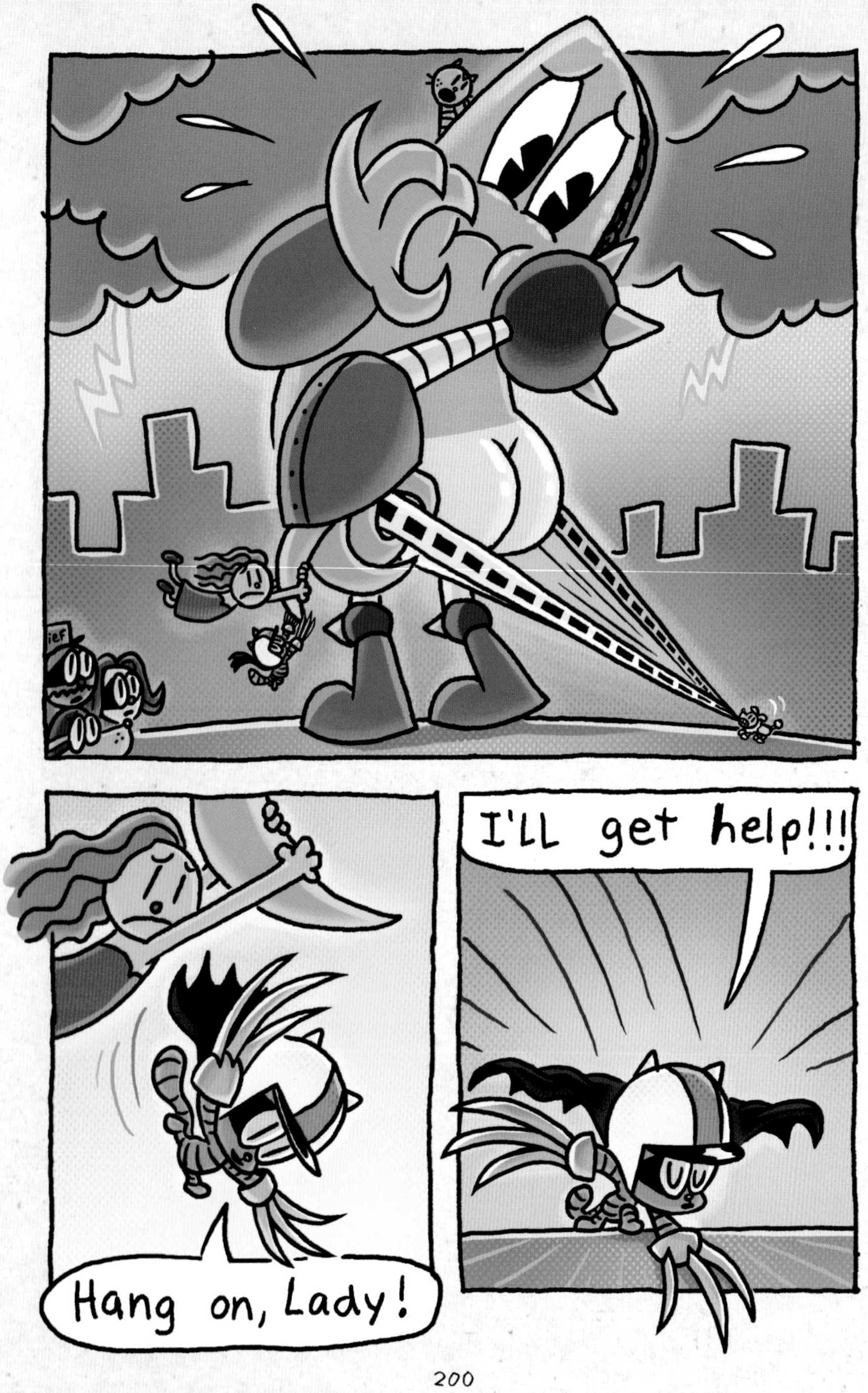
Hang on, Lady!
I'LL get help!!!

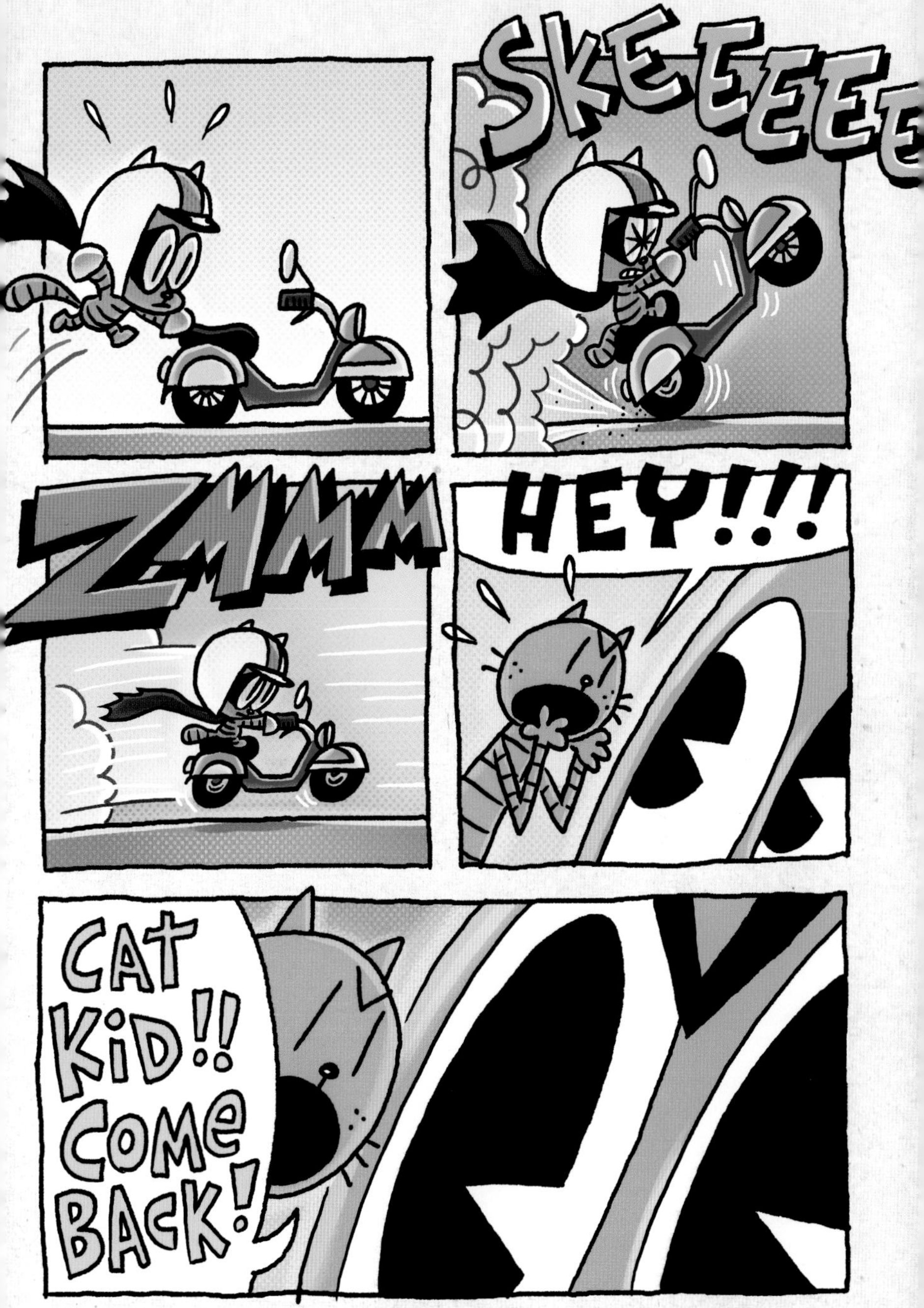
SKEEEEEE
ZMMMM
HEY!!!
CAT KID!! COME BACK!

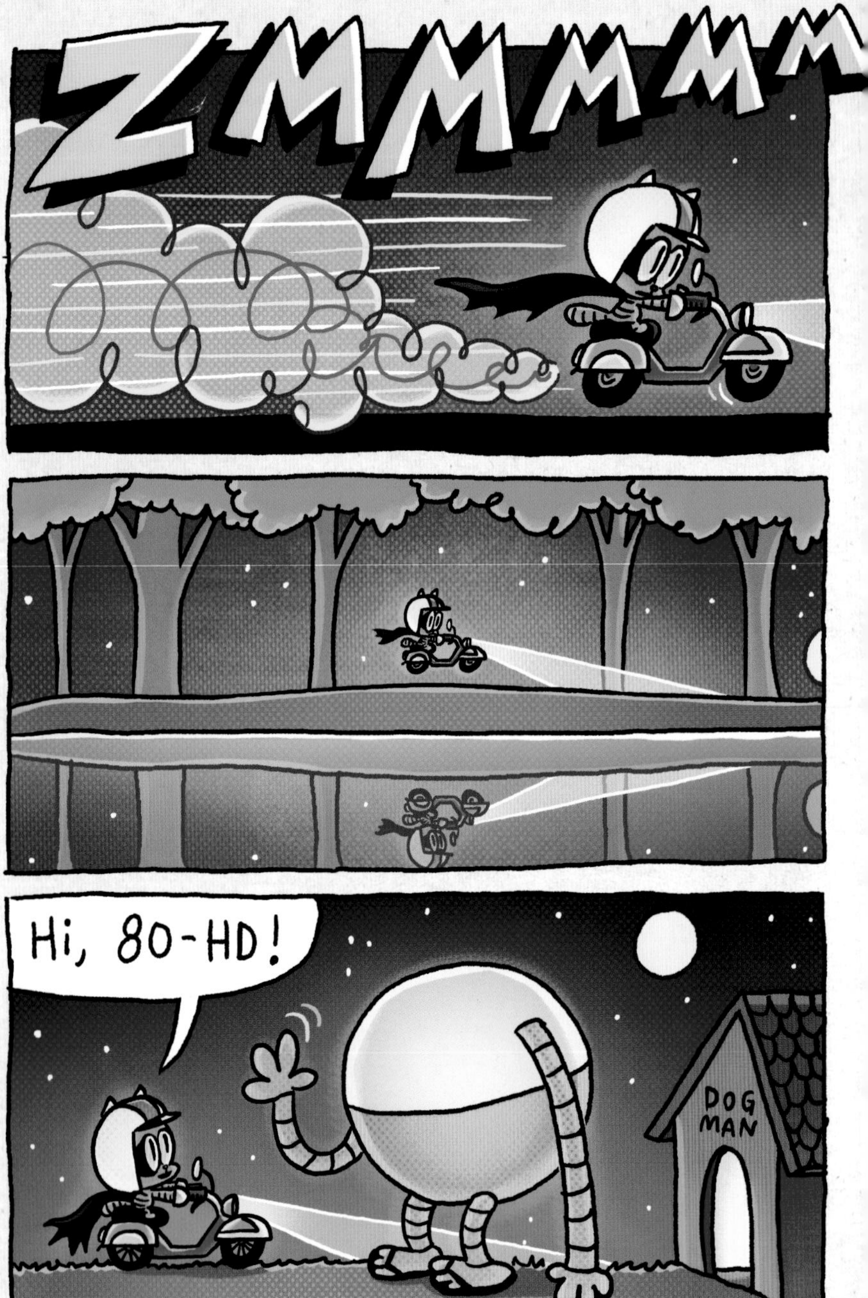
ZMMMMMM
Hi, 80-HD!
DOG MAN

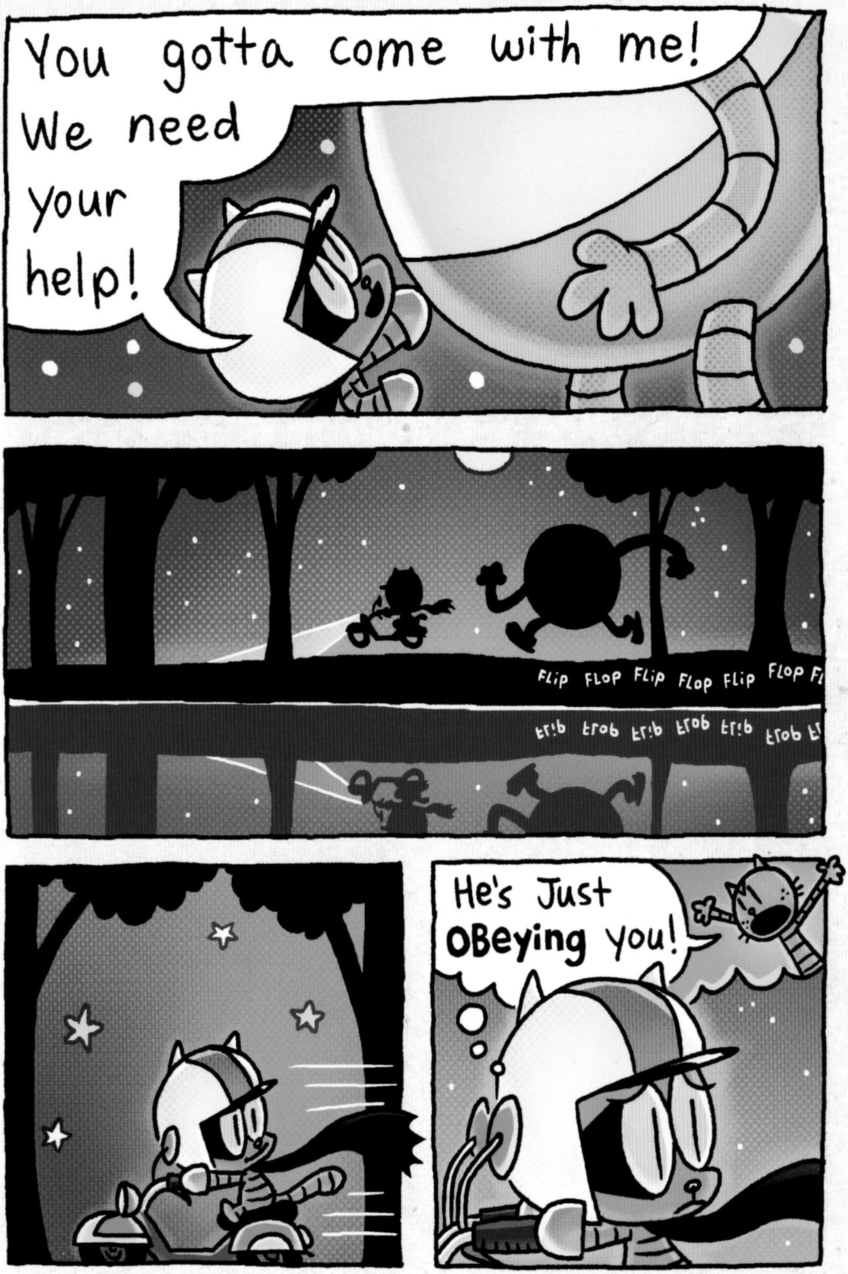

You gotta come with me! We need your help!
FLip FLOP FLip FLop FLip FLOP
He's Just OBeying you!

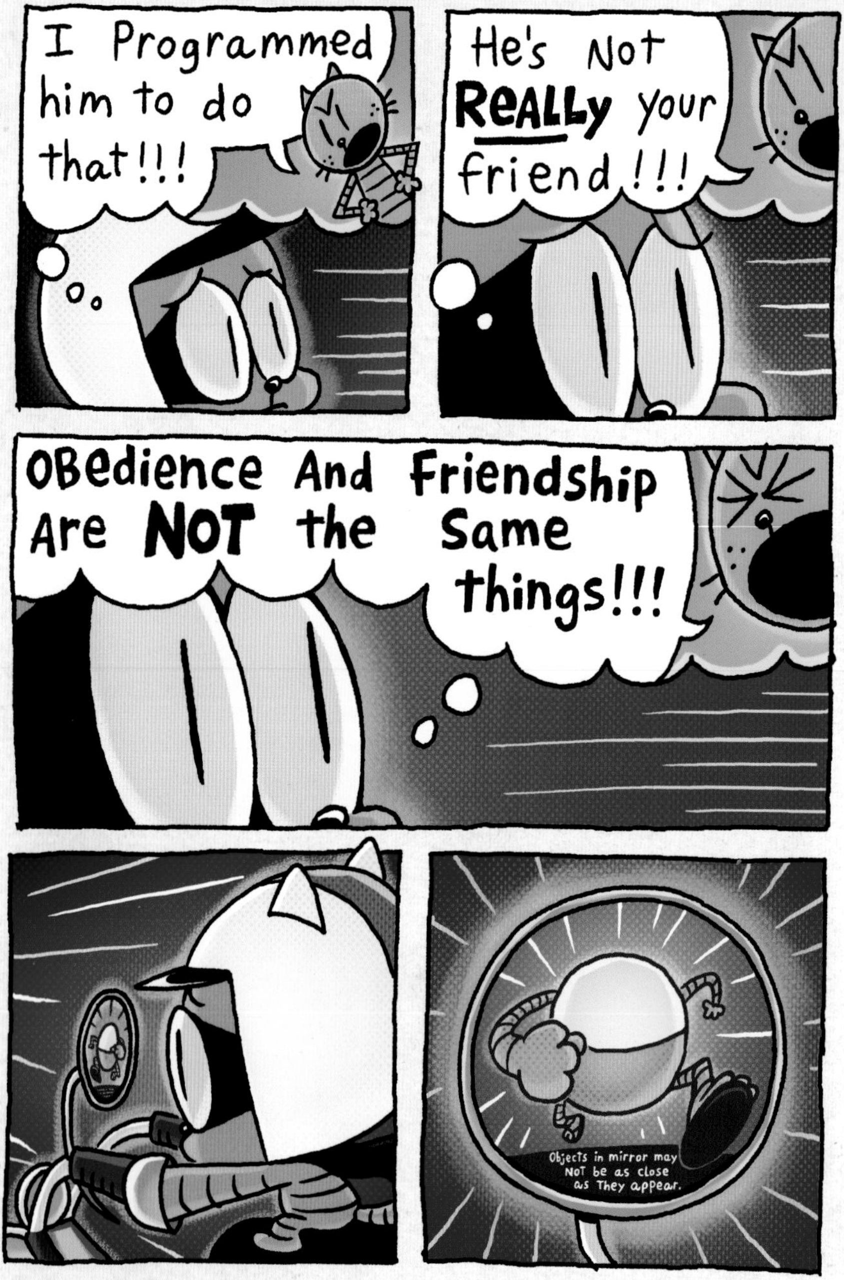
I Programmed him to do that!!!
He's Not REALLy your friend!!!
OBedience And Friendship Are NOT the Same things!!!
Objects in mirror may NOT be as close as They appear.

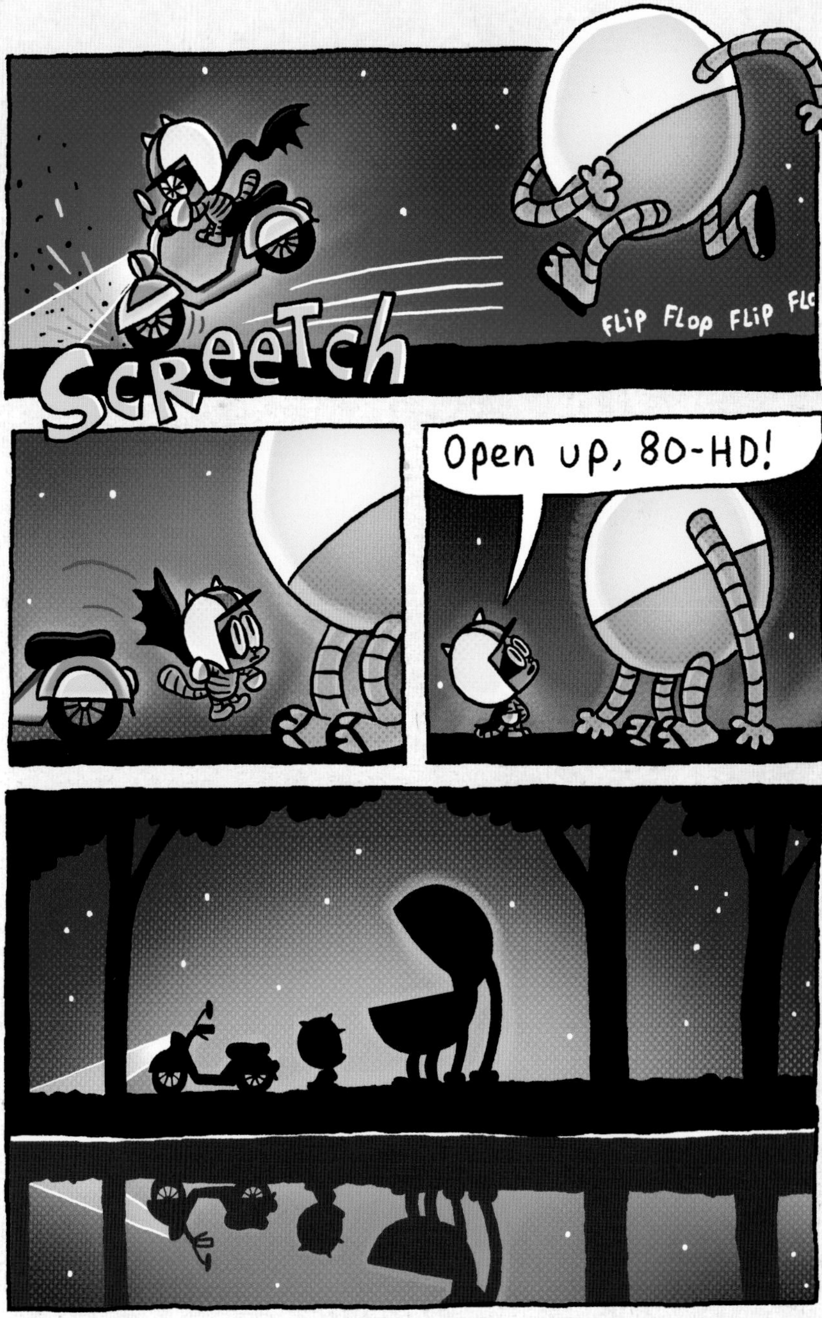
SCREETCH
FLIP FLOP FLIP FLO
Open up, 80-HD!

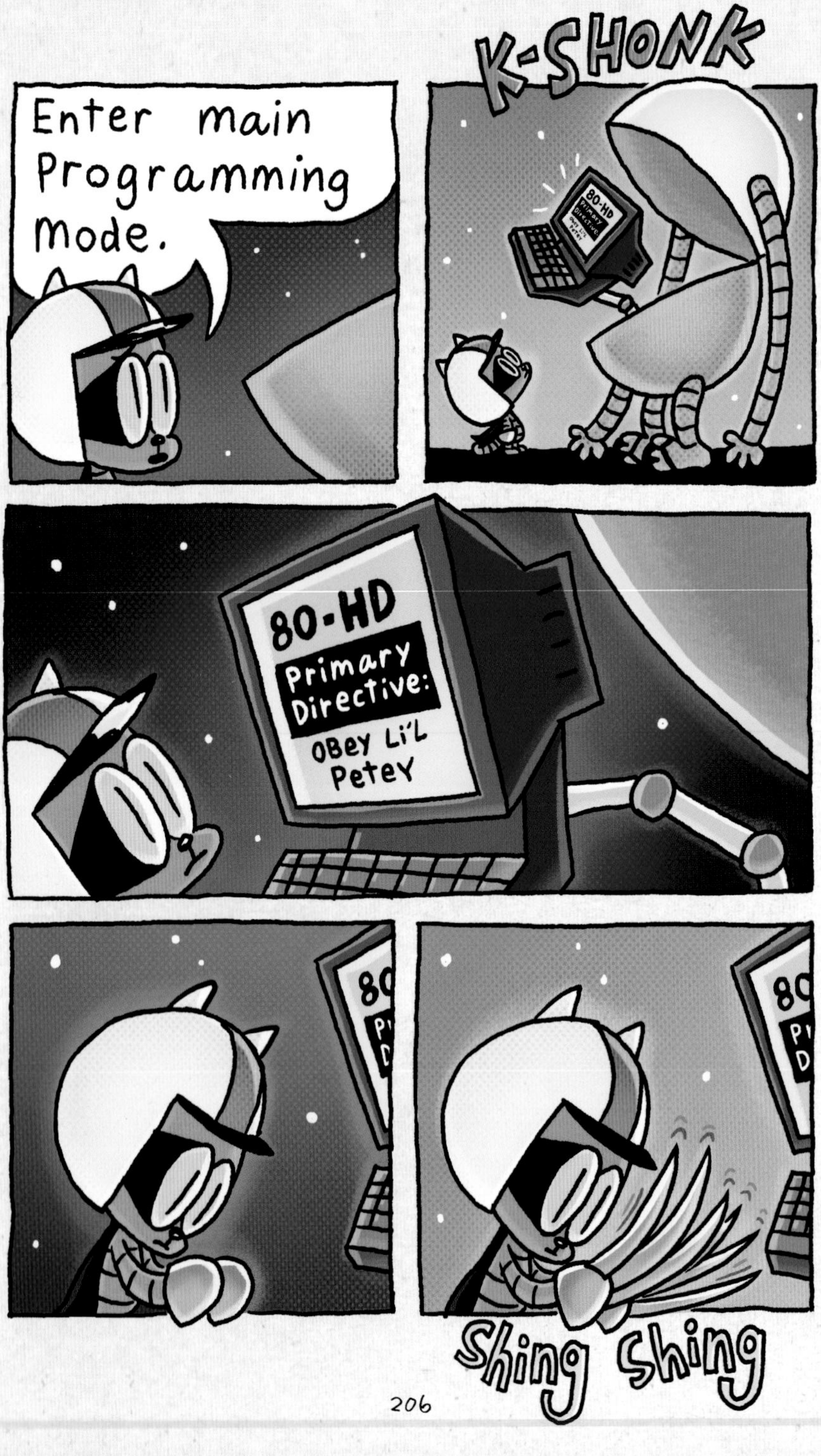
Enter main Programming mode.
K-SHONK
80-HD
Primary Directive:
OBey Li'L Petey
Shing Shing

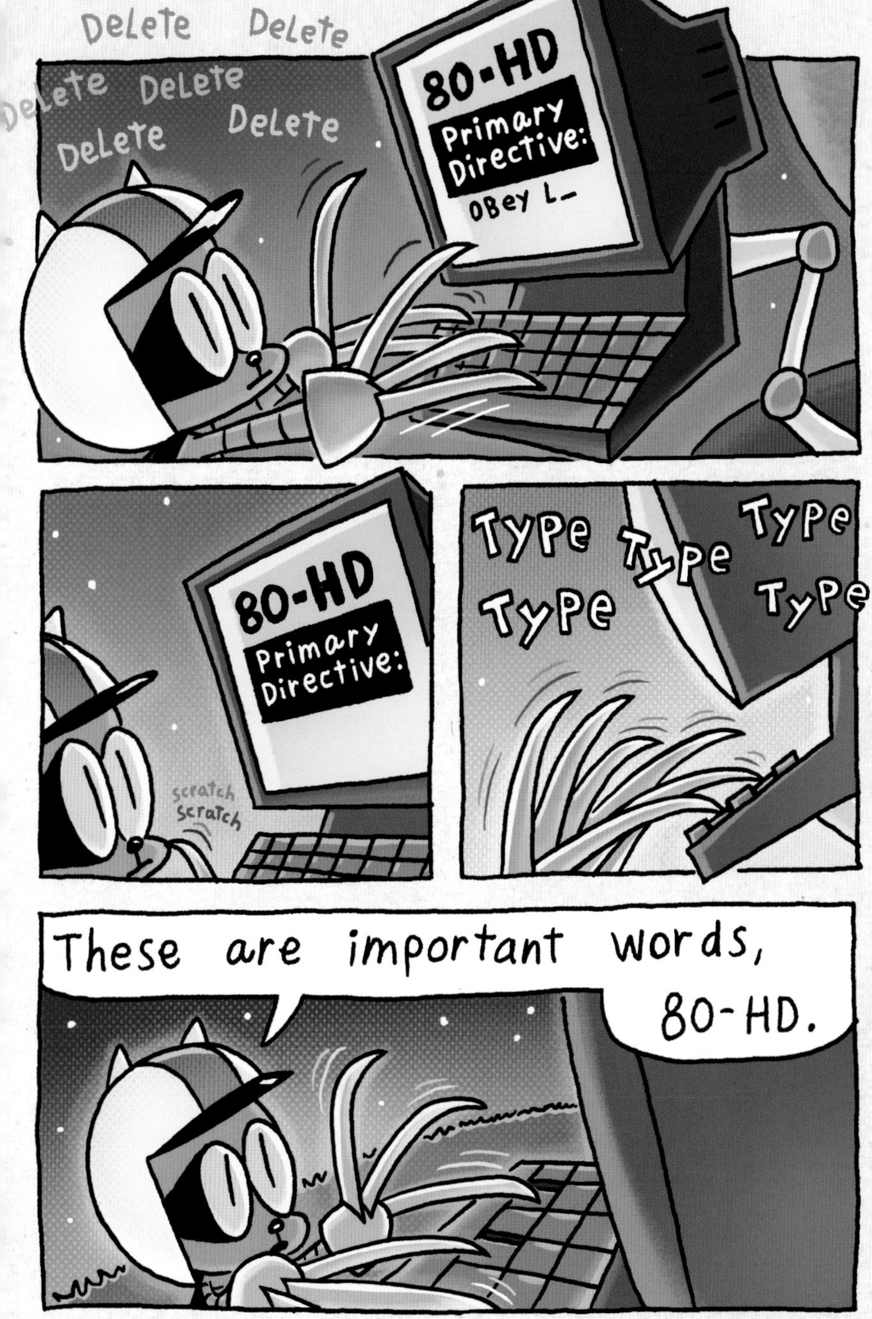

Delete Delete
Delete Delete
Delete Delete Delete
80-HD
Primary Directive:
OBey L_
80-HD
Primary Directive:
scratch scratch
Type Type Type
Type Type Type
These are important words, 80-HD.

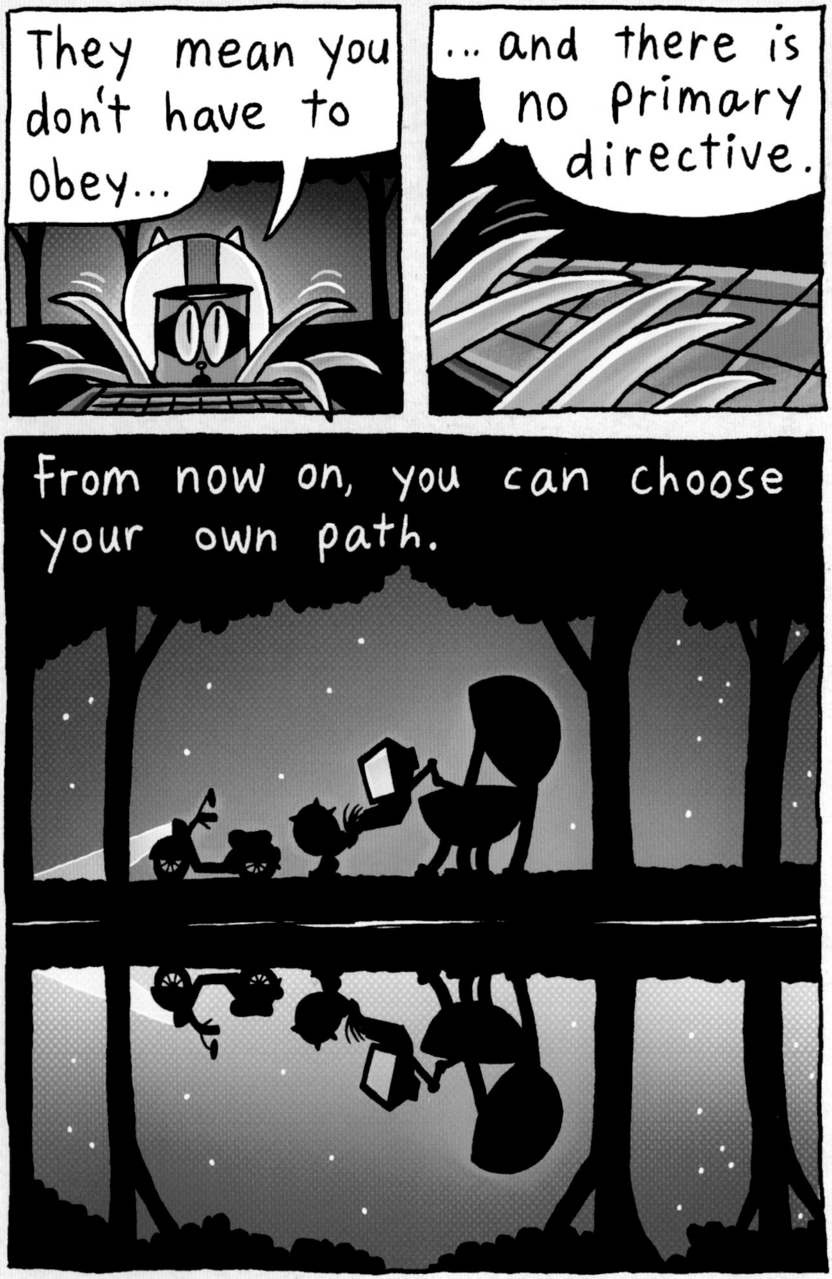
They mean you don't have to obey...
...and there is no primary directive.
From now on, you can choose your own path.

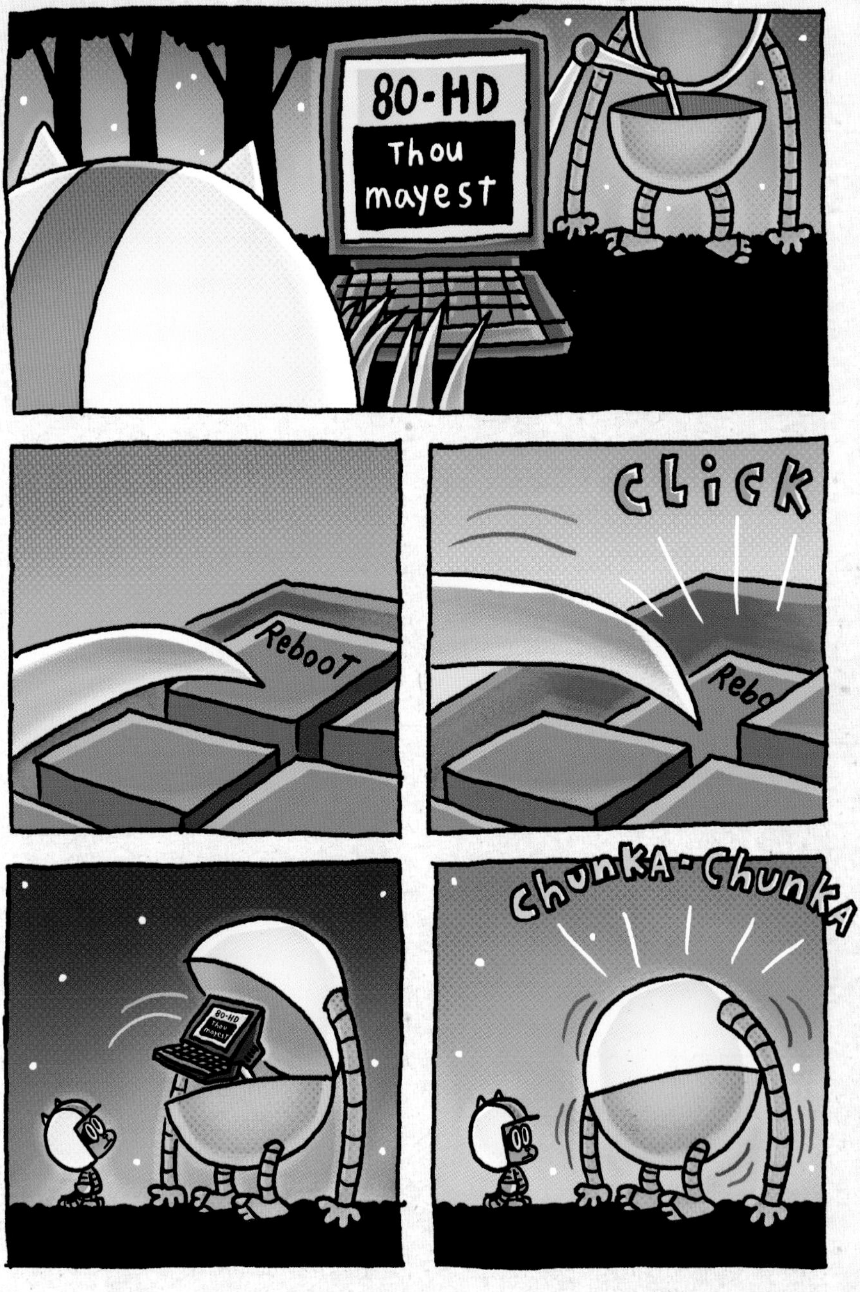
80-HD
Thou mayest
ReBooT
CLICK
Rebo
80-HD
Thou mayest
CHUNKA-CHUNKA

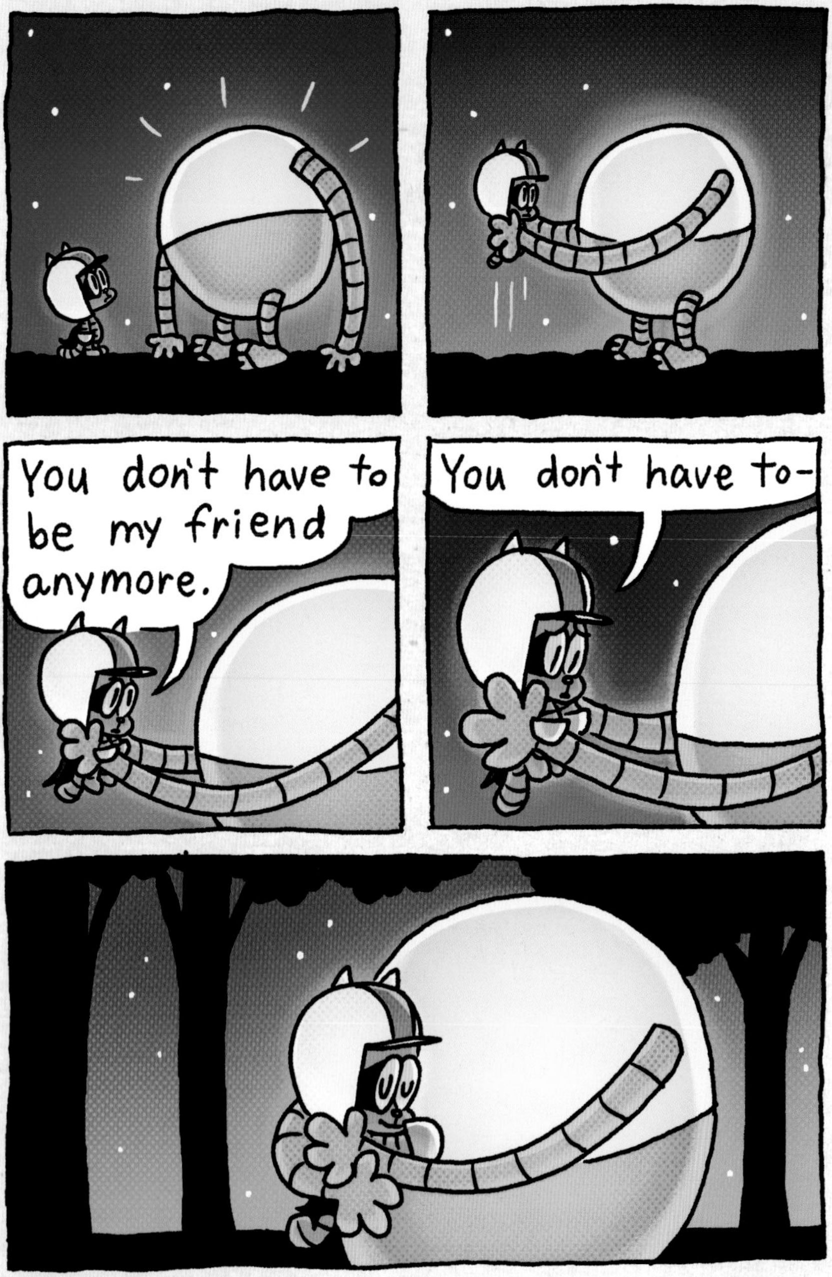
You don't have to be my friend anymore.
You don't have to-

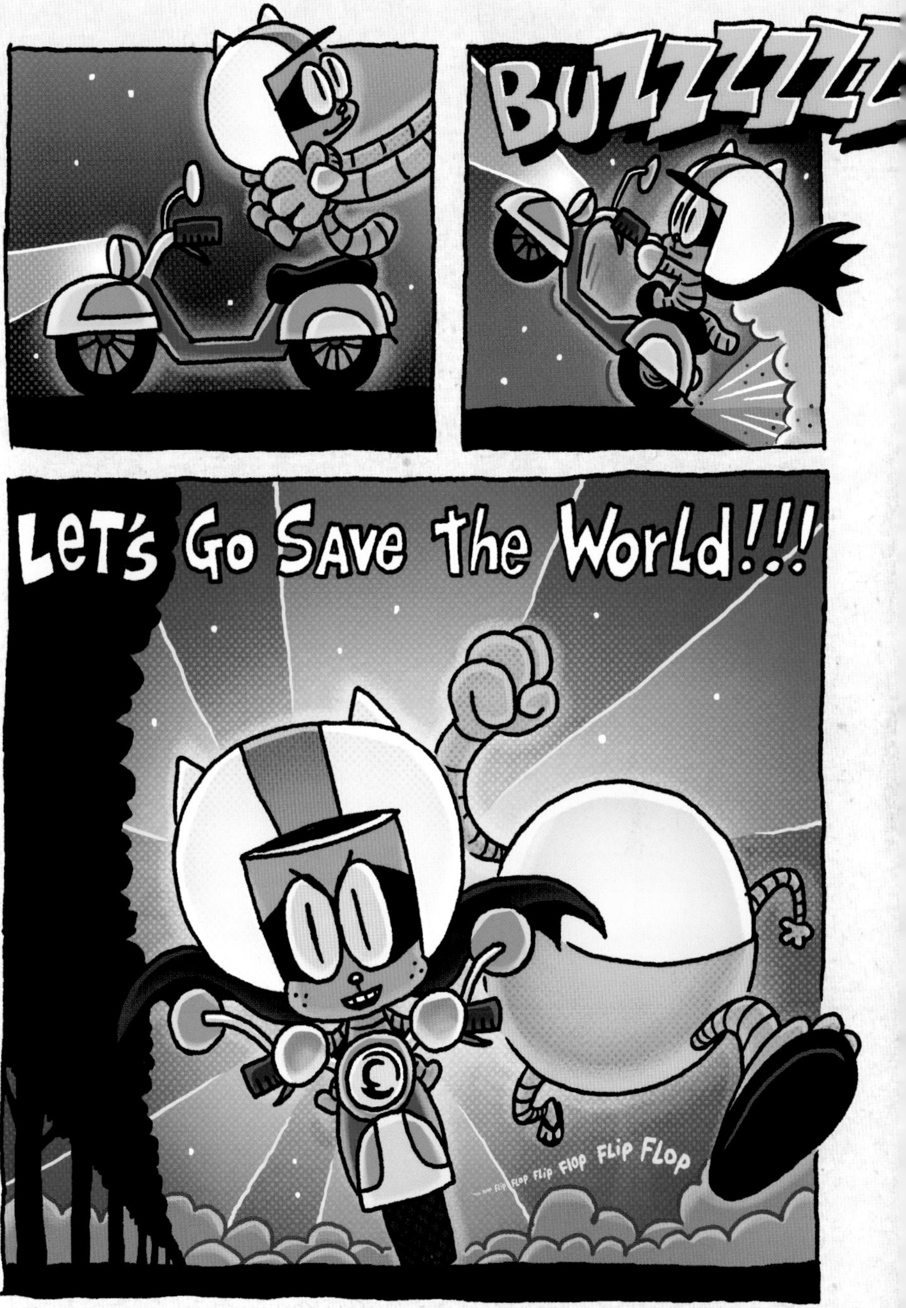
BUZZZZZZ
LET'S Go Save the World!!!
FLip FLop FLip FLop FLIP FLOP

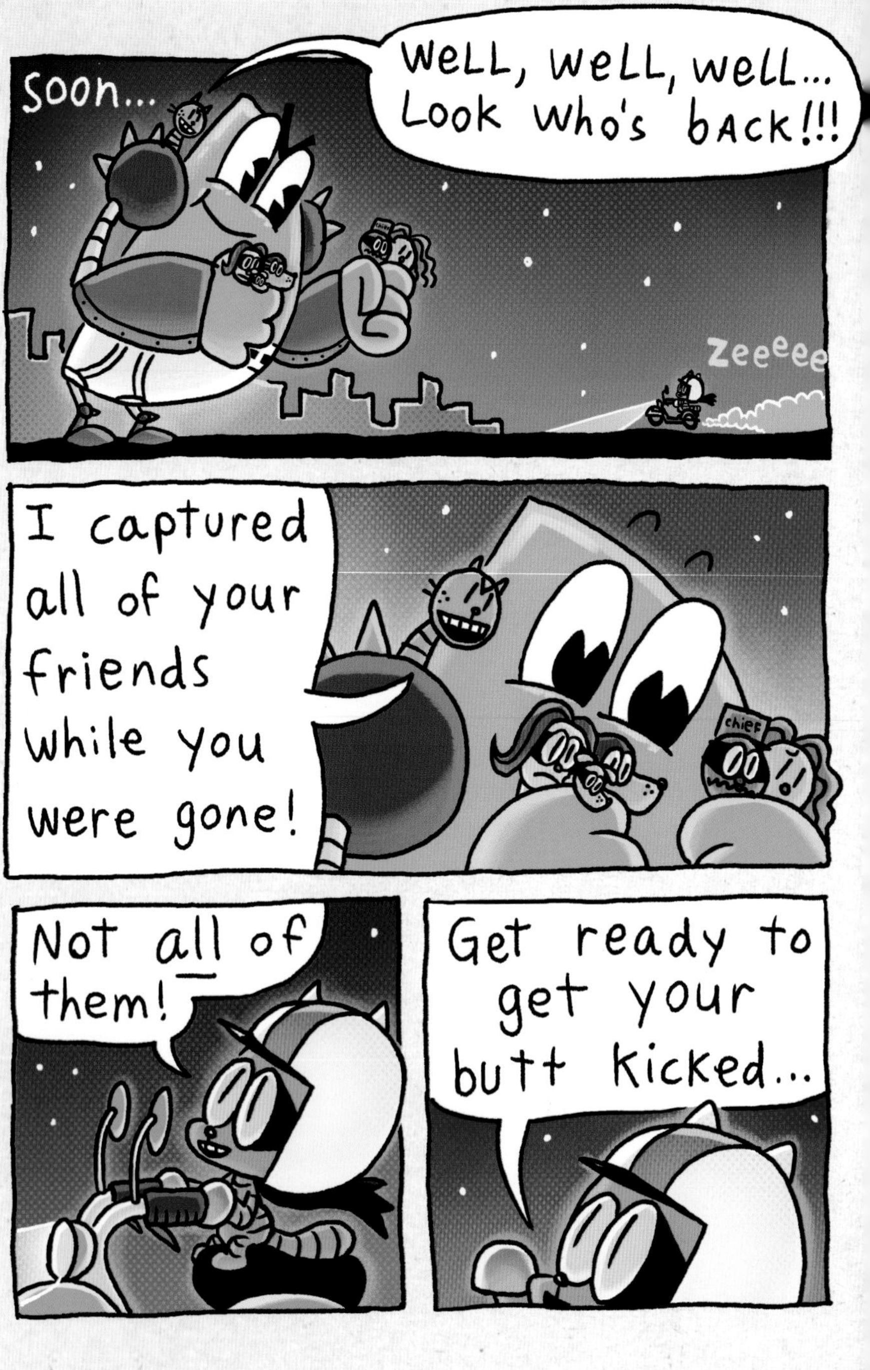
Soon...
WELL, WELL, WELL... Look who's BACK!!!
Zeeeee
I captured all of your friends while you were gone!
chief
Not all of them!
Get ready to get your butt kicked...

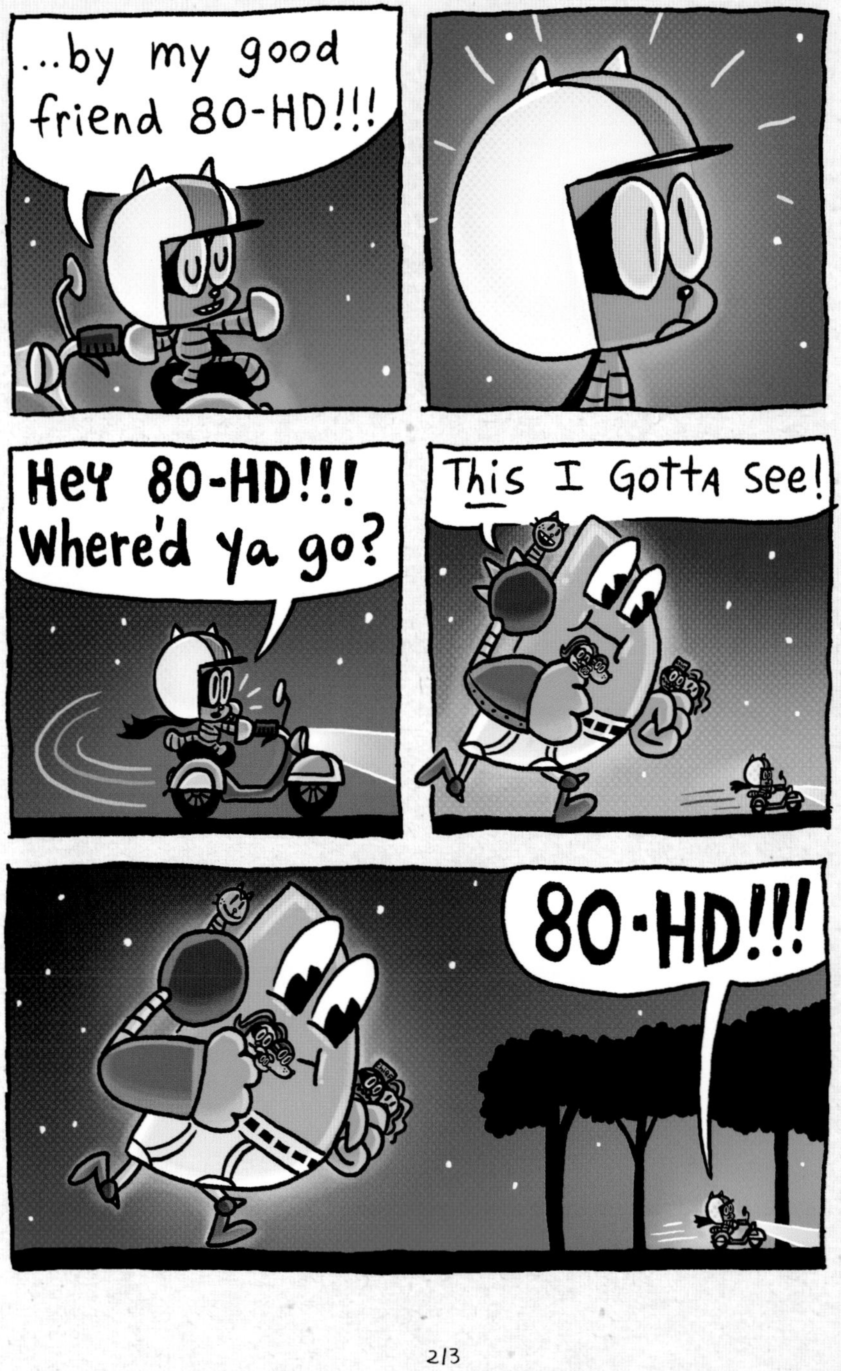
...by my good friend 80-HD!!!
Hey 80-HD!!! Where'd ya go?
This I Gotta see!
80-HD!!!

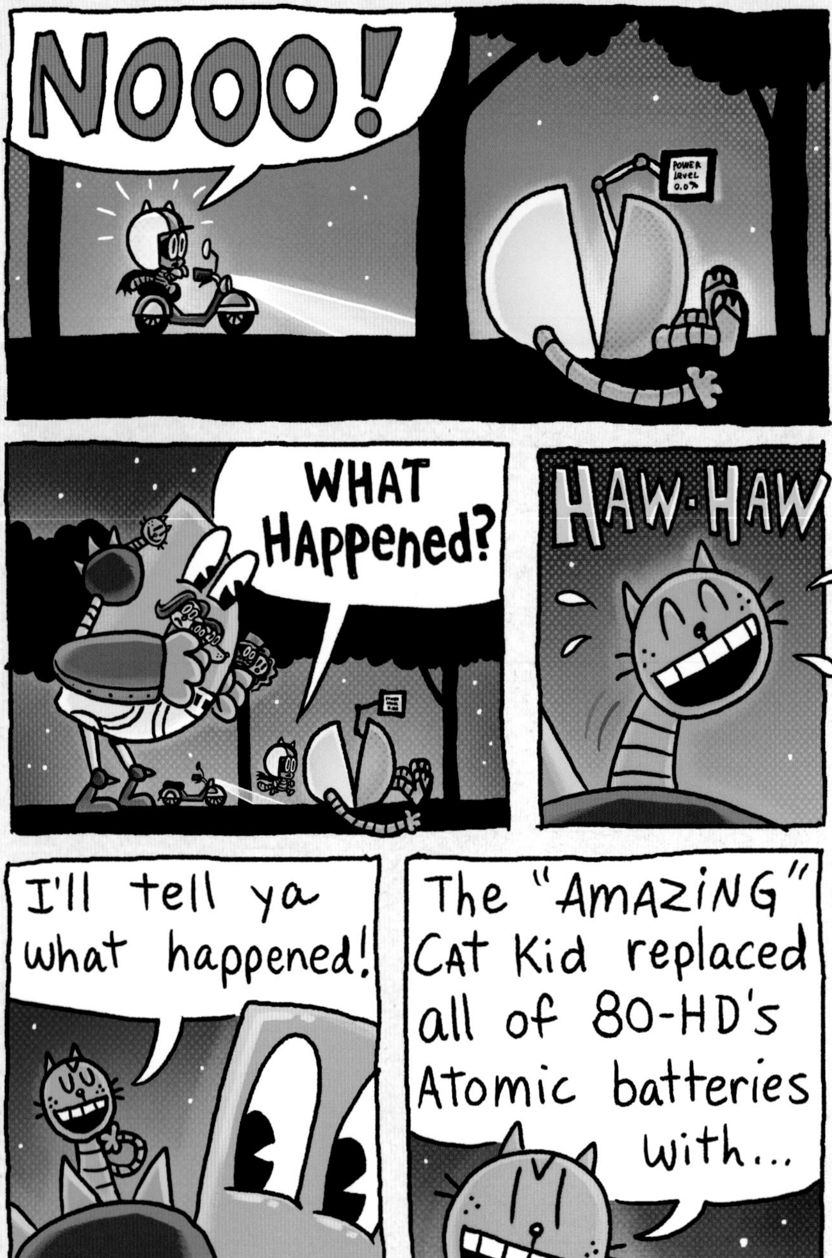
NOOO!
POWER LEVEL 0.0%
WHAT HAPPENED?
HAW-HAW
I'll tell ya what happened!
The "AMAZING" Cat Kid replaced all of 80-HD's Atomic batteries with...

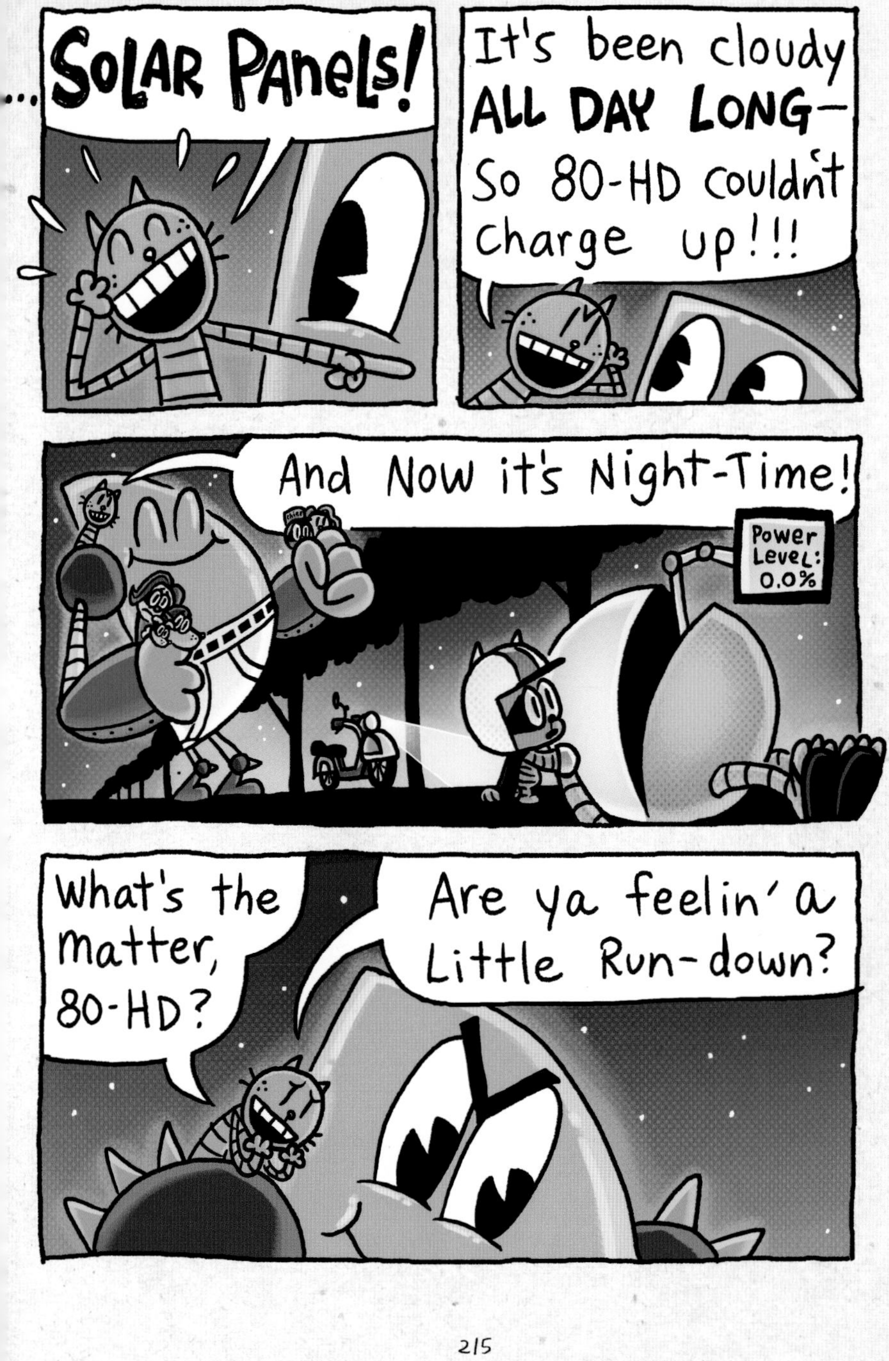
...SOLAR PANELS!
It's been cloudy ALL DAY LONG— So 80-HD couldn't charge up!!!
And Now it's Night-Time!
Power Level: 0.0%
What's the matter, 80-HD?
Are ya feelin' a Little Run-down?

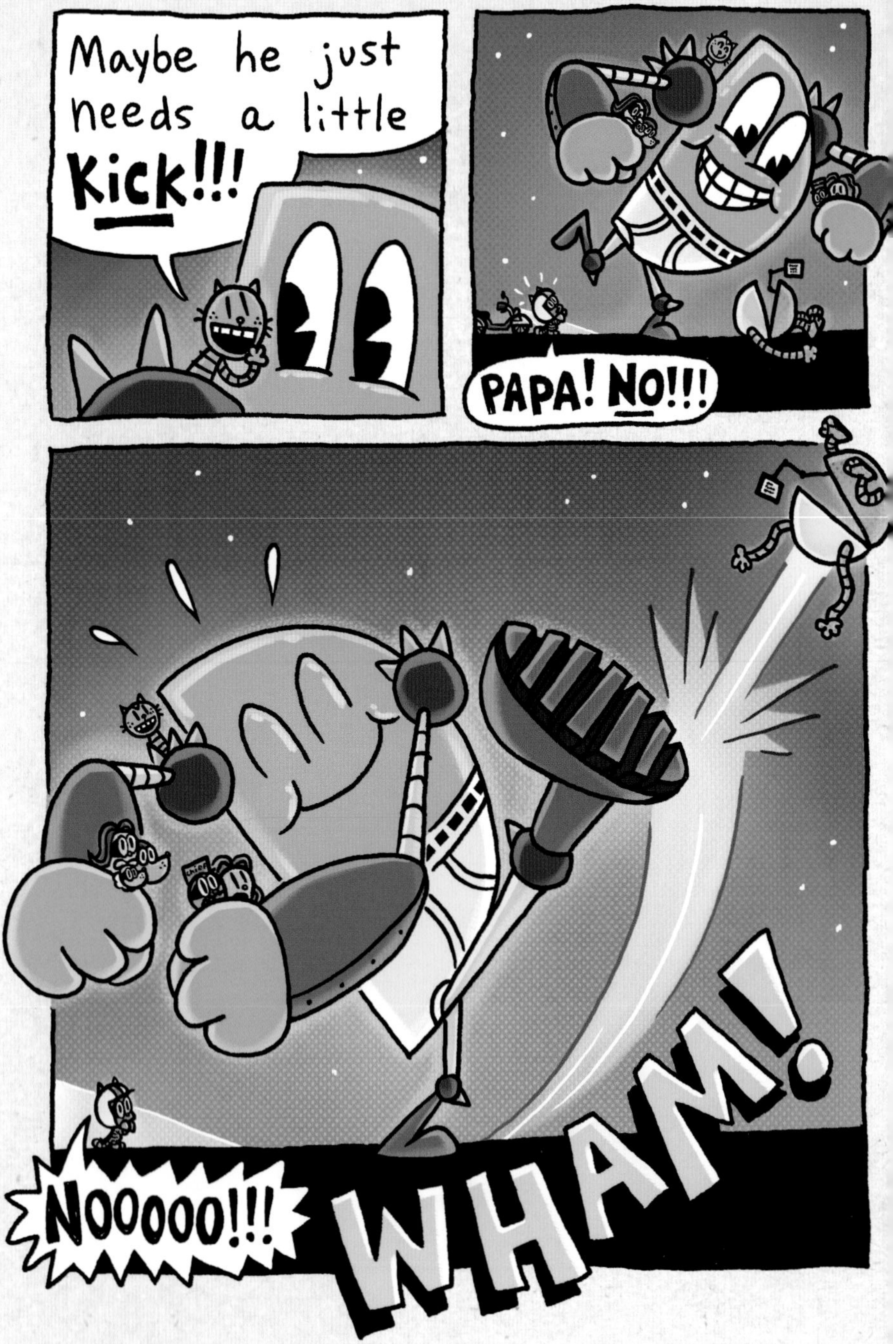

Maybe he just needs a little KICK!!!
PAPA! NO!!!
NOOOOO!!!
WHAM!

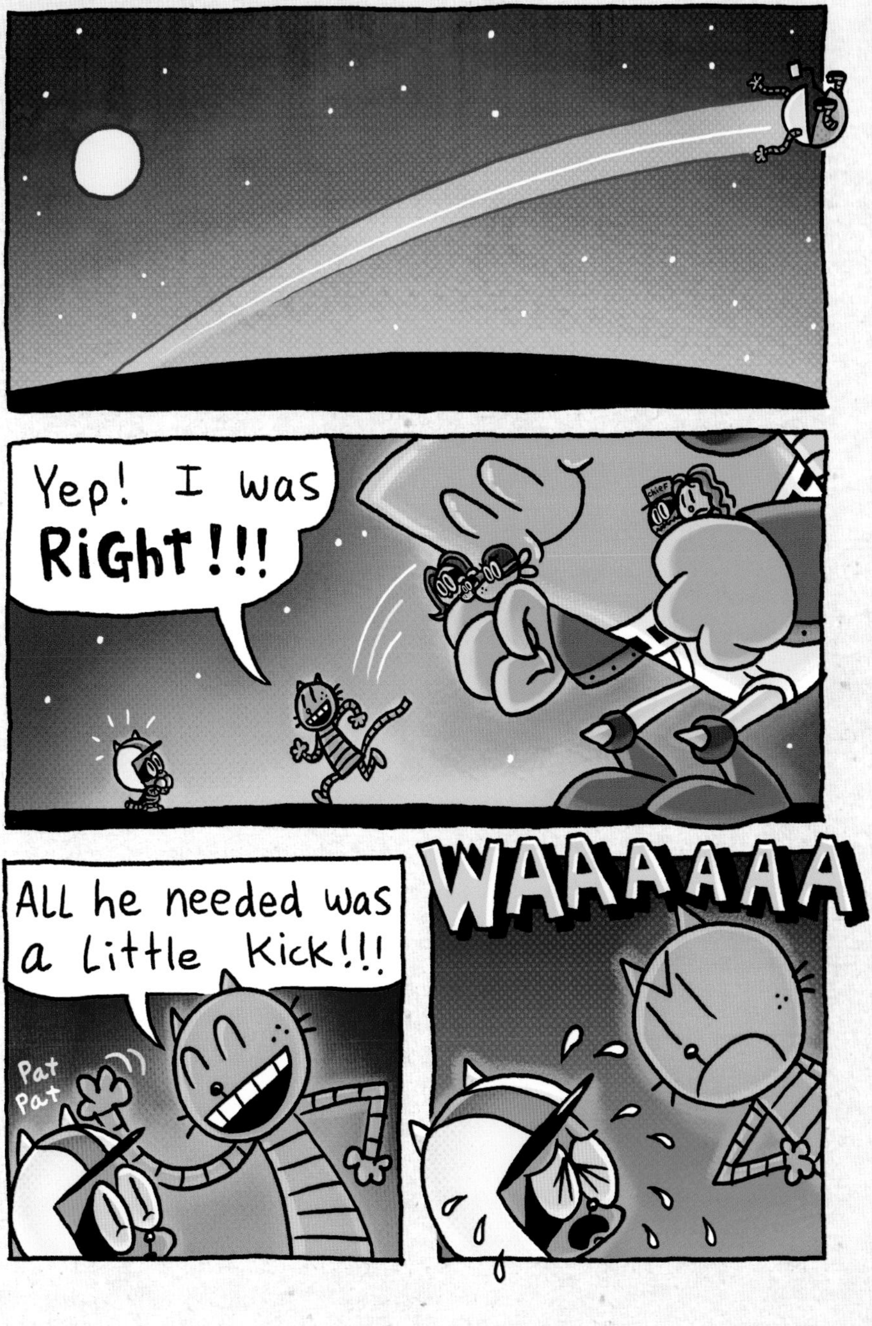
Yep! I was RiGht!!!
All he needed was a Little Kick!!!
Pat Pat
WAAAAAA

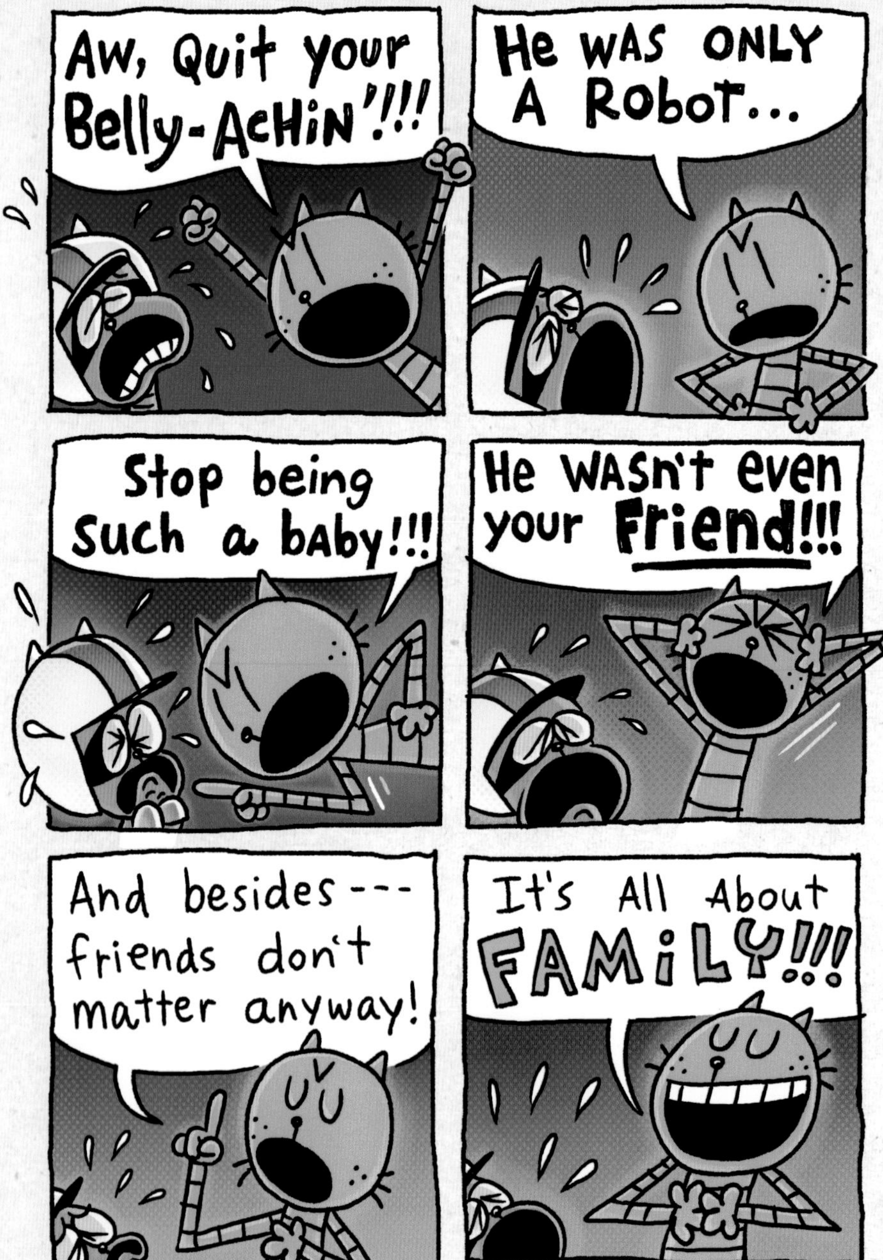
Aw, Quit your Belly-AcHiN'!!!
He WAS ONLY A RoboT...
Stop being such a bAby!!!
He WASn't even your Friend!!!
And besides--- friends don't matter anyway!
It's All About FAMiLY!!!

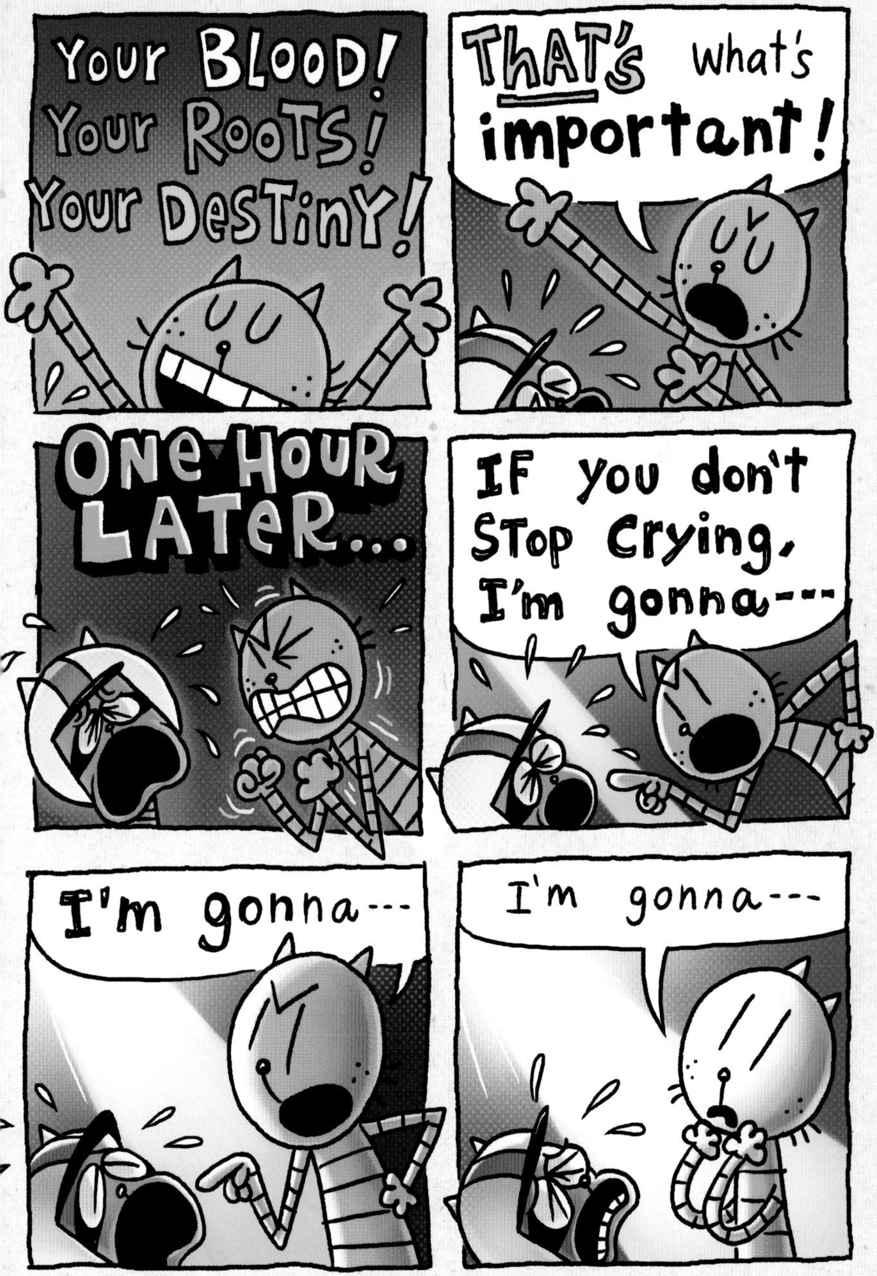
Your BLOOD! Your ROOTS! Your DESTINY!
THAT'S what's important!
ONE HOUR LATER...
IF you don't STop Crying, I'm gonna---
I'm gonna---
I'm gonna---

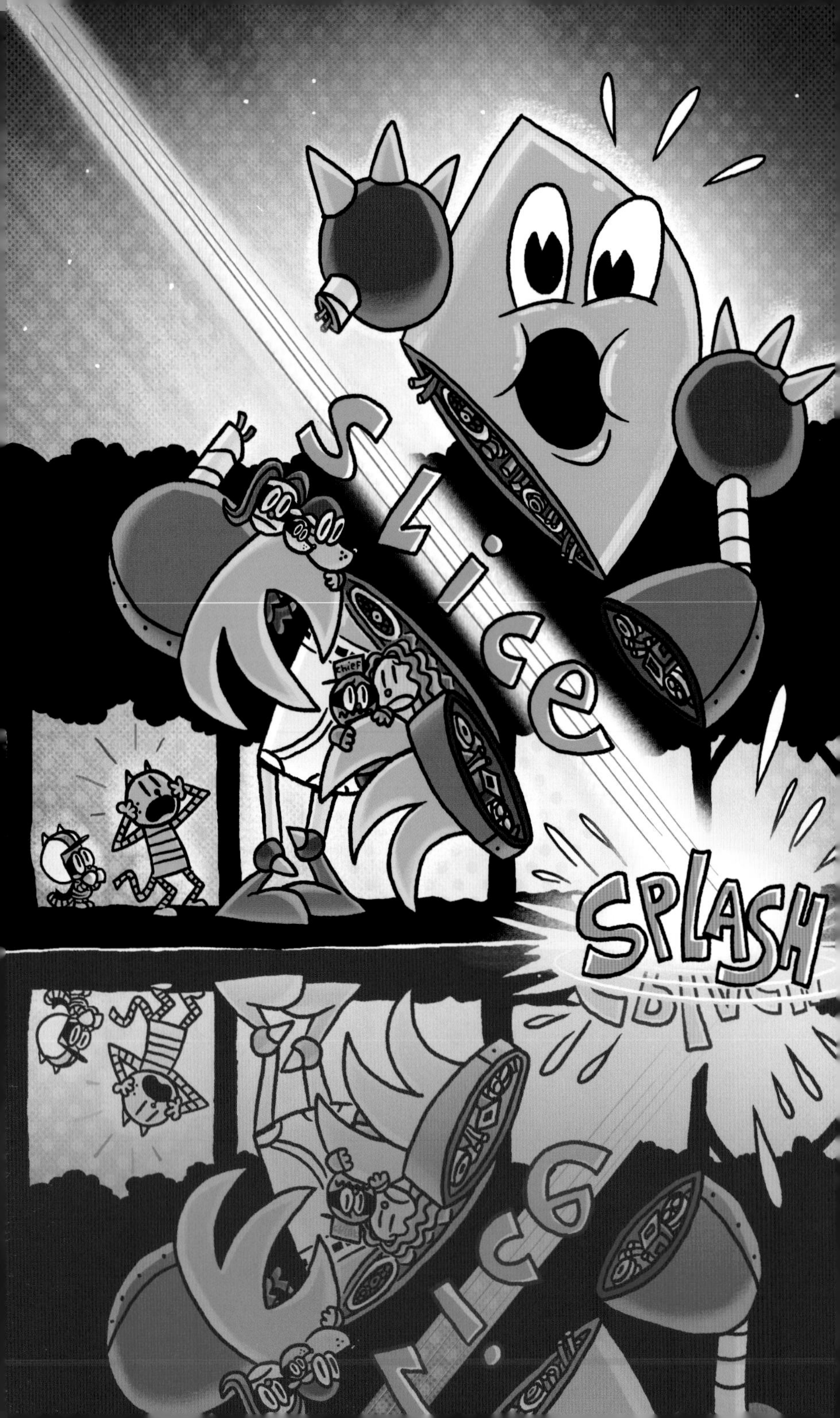
SLICE
chief
SPLASH

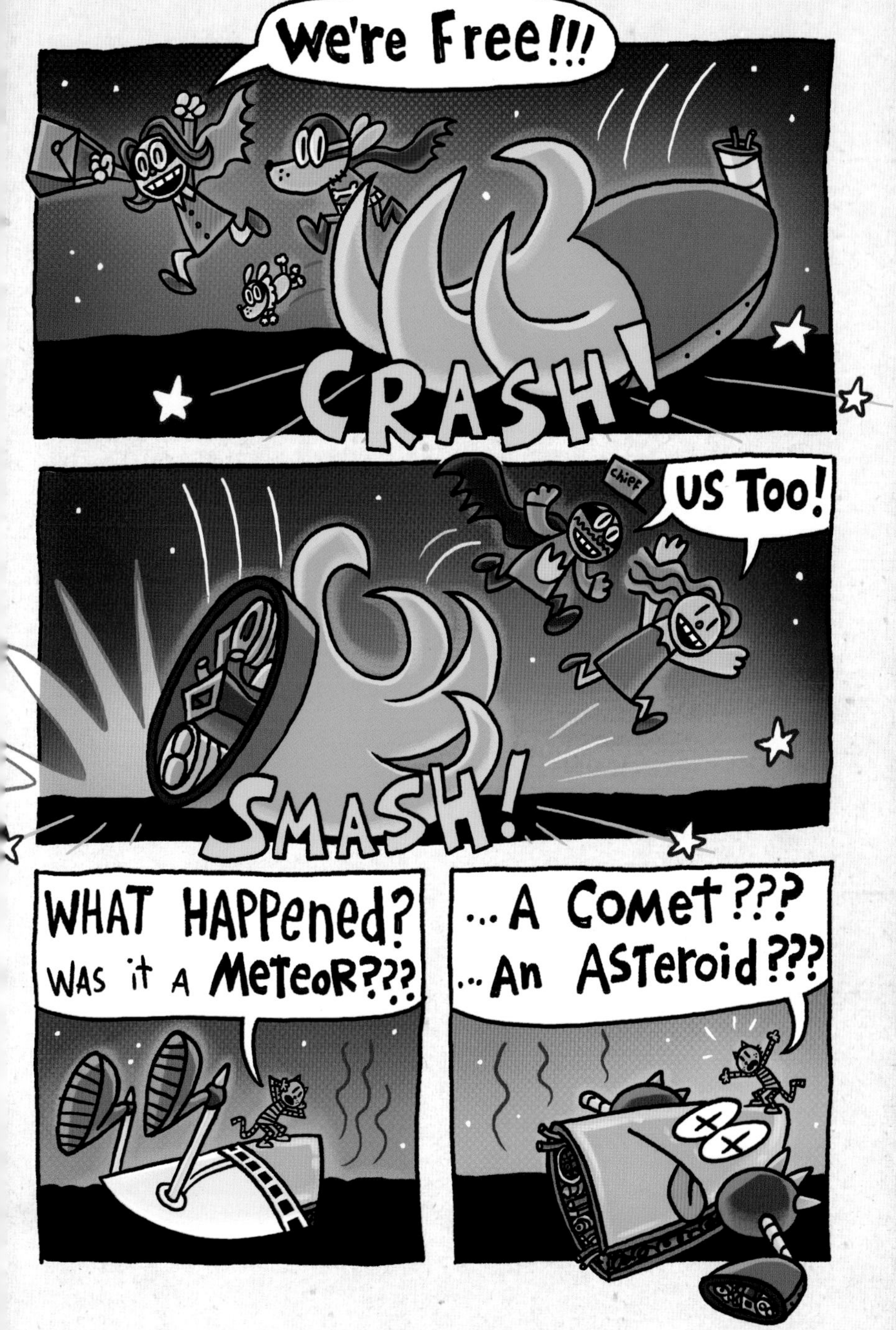
We're Free!!!
CRASH!
CHIEF
US Too!
SMASH!
WHAT HAPPened? Was it A MeTeoR???
...A Comet???
...An ASTeroid???

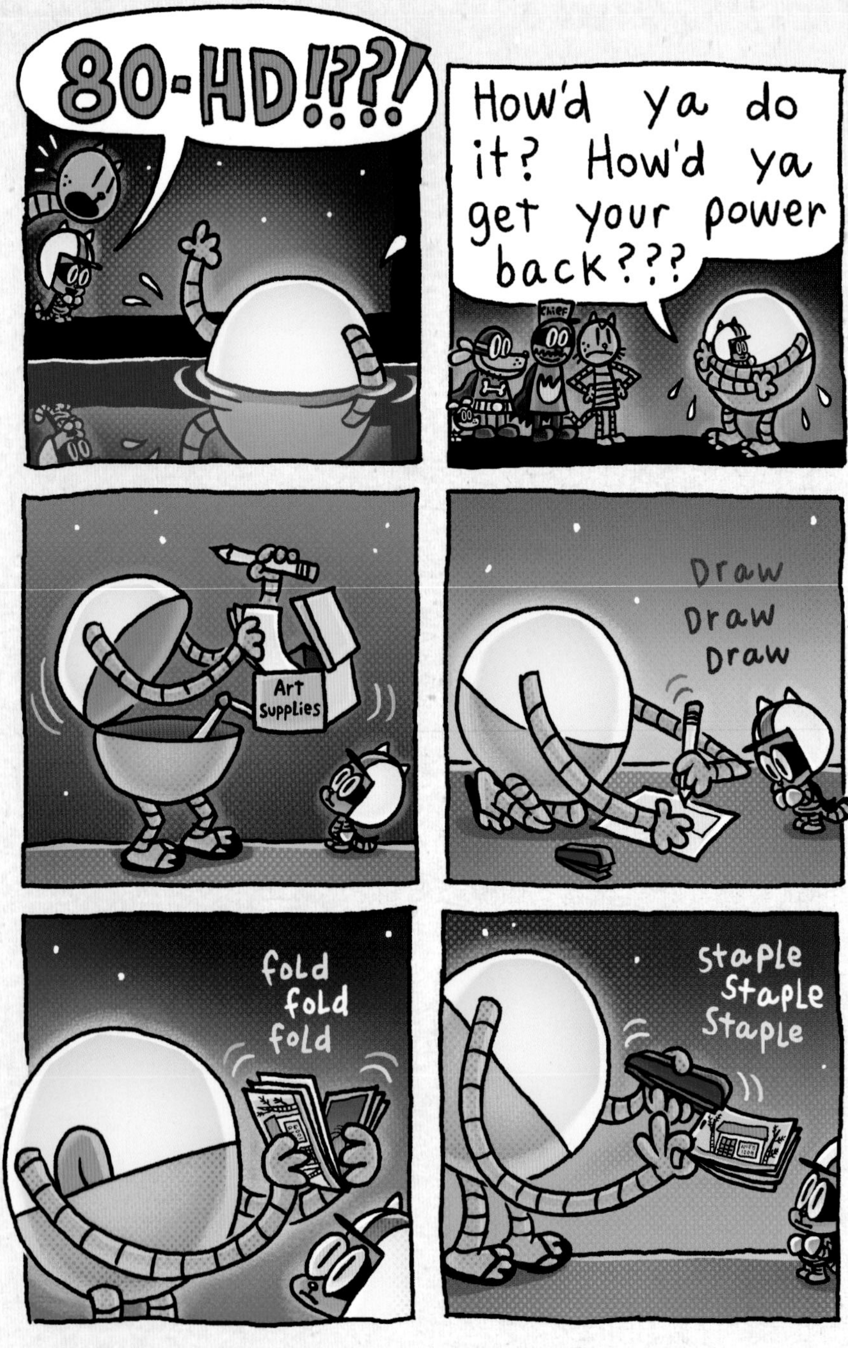
80-HD!??!
How'd ya do it? How'd ya get your power back???
Chief
Art Supplies
Draw
Draw
Draw
fold
fold
fold
staple
staple
staple

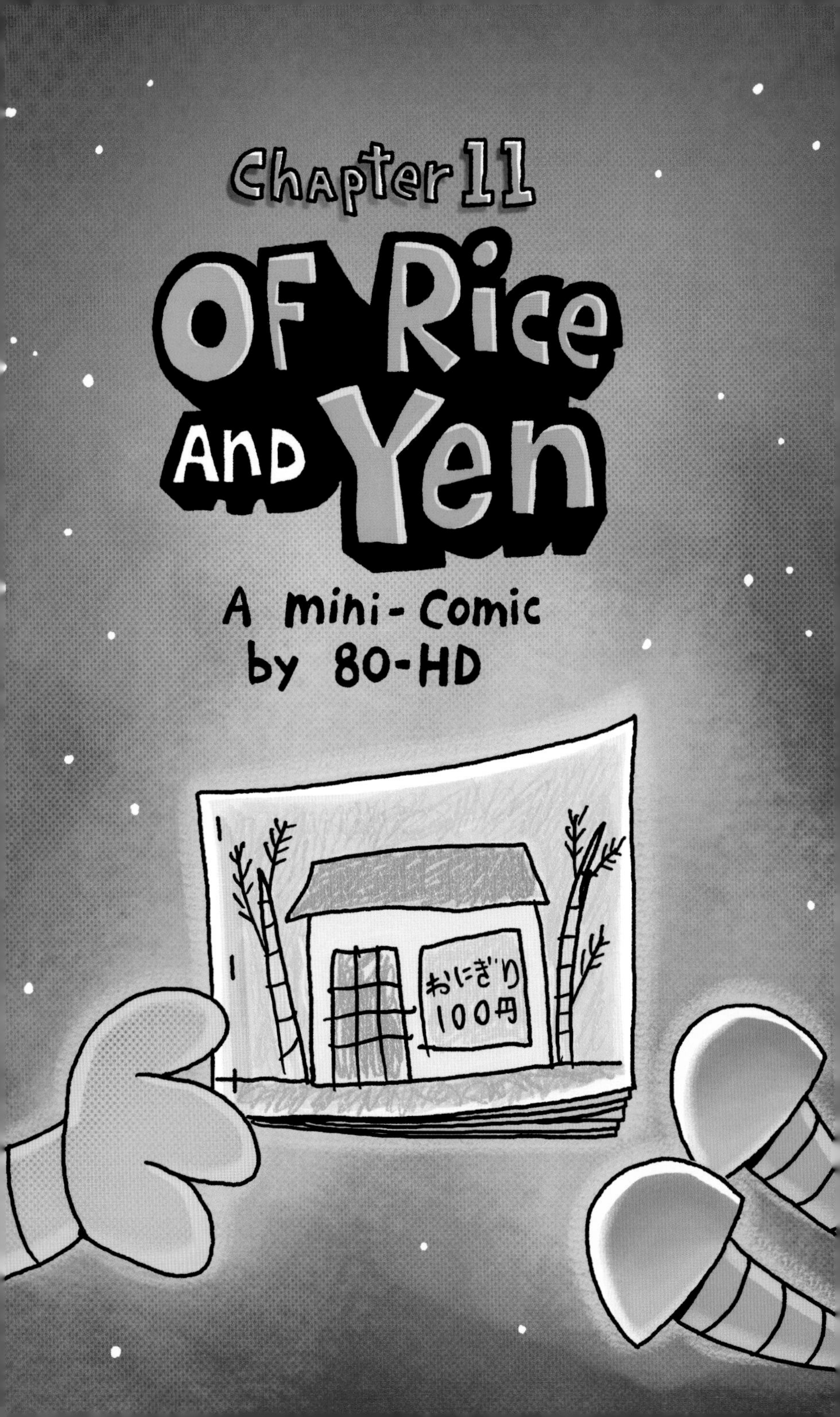
Chapter 11
Of Rice And Yen
A mini-Comic by 80-HD
おにぎり
100円

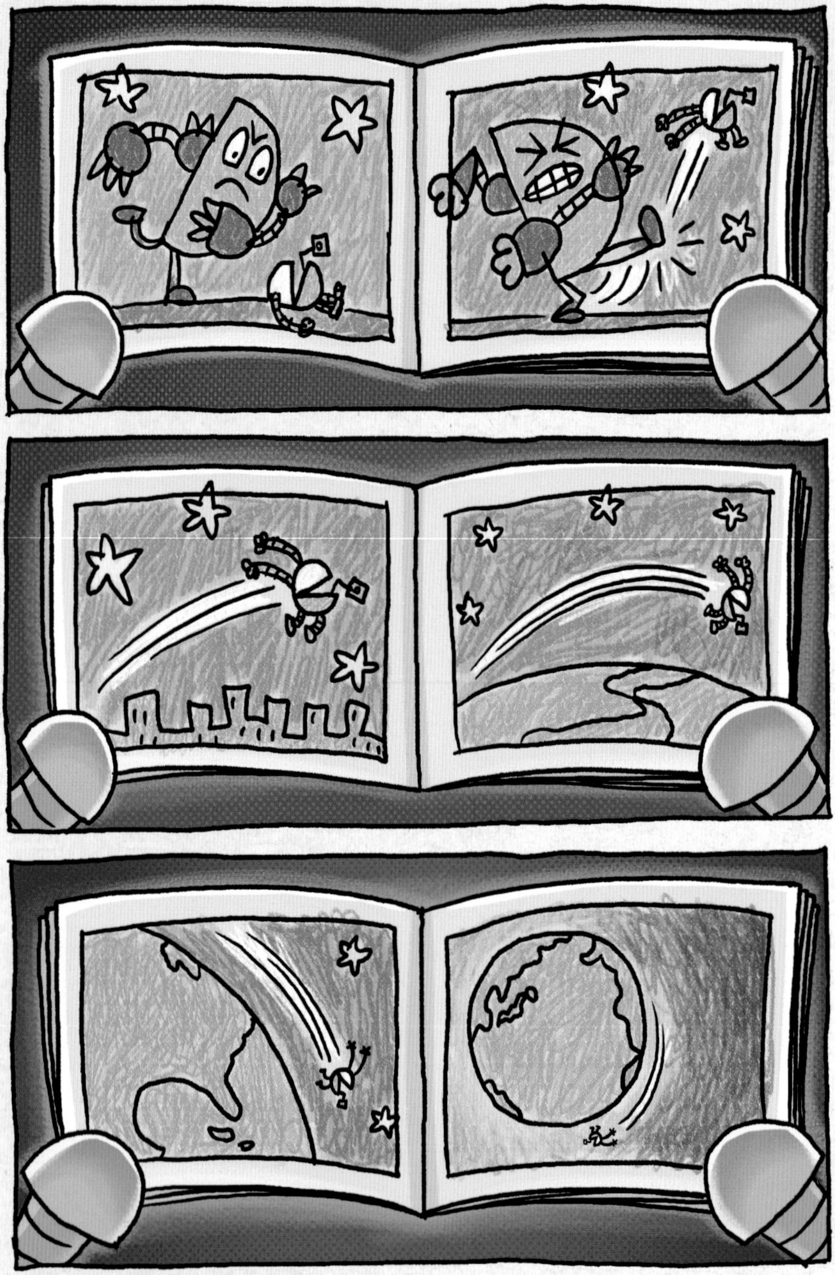

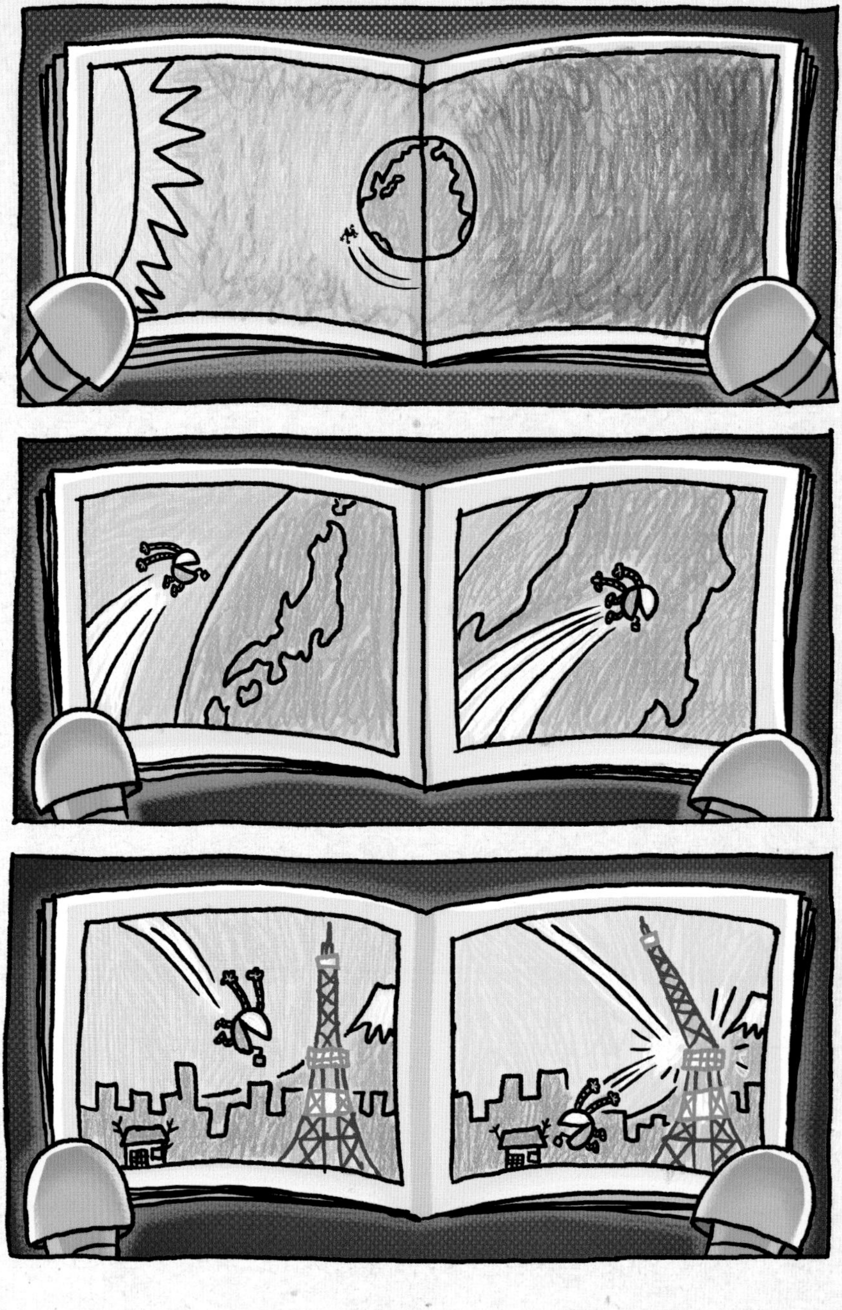

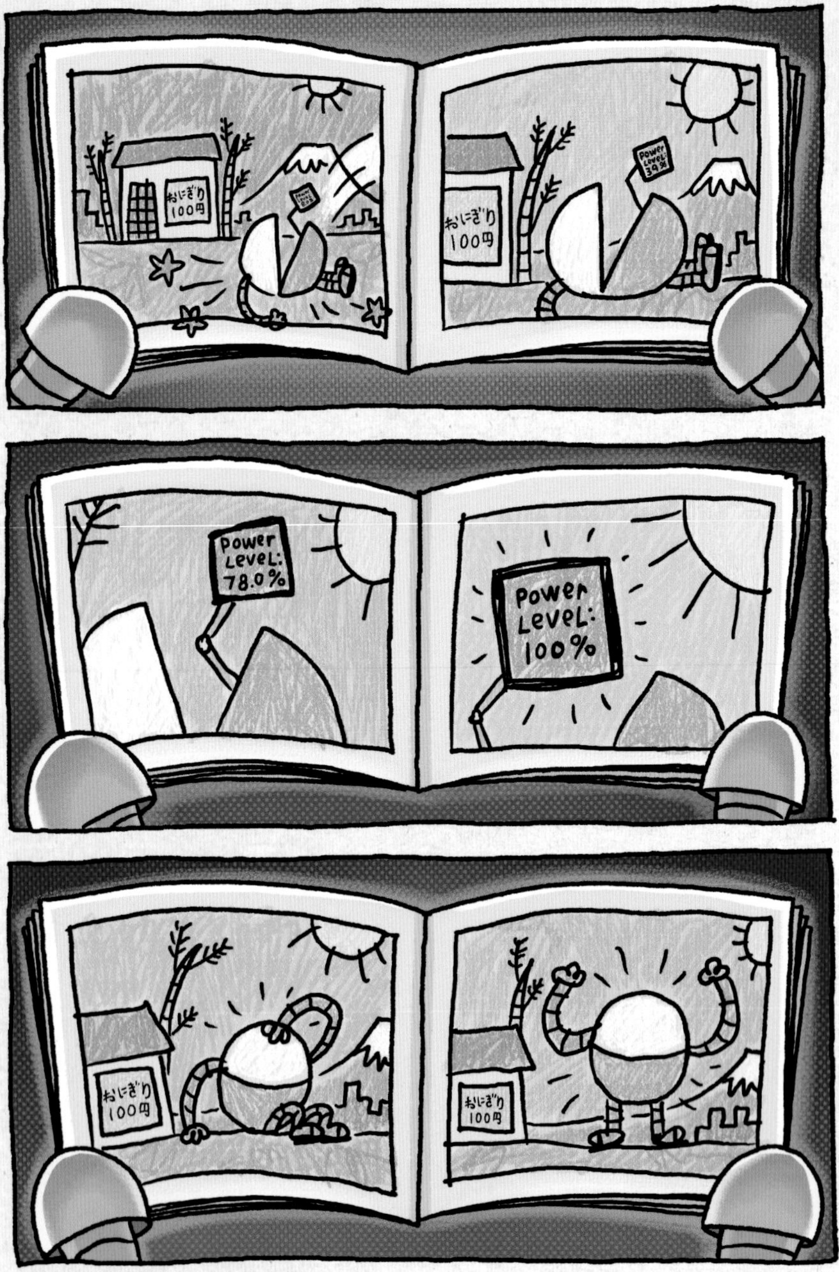
おにぎり
100円
おにぎり
100円
Power
Level:
78.0%
Power
Level:
100%
おにぎり
100円
おにぎり
100円

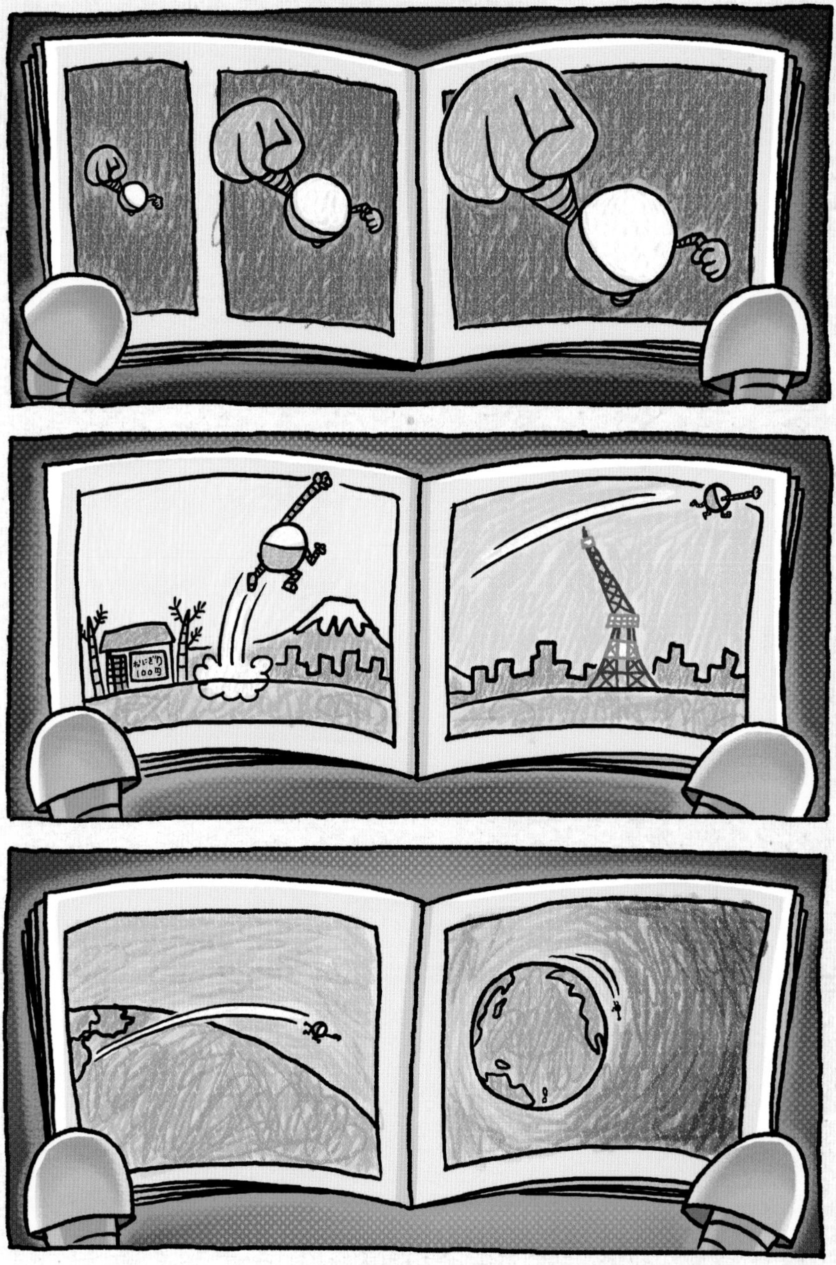
おにぎり
100円

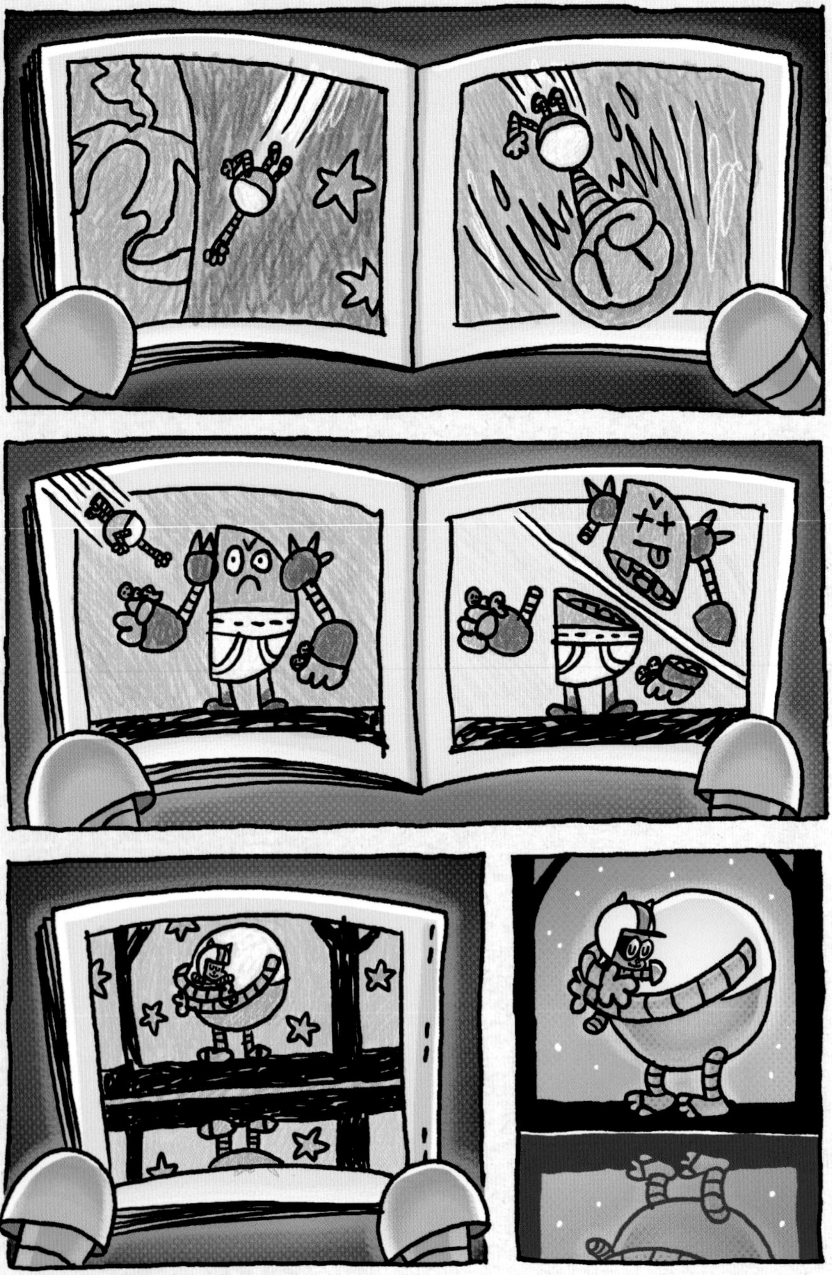

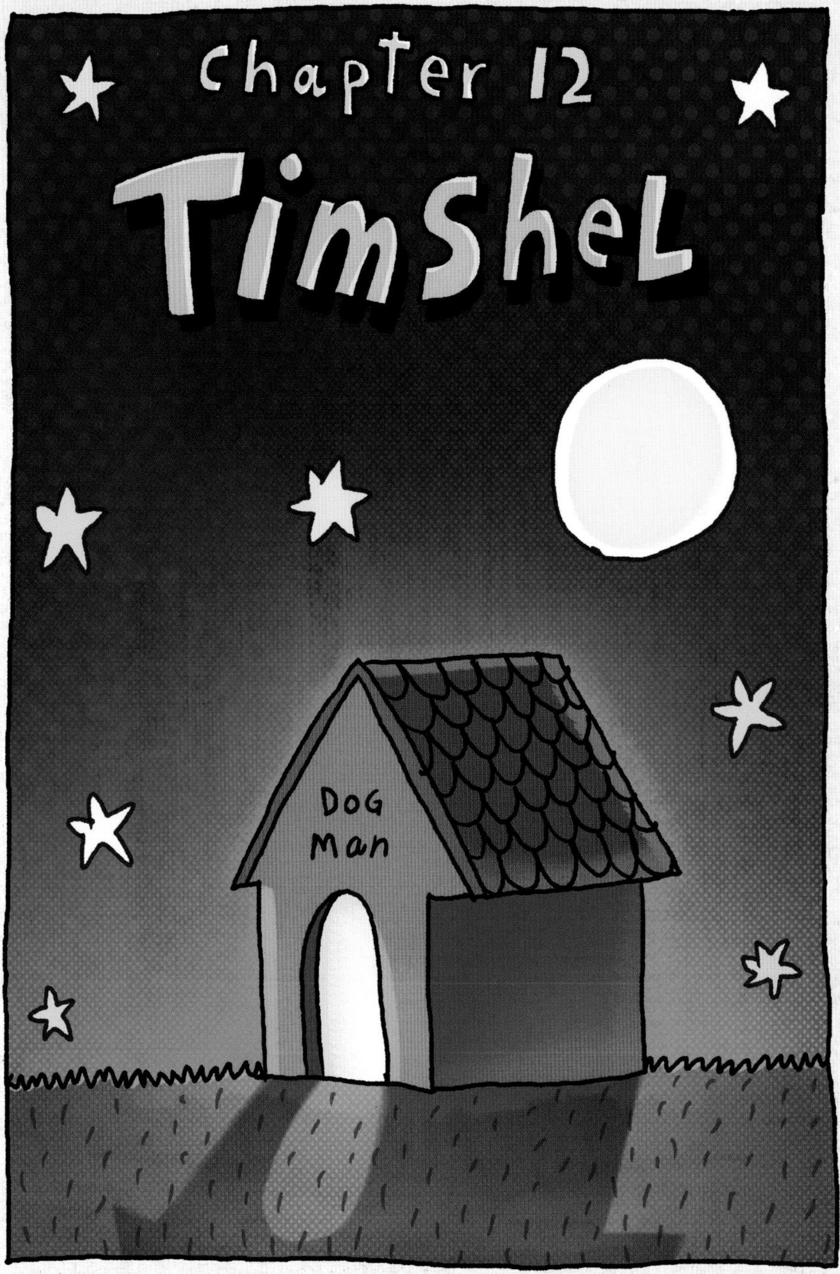
Chapter 12
Timshel
DOG
Man

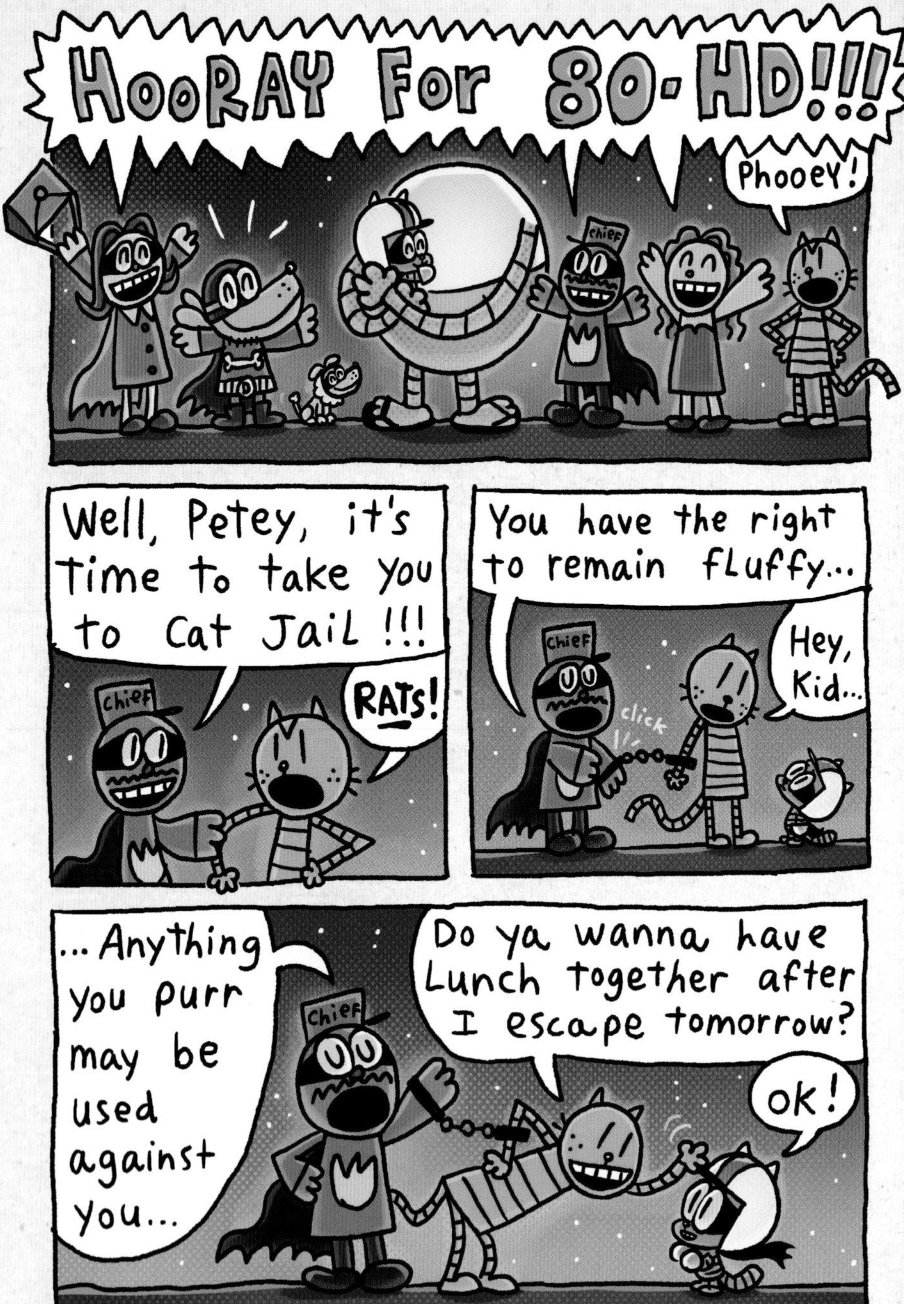
HOORAY For 80-HD!!!
Phooey!
Well, Petey, it's time to take you to Cat Jail!!!
RATS!
You have the right to remain fluffy...
Hey, Kid...
click
...Anything you purr may be used against you...
Do ya wanna have lunch together after I escape tomorrow?
OK!

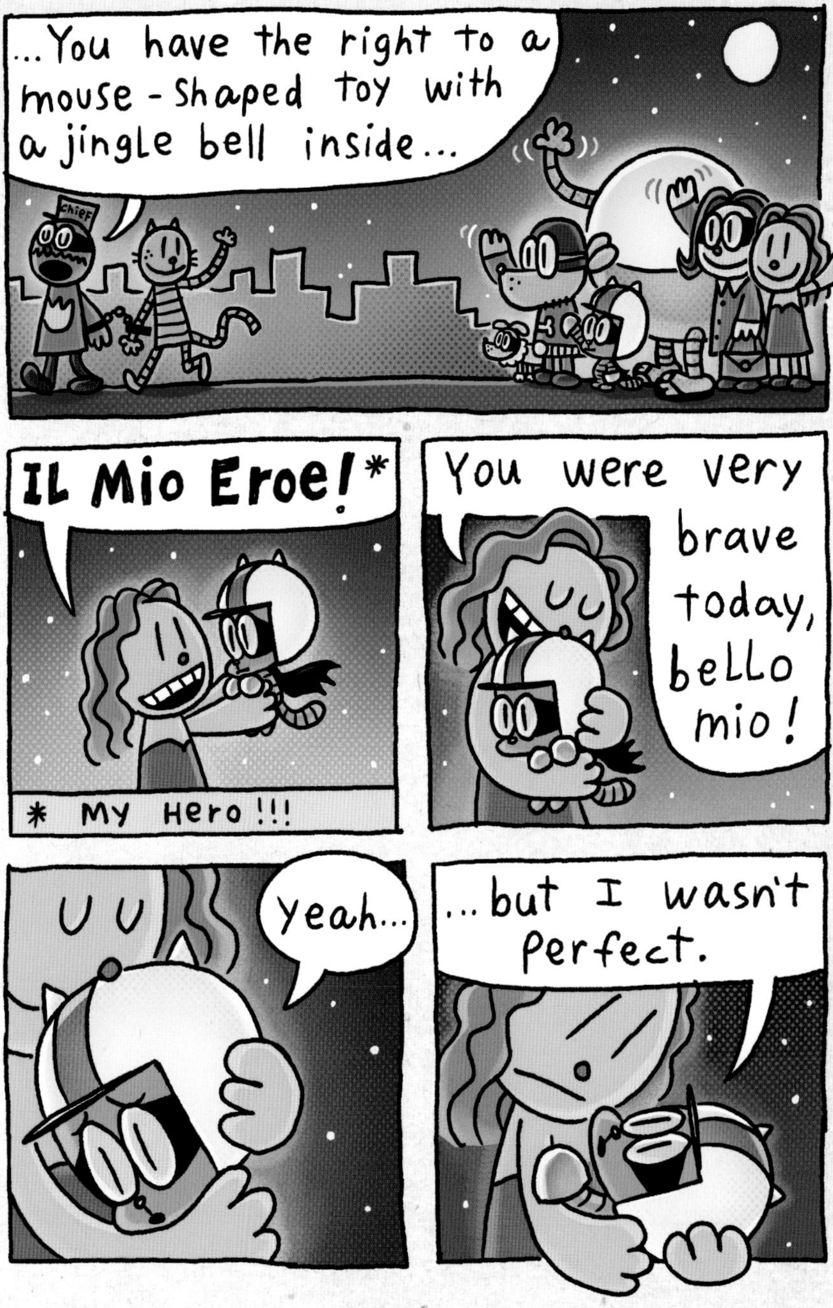
...You have the right to a mouse-shaped toy with a jingle bell inside...
CHIEF
IL Mio Eroe!*
* My Hero!!!
You were very brave today, bello mio!
yeah...
...but I wasn't perfect.

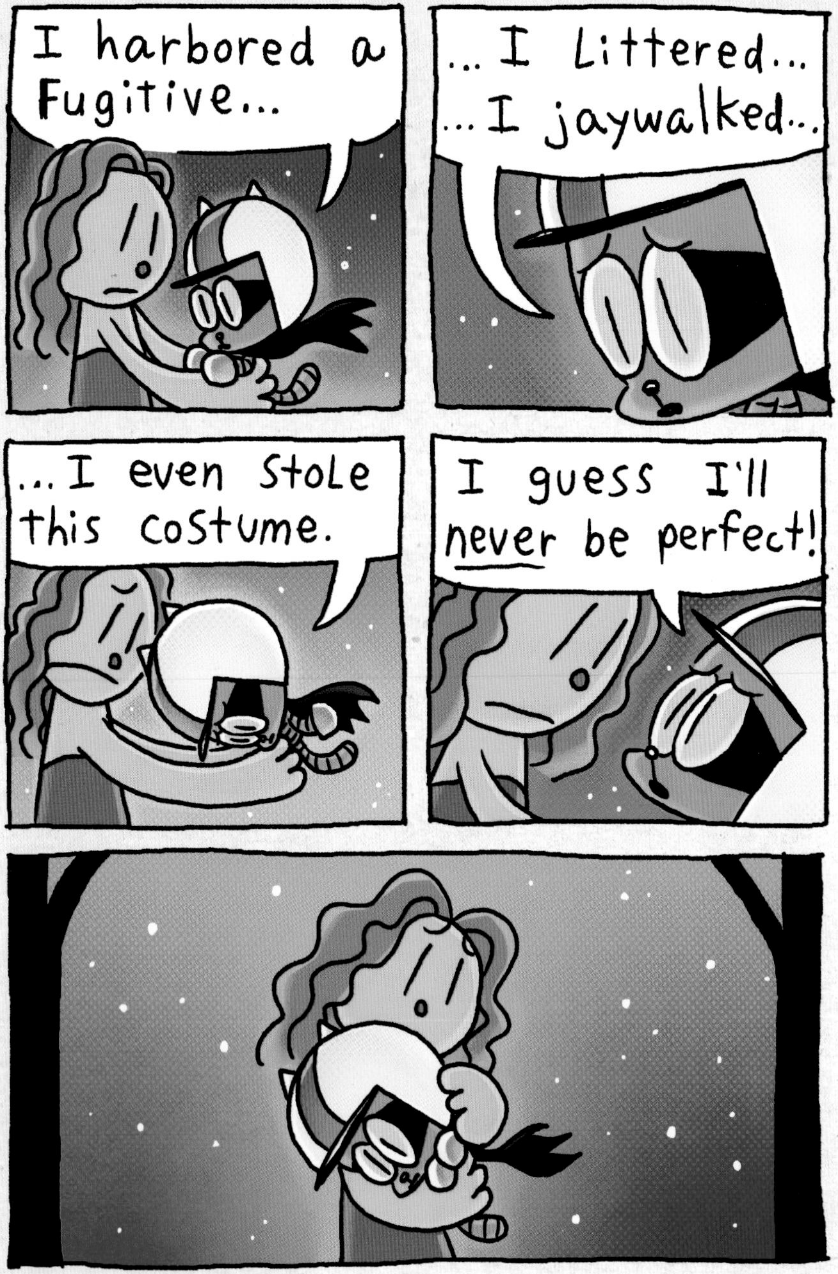
I harbored a Fugitive...
...I Littered...
...I jaywalked...
...I even stole this costume.
I guess I'll never be perfect!

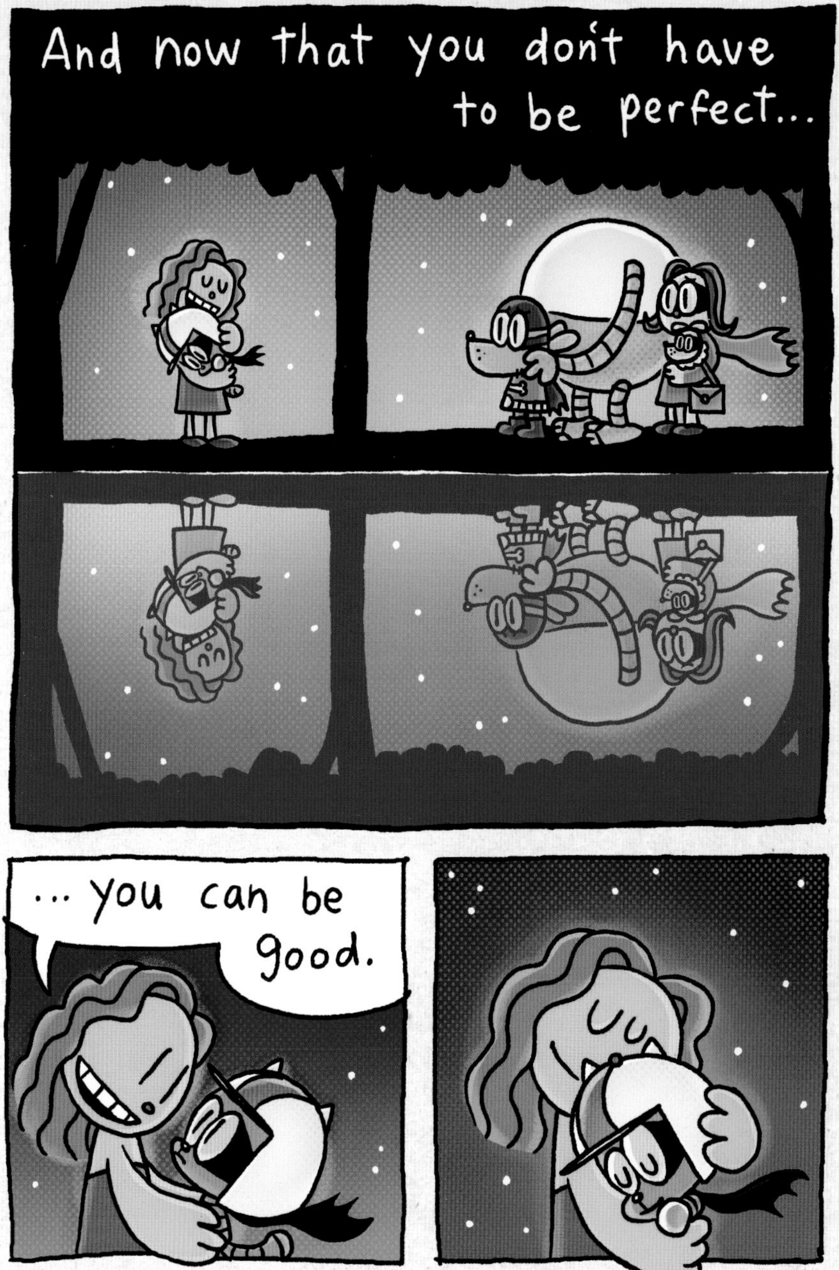
And now that you don't have to be perfect...
...you can be good.

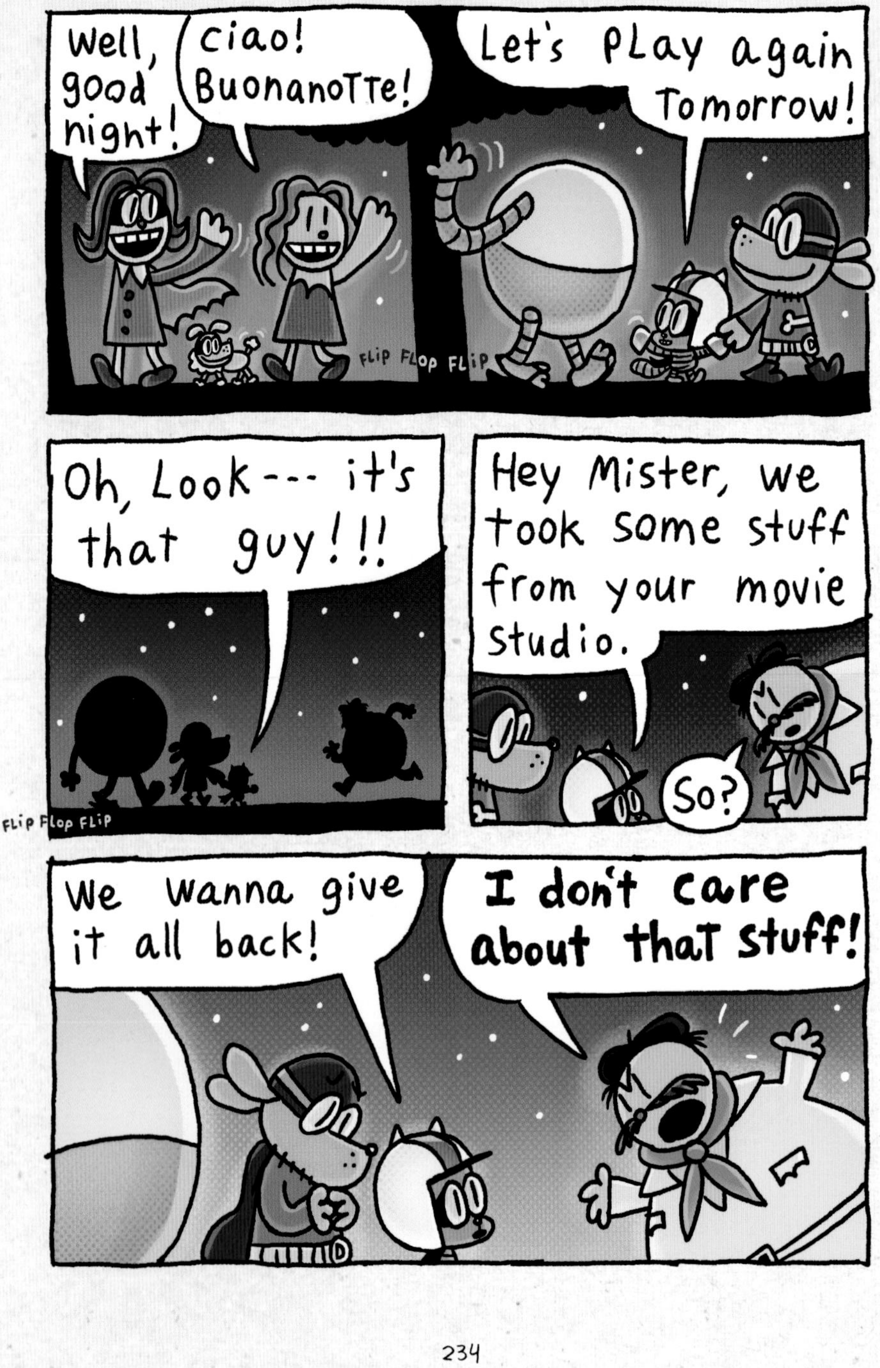
Well, good night!
ciao! BuonanoTTe!
Let's PLay again Tomorrow!
FLip FLop FLiP
Oh, Look--- it's that guy!!!
FLip FLop FLip
Hey Mister, we took some stuff from your movie studio.
So?
We wanna give it all back!
I don't care about that stuff!

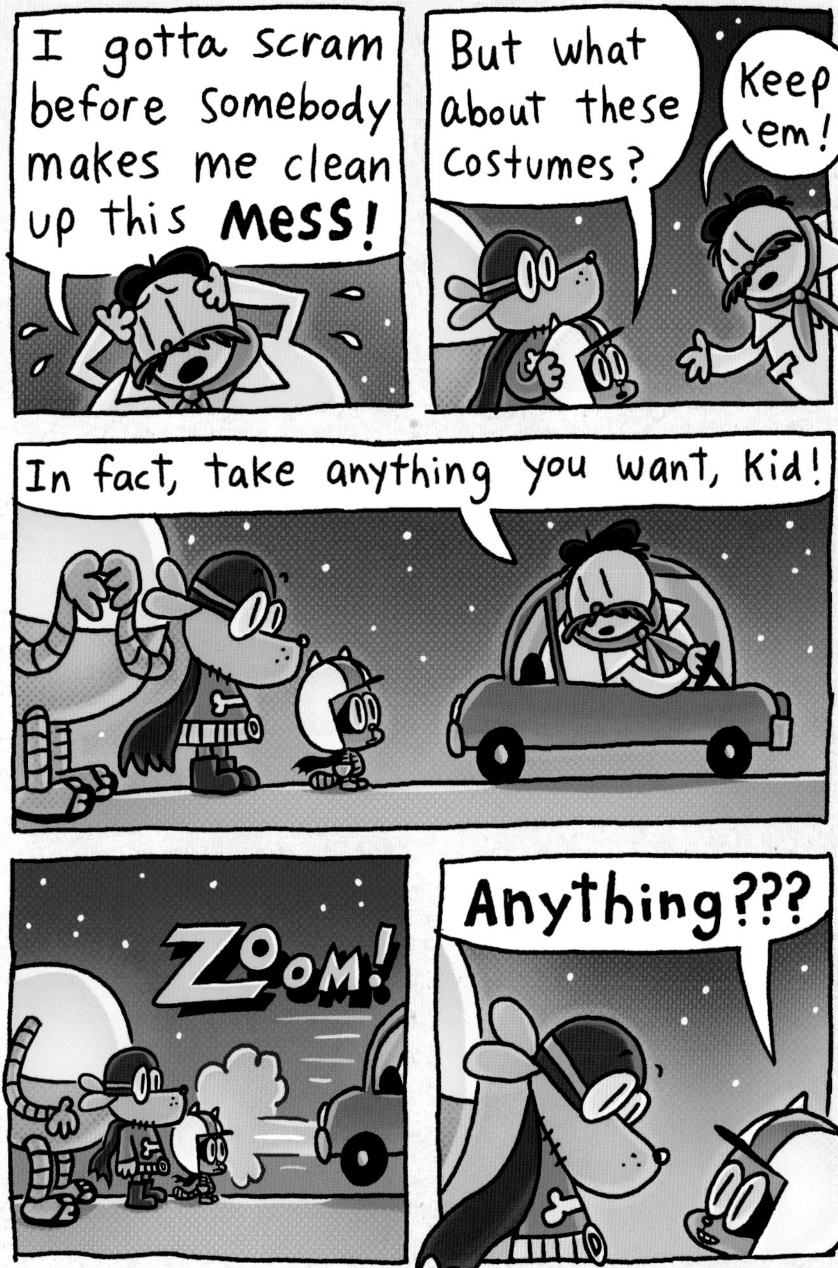

I gotta scram before somebody makes me clean up this MESS!
But what about these costumes?
Keep 'em!
In fact, take anything you want, Kid!
ZOOM!
Anything???

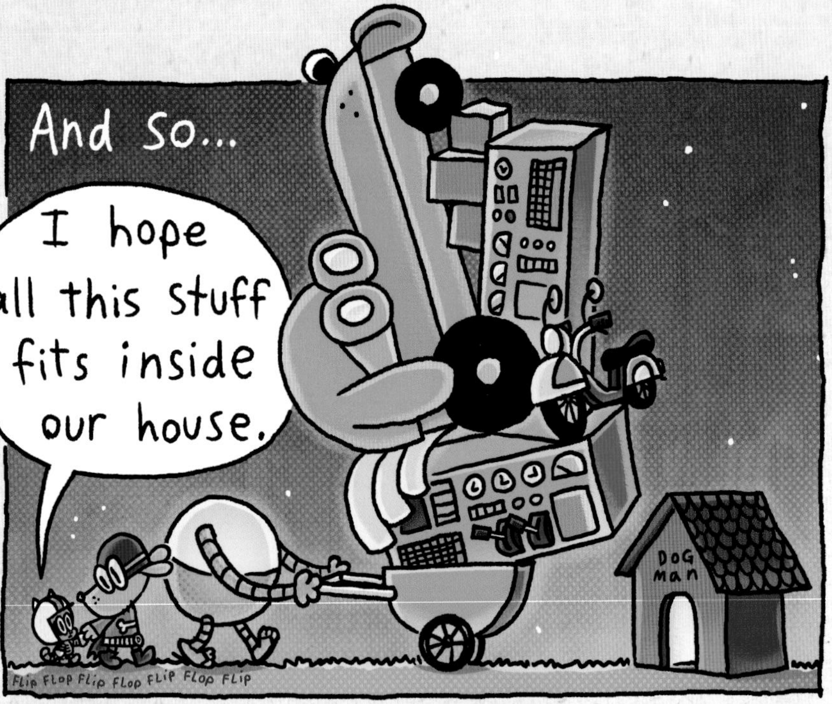
And so...
I hope all this stuff fits inside our house.
DOG Man
FLIP FLOP FLIP FLOP FLIP FLOP FLIP

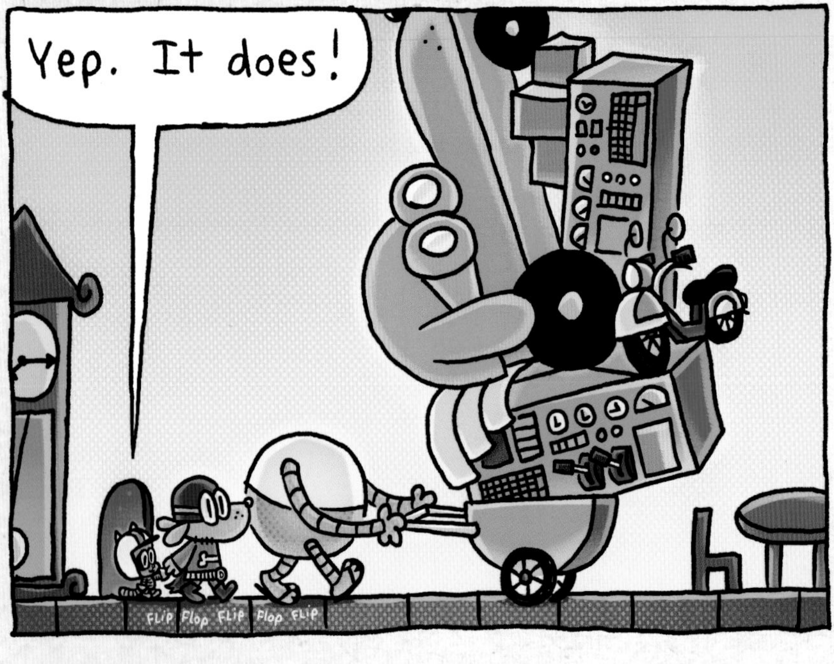
Yep. It does!
FLIP Flop FLIP Flop FLIP

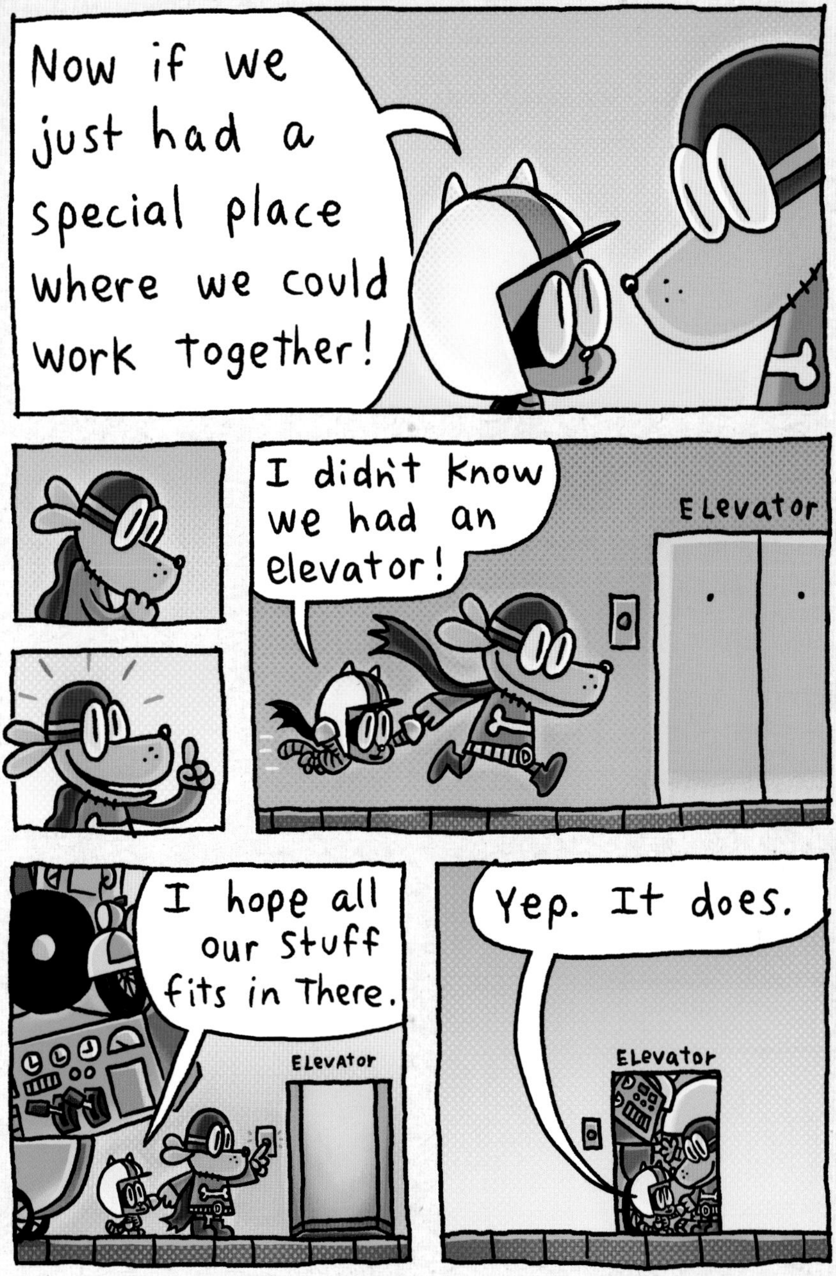
Now if we just had a special place where we could work together!
I didn't know we had an elevator!
Elevator
I hope all our Stuff fits in There.
Elevator
Yep. It does.
Elevator

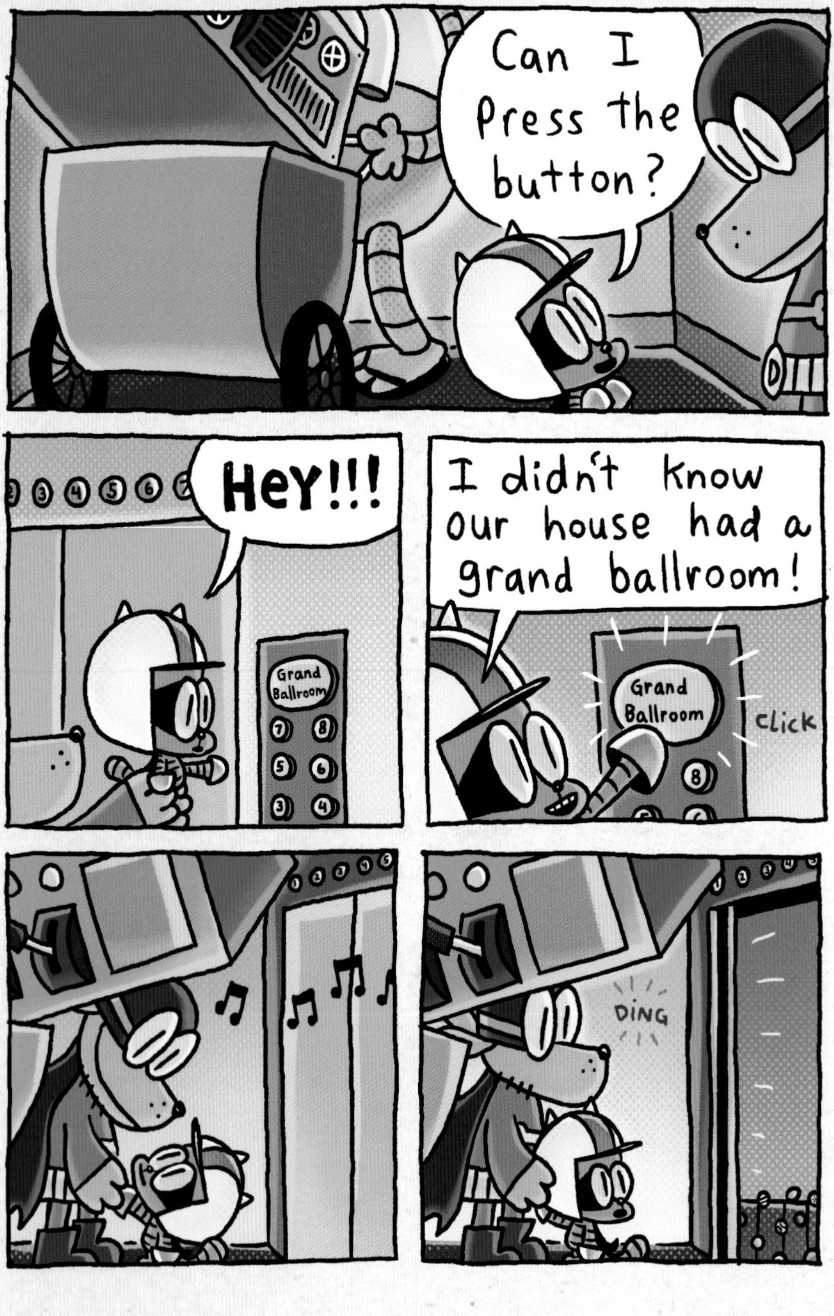
Can I press the button?
HEY!!!
Grand Ballroom
I didn't know our house had a grand ballroom!
Grand Ballroom
CLICK
DING

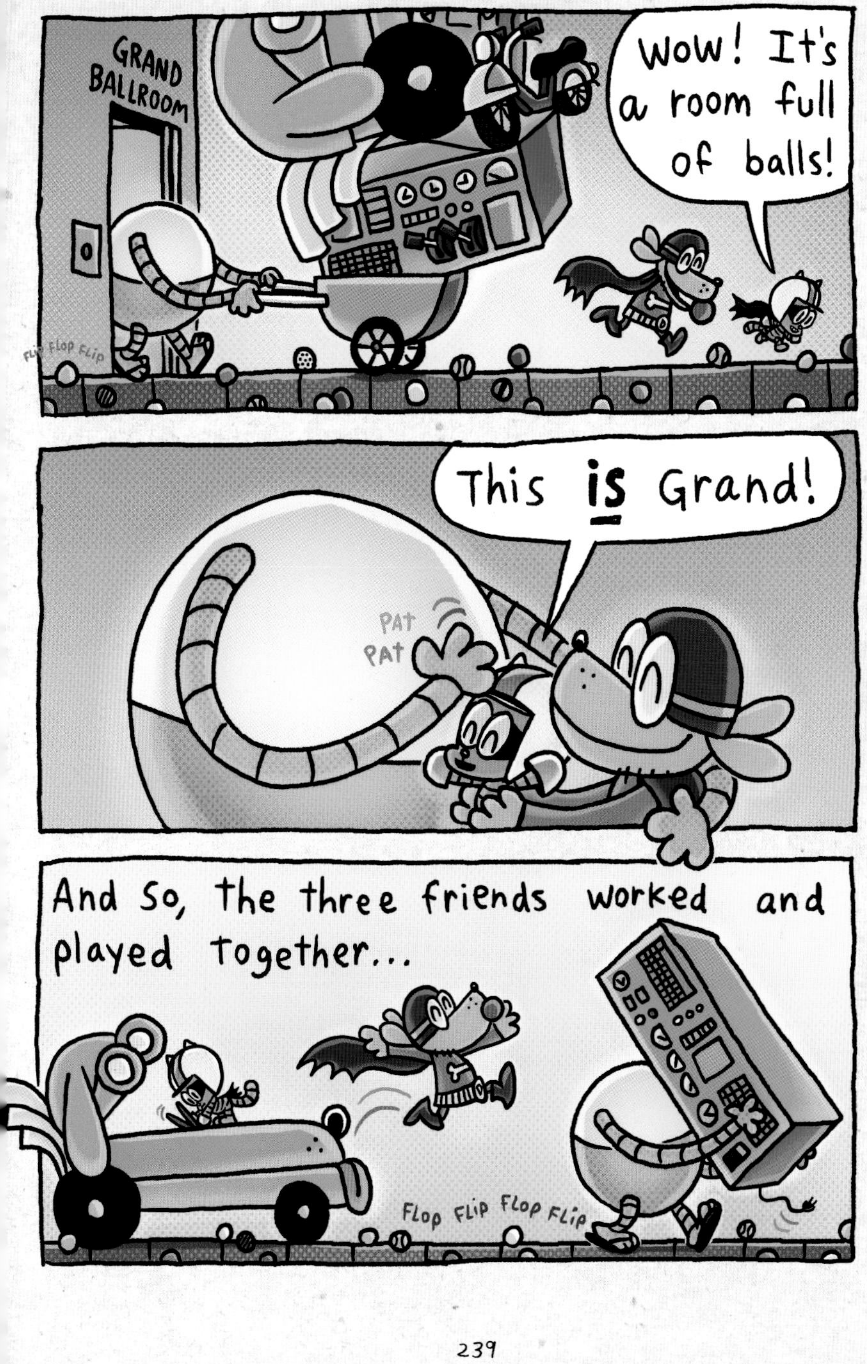
GRAND BALLROOM
FLIP FLOP FLIP
Wow! It's a room full of balls!
This **is** Grand!
PAT PAT
And so, the three friends worked and played together...
FLOP FLIP FLOP FLIP

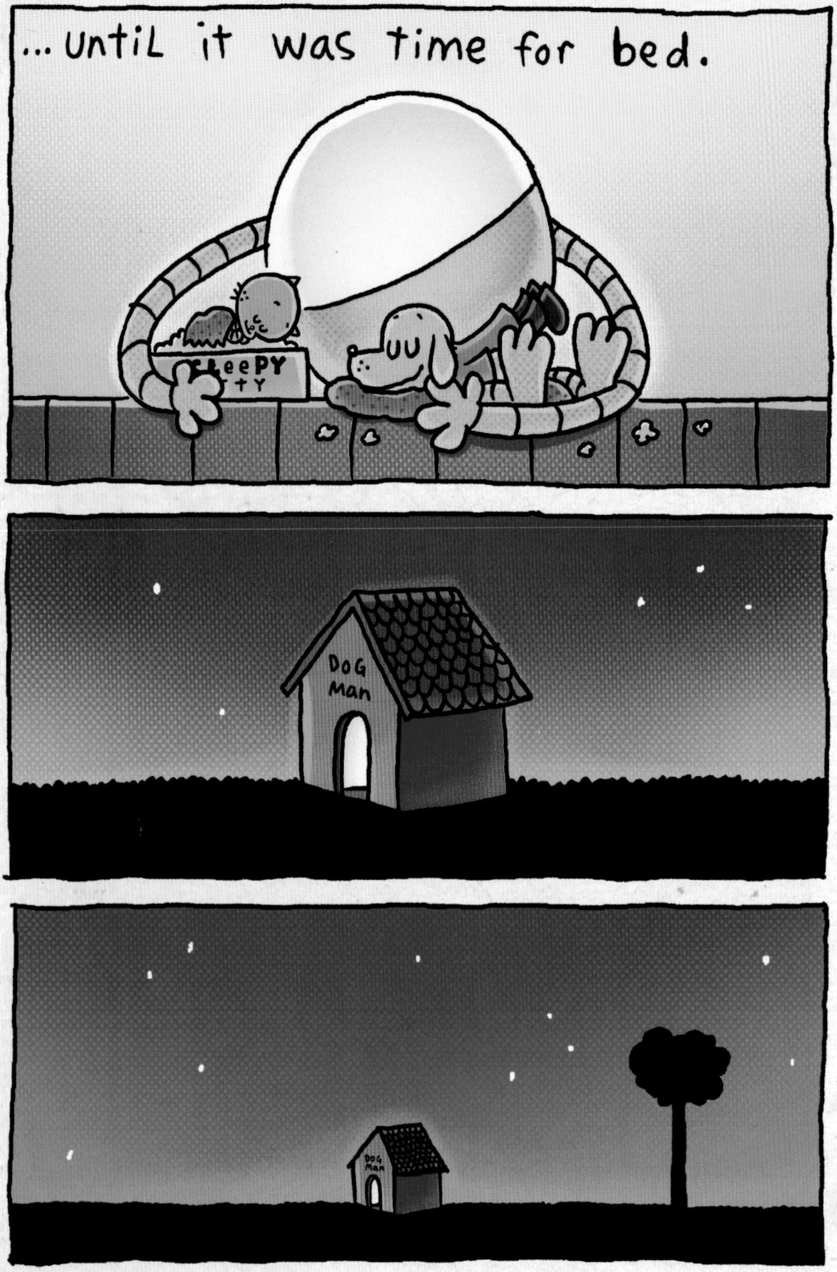
...until it was time for bed.
DOG Man

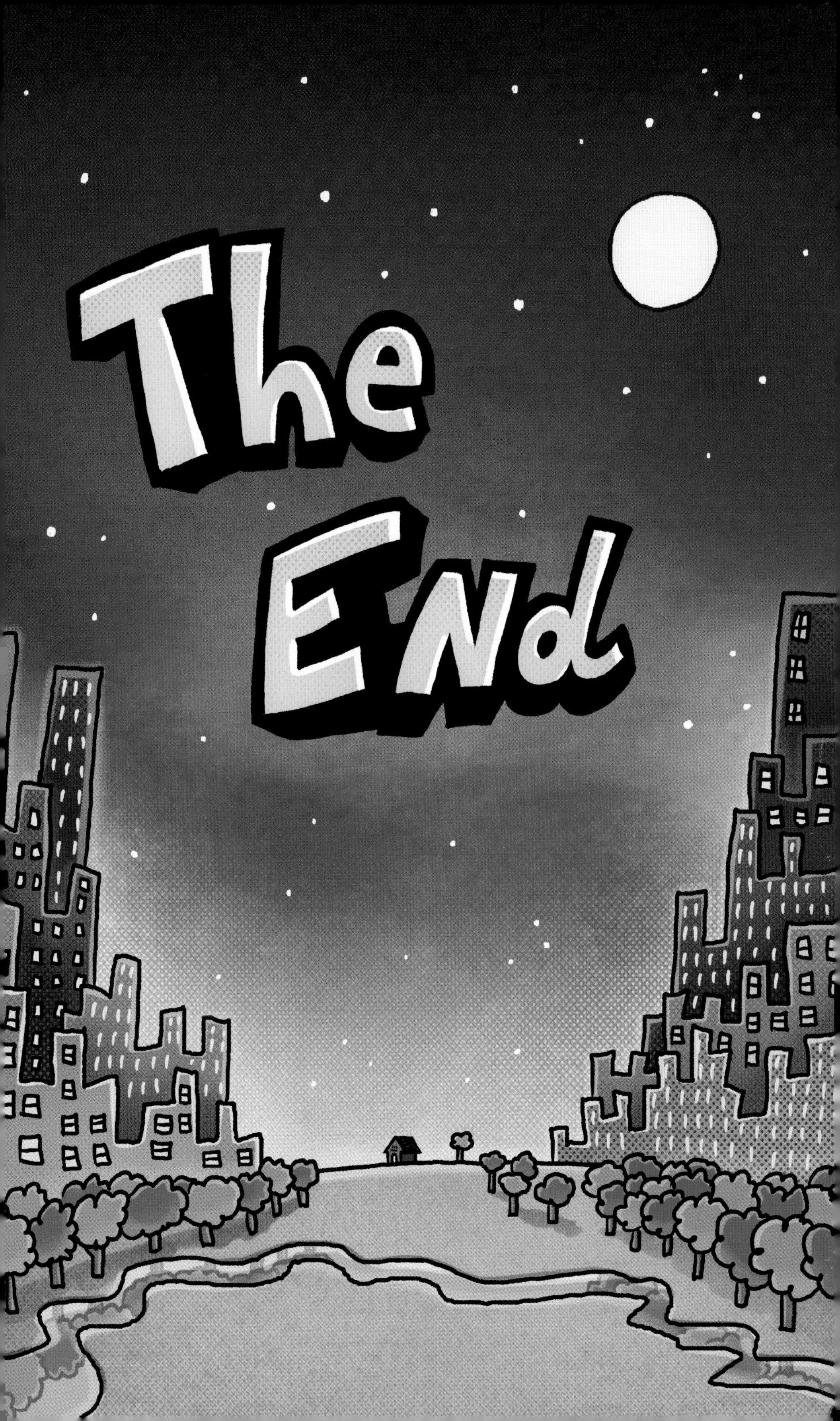
The End

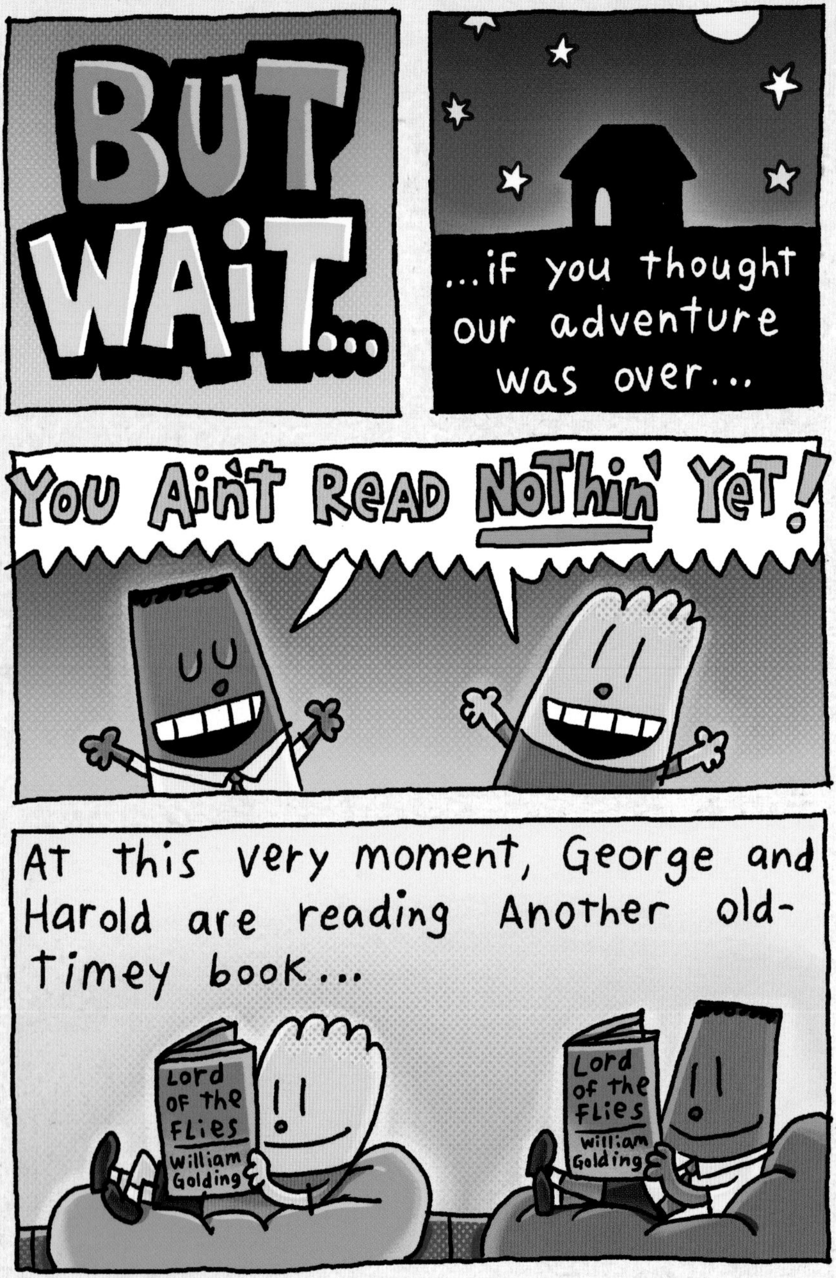

BUT WAIT...
...if you thought our adventure was over...
You Ain't Read NOThin' YeT!
At this very moment, George and Harold are reading Another old-timey book...
Lord of the Flies
William Golding
Lord of the Flies
William Golding

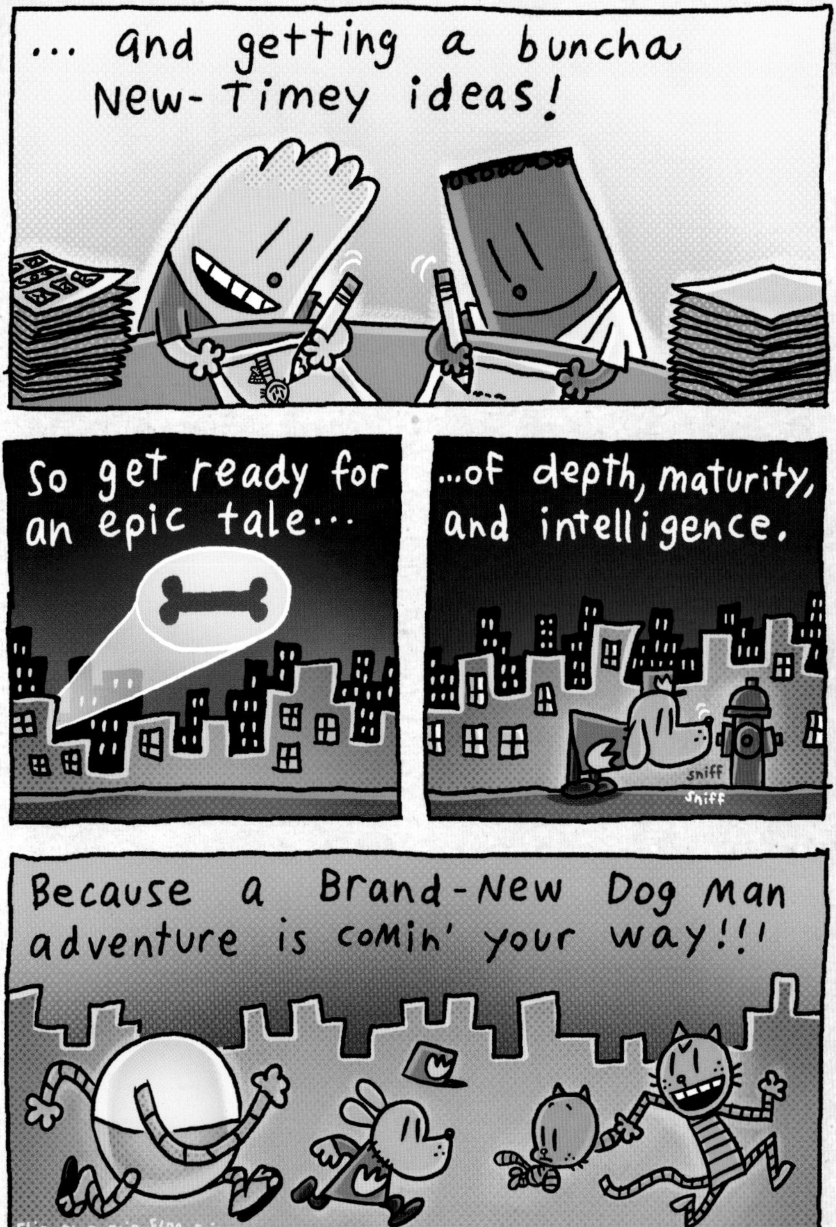
... and getting a buncha New-Timey ideas!
So get ready for an epic tale...
...of depth, maturity, and intelligence.
sniff
sniff
Because a Brand-New Dog Man adventure is comin' your way!!!
FLIP FLOP FLIP FLOP FLIP

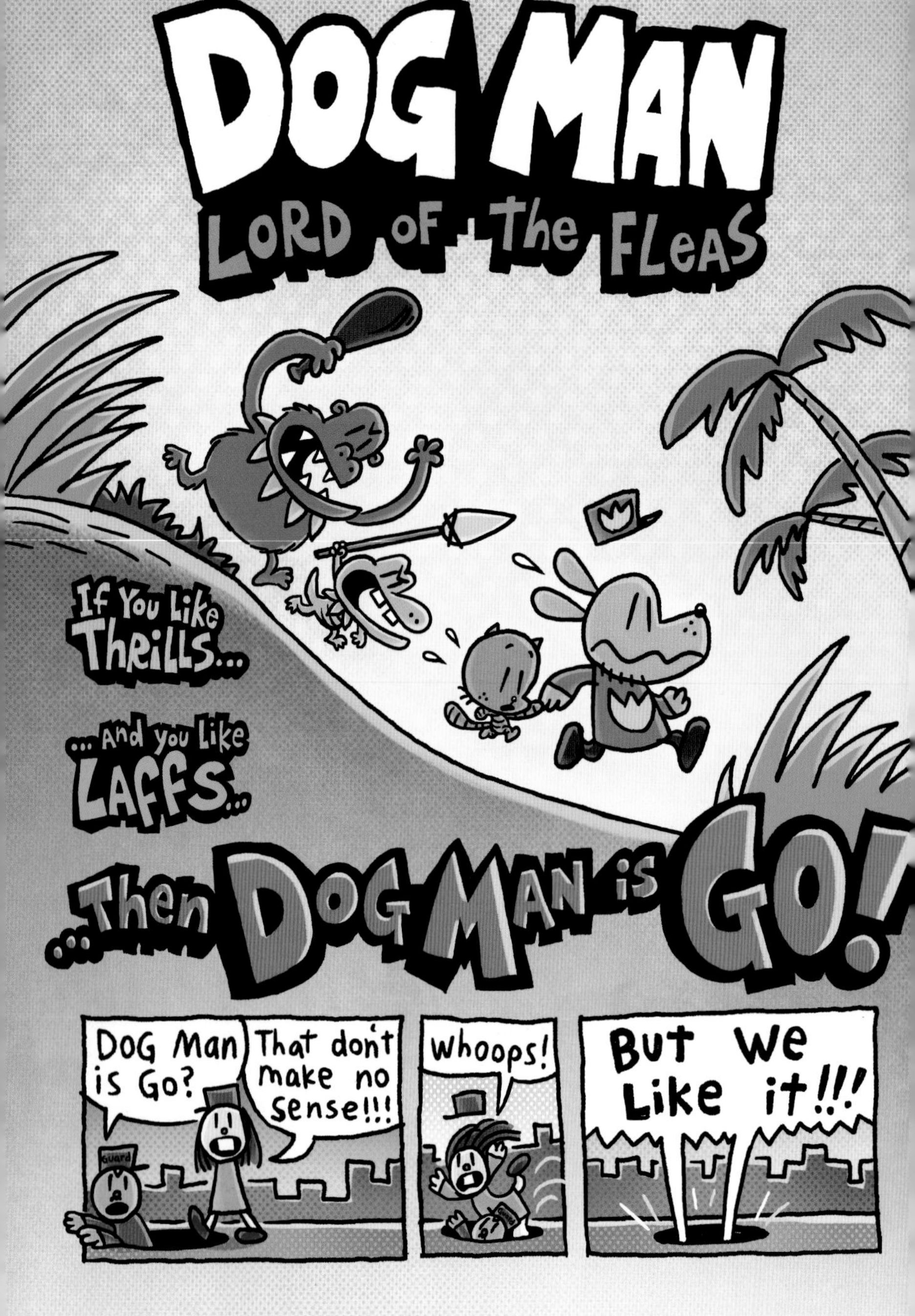
DOG MAN
LORD OF The FLEAS
If You Like THRILLS...
...And you like LAFFS...
...Then DOG MAN is GO!
DOG Man is Go?
That don't make no sense!!!
Whoops!
But we Like it!!!

HOW 2 DRAW THE BARK KNIGHT

in 46 Ridiculously easy Steps!

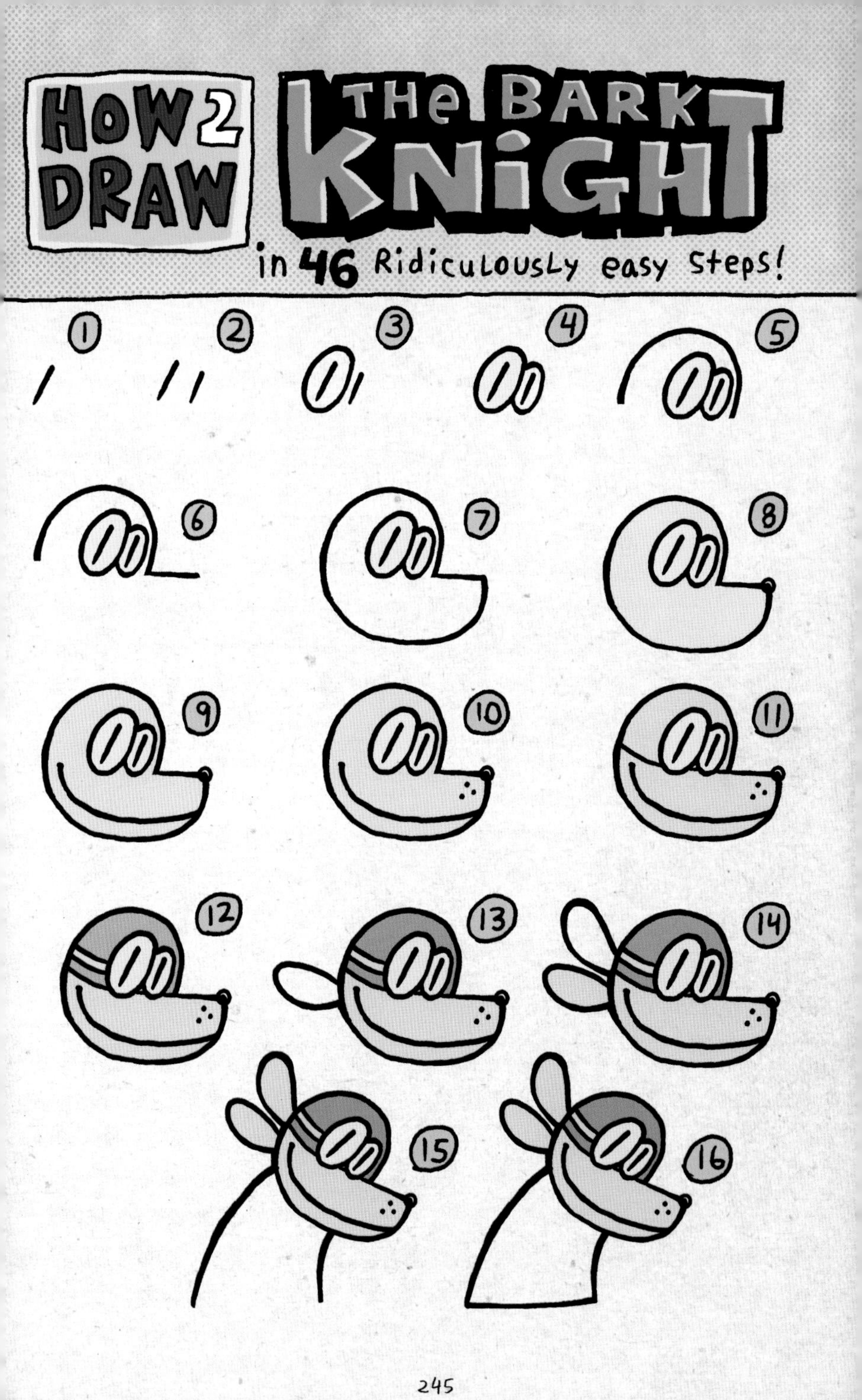
1
2
3
4
5
6
7
8
9
10
11
12
13
14
15
16

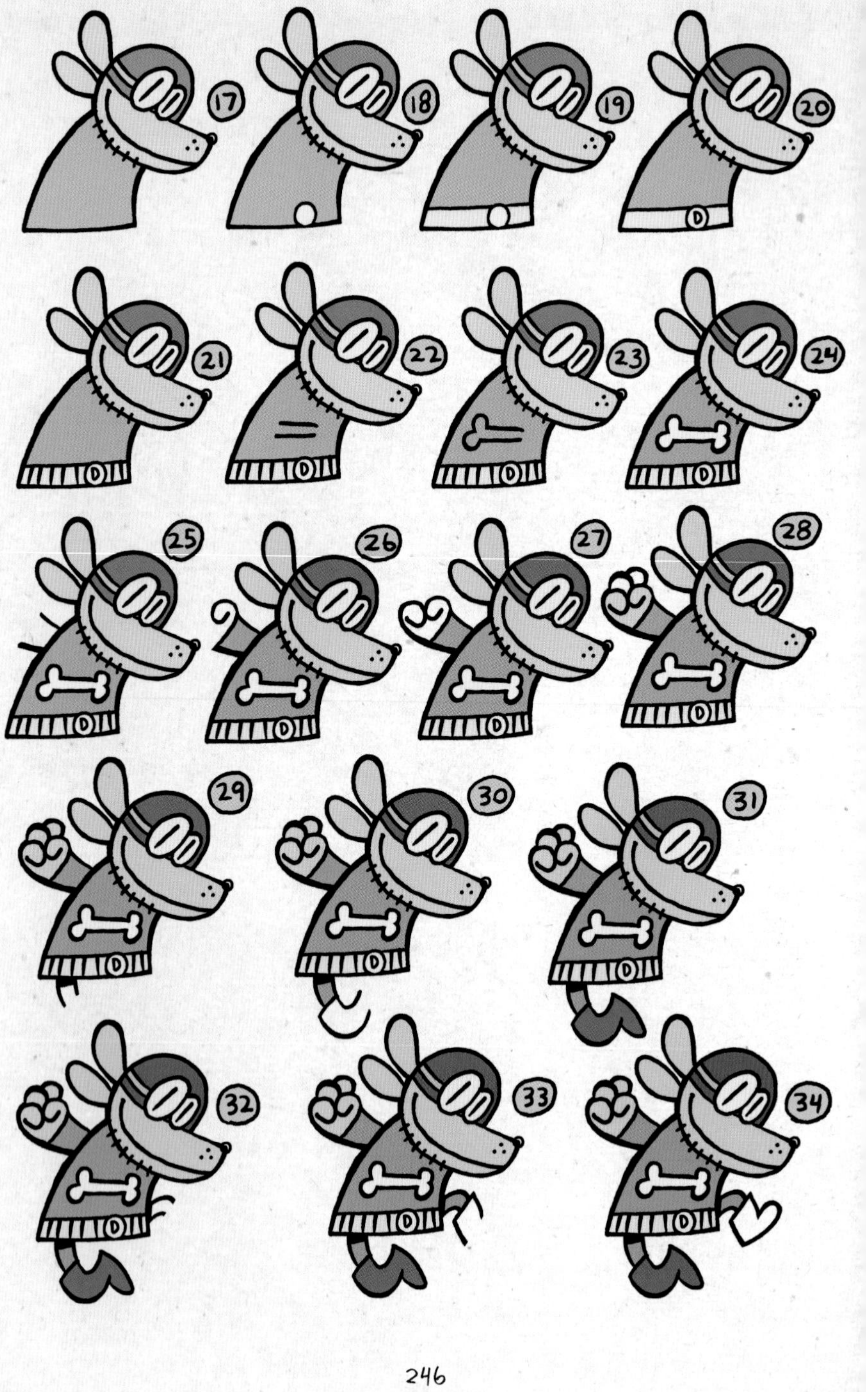
17
18
19
20
21
22
23
24
25
26
27
28
29
30
31
32
33
34

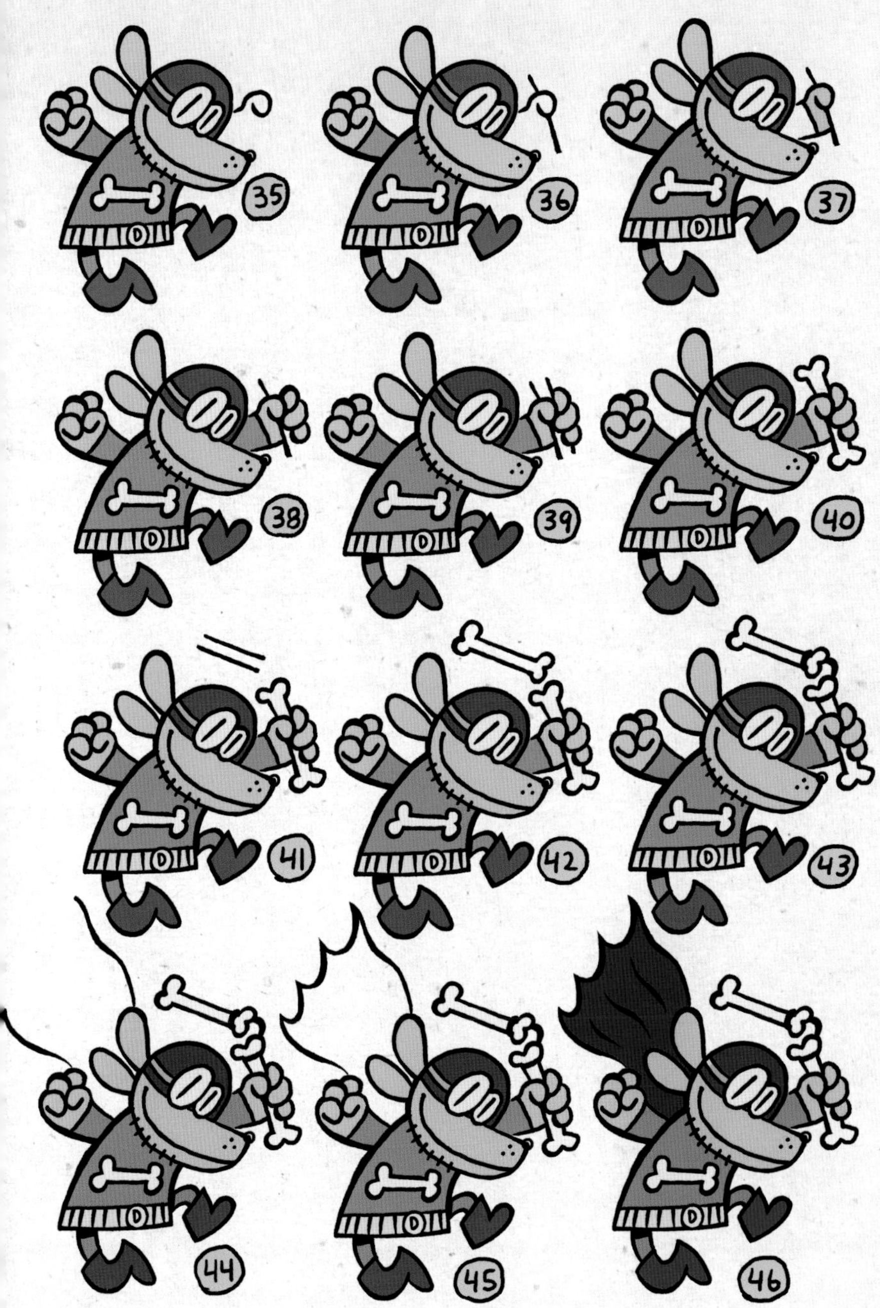
35
36
37
38
39
40
41
42
43
44
45
46

HOW 2 DRAW SUPA-MECHA PHILLY

in 37 Ridiculously easy steps!

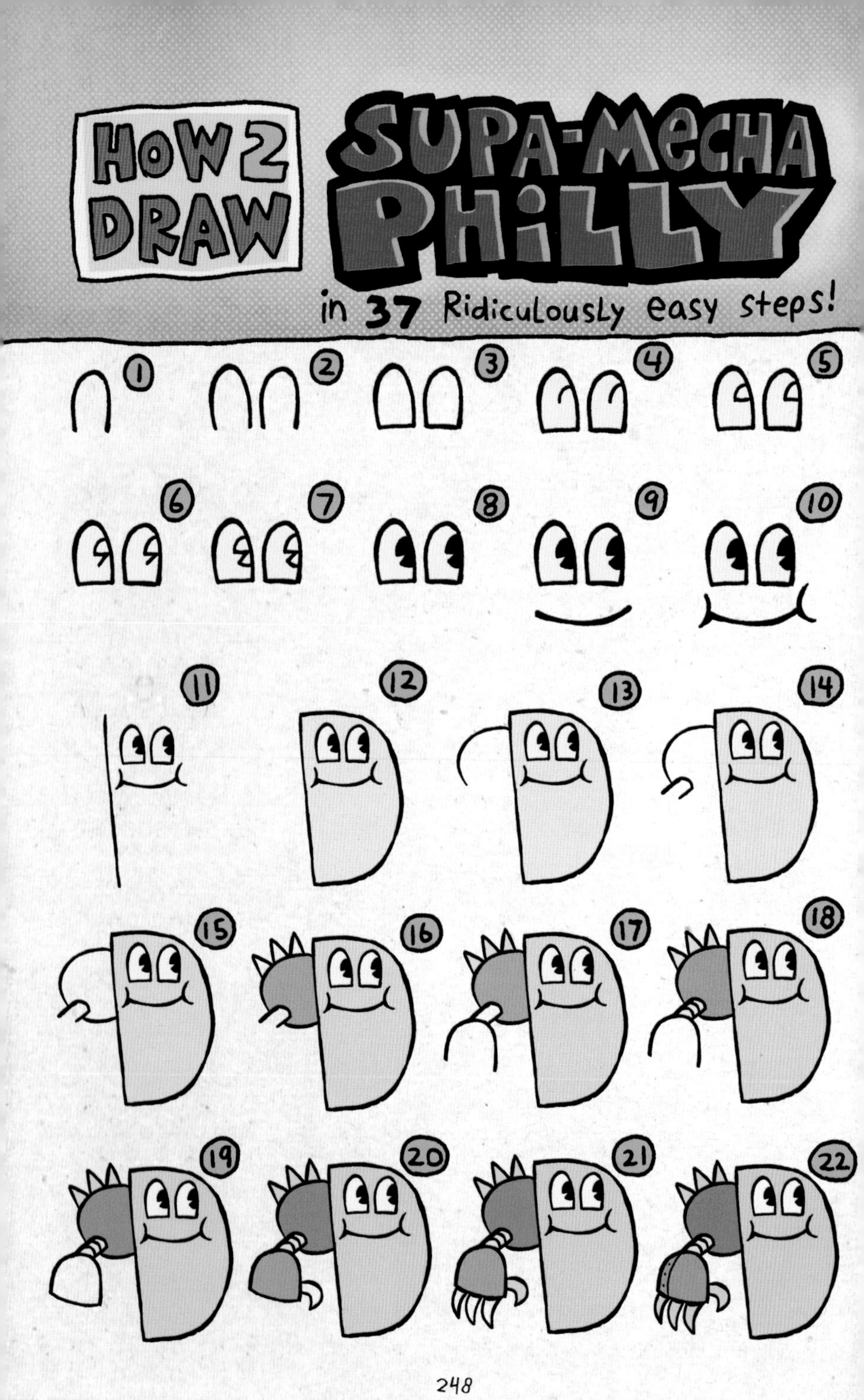
1
2
3
4
5
6
7
8
9
10
11
12
13
14
15
16
17
18
19
20
21
22

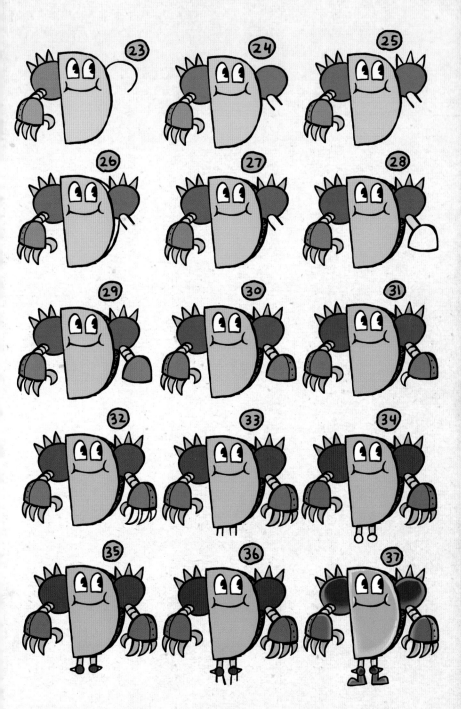

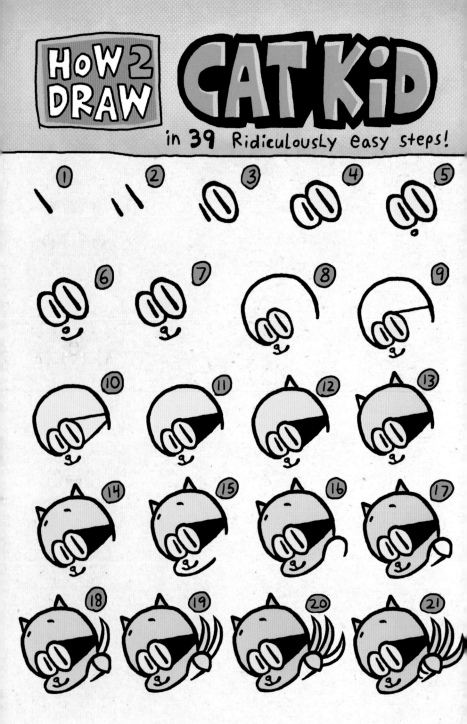

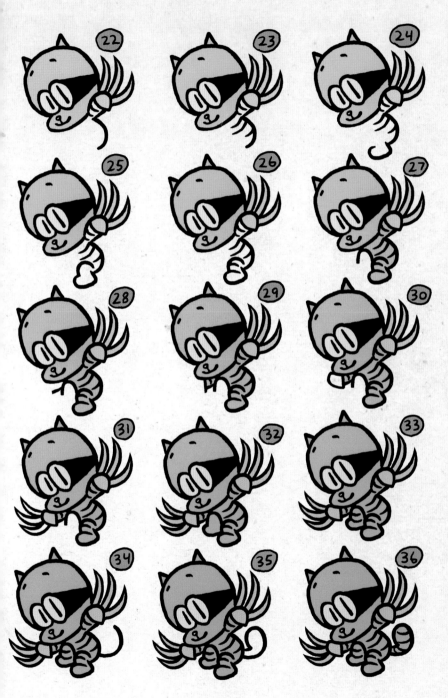

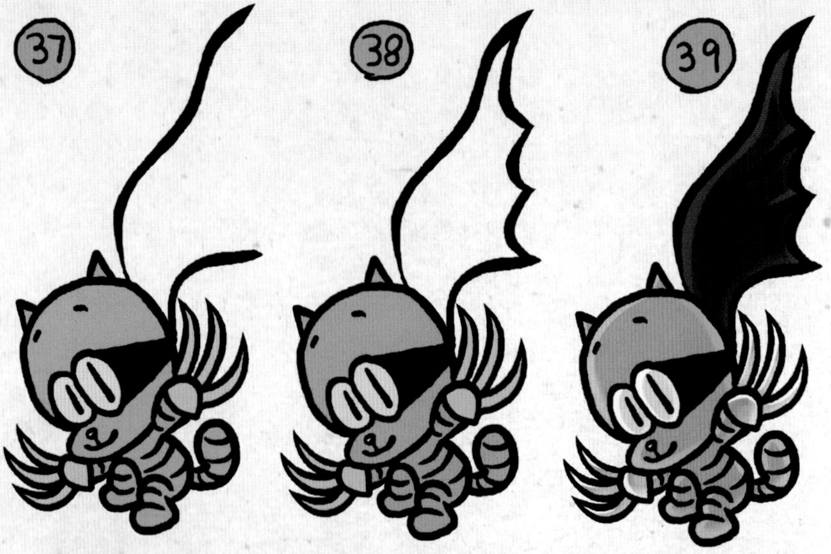
37
38
39

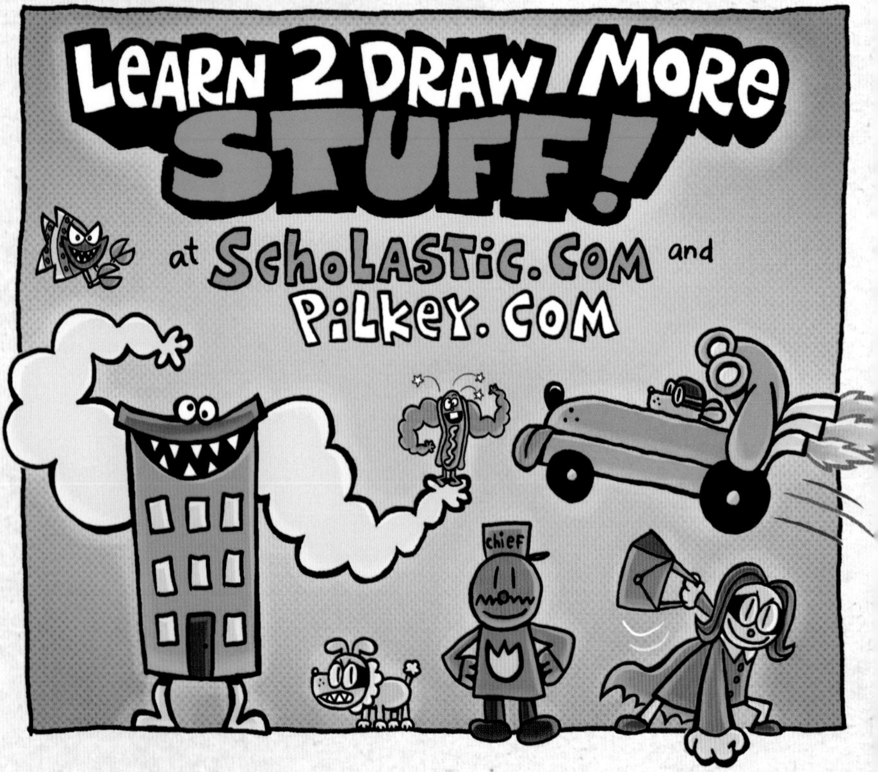
LEARN 2 DRAW MORE STUFF!
at SCHOLASTIC.COM and
PILKEY.COM
chief

NOTES

by George and Harold

★ The titles of chapters 9, 10, and 11 are parodies of the titles of <u>Other</u> books by John Steinbeck.

★ The words on pages 57 and 233 are direct Quotes From <u>East of Eden</u> by Steinbeck.

★ The Japanese words in chapter 11 mean: Onigiri (rice balls), 100 yen (about a dollar).

★ "Timshel" is the Hebrew word for "Thou mayest."

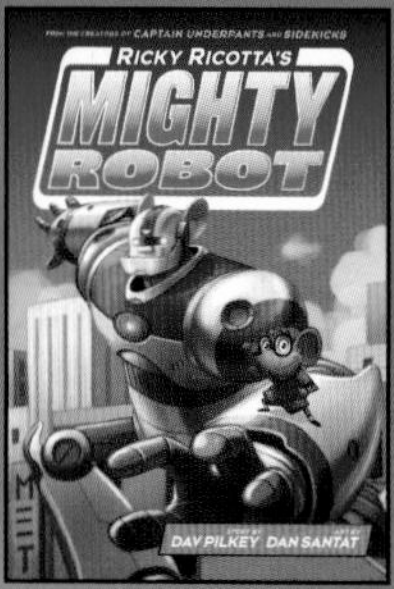
RICKY RICOTTA'S
MIGHTY ROBOT
DAV PILKEY DAN SANTAT

GET READING WITH RICKY RICOTTA!

"A fun introduction to chapter books."
— School Library Journal

"Has all the classic Pilkey hallmarks: comic book panels, superhero action, and Flip-O-Rama." — Booklist

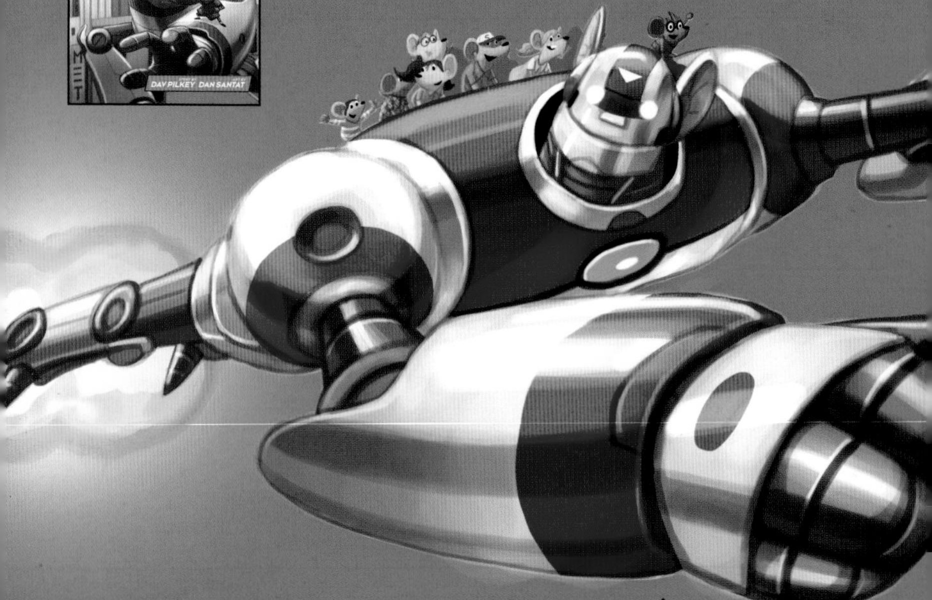

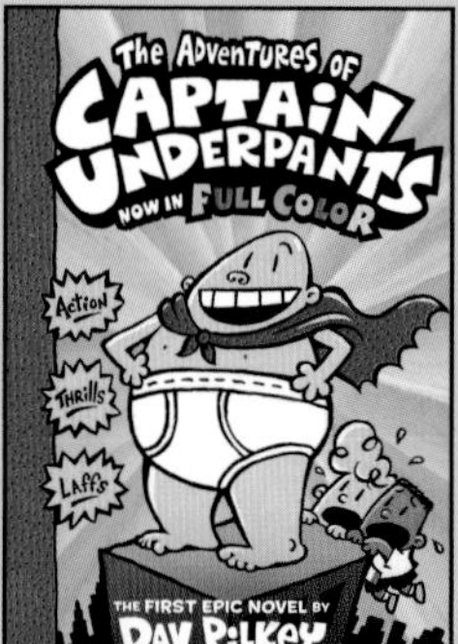
The Adventures of
CAPTAIN UNDERPANTS
NOW IN FULL COLOR
Action
Thrills
Laffs
THE FIRST EPIC NOVEL BY
DAV PILKEY
CALDECOTT HONOR ARTIST

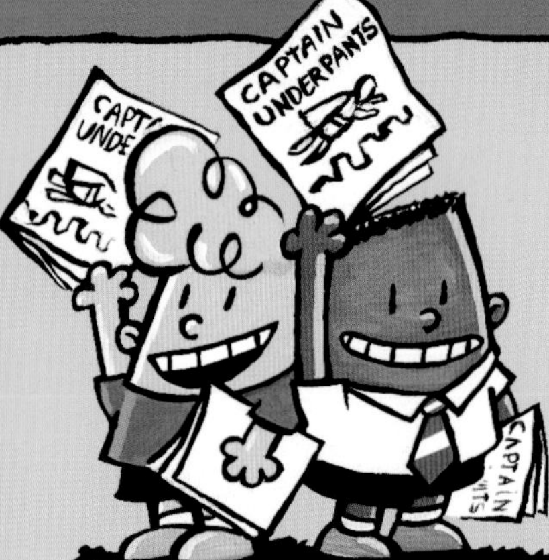
CAPTAIN UNDERPANTS

THE CRITICS ARE CRAZY ABOUT UNDERPANTS!

"Pilkey's sharp humor shines, and is as much fun for parents as their young readers." — Parents' Choice Foundation

"So appealing that youngsters won't notice that their vocabulary is stretching." — School Library Journal

ABOUT THE AUTHOR-ILLUSTRATOR

When Dav Pilkey was a kid, he suffered from ADHD, dyslexia, and behavioral problems. Dav was so disruptive in class that his teachers made him sit out in the hall every day. Luckily, Dav loved to draw and make up stories. He spent his time in the hallway creating his own original comic books.

In the second grade, Dav Pilkey created a comic book about a superhero named Captain Underpants. His teacher ripped it up and told him he couldn't spend the rest of his life making silly books.

Fortunately, Dav was not a very good listener.

ABOUT THE COLORIST

Jose Garibaldi grew up on the South Side of Chicago. As a kid, he was a daydreamer and a doodler, and now it's his full-time job to do both. Jose is a professional illustrator, painter, and cartoonist who has created work for Dark Horse Comics, Disney, Nickelodeon, MAD Magazine, and many more. He lives in Los Angeles, California, with his wife and their cats.